Books by Janis Reams Hudson

WILD TEXAS FLAME
APACHE MAGIC
APACHE PROMISE
APACHE TEMPTATION
APACHE LEGACY
APACHE HEARTSONG
APACHE FLAME
WARRIOR'S SONG
HAWK'S WOMAN
WINTER'S TOUCH

Published by Zebra Books

HUNTER'S
TOUCH

JANIS REAMS HUDSON

Zebra Books
Kensington Publishing Corp.

http://www.zebrabooks.com

ZEBRA BOOKS are published by

Kensington Publishing Corp.
850 Third Avenue
New York, NY 10022

First Printing: October, 1999
10   9   8   7   6   5   4   3   2   1

Printed in the United States of America

CHAPTER ONE

He was bronze from head to toe.

But for breechclout and moccasins, he was naked.

She should be scandalized—*shocked*—to see him unclothed as he was. She should turn her face away and not look. She should turn her horse around and ride the ten miles back home and stay there until he decided he was ready to come and see her—*with his clothes on.*

That was what a proper young lady would do, and Bess Dulaney struggled every day to be proper. It was what her family expected of her, what Hunter wanted of her. But oh, sometimes it was so hard, this being proper. She bit her tongue on swear words. She dug her fingernails into her palms to keep her boisterous laugh down to a polite chuckle. She clenched her jaw whenever anger tempted her to raise her voice.

And when she thought of Hunter and felt her heart pound, her blood race hot and fast through her veins, she very deliberately brought to mind the last time she had pricked her finger while sewing, or cleaned the feathers off a newly killed chicken, or took her turn at pouring lime down the seat holes in the privy. Anything to stifle the urge to reach out and touch him, to let him know how much she missed his touch, his smile, his laughter.

It was slowly killing her, this denying of her own feelings. She was shriveling up inside like a rosebud pulled from the vine and left lying for days in the sun.

Just this once, she would let herself feel. Hunter was too far away to be able to read the yearning she knew was visible in her eyes. She should turn her horse around and go home. At the least, she should look away from that glorious display of bronze skin. Why, a proper young lady probably wasn't even aware that a man had that much skin. Underneath his outer clothes was only another layer of clothes, made of flannel. And that, or so others would have her believe, was as deep as any man went.

But Bess did not turn her horse around, nor did she look away. She stared in utter fascination at the way the morning sun gleamed off sleek muscles. The way his strong, bare legs clamped tightly around the horse's sides. The way his long black hair streamed away from his face in the wind.

She was not scandalized or shocked. She was, quite literally, breathless.

She drew her mare to a halt at the mouth of the canyon and watched as Hunter leaned low over his mustang's neck and urged the horse into a flying leap over the steep-banked creek that ran the length of the canyon. Together, man and horse soared.

Heavens, how she loved to watch him ride. The way he and the horse became one, moved together, anticipated each other.

Standing on his own two feet, Hunter MacDougall was a man to be reckoned with, strong and capable, honest and loyal. On horseback, he was, she thought, nothing short of poetry. He was magnificent. He had only to whisper in a horse's ear, and the animal was his to bid.

He was half Arapaho, half white, and everything Bess Dulaney had ever wanted. She had loved him since they met, when she was thirteen and he was fifteen. At one time, long ago, he had felt the same. Until that night two years ago, when she had let her passions overrule her good sense and let him know just how much she wanted him.

Lord, it had been sweet. Heavenly. They had touched and kissed in a way they never had before. Her blood sang with the memory. Her breasts swelled and tightened when she recalled his touch.

Then, abruptly, he had pulled away from her.

To Hunter's credit, he had tried to take the blame for her shameless behavior. He'd said, "You're a lady, Bess. A proper young lady should slap a man's face for pawing her like an animal the way I've done you."

Bess had wanted to cry out that she *wanted* him to paw her, that she craved his touch. But shame over her own brazenness and pain at his rejection had strangled the words in her throat.

Nothing had ever been the same between them again. Since that night, they still spoke of marriage, but in stilted voices and with eyes that looked aside. They never touched anymore, never laughed together, dreamed together. They never even argued.

She wasn't used to seeing Hunter like this, naked but for breechclout and moccasins. Except for his long hair, which hung below his shoulders, he seldom flaunted his Arapaho heritage. Not that he was ashamed of his mother's people. He wasn't. And not that he could pass for white if he tried. He couldn't. One look and there was no doubting he was part Indian.

But he didn't usually dress like an Indian because, according to him, rubbing the fact that he was Arapaho in the faces of whites who hated Indians was asking for trouble he could do without. He preferred to go his own way and mind his own business. It was easier to do that, he said, if he dressed like everyone else.

Yet here he was, riding hell-bent across his canyon, dressed as he had been the first time she'd seen him seven years ago, the day he and his sister helped their father free Bess and her family from the Arapaho warriors who had captured them.

That he would dress this way, when any casual rider might happen along and see him, troubled her. Did it mean he was looking for trouble? Was he daring anyone to taunt him? But why?

Bess shook her head. It made no sense. But then, most things Hunter did these days made no sense to her. She straightened in the saddle and gripped the reins tightly in her gloved hands. Last week she'd returned home after being gone a month, and he had yet to come see her. Now she found him dressed like an Indian, riding like one.

Fine. He *was* Indian, after all. Half Indian. But she figured it was his Scots blood that made him so blamed stubborn.

Well, she could be just as stubborn.

She didn't like to cry. It made her eyes red and puffy, her nose clog up, and her head ache. But Hunter had hurt her last week—again—by not coming to see her. She'd cried for days. Waited for days. Waited for him to come to her, to say he had missed her, that he still cared for her. That he didn't want her to go away again. And more. She wanted so much more from him, but a simple show of interest on his part would go a long way toward soothing her aching heart. That was why she had gone with Aunt Gussie to Atlanta in the first place—in hopes that Hunter would miss her enough to break once and for all this terrible restraint between them.

Yet when she'd returned, he hadn't come. His absence had nearly crushed her.

He might very well hurt her again today, if her plan didn't work.

What, she asked herself as she watched him ride, had gone

wrong? They had been so close in those early years when they'd first come to live along the banks of the Huerfano River, where her brother had brought them to revive their father's ranch. Bess and Hunter had spent many an afternoon, and yes, if the truth were known, more than a few nights, walking along the banks of the river hand in hand, sharing their dreams of being together, of starting their own ranch. He would raise horses, train them. She would make a home for them. They would have children. Lots of black-haired children.

Oh, Hunter. What happened to our dreams?

She would have liked to blame it all on that night she'd lost her head and thrown herself at him. But in all honesty, things had not been quite right between them even before that.

Maybe if she hadn't started going to school in town. Hunter had refused to go, claiming he was too old—and at fifteen, he was probably right—and too far behind everyone else, since he couldn't read at all.

Somehow, after that, there seemed to be a distance between them. Bess hadn't realized it at first. She'd been busy making new friends. Hunter had been busy working for her brother and getting to know his father for the first time in years. But Bess's feelings for Hunter had never changed. She had never stopped loving him.

She was twenty years old; he was twenty-two. It was time, in her mind, for her to find out if there was any hope for them.

She worried for a moment that what she was about to do was childish or mean, but she was desperate. She didn't know what else to do to get Hunter's attention. She had tried Aunt Gussie's way. For years, for as far back as Bess could remember, Aunt Gussie had told her she must always be a lady, must never raise her voice, must be sweet and agreeable—while still getting her own way.

Bess had been as sweet and agreeable as she possibly could with Hunter over the years. So sweet and agreeable that at times she feared she might choke on it. Every now and then, life seemed to call for the utterance of an expletive. Men certainly seemed to find plenty of occasions when nothing else but a strong swear word would do.

Oh, her brother and his men, and Hunter and Mr. Mac, took care most of the time to refrain from such language around females, but Bess had heard her share over the years. Every now and then, she found herself biting her tongue to hold back a choice swear word of her own.

But dignity, Aunt Gussie's teachings, and Hunter's comment about proper young ladies prevailed. Bess Dulaney did not swear. Dammit.

Oh, she was no pushover. She could hold her own in any argument, but she did not raise her voice, did not lose her temper. Did not let her emotions show at any time. A lady simply did not do such things.

Still, her calm, steady manner had so far failed to bring Hunter back to her. She wanted to see him look at her the way he used to, as if she were the stars and moon in his own personal heaven.

Since calmness and agreeability had not worked, Bess had decided to try Mary Sue Baxter's way. Mary Sue was her childhood friend from Atlanta, and Bess had just spent two weeks with her, regaling her with tales of life on a Colorado ranch. When Bess had told her about Hunter, about the way he had helped save her family years ago, about his dark good looks, his gentleness, his strength, his smile, his eyes, his deep voice . . . Well, Mary Sue hadn't believed Bess at first, but she had come up with a way she swore would get his attention and force him to declare himself.

Overhead, dark clouds rolled across the sun. Bess hoped that wasn't a sign of things to come.

Taking a deep breath for courage, she nudged her mount forward. She was about to make the biggest gamble of her life.

* * *

Halfway up the canyon, Hunter slowed his horse to a trot. The animal mouthed the bit and tried to turn his head.

"Easy, boy," Hunter crooned, patting the horse's neck.

The mustang fought for control.

"None of that, now." Hunter held firm on the reins and kept the horse moving forward toward the corral. "I see her. That long-legged filly's not for the likes of you, lad." *And the long-legged woman on her back is not for the likes of me,* he thought grimly. *At least, not yet.*

The mare was a Thoroughbred, destined to mate with a Thoroughbred, to produce Thoroughbred foals.

The woman was a Southern lady, transplanted to the Colorado Territory. She was meant for a gentleman. A rich man who could give her everything she deserved. A white man, at whose side she could walk and not have to suffer other white ladies drawing their skirts aside when she walked by on the arm of a half-breed. She was meant for a man who could control his own passions and not take advantage of her youth and innocence.

Hunter knew he was none of those things. He wasn't a gentleman, he wasn't rich, and he wasn't white, never would be. Like the stallion beneath him, he was a mongrel. The horse was a once-wild, range-bred mustang, still not sure about the two-legged creature on his back.

The man was a half-breed.

She deserved a man who could control the fire she ignited in his blood. Hunter MacDougall was not that man. To his shame, he had proven that to both of them. He would not allow himself to touch her again unless and until they were properly married.

In the language of his mother's people, the Inuna-ina, whom the whites called the Southern Arapaho, Hunter quietly urged the mustang to ignore the visitors behind them. In the language of his father's people, the wild highland Scots, Hunter let loose a few Gaelic terms better not uttered in polite company. For good measure, he threw in a few choice Anglo-Saxon swear words.

Bess.

What was she doing here?

Man-Above, she was beautiful. She was trouble. She was killing him. He cursed again beneath his breath. If she'd just given him a little more time, he might have been able to outride the demons that had pounced on him the instant he learned she was home from her trip. The demons that urged him to go to her, claim her, make her his for once and forever.

But he wasn't ready. What did he have to offer someone as fine as Elizabeth Dulaney? Nothing. A one-room log cabin with a dirt floor. He couldn't—wouldn't—ask Bess to live like that. Not when she was used to better.

But soon, soon, he thought, he would have money. White man's money that would pay for building a house—a real house, with smooth walls and wooden floors, a bedroom separate from the rest of the house. More bedrooms. For the children he wanted some day to give her.

Soon. At the far end of the canyon, he had a new herd of mustangs he'd brought in last week. The stallion he now rode was one of the youngsters from the herd. As soon as Hunter settled them down and worked with them, taught them to accept a saddle and rider, he would sell them and build a house for Bess.

He would not, however, sell them to the Army, to be used against the tribes still fighting for their freedom on the plains. But ranchers would pay for good horses to work their cattle. Hunter's reputation with horses was spreading. The horses he sold were good, reliable mounts, not ''green-broke,'' as some called them.

But to do any of the things he planned, he had to stay away

from Bess. The last time he'd seen her, about a week before she and Gussie left for Atlanta last month, Bess had met him at their old meeting place beside the river near her house.

He'd been a fool to meet her there, in the trees, in the moonlight. Bess in the moonlight was more temptation than Hunter had been able to resist. He had very nearly taken her there on the ground once before. And she would have let him. This last time, just before she left for Atlanta, he hadn't dared to touch her. Had he *known* she was leaving, things might have been different.

But despite the pain he suffered over her not telling him about her trip, he figured it was just as well that he hadn't known. He might have ruined everything.

She probably thought he was crazy. She was probably riding out here today, despite a storm coming on, to tell him she never wanted to see him again. He couldn't say he would blame her. He had hurt her so many times over the years. He'd watched her go off to school in town, and he'd stayed behind when she had begged him to go with her. He'd watched other boys strut around her, and he'd done nothing about it. Yet still she had loved him.

Man-Above, he didn't deserve a woman like her.

She'd been gone a month, and he hadn't gone to see her when she returned. If she still cared for him at all, his absence from her homecoming must have hurt her.

But no more than her departure had hurt him, he thought grimly, since she hadn't bothered to tell him she was leaving. That should have given him a clue as to how she really felt about him. She didn't care anymore.

But he hadn't been able to go to the Double D since he heard she was home a few days ago. Just thinking of her, of how he wanted to greet her, with his hands and his mouth all over her, started a fire in his blood so hot and powerful that it shook him. Every day since she had returned, he had ridden hard and fast, changing horses often to keep from injuring them, trying to outrun the fever in his blood. The fever for Bess.

Now, here she was, riding right up to his house. He didn't know what to hope for, but he prayed for strength.

While she was still some distance away, he slipped into the barn for his white-man clothes. He wouldn't have it said that he treated her with anything less than proper white man's respect by greeting her bare-chested. What covering up his chest had to do with showing respect to a woman, Hunter never had figured out, but he had resigned himself years ago to not understanding everything he knew about white men's ways.

He was only half white. Which fit, since he understood only about half of the white man's way of doing things. He wondered what a white man would do now in his place. Should he go with his heart and give in to what he knew he and Bess both wanted, or should he listen to his head, which kept pointing out that he wasn't ready to support a wife. Not when the wife would be Bess Dulaney, who was used to having everything she needed or wanted just for the asking.

Hunter snorted—sounding a lot like his horse—and watched as Bess rode nearer. What did he have to offer her? Not very damn much, that was for certain. A one-room, dirt-floor cabin and no income. He wouldn't subject Bess to that. Couldn't. He had loved her from the day they met, seven years ago, during his fifteenth summer, when she was thirteen. From that day forward he had known that she was his destiny. There would never be another woman for him.

He knew that she felt the same. Or once had. But Bess wasn't always reasonable.

Now there's an understatement.

She didn't see any reason to wait. As far as she was concerned, they should have gotten married years ago.

Hunter knew that she thought she meant it. She had some vague idea that they would live on her brother's ranch and everything would be the way it always had been, except the two of them would be married.

But Hunter would be damned if he would live off her brother's charity. Not that Carson had ever offered, Hunter thought grimly. Carson was a good man, one whom Hunter was proud to call friend. But he would never offer to support his sister's husband. If the man couldn't support himself, and support Bess in comfort, then he wasn't the man for Bess. Hunter did not blame Carson in the least for that attitude. In fact, he agreed with him wholeheartedly.

This cabin was Hunter's start. It was not, as Bess believed, merely a means to add another one hundred and sixty acres to her brother's ranch. This was Hunter's ranch. Or the start of it. He wanted to raise and train horses. He had a gift with horses, and a good reputation, even if he was a half-breed in a territory that had no use for anyone with Indian blood. If the name MacDougall opened doors for him that would otherwise be closed to a half-breed, he wasn't shy about walking through. It was his name, his father's name.

The one thing Hunter would not do was trade on his relationship with Carson Dulaney. He and Bess had had more than one argument about that. She said he had too much stubborn pride, and maybe she was right. But if so, he wasn't willing to do anything about it.

Talk about stubborn. He'd been told that Bess was supposed to stay in Atlanta for two months, but she had come home after only one. He wondered how she had convinced Gussie to cut short her trip.

Ah, Gussie. She was Bess's aunt, but she had married Hunter's father. The poor woman was bound to feel divided loyalties before all the shouting was done.

Not that Bess ever shouted at him anymore. That was how bad it was for him—he missed her shouting.

Before Bess got any closer, Hunter slipped on his shirt and used his fingers to comb his hair. If he was lucky, he smelled so much like a sweaty horse that Bess wouldn't want to get near him.

But then, he'd never been that lucky. Not with Bess. She had never minded the smell of sweat and horse on him before.

The closer she came, the drier his mouth, the damper his palms. Damn her. He wanted this girl like there was no tomorrow. She was going to tease him, torment him, either consciously and deliberately, or unconsciously, without even trying. Either way, he was in for a rough time.

She was so beautiful. She wore her coal-black hair in a pile of curls, with some kind of frilly straw hat perched on top, while she herself sat perched on the side of that ridiculous lady's saddle. A sidesaddle, they called it.

Nonsense, as far as he was concerned.

Her dress and parasol were pink-and-white striped, reminding him of the soft pink roses Gussie grew outside her door. And if he got close enough, he knew she would smell that way, too.

She walked her horse right up to him, then drew to a halt. She sat there for a long moment, looking down at Hunter, studying him. "Aren't you going to say anything?"

"Hello, Bess."

Her bottom lip quivered, making him ache inside. Making him feel small. Which, he supposed, was her intent, damn her. She always did have him wrapped right around her little finger. And they both knew it.

"You don't look happy to see me," she said.

"I wasn't expecting you. I've been busy. Now there's a storm moving in."

In the manner of a woman used to having her wishes granted, she held out her arms to him. "Are you going to help me down?" she demanded.

Hunter huffed out a breath. The way those clouds were sweeping in behind her, he couldn't send her home the way he wanted to. She'd get drenched before she made it halfway

back. And even if a storm weren't about to strike, there was
no way he could refuse her when she held out her arms to him.
He wasn't strong enough, not nearly strong enough, to turn
away from the honest plea in her eyes.

In the manner of a man looking for any excuse to get his
hands on her, even knowing he shouldn't, Hunter placed his
greedy hands around her waist to lift her down. When her
gentle hands settled on his shoulders, he pulled her from the
saddle, much more slowly than was wise, and stood her before
him.

"Hunter?" Instead of stepping away, she moved closer. Her
fingers dug into his shoulders.

As if she had suddenly turned to fire beneath his touch, he
dropped his hands from her waist and stepped back.

She looked up at him with those big blue eyes. "Why didn't
you come to see me when I got back?"

Hunter had to reach down deep inside himself for the strength
to keep from crushing her to his chest. He'd been right—she
smelled slightly of roses. He had a weakness for the smell of
roses. "Why didn't you tell me you were leaving?" he finally
asked, doing his best to keep the hurt and weakness from his
voice.

She looked down and away. "I guess I had that coming. So
you stayed away to get even."

"I stayed away because I had things to do."

Her eyes widened. There was hurt in those deep blue depths,
but the storm of rage overpowered it. Hunter thanked Man-
Above for that. He would rather have her angry any day. He
hated himself for hurting her.

He often wondered if any of this was worth what it was
doing to both of them. He loved her. More than his life, he
loved this woman. Yet he had to push her away, and it hurt
her, angered her.

Who could blame her for that, with the way he treated her?

"Well," she said, arching her neck and tugging on the hem

of first one kid glove, then the other. "I guess that tells me how important I've become to you lately, doesn't it?"

To play the game, he should have kept his mouth shut. But he couldn't. "Dinna be puttin' words into ma mouth, lassie."

"Dinna be givin' me yer Scottish burr, laddie," she countered. "I guess since you didn't care enough to come see me, then it won't bother you if I go to the Independence Day celebration in Walsenburg with Virgil Horton."

Everything inside Hunter turned to ice. Had he been so wrong? Had he taken too long to claim her, that she could throw a rich white man like Virgil Horton in his face?

Hunter thought of the cabin a few yards behind him, its single room, its dirt floor, its narrow rope bed, its lone chair. How the hell was he supposed to compete with a banker's son?

Hunter learned something about himself in that moment that he didn't particularly like—but didn't necessarily dislike, either. But it was a part of him, and he wouldn't be denying it. His love for Bess, while the guiding force in his life, was not as selfless and altruistic as it perhaps should have been. If Virgil Horton could make her happy, could provide better for her than Hunter could, then the best thing for Bess would be for Hunter to step back and wish her well.

The hell he would.

When it came to Bess, Hunter was anything but selfless and altruistic. He was out-and-out possessive. And she knew it, the little minx. She was doing this to get his attention.

Well, it worked, damn her, but he wasn't going to let her off easy. "Virgil Horton is a son of a bitch."

"He's an important man. He had nothing to do with putting that sign up at the bank that said 'No Indians Allowed.' In fact, he's the one who got it taken down."

"So you like him?"

Bess frowned. "Of course I do. If not, I wouldn't be planning to attend the picnic with him. Why would you think otherwise?"

Hunter gave his best imitation of a negligent shrug. "I just figured that if you liked him, you really wouldn't want to see his scalp dangling from the end of my lance."

"You don't have a lance," she pointed out.

"I'll make one. Just for the occasion."

She smiled softly and took a step closer. "Then you don't want me to go with him."

"I didn't say that."

Her jaw squared. "You look me in the eye, Hunter MacDougall, and tell me you don't care if I go with Virgil."

Hunter gave her a narrow-eyed glare. The muscle along his jaw bunched. "I'm looking you in the eye."

"Say it," she demanded. "Go ahead. I dare you."

He leaned closer and glared at her. He spaced his words slowly. "I . . . don't . . . care."

Bess sucked in a sharp breath that barely made it past the lance of pain from his words. It was all she could do to choke back a cry of protest. He didn't mean it. He couldn't mean it. He had loved her since she was thirteen and he was fifteen. And she loved him. "Liar," she said in a broken whisper.

Hunter looked away, glanced at the sky. "It's gonna storm. You shouldn't have come."

Bess angled her chin. "Do you expect me to ride home in the rain just because you don't want me here?"

"Go in the house, Bess, before you get soaked. I'll see to your horse."

She opened her mouth, then snapped it shut. Her chin quivered.

"Please," he said.

Bess read the plea in his eyes, eyes the same dark gray as the thunderheads building in the sky. She turned and headed toward the cabin.

She had her answer. His jealousy had risen instantly when she mentioned Virgil's name. But the distance was still there, that damn distance he'd been keeping between them for months.

Years. She wasn't leaving until she found out once and for all what was wrong.

A chilly gust of wind nudged at her back and hurried her into the cabin. She pushed the door closed behind her and waited for her eyes to adjust to the dim light from the front window.

Her heart contracted as she looked around. Oh, how she wanted to make his heart soften so that she and Hunter could marry and she could live here with him.

It wasn't much, to be sure, but they didn't need much. This one room, with its bed in the corner, the fireplace along one wall, the waist-high counter, the curtains she had made and hung over the front window beside the only door, would do nicely until they could enlarge it. Until they had a need to enlarge it. A need such as a child.

Bess closed her eyes and pressed a hand to her abdomen, dreaming deeply, hotly, of the time Hunter would make her finally, irrevocably, his. Of the child that would one day, God willing, grow within her womb. A child with black hair, bronze skin, and deep gray eyes.

"Oh, Hunter," she whispered. "Do you still love me, even a little?"

Hunter wasn't there, of course, so he could not answer.

It had been warm outside, but the cabin was cool. When the rain started a moment later, she knew it would get cooler. She started a small fire in the fireplace, then peered out the front window to watch for Hunter. When she spotted him sprinting through the rain, she rushed to open the door for him.

He came in on a gust of wind and rain. He slammed the door shut behind him, then stood, looking at her with expressionless eyes. Water dripped off him, turning the floor of the cabin to mud. Bess grabbed a shirt hanging from a peg next to the fireplace and reached toward him to blot the water from his long black hair.

Something so simple, Hunter thought, as her wiping a shirt

over his hair, should not ignite the fire in his blood, but it did. She didn't actually touch him flesh to flesh. All she did was press the shirt to his head, stroking his hair, soaking up the water. But it felt so damn good that for a moment, only a moment, he closed his eyes and reveled in her touch.

Then she moved closer, until he could feel her breath on his chin. She couldn't have been any more surprised than he when he reached out and grasped her shoulders. Instinct, and the fire in his blood, told him to pull her closer, pull her flush against his chest and hold her tight, kiss those sweet lips.

But one of Hunter's greatest fears was that he would lose control and dishonor them both by taking things farther than he had any right to. Among his mother's people, the Inuna-ina, dishonoring a young maiden was simply unheard of. His grandfather had raised him to respect a girl's highly prized chastity. Since leaving the tribe at age fifteen to live in the white world with his father, Hunter had learned that in this, as in many other things, whites and Arapahos thought alike. Making love with Bess now, before they were married, would dishonor them both. Before he could do anything to shame himself, he pushed her away.

"Hunter?" Hurt and confusion darkened her blue eyes.

"Don't get so close to me," he said, his voice harsher than he intended. "Look at your dress."

She glanced down at the mud on her hem, then frowned up at him. "So?"

He dropped his hands from her shoulders and stepped back, away from her. "It's ruined."

"Is that why you pushed me away?" Suddenly the hurt in her eyes was replaced with anger. "Is that your excuse this time?"

Hunter stiffened. "I don't know—"

"Don't you dare say you don't know what I'm talking about," she said tightly. "You push me away every chance you get."

"I obviously don't push hard enough," he said bitterly, "or you wouldn't be here."

"Is that what you want?" Her shoulders drooped, her eyes dulled. "Do you want me to just go away and never bother you again?"

"Look around you, Bess." He made a sweeping motion with his arm. "You dinna belong in a place like this."

Outside, thunder crashed and the rain pounded. Bess blinked, then stared at Hunter, her mouth hanging open. The Scottish wording and the soft burr in his voice told her his emotions were running high. She just didn't know which emotions they were. "What," she said carefully, "are you talking about?"

Abruptly, he turned away from her. "Forget I said anything."

"I won't forget it." Disregarding his wet clothes and the mud he left in his trail, she followed and plucked at his arm. "What do you mean, I don't belong in a place like this?"

"It's fair plain, isna it?"

"Not to me, it isn't. Are you saying you don't want me here?"

Hunter forced himself to turn and face her. "I'm saying you don't belong here."

Bess felt her heart stop. What was he saying? He couldn't mean . . . "Don't belong where?" she whispered. "With you?"

"It's true, isn't it?"

"No. Don't say that."

"You belong with some rich white man like Horton, who can give you a nice house and fancy clothes."

"You hate Virgil Horton."

"Aye, but obviously you don't."

For a moment, Bess was speechless. Rage and pain left her unable to utter anything more than a strangled squeak. "Well, aren't you the lucky one, then, that he asked me to the picnic and not you. I guess I should have known," she said, turning from him to pace before the fire. "Every chance you get, you put more distance between us. I've been gone a month and you didn't care enough to come see me when I got home.'' She whirled on him. ''Now you tell me I should go with Virgil.''

She waited, hoping, praying he would say something, anything. But he merely stood there, looking at her, through her. His fists, opening and closing at his sides, were the only indication that he felt anything at all.

She had to stop and wait for the ache in her throat to ease before she could go on. ''It was so wonderful, the way it used to be before you started pushing me away. I thought ... I thought, hoped, that maybe you still loved me, maybe just a little.'' Even to her own ears, she sounded pitiful, and hated it. But her heart was breaking, and she simply couldn't help it. ''I guess I was wrong.''

Hunter closed his eyes briefly against the pain he saw in hers. She really didn't know. She had no idea how she affected him. If she ever realized the truth, he would be lost. Keeping his hands off her had been difficult enough over the past two years. If she ever turned the full power of her womanhood on him again the way she had that night beside the river, he knew he would lose all control. Yet he could not stand to hurt her this way.

''I guess,'' she said, with a little waver in her voice that shamed him, ''you really don't care if other men court me.''

''No more than I care if I never draw another breath.''

He said it so quietly that it took Bess a moment to realize his meaning. But when she did, her entire face glowed. ''Hunter?'' she breathed.

''I would rather cut out my own eyes than watch another man so much as touch you,'' he said furiously.

''Oh, Hunter,'' she cried. With her arms raised, she threw herself at his chest.

Unable to stop himself, Hunter caught her and held her tightly to his chest. ''Bess ...''

''I love you, Hunter,'' she said.

The words went straight to his heart, piercing him, making him yearn for a life with her. The life he couldn't yet provide.

When he didn't respond to her declaration, she looked up at him. Man-Above, there were tears in her eyes.

Hunter knew what she wanted. She wanted him to say the words, too. Needed them, if her feelings ran as deep as his. "I have no right, Bess."

"No right? No right to what? Love me back?"

"I can't help doing that," he told her, looking into her eyes. A man could drown in those blue, blue eyes. "But I have no right to say it. The man who holds you like this, kisses you, feels what I feel for you, should be asking you to marry him, and I can't do that, so I have no right to be doing any of this."

In his arms, Bess stiffened. Slowly, she raised her head and looked at him. Her lower lip trembled. "You . . . you don't want to marry me?"

"Not until I have something better to offer you than this one-room cabin."

"This cabin?" she asked, bewildered. "What does this cabin have to do with whether or not you love me?"

His fingers flexed against her shoulders. "It has everything to do with it. If I didn't love you, I wouldn't care that you had to live like this when you're used to so much better. But I do love you, Blue Eyes, you know I do. And when I have the money to build you a real house—"

"Money?" She came close to shrieking the word as she tore herself from his embrace. "This is about money? Hunter, I would live with you in a tepee. You know that. I would live with you in the open. What do I care what kind of house we have?"

"I care," he said fiercely, pounding a fist against his chest.

"Well that's just the most ridiculous thing I've ever heard of," she protested.

"It's not ridiculous," Hunter said harshly. "How long do you think you'd last before you got tired of ruining another dress every time it rained?'' He waved toward the mud at the hem of her dress.

"Hunter, why are we discussing my dresses? If they get ruined, I'll make new ones."

"And how," he said, folding his arms across his chest, "will you manage that?"

"With a needle and thread."

Hunter narrowed his eyes at her. "You're not stupid, Bess."

"Thank you."

"If you were married to me, there wouldn't be any money for needles and thread, much less the material."

"You're not stupid, either," she told him, with a slight edge in her voice. "You know that if we married, Carson would give you a raise."

Hunter's eyes widened. "Ye gads, lass, I willna be askin' yer brother for money to provide for ma own wife."

"I didn't mean you should ask him," she said with what she thought was great patience.

"When we get married—"

"When?" she repeated with enthusiastic emphasis.

"I don't work for your brother any longer," Hunter said, his jaw flexing. "In case you haven't noticed, I'm my own man now. I have my own ranch."

"Of course you do. But I know you still do work for him. And you've only just started here. I thought . . ."

"You thought?"

"I guess I thought we would build a ranch together. You and me."

"Ah, Bess," he said softly. "We will, you'll see. But we're not ready, neither of us, not yet. I have to do better by you than this, don't you see?"

"No," she whispered, her heart aching. "I don't see, Hunter, I don't see at all."

"Think of those women you see in town. The ones from the small outlying farms and ranches."

"What about them?"

"Most of them are so worn down from struggling to feed themselves and their children, they're old before their time. Their skin looks like tanned leather, and their eyes—Bess, their eyes look all hollowed out and lifeless. I refuse to do that to you. I want better than that for you."

She gave a toss of her head. "And I have nothing to say about it?"

"Not until I can build you a real house. Then you can have all the say you want."

She narrowed her eyes. "I like this house."

"It's not good enough."

"Oh, I get it. This isn't about me at all, is it? It's about you, and that monumental pride of yours."

Hunter stiffened. "I'm not ashamed to admit I'm a proud man."

Bess ground her teeth in frustration. "Oh, you . . . you—"

A gust of wind pelted the cabin with rain. Hunter turned away from her to check the shutters. Bess, fighting the sting of tears, moved to light the lantern hanging on a nail beside the fireplace.

Something large and heavy slammed against the door, and then the door crashed open. A man burst into the cabin, streaming rain water from his hat brim and his long yellow slicker. Behind him, two more men stumbled in, with another man supported between them. Rainwater streamed from all four, turning what was left of the dirt floor after Hunter's entrance earlier even more muddy.

Startled, Bess dropped the match she'd been about to light. She barely had time to stiffen at the effrontery of strangers who would barge into someone's home when she noticed the guns. Three of them, pointed at her and Hunter.

CHAPTER TWO

If he'd been alone, Hunter might have chanced a dive for his revolver in the trunk at the foot of his bed across the room. He probably would have had at least a half dozen bullets in him before he reached it, probably would have been dead before he got the gun out and aimed it, much less fired it. Still, alone he might have tried.

But he wasn't alone. He had Bess to think of. Fear for her safety seized his chest, shortened his breath.

"See, Ned?" said the freckle-faced man. "A half-breed and a woman, just like ol' Gonzales said."

The name Ned raised Hunter's hackles. The wanted posters, depicting cold eyes and bushy black hair and beard, were eerily accurate. Ned Rawlins. Leader of the Rawlins gang. They robbed banks, merchants, stagecoaches, any place with enough money to make it worth their while. In the last couple of years they'd been making some big hauls, and they had no qualms about shooting their way out of tight situations. From the looks of the injured man with them, somebody must have shot back this time.

Hunter glanced swiftly at Bess and bit back a curse. She was whiter than fresh milk and her eyes looked big enough to swallow her face.

"So you said, Woody," Rawlins answered, keeping his gun leveled on Hunter while taking off his hat with the other hand and shaking the water from its brim. "But I still say there's no such thing as a woman who can do magic like he said."

"I thought he said the half-breed *was* a woman," one of the men muttered.

"As liquored up as he was, who knows what he said. All I know is we're on a fool's errand, and if there ain't a posse on our trail by now, I'll kiss somebody's ass. Dammit, don't stand there gawkin'," Rawlins ordered the other two men. "Put Cecil down. Woody, get back out to the barn and guard the horses. Fire off two rounds if you see anybody. Billy, cut that bullet outta Cecil and let's get ourselves gone."

They laid the injured man down before the fireplace, and his slicker fell open. The two men squatted beside him and stared.

Bess wasn't a squeamish person, but at the sight of all that blood soaking the man's shirt, her stomach rolled over. "Gracious," she whispered, covering her mouth with one hand and stepping back.

"I'll guard the horses," said the one who was missing the lower half of one upper front tooth. "Woody can take care of Cecil."

"How come you get to guard the money?" Woody protested.

"Cuz you're too damn dumb," Billy shot back.

Woody turned his gun on Billy. "Don't you be callin' me dumb. I ain't dumb, damn you."

"You're dumb as a fence post, and everybody knows it. We'd a got away clean if you hadn't been late with the damn horses."

"I weren't late, y'all was early," Woody cried. "Ned said five minutes, and I timed it on Pa's watch."

"Since when can you tell time?"

"Why, you—"

"Shut up, both of you," Ned Rawlins said with a snarl. "Billy, get out to the horses. Woody, either patch Cecil up, or we're leaving him here. We gotta be at the hideout on time, or there'll be hell to pay."

The one called Billy, the one with the broken tooth, pushed himself to his feet and grinned at Bess. "I think I'll take this little filly with me." He took a step closer to Bess and used the barrel of his revolver to stroke her cheek.

The steel was cold. His eyes were hot. Bess nearly gagged on terror so great that her knees threatened to give way.

"She can keep me warm in the barn," he added.

Across the room, Hunter growled and started to lunge.

Ned Rawlins jabbed the barrel of his gun against Hunter's cheek. "Not smart, half-breed."

Bess wanted to scream, shout, anything to take the man's attention from Hunter, but the only sound she could force through her fear-tightened throat was a small squeak. She could see the rage in Hunter's eyes, the fear—fear for her. She prayed that he wouldn't do anything foolish. *Don't be brave,* she silently begged. *Hunter, please don't be brave.*

With a nod toward Hunter, Rawlins said, "Forget the woman and get over here and tie him up."

"Ah, come on, Ned, she wants to go with me, don'tcha, honey?"

The barrel of Billy's gun stroked Bess's cheek again. She could not suppress the shudder of revulsion that ran through her. Nor could she stop herself from taking a step backward, away from the foul-smelling man with the broken tooth. But the backward step took her straight into the corner near the foot of the bed. There was nowhere else to go. She was trapped.

"Billy," Rawlins said threateningly.

"Awright, awright." Billy gave Bess's cheek one final stroke with the barrel of his revolver, then turned away.

Bess nearly sagged in relief.

"I'm coming," Billy whined. "But when we leave, we oughta take her with us. She's a damn sight prettier to look at than any of the rest of you bastards."

Billy holstered his revolver and crossed the room. He stood beside Hunter, then flapped his arms. "I ain't got nothin' to tie him up with. Be easier just to shoot him."

"No!" Bess cried, her heart stopping. She rushed to Rawlins's side.

"Bess," Hunter warned. "Stay back."

"Shut up," Rawlins snarled at Hunter, poking the tip of his gun barrel deeper into Hunter's cheek.

"Hunter, please," Bess begged. "Wait," she said to Rawlins. She rushed to the bed in the far corner and tore a strip from the sheet. "Here." She rushed back to Rawlins and held out the strip. "Please. Here. I'll tie him for you."

"Bess," Hunter growled.

Ned Rawlins snorted. "Look at that, Billy. I think they're sweet on each other. You still want her, even if she's been with a breed?"

"Don't nobody get her," Woody called from where he knelt beside the wounded man before the fireplace. "Leastwise not 'til she fixes Cecil. Get over here, girl, and touch him so's his wound'll heal."

While Billy took the strip of sheet from Bess and tied Hunter's hands behind his back, he sneered at Woody. "You dumb shit. I told ye, there ain't no such thing as healin' a wound just by touchin' it. Juan Gonzales is nothin' but a lyin', no-account drunk."

Hunter flinched. Not because Billy chose that moment to yank tight on his wrists with the strip of sheet, but because of what the outlaw said. There must be two dozen men named Juan Gonzales just in the southern half of Colorado Territory alone. But there couldn't be more than one who would speak of a woman, a half-breed, who could heal wounds with a touch.

Bloody hell! They were talking about Winter Fawn! Hunter's sister had been born with a mysterious gift that no one understood. With the touch of her hand, she could heal a wound. That was all it took—the touch of her hand. Several years ago she had been forced to heal their father in full view of the Southern Arapaho tribe. Gonzales traded with the tribe. Someone must have told him about it. Or maybe he'd been there at the time. It didn't matter. All that mattered to Hunter was that these bastards not get anywhere near his sister.

But Man-Above, they thought Bess was Winter Fawn. They thought she could heal this man.

"Come on, girl, hurry it up," said the red-haired man kneeling beside his fallen partner. "Get over here and touch him so's we can git gone."

Bess glanced at Hunter, then started across the room. Her hands were visibly shaking. The terrified look in her eyes cut him to the bone. Man-Above, was he to see Bess sacrificed in order to keep these men from his sister? Or was he to tell them they had the wrong woman, and send them to Winter Fawn?

But dammit, there were more people at the Double D. Carson, the ranch hands. Maybe even Hunter's father. Rawlins and his gang wouldn't be able to take the place by surprise the way they had here. And in any case, unless they killed him, he would be able to ride around them and warn those at the ranch.

It was a chance. A slim one, but Hunter didn't see anything else he could do. He would gamble his sister's safety on the chance to protect Bess.

"You've got the wrong woman," he said to Woody, the one who had called to Bess.

At Hunter's words, Bess thought her knees would buckle. She swayed and had to brace one hand on the rough log wall to steady herself. "No," she cried to Hunter. He couldn't mean to send these men to Winter Fawn.

Or perhaps he did. He couldn't know that Carson, his two top men, and Hunter's father had ridden to Pueblo two days ago to look at a new bull. Winter Fawn and the children were home alone.

There were other men on the Double D, of course, but they would be out checking on the cattle.

No. Bess refused to even think of what might happen if these men rode to the house.

"Bess—"

"It's no use, Hunter," she said hurriedly, silently pleading with him to go along with her. "They know I'm the one they're looking for. We can't lie to them."

To the outlaws she said, "There is no need for guns here, gentlemen. I'll be glad to help your friend."

The leader of the gang, the man called Ned, gave her a narrow-eyed stare that sent chills of foreboding down her spine.

"Then get on with it," he ordered. "We don't have all day." He did not put his gun away, but at least he no longer had the barrel pressed into Hunter's cheek.

With a quick, fervent prayer for courage, Bess knelt beside the wounded man, then looked back at their apparent leader. "If you're in a hurry, you're welcome to leave this man here. We'll see that he is taken care of."

Ned gave her a mocking grin. "Taken care of by the nearest sheriff, you mean."

Bess gave her best imitation of a blink of innocence. "Sheriff? Why ever would a sheriff take care of him? Unless, of course, the sheriff is also a doctor, but I'm not aware of anyone in the county who fits that description."

Billy had yet to leave for the barn. He stood at the door and cackled. "Whooee, listen to the uppity way she talks. She don't expect us to believe her, does she?"

"I told you to get outside," Ned said sharply. "Before we have a sheriff surprise us for real. And you"—he waved his gun at Bess—"shut up and get busy."

"We ain't leavin' him, Ned," said Woody.

"No, Wood, we ain't leaving Cecil here. If he's still breathing when she's done with him, we'll carry him with us. But we're not letting him slow us down any more than he already has. You hear that, Cecil?" he called to the wounded man. "You gotta keep up."

The man on the floor blinked up at Bess, but answered Ned. "I hear ye. You can tie me to the saddle if you have to. You ain't leavin' me here. You ain't cuttin' me out of my share of the take."

Bess was certain that she didn't want to know what he meant by his share of the take. She didn't want to know who they had robbed or how this man came to be bleeding all over the floor of Hunter's cabin. She had enough to deal with. Somehow she had to get these men to leave before something terrible happened.

If she hadn't been so terrified, she might have laughed at her own thoughts. Something terrible had already happened! These . . . *outlaws* had burst in at gunpoint, threatened her and Hunter, tied Hunter up, and now expected her to heal a bullet wound.

But she knew that something much worse could happen. *Would* happen if she didn't think fast.

Outside, the rain sounded as though it was tapering off. When Billy opened the door a moment later to head for the barn, a gust of chilling air swept through the cabin.

Bess stared down at the man on the floor. Like the one kneeling on his other side, he had freckles all over his face. The spots stood out vividly; the skin beneath was pasty gray. She suspected the dampness across his face was more from pain-induced sweat than rain.

What she could see of his hair beneath his hat was a dark, rusty red. His eyes were cloudy blue, and the top half of his right ear was missing. It looked as though it had been chewed off by some wild animal. She forced herself to look into his eyes rather than at that ear or his bloody chest.

"Did I hear them call you Cecil?" she asked, trying with all her inner strength for a calm, polite tone while she clenched her fists in the folds of her skirt and prayed they would stop their violent shaking.

The man swallowed, then grimaced, as though the simple action caused him pain. "Yes, ma'am." His voice was breathless.

"My name is Bess."

"You sure are pretty, Miss Bess."

"Why, thank you, Cecil. We're going to take care of you now. All you have to do is lie still and relax as best you can." She nodded to Woody. "I believe you were going to remove the bullet?"

Woody had those same cloudy blue eyes, and they were fixed on her with an intent that spoke of a new threat. He simply stared at her and grinned.

Think like Aunt Gussie, Bess told herself. No one intimidated Aunt Gussie. What would she do if she was here right now?

What Gussie wouldn't do, Bess thought, was show her fear to these men. Bess strove for an air of distant politeness. "The bullet?" she prompted again.

"I thought you were going to heal him," Ned sneered.

Bess peered over her shoulder at the outlaws' leader. The rain might have let up until it was now no more than a slight drizzle, but the room was growing darker. Ned loomed like a menacing shadow halfway between her and where Hunter stood across the room.

"The bullet must come out first," she stated as though explaining that one plus one equaled two.

"Hear that, Woody?" Ned said in his same sneering tone. "Your magic healer can't even dig out a bullet."

Woody blinked. "Cecil's right, Miss Bess—you sure is pretty."

"Son of a bitch." Ned crossed the room. "Get out of the way." After holstering his revolver, he shoved Woody aside and took his place across from Bess. "Go keep an eye on the breed."

"Ah, hell, Ned, he's tied up. He ain't goin' nowheres. He don't need watchin'."

"Then I guess you won't care if he runs over here and bumps into me while I've got my knife blade buried in your brother's chest."

"I don't think I'd like that none, Ned," Woody decided. "I'll watch the breed."

Ned pulled a hunting knife from the top of his boot and leaned over Cecil.

Bess braced herself for whatever was to come. She had never tended a bullet wound herself before. Nor any serious wound at all, for that matter. Aunt Gussie and Winter Fawn always dealt with anything serious. But Bess had assisted them several times. She knew what needed to be done.

If possible, Cecil's face turned more gray than before. "I want a drink first."

"Quit yer whining," Ned told him. With that, Ned tore open Cecil's bloody shirt.

Cecil passed out.

Ned sneered. "Lily-livered jackass fainted." Shaking his head, he poked the tip of his knife into the small hole in Cecil's chest.

The shirt of Hunter's, which Bess had used to wipe his hair, lay next to her in a muddy mess. She grabbed it and used it to soak up the fresh flow of blood.

Ned must have had considerable experience in digging out bullets, for he had the lead out in a matter of seconds. He tossed the bullet aside, then braced his forearm across his raised knee, bloody knife dangling in his hand, and looked up at Bess. "Now bandage him up, girl, and be quick about it."

Bess tore more strips from the sheet. Ned and Woody held Cecil up while she wrapped a bandage tightly around his chest.

While the three of them worked to bandage the wounded outlaw, Hunter struggled to free himself from his bonds. If he could get his hands loose, now would be the best time to jump them, when their hands were busy, their guns holstered.

But bloody hell, that bastard Billy had tied him tight.

"Okay," Ned said. "That's it. Let's get him on his horse and get out of here."

Bess held her breath. Oh, yes, please, Lord, they were leaving!

"But she's supposed to heal him," Woody protested.

"Given proper rest and adequate food," Bess said calmly, "he should heal nicely, if he hasn't already lost too much blood."

"Come on, Woody," Ned said.

"But . . . no," Woody whined. "That ain't how it's supposed to work. Gonzales said she would put her hand on the wound and it would disappear."

Ned rolled his eyes in disgust. "How 'bout it, girl? Are you some kind of miracle worker?"

"The healing of human flesh is a miracle on its own," Bess told him. "I've done all that can be done."

"Why, you lyin'—"

"Save it," Ned said, cutting Woody off. "Either help me get him up, or we leave him here."

"We ain't leavin' him, Ned. He's my brother. What if it was Billy that was shot? Would you be leavin' him?"

"It's not Billy that's shot," Ned bit out. "Now get over here, or get out. We're leaving."

They hauled the wounded man none too gently to his feet, and Woody, grumbling that Bess was supposed to heal his brother, not just bandage him, braced himself beneath Cecil's arm and took his weight. Ned threw the door open, and Woody and Cecil stumbled out into the rain.

Bess's heart started pounding as hope rose in her. They were really going to leave!

"Let's go, girl." Ned nudged her toward the door.

Bess jerked as though he had slapped her.

Hunter leaped forward, arms still bound behind his back. "No!"

Ned jerked his gun from his holster and took aim at Hunter's chest.

Hunter halted halfway to Bess, every muscle, every nerve screaming in impotent fury—and a fear he tried not to acknowledge lest it cripple him. Whatever it took, he couldn't let them take Bess.

Bess saw in Hunter's face that he was prepared to do something brave and foolish to save her from being taken away. She couldn't let him. This outlaw beside her would have no qualms about shooting anyone who got in his way. She scrambled for what to do, what to say. *Think like Aunt Gussie,* she frantically reminded herself.

She arched a brow at the outlaw in her best Aunt Gussie imitation. "He's right, of course, sir. I won't be accompanying you. I can be of no further help to your man. He has no more need of my services."

Ned Rawlins grinned. "Hell, darlin', there's services, then there's *services.* Ol' Cecil ain't the only one with needs."

Bess blinked in shock. She didn't need an explanation. His meaning was more than obvious. "I beg your pardon!"

Rawlins didn't argue, didn't try to convince her to go with him. He simply grabbed her arm. With the gun pointed at her side, he pulled her out the door.

Hunter's bellow of outrage echoed down the canyon. As he barreled out the door after Bess, he finally worked free of his bonds. "Goddamn you, Rawlins!"

Rawlins turned and leveled his revolver at Hunter as Hunter burst from the cabin.

"Hunter, no!" Bess screamed.

Rawlins pulled the trigger.

For a moment, Hunter hung there in the air, as if he had run into an invisible wall. Rage contorted his face. Blood blossomed in the center of his chest. Then he fell. Face down in the mud.

Bess went wild. She didn't care any more if Rawlins threatened her with his gun. He'd shot Hunter! *Oh God oh God oh God.* He wasn't moving. She couldn't see him breathing. *"Hunter!"* She screamed his name and fought frantically to free herself from the outlaw's hold. Then pain exploded in her head and everything went black.

CHAPTER THREE

It was the mud that kept Hunter from bleeding to death. When he fell facedown in it, it plugged up the hole in his chest.

It was the horse that brought him from the dark depths of unconsciousness with a hot, wet blowing in his ear.

It was the pain that nearly sent him back under. Enormous, suffocating agony burning outward from the center of him like a raging wildfire out of control. He lay still for long moments, trying to breathe past the pain, wondering what had happened to him.

It had rained, but the storm was gone now. The sun was setting. The mud was cold, the air warm. And . . . and what?

Bess is gone!

In a rush, it came back to him. The Rawlins gang. They took Bess. Man-Above, *they took her.*

He tried to get up. Dark spots swam before his eyes. Pain stole his breath. He'd been shot, and it was bad. The darkness of oblivion called to him, tempting him to surrender, to sink down once again below the pain, where there was nothing but blackness, nothing to hurt him.

But he had to get to Bess. He had to save her. The least they would do would be to kill her—but not, he knew, before she begged for death.

Bess!

If he lay there and died in the mud, no one would ever know what had happened to her. No one would know to go after her.

Bess!

"Horse," he whispered in the language of his mother's people. "You must help me."

The half-wild mustang stood beside him and did not move while Hunter used first the animal's foreleg, then its mane, to pull himself up. By the time Hunter made it to his feet, sweat soaked through the mud coating him. Pain blinded him, and he shook violently. He was losing blood, fast.

"Take me," he gasped, "to the log."

Like a trained dog, the horse moved toward the log near the cabin door barely an inch at a time, so as not to outpace the man stumbling along beside him, clinging to him.

Hunter had never understood where his gift with horses came from. From Man-Above, he supposed, the same as his sister's gift of healing. In that moment it was not important that he understood his gift. He was only grateful, as grateful as a man could be, that when he whispered to a horse in the language of the Arapaho, the horse understood. The gift had come in handy during his boyhood with the Arapaho, helping him win many a race. Since coming to the white world, Hunter had used the gift to make money, and to start his ranch. Never had he dreamed the gift might save his life.

Each step was agony, but eventually Hunter, leaning heavily on the horse, made it to the short, up-ended log he used for a chopping block.

"Help me, my friend," he whispered.

The mustang moved gently, and somehow, Hunter made it onto the block.

"My friend," he whispered, panting for breath, holding on to consciousness by a bare thread. "Take me to Winter Fawn. Take me to the house along the river. The place where you had the good corn the last time the moon was full. Take me there, my friend."

Hunter was about to pass out. He knew he would never be able to stay astride the horse without falling off. He leaned forward until his own weight tipped him over and he fell belly-down across the horse's back. His breath left him, and so did all conscious thought, as the pain slammed into him and sucked him back into the darkness.

Winter Fawn Dulaney crooned softly to her son. Finally, finally he was resting. He'd been in such pain. Never had she felt so helpless. What good was the gift of healing if she could not use it to take the pain from her baby?

He was so beautiful, this son of hers. Every bit as beautiful as his two sisters, although it wouldn't be too many years before he would object to the term and the comparison. For now, however, he was only three and didn't know that beautiful was not a suitable word with which to describe a young man. For now, all three of the bairns Carson had given her were beautiful.

She leaned down and kissed Innes Edmond's forehead. Poor wee laddie, he'd had the earache something fierce since yesterday. He was so tired, he would probably sleep late into the morning tomorrow.

Quietly she made her way to the bed across from his and kissed each of her sleeping daughters. April had been disappointed at not getting to go with Carson yesterday to Pueblo. But April, who had turned six only a few weeks ago, was so even-tempered that she had taken the disappointment in stride.

Four-year-old Bonnie, on the other hand, was not so even-tempered. Winter Fawn could smile now at the tantrum her youngest daughter had thrown yesterday when she learned her da was leaving, but at the time, what with little Innes crying so pitifully, it had almost been more than Winter Fawn could take. Were it not for Megan, Winter Fawn might have thrown herself on the floor beside Bonnie and screamed and cried right along with her.

Pressing a hand to the ache in the small of her back, Winter Fawn straightened and picked up the lamp. After a final look and a prayer of thanks, she stepped out of the room and placed the lamp on the high shelf between their door and the door to her and Carson's room, where it would be out of the reach of little hands. Then she turned down the wick and went to the kitchen.

There she found Megan giving a final wipe to the dishpan. Every day Winter Fawn gave thanks for this daughter of Carson's. Winter Fawn had loved her at first sight, when Megan had been six and terrified at seeing her father captured by Arapaho. The poor girl had already lost her mother and grandfather, and suddenly now her beloved father had been in danger. Yet, despite her fear, Megan had been a brave little thing. She was thirteen now, a beautiful young lady, always eager and willing to help Winter Fawn with the children and the chores. Especially, Winter Fawn thought fondly, if doing so meant avoiding schoolwork.

"You're all finished," Winter Fawn observed, looking around at the tidy, clean kitchen.

"Yes," Megan said. "Is it all quiet in there?"

Winter Fawn smiled. "Aye," she said, her father's Scottish burr slipping into her voice, as it always did when her emotions ran high, or when she was tired. "They all be asleep finally."

Megan gave her a smile. "You look like you could use a little sleep yourself."

Winter Fawn's smile turned wan. "I think I'm too tired to sleep. Besides, I have mending to do."

"I can do it, if you want."

Winter Fawn pursed her lips. "Don't you have an essay to write for school?"

Megan grimaced. "Don't remind me."

Winter Fawn laughed. "It sounds as if someone needs to."

A loud thump, then another, came from the front porch.

Winter Fawn turned toward the door. "Bess," she breathed in relief.

"You should scold her for being so late. It's well past dark. She said she'd be home for supper."

Winter Fawn rushed toward the door, eager to make sure Bess was all right. It wasn't like her to be gone so long.

As she reached for the latch, Winter Fawn paused. A feeling of uneasiness swept over her.

Megan picked up on the feeling instantly. "What is it?" she whispered.

"I don't know," Winter Fawn answered, her voice low. There hadn't been another sound since those two footsteps on the porch. If they were footsteps. But what else could they be?

Yet if that was Bess out there, she wouldn't just stand out on the porch. She would come on into the house.

It could be Carson, returning early for some reason. He wasn't due for another day or two, but something could have brought him back early. But if it was him, he would have called out or entered the house by now.

It could be a drifter trying to decide whether or not to knock and ask for a meal. Except an honest drifter would have called out before clomping up the porch steps. And he most likely would have gone to the bunkhouse at this time of night, rather than the big house.

Another sound, a shuffling noise, came through the door.

Truly alarmed now, Winter Fawn glanced to make certain the bar was secure across the door. It wasn't.

The latchstring. She had left the latchstring out. Anyone

could open the door and walk in. Anyone on earth. Why hadn't she pulled in the bloody latchstring?

Carefully, she backed away, edging toward the gun rack beside the fireplace.

"Megan," she said softly, "go upstairs."

"No." Megan hurried to her stepmother's side. "I can shoot. I'll do more good down here with you."

"Aye, and won't we feel foolish when yon visitor turns out to be a lost steer."

"If it is, it can be our little secret," Megan said, her voice shaking with nerves as she reached for the shotgun. "Nobody has to know what 'fraidy-gooses we were."

Winter Fawn wasn't very good with a rifle. She rushed into the bedroom and dug out Carson's pistol, fumbling for a moment to make sure it was loaded. Then quietly, except for the thundering of her heart, she went to the door and gingerly, a fraction of an inch at a time so that maybe, if someone were out there, they wouldn't notice, she pulled in the latchstring.

With that done, she leaned against the door until her knees stopped trembling.

Behind her, Megan turned down the wick on the kitchen lamp until it emitted only a small glow.

Out on the porch there was another shuffling, scraping sound, then another hollow thud. Like a large man's heavy footfall on the step.

Man-Above. What should she do? Stand there all night until whoever it was went away? What if someone was hurt out there and unable to call for help?

What if it's Carson?

Ach, she couldn't just hide and do nothing. Yet she must, at all costs, protect Megan and the children.

Taking a deep breath for courage, she motioned Megan across the room, so the girl would have a clear shot at the door. From there she could also see the window. Just in case.

Then Winter Fawn straightened and cocked the pistol. "Who's there?" she demanded.

The only answer was another shuffling sound.

"We're armed in here," she warned. "We'll be shooting through the door if you don't speak up."

This time, there was a loud snort.

"A horse?" Megan asked, her voice tight.

Before Winter Fawn could answer, there came a loud crashing on the porch, and a low groan. It sounded like—

"Hunter?" Winter Fawn called, her heart racing. "Hunter? Is that you? Did you bring Bess home?"

Another low moan came in response.

Man-Above, it *was* Hunter, and something was terribly wrong. Winter Fawn flung open the door. "Bring the lamp," she cried to Megan.

A horse with no saddle stood with its forelegs on the middle step. Before him Hunter lay sprawled on the porch.

Winter Fawn reached out and touched her brother and jerked her hand back, unnerved by the unexpected feel of something hard and crusty. Mud, she realized a moment later when Megan arrived with the lamp. Dried and caked from his head to the soles of his moccasins. But something darker covered his shirt. Blood.

"Hunter," she called anxiously, feeling along his neck for the pulse that would reassure her.

"Bess," he groaned.

"What about Bess?" Winter Fawn leaned closer. "Where is she? What happened? Where are you hurt?" The last question was unnecessary and unkind. She could find the center of his pain herself without asking him to concentrate and speak. Ignoring the dried mud and fresh blood, she ran her hands over his chest, searching for injury.

"Took . . . her," he managed on a short breath.

Ach, Winter Fawn thought with anguish. It was hard to concentrate on his pain and at the same time worry about what his words meant. And then she found it as she ran her hand down his chest. Sharp and dull at once, enormous pain that doubled her over.

"Mama!" Megan cried.

"I'm . . . all right." Winter Fawn forced her hand away from the hole in Hunter's chest. Man-Above help her, it was a bullet hole. "Inside. Help me get him inside."

Megan plunked the lamp down on the porch. "I'll go get help."

"No!" Winter Fawn snagged the hem of Megan's skirt before the girl could leap from the porch and run to the bunk-house.

"But—"

"There's no time," Winter Fawn said urgently. "They can't help him. I can. Just help me."

Megan's eyes widened. "You're going to . . ." The girl swallowed hard. "The secret?"

"You remember that?"

"Yes." As if it were yesterday, Megan thought. She'd been six at the time. They had just come to Colorado—Megan, her father, and Aunt Bess. That was before Winter Fawn and her father had married. Megan had sliced her hand open on a broken plate. Winter Fawn had rushed to her side and pressed her own hand over the cut. Megan remembered heat, and an instant easing of the pain. When Winter Fawn had taken her hand away, the cut on Megan's palm was gone. Just . . . gone. As though it had never been there. Except for the traces of blood and the remembered pain, she might have thought she'd imagined the entire incident.

Then, too, there had been the stunned faces of Megan's father and Aunt Gussie, who had been standing behind Winter Fawn at the time, although Winter Fawn hadn't known they were there.

Afterward, Winter Fawn had sworn Megan to secrecy. She

wasn't to tell anyone what had happened, or the magic might not work the next time.

Megan looked down at Hunter, at the blood on his shirt, the pain in his face. If ever there was a need for magic . . .

"I never told anyone," she whispered. "But Mama, this is . . . this is no cut on the hand. This is—"

"I know." Winter Fawn bit the inside of her cheek. There were men in the bunkhouse. If one of them should wander outside and stroll this way, they would surely be curious about what might be happening on the porch at night that required a light, and had Winter Fawn and Megan on their knees.

It was impossible, of course, to keep a gift such as the one Winter Fawn had been born with a secret. But it was not something that she spoke about. Her mother's people, the Southern Arapaho, knew because it had been necessary a number of years ago for Winter Fawn to heal her father in full sight of the tribe.

Afterward, many of the people she had lived with her entire life began to look at her strangely, to shy away from her.

In the white world, Winter Fawn chose to keep her gift as private as possible. She used it when necessary, but she did not speak of it, nor did those around her. If the men in the bunkhouse knew, they said nothing. If they did not know, it was better—safer for her—that they remain in ignorance.

Yet to drag Hunter into the house where others could not see would take time and cause him extra pain he did not need. Her brother's life was much more important than her privacy.

"Never mind about moving him inside," she said briskly. "I'll do it here. But I may need your help, Megan."

Megan set the lamp beside Hunter and knelt next to Winter Fawn. "What can I do?"

"If I faint—"

"Oh, no!"

"Aye," Winter Fawn said firmly. Hunter's wound did not look as bad as that horrible hole in her father's gut that she had healed years ago. That bullet had gone clear through her father and torn a large hole in his back on its way out. This did not appear as severe. She had yet to see Hunter's back, but he would never have made it to the ranch alive with a wound that bad. Her father had barely lived the few moments it had taken her to get to his side.

Also, Winter Fawn knew that each year, her gift grew stronger within her. She did not believe she would be endangering herself to heal her brother, but if the reverse were true, she would still do it. She could not sit by and let her brother die. Not if there was anything she could do about it. And there most definitely was.

Still, the wound was bad enough that she had to warn Megan of what might happen. "I may faint, Megan. If I do, you must make certain that my hand stays on his wound, even if you have to hold it there yourself. Can you do that?"

Megan swallowed. "I can do it."

"Bless you, lass." Winter Fawn looked down and saw that Hunter's eyes were open. "Hunter? Can you hear me? You're going to be all right."

Through gritted teeth, he asked, "Can you do this?"

"Aye."

"I dinna ask for maself. 'Tis for Bess. I hae to go after Bess." He struggled as if to rise.

"Nae." Winter Fawn held him down easily.

Hunter was appalled at his own weakness. For a minute, he'd felt all right. The pain had dulled and spread out, no longer centered in that one hot, tight knot in his chest. But that one effort at moving had centered the pain again and brought it into sharp focus.

Then his sister placed her hand over the hole in his hide. First he felt heat, then an easing of the pain. He watched, almost dispassionately, as his sister took the pain, and the wound, into herself. Her face contorted with it. Her body flinched. As he grew stronger, she grew weaker. Blood blossomed across the front of her dress. She moaned in agony.

Hunter hated himself for putting her through this.

Winter Fawn's eyes rolled back, and she fell in a slump across him.

Hunter swore.

Megan cried out in dismay.

Hunter struggled to rise.

"No," Megan cried. "You have to stay still. She said to keep her hand on you." She lifted Winter Fawn's limp hand and placed it back over the wound in Hunter's chest.

"She's fainted, lass."

"I know that. But feel. Her hand is still hot."

It was true, Hunter realized. Winter Fawn was out cold, yet, through her warm touch, she was still healing him.

He must have passed out or dozed off, because the next thing he knew, he was blinking his eyes open to find Winter Fawn still out and draped across him, with Megan crying at his side.

Suddenly frantic, Hunter reached out and pressed his fingers against Winter Fawn's throat. There. Relief left him weak. Her pulse was strong and steady.

He gripped Megan's hand and squeezed. "She's going to be all right," he assured her.

Feeling dazed, he ran his hand over his chest. The pain was gone, and so, by the grace of Man-Above and Winter Fawn, was the bullet wound. The very thought of what had just happened there on the porch staggered him. He'd known of her gift, had seen her heal a wound or two in recent years. But he'd never been on the receiving end of it before. He felt humbled. Undeserving.

What had it cost his sister to save his worthless hide? She should have let him die.

But he couldn't die, not yet. He had to find Bess, had to bring her home. Had to kill four men.

After a moment, strength surged through him. He sat up and scooped his arms beneath his sister. "Let's get her inside."

It was two hours before Winter Fawn came around. As anxious as Hunter was to go after Bess, he could not leave the ranch until he knew for sure that Winter Fawn was all right.

In any case, he couldn't track in the dark. Dammit.

He had carried Winter Fawn to her bed, where Megan had cleaned her up and dressed her in her nightgown. Only then did Hunter learn that Carson was away from the ranch for a few days. Bess would have known that, which explained why she had let the outlaws believe she was the woman they were looking for, the one who could heal wounds by touching them.

"What about the rest of the men?" Hunter had asked sharply. "Where are they?"

"In the bunkhouse."

While Hunter was grateful the hands hadn't come out to witness Winter Fawn's healing him—some people believed such gifts were evil rather than sacred—he intended to have a sharp word with them about keeping a better watch over the place. From the looks of it, if the Rawlins gang had come here, they could have made off with everything and everyone in the damn house while the men played cards around that old, scarred table in the bunkhouse.

After he and Megan had Winter Fawn settled, and Hunter had put his horse in a stall in the barn—with an extra measure of oats and a handful of corn—Megan heated wash water for him and gave him some of Carson's clothes, since what little of his own weren't covered in blood were caked with dried mud.

When Winter Fawn finally roused, Hunter was at her side. "How do you feel?" he asked anxiously.

She frowned up at him and rested a forearm across her

forehead. "Hunter? Wha—?" Memory darkened her eyes. She sprang up in bed and reached for him. "Are you all right?"

"Thanks to you," he told her. "How about you?"

"I'm fine. What happened? Who shot you? Where's Bess?"

In clipped tones filled with anger—at himself, mostly—he told her.

"Took her?" she cried. "They took her?" She threw the bedcovers aside and swung her feet to the floor. "We'll send one of the men for the sheriff. Surely if they've just robbed a bank, there's a posse after them."

"They seemed to think there was. But I'm not waiting for the sheriff or a posse. Now that I know you're all right, I'm heading out."

"Now?" she protested. "You can't track in the dark, and it's—what time is it?"

"It's after midnight. I'm going back to my place. I want to be ready to follow their trail at first light."

"Alone? You canna mean to go alone. You'll need help."

"Do you forget, sister," he said in Arapaho, "that I am called Hunter?"

"Because you tracked a rabbit through heavy snow to its den," she cried in protest. "Hunter of Rabbits."

"Yes. In my third winter. Now I am a man, and I will hunt these men to their den."

Winter Fawn did not waste any more time trying to dissuade him. She knew in her heart that if anyone could find Bess and bring her home, it was Hunter. She reached for the robe lying across the foot of the bed.

"You'll need supplies."

CHAPTER FOUR

When dawn came, Bess was sitting in the same spot she'd been in all night, shivering beside the fire—or what was left of it—in a small clearing beside a mountain stream. She stared dully at the remaining embers, wondering why she was still alive. She would have screamed at God, protesting that she did not want to live in a world without Hunter, but screaming would take effort. Screaming would indicate that she cared, and she didn't. She didn't care about anything. She just wanted to sit there and die with what was left of the fire.

It was her fault. After everything was said and done, Hunter's death at the hands of Ned Rawlins was Bess's fault. Hunter hadn't wanted her there. If she had stayed home, as she knew she should have, he would have been alone in his canyon. He would have been paying attention, as he normally did, to everything around him, rather than having to shut himself up in the cabin because of a little rain and having to listen to her try to wheedle a declaration out of him.

Had she not been there to distract him, he would have seen

the riders coming and been ready for them. No one would have been able to sneak up on him.

Over and over in her mind she kept seeing that instant when Hunter had been stopped cold—shockingly so—by the impact of the bullet from Ned Rawlins's gun. The look on Hunter's face—sheer rage, and fear, and stunned disbelief when he looked down and saw the blood on his chest. The way he had fallen face down in the mud, never to stir again.

She supposed she had gone a little mad then. More than a little. She had fought, kicking and biting and scratching, disregarding the gun Rawlins pointed at her. She only knew she had to get to Hunter.

But it had been too late. Even as she had dug furrows down Rawlins's cheek with her fingernails and torn out a hunk of his beard scrambling to free herself from his hold, she had known it was too late.

She had screamed Hunter's name until there had been nothing left of her voice.

Rawlins had thrown her onto her horse, tied her hands to the saddle horn, and taken her reins himself. Everything after that was a blur, including the night that had followed. She knew they had stopped to camp at dusk somewhere in the mountains, but she couldn't bring herself to care where, or what might happen to her.

Yet gradually, as the eastern sky lightened, she became aware of little things that penetrated her numbness, and she resented them. Something heavy and reeking of sweaty horse lay draped across her shoulders. It scratched through her dress. She thought perhaps her hands were gripping it, but looking down to see would take too much energy, and frankly, she didn't particularly care what her fingers were clamped around. They were numb, anyway.

In a nearby tree, a bird woke and flitted from branch to branch. Behind her men stirred in their bedrolls. And from inside her own body she became aware of a growing, desperate need to relieve herself. But to do that, she would have to rise. She would have to take deliberate action. Stand up. Walk. Look around at a new day.

Something pink dangled in the corner of her vision. She nearly smiled, realizing it was one of the gingham roses on her hat. Imagine that. She still had her hat on.

She'd taken such care with her appearance—was it only yesterday? A new dress, a new hat. She had wanted every advantage possible in her campaign to breach Hunter's defenses.

Hunter.

Oh, God, Hunter.

"Get up, lady."

Someone was speaking to her, hitting her on the shoulder.

"Get up, damn you, and take care of my brother."

Involuntarily, Bess looked up. Woody looked down at her with anger in his eyes.

"You been sittin' there all goddamn night. You shoulda fixed him by now. I want you to fix him like Gonzales said you could."

"I don't know any Gonzales," she said dully. It was a lie, of course. She had met a man named Gonzales years ago. He used to trade with the Southern Arapaho and Cheyenne, and he had known Winter Fawn and Hunter from the days when they lived with the tribe, as well as after they had come to live on the ranch. If there was a Gonzales who knew about Winter Fawn's healing gift, it would be him. "I know a Juanita Gonzales from Badito. She's ninety-seven and has no teeth."

Woody Smith knew he wasn't real smart. Folks had been calling him a dummy ever since Pa had knocked him out of the hayloft and he'd landed on his head. Cecil always swore that before that, Woody had been as smart as the next fellow.

But dummy or not, Woody knew when somebody was lying to him, and this damn girl was lying, sure enough. "I say you do know the man I'm talkin' about."

"You're wrong." Bess stared up at Woody until pain exploded along the left side of her ribs and she went sprawling across Woody's boots. Dumbfounded and disoriented, she looked around and realized that Ned Rawlins had kicked her.

Ned had been watching her for some time. The last watch had been Billy's, but Billy was a screw-up from the word go, so Ned had made sure to be awake for the past hour or more. Besides, he'd been eager for first light so they could get on up the mountain to the hideout.

As far as he was concerned, women were nothing but trouble. The girl and Woody might think he'd brought her along to take care of Cecil. If she could help Cecil, that'd be fine, 'cause Ned had a fondness for his oldest partner. But Ned figured Cecil was probably a goner, no matter what anybody did for him.

It was too damn bad about Cecil. If Ned had ever thought of any man as his friend, it was Cecil Smith. Friend, and more, if the truth were known. Which it wasn't, except between Ned and Cecil.

No, Ned had brought the girl for Billy. They hadn't gotten to stay in a town in days, and Billy tended to go a little crazy when he went too long without a woman to poke his pecker in. He'd got so rowdy down in Trinidad last month, the damn whore had up and died while Billy was still pounding on her. That little trick had got them run outta town. Ned hoped this girl here would take the edge off for his little brother before they met J.T. and headed on up to Pueblo.

Still, he figured she might as well take care of Cecil 'til they got to the cabin. "Get your useless ass over there and see about Cecil, girl," he snarled, "before I turn Billy loose on you."

As Bess lay there hugging her side, she thought it strange that she could actually feel her lethargy deserting her. She didn't mind dying. Had been wishing for it all night. But she was forced to acknowledge that she did not care for pain, and cared even less for being kicked. She refused to even think about what Rawlins might have meant about turning Billy loose on her.

She had survived Sherman's march on Atlanta and capture by Arapaho dog soldiers. It suddenly seemed important to her that she not allow the Rawlins gang to defeat her. They were so much less than those other enemies, yet they had taken more from her than anyone should have to lose. They had taken Hunter, and along with him, her chance for true love.

For Hunter, she decided, pushing herself up from the ground. She would survive to avenge Hunter. Somehow, some way, she would make Ned Rawlins pay. They would all pay.

The horse blanket that had been around her shoulders tangled around her ankles. Once she made it to her feet, she swayed before gaining her balance.

The insides of her thighs screamed in agony. They had put Hunter's saddle on her horse yesterday, rather than her own sidesaddle. It was a good thing, she supposed, that she hadn't cared what happened to her yesterday, else she would have realized how physically miserable she was just that much sooner.

Not that she'd never ridden astride before. Of course she had. Once. Seven years ago.

She turned away from the men and headed for the limited privacy offered by the scrub growing among the trees.

Rawlins grabbed her arm and yanked her off balance so that she stumbled into him.

"Where the hell do you think you're going?" he demanded.

Everything about this man repelled her. His hair was so greasy that she couldn't tell what color it was. His breath was rancid, his hands were cruel, and there was no telling what was beneath that repulsive, snarled beard.

She narrowed her eyes and jerked free of his hold. "To the bushes," she stated.

No one tried to stop her, but Rawlins warned her that she

better not go far. "You get outta sight, I'll send Billy after you."

"Maybe I just better go with her," Billy said with a leer. "I wouldn't mind watchin' her lift those skirts. Maybe she needs a little help."

"Maybe," Bess said coldly, "she doesn't."

Turning her back on them again, she walked slowly into the trees, praying with every step that no one would follow.

No one did.

When she returned to camp, she went to Cecil's side and knelt. His eyes were open. Woody came and stood beside her. To him she said, "I'll need water, something clean, if possible, to replace the bandage, and some willow bark."

"To hell with that. All you gotta do is put your hand on the wound and heal it."

"There's a stand of willows down there." She pointed downstream to the thick stand of willows. "I need some bark. Enough to make a tea."

"We ain't sittin' around for no damn tea party," Billy said with a snarl.

"You've got five minutes, girl," Rawlins said. "Then we're riding out."

Bess took a deep breath and looked up at the outlaw leader. "Your friend is never going to recover if he doesn't get some rest."

"He'll get permanent rest—we all will—if we stay out here in the open and let some trigger-happy posse catch us."

"Perhaps you should consider a less risky line of work."

Rawlins laughed. "You sure are something, with your fancy talk and snooty ways. You just do what you can for Cecil before we load him up on his horse and ride out. He's one tough son of a bitch. He'll make it fine. Won't ya, Cecil?"

"Sure, Ned," Cecil managed with a grimace. "I'll make it fine." He motioned for Woody to go after the things Bess wanted.

She did what she could for Cecil, but the wound was seeping an ugly, gray ooze that had a rotting smell to it.

"How . . . how bad is it?" Cecil asked.

Bess met his pain-filled gaze steadily. "I won't lie to you. It's pretty bad."

"Am I gonna die?"

"I honestly don't know. With proper rest and care, I believe you might recover. But . . ."

"We'll be at the hideout today. Once we get there, you can take proper care of me, can't you?"

If either of us lives that long, she thought. But she said, "I'll do my best."

Then he smiled at her, a trembling smile of gratitude. Flustered, Bess finished with the new bandage, torn from the tail of Woody's shirt. When she stood and turned away, Billy was waiting for her. He gave her a leer that sent chills of fear down her spine while he rubbed one gloved hand up and down along his crotch.

"I gotta ache you can see to now, girl."

Bess nearly strangled on the terror that rose to her throat. To die, to welcome the idea of death, was one thing. To be raped by this man—these men, she amended, seeing Rawlins grin from behind Billy . . .

"Lay down and spread those pretty legs for me, girl."

Bess tried to swallow, but her mouth was as dry as the plains in drought. Suddenly she knew that she did not want to die. But if that was her only alternative to what Billy had planned for her, then she would welcome death with open arms. She could do nothing now but fight.

"I think not," she said to Billy.

The outlaw, younger than Rawlins and Cecil, but older looking than Woody, blinked at her in surprise. "You— Well, hell. Ya hear that, big brother?" he said to Rawlins. "She thinks not." He rubbed his crotch again and grinned. "Damned if she don't make me harder than a fence post."

Then Billy lunged at her, those gloved hands reaching for her. They went down in a tangle of arms, legs, and skirt. Bess bit and clawed and kicked. Billy cursed and laughed and used his weight to hold her down. With one dirty hand, he squeezed her breast so hard that tears stung her eyes. He pinched her waist and clutched at her inner thighs.

Frantic, terrified, Bess increased her efforts to be free of him. Her knee found, with all the force she could muster, that fence post he'd bragged about.

Billy screeched and rolled away, this time grabbing himself with both hands.

Bess rolled the opposite direction. Her breath came hard. Her heart thundered in her ears, sounding like a herd of stampeding cattle.

While the other men looked on avidly, Billy slowly crawled to his feet. "Damn you, bitch," he said, stripping off his gloves and flexing his fingers. "I'll kill you for that."

Before he could throw himself on top of her again, Bess made it to her feet. When he reached out with one hand to grab her again, Bess reached up and whipped the twelve-inch hatpin from her hat. Holding the thin, sharp steel in both hands to give it stability, she jabbed him in the hand.

Billy howled in rage. A thin line of blood streamed from the center of his right palm. In his eyes, Bess saw her death.

"Looks like she's a little livelier than we thought," Rawlins said with a chuckle. "You set out to poke her, and she poked you first." He laughed harder at his own joke. "Want me to hold her for you, Billy Boy?"

Billy snarled. "I ain't never needed your help yet with a woman, big brother." He crouched before Bess and held his arms out to his sides, never taking his eyes off her. "Don't reckon I need it now."

"Well, hurry up and get to it," Ned said with disgust. "We need to get a move on."

Their conversation distracted Bess just enough to slow her

down when Billy moved. It was so fast, she didn't really see
his arm swing out. But she felt the impact of the back of his
hand against her cheek. The force of the blow knocked her to
the ground. He was on her again before she knew it, his heavy
weight crushing the breath from her lungs. One of his hands
gripped her wrist and held it to the ground above her head,
pinning down the hand that held the hatpin. She felt his other
hand tugging her skirt up toward her waist. She screamed.

Through the haze of pain that felt as though it was eating
him alive, Cecil Smith watched as Billy backhanded the girl
yet again. Woody might have thought they'd brought the girl
to take care of Cecil, but Cecil knew better. Ned had brought
her along for sport. For Billy's sport, and maybe Woody's. As
for Ned—well, Ned had other tastes, but they would have to
wait until Cecil got better. If Cecil survived.

Cecil knew he was bad off. He figured his chances of seeing
another sunrise were slim to none. His little brother would try
to take care of him, but Woody never had been any good at
doctoring. Or any other thing, for that matter, but none of that
was Woody's fault.

As for Ned and Billy, Cecil figured they were already counting his share of the loot as theirs.

Near as he could figure, he had one chance of surviving, and
that was if the girl took real good care of him.

It cost him considerable, but he managed to pull his revolver
from the holster at his hip and cock it.

Despite the noise of the struggle, the sound of the hammer
being pulled back echoed through the little clearing like a
church bell.

"Let her be, Billy," Cecil managed.

Sprawled across the girl, Billy raised his head and stared
down the barrel of Cecil's Colt. "Put that thing away," he
snarled. "What the hell's the matter with you? I'm just havin'
a little fun."

Sweat coated Cecil's face. "I said let her be. You hurt her

too bad, she won't be able to take care of me. I seen a girl raped by a bunch of fellows once over to Kansas. After they was finished with her, she just laid there and stared up at the sky. From then on, her mama had to dress her and feed her and do everything for her. The girl never spoke another word, not 'til the day she throwed herself in front of the train.''

"Ah, hell, Cecil, you know you're done for, anyway. 'Sides,'' Billy said, "this 'un's got too much spit and vinegar to turn into a idiot over a little pokin', don't ya, girl?''

"I said get off her.''

"Cecil,'' Ned said. "What the hell you think you're doing, drawing down on Billy like this?''

"Tryin' to stay alive, Ned. Just tryin' to stay alive.''

"Well, you picked a piss-poor way to go about it.'' Ned drew his gun and leveled it at Cecil. "I'll admit Billy ain't no prize, but I don't stand for nobody drawing down on my brother. Not even you.''

"Same goes,'' Woody said, drawing his own gun and pointing it at Ned. "You ain't got no call to go aimin' that thing at Cecil.''

For a long moment, no one moved. Then suddenly Ned laughed bitterly and holstered his revolver. "A bunch of damn fools, that's what we are, letting a woman get us all in an uproar. Her screaming was loud enough to wake the dead. Go adding gunshots to it when we all start firing at each other, and we'll bring every prospector and who knows who all down on our heads quicker than spit. 'Course, it won't matter none, 'cause we'll have all killed each other by then. Billy, unhand that girl and get her up on her horse. We're pulling out.''

"I'll unhand her when I'm done pokin' her.''

Ned gave his little brother a steely-eyed look. "If I have to tell you again, I'm taking half your share of the money.''

Billy braced a forearm across Bess's throat to hold her still. "What the hell would you do a damn thing like that for?''

"Let's call it a fine. An asshole fine. You act like an asshole, and I fine you."

"Ah, hell, Ned." Billy grinned and rolled off Bess. "I've always been an asshole. You know that."

"That doesn't mean you have to act like one, little brother."

Billy grunted and pushed himself to his feet. He headed for his saddlebags and started digging around in one of them until he pulled out a bottle of whiskey.

"Dammit, Billy." Ned swiped the bottle out of his hand. "You know the rules. No hootch 'til we get to the cabin."

"Goddammit, Ned, it ain't fair. I got a woman and a bottle right under my nose, and you won't let me have neither one of 'em."

Ned stuffed the bottle back into the saddlebag. "I shoulda left you at home. You don't settle down some, boy, I'll send you there, sure as shit."

Billy made a face, then stumbled off into the bushes.

Sensing the trouble was over, at least for the time being, Cecil and Woody holstered their guns.

Woody laughed. "An asshole fine. That's a good one, Ned."

Cecil looked over at the woman. "I expect you to take real good care of me."

Bess swallowed hard. This man had just saved her from rape, possibly death. She swallowed again. "I'll do my best."

Two hours after sunup, Hunter lost their trail. He knew he would pick it up again, but he cursed at the need to slow his pace.

They had left his barn and ridden due north out of the canyon. The tracks of six horses—four for the men, one packhorse, and Bess's mare—were easily followed. When they'd hit the road that more or less paralleled the river, they had taken it west. On the road, their tracks were obliterated by a freight wagon and the six mules pulling it.

Now he had to watch both sides of the road carefully so as not to miss the spot where the Rawlins gang had turned off. Logic told him they would head north again, into the Wet Mountains, but he wasn't taking any chances. He searched both sides, concentrating on the task at hand, deliberately blocking thoughts of what Bess might be going through. If he let himself think, for even a moment, about Bess, he would be useless to her. Such rage and fear as he'd never known in his life would surge inside of him, and he would miss the very sign he was looking for.

In the end, he nearly missed it anyway. Rawlins, it seemed, was no fool. They had left the road—heading north, as Hunter had guessed—singly and in pairs. Not until Hunter recognized the track made by Bess's mare did he realize that the two previous single horses were not just lone riders leaving the road. A mile north, the separate tracks came together and headed into the foothills.

Grimly, Hunter followed.

It was early afternoon when he found her hat. The sight of it, filthy and bedraggled, lying tangled in the brush along the tree line, nearly stopped his heart.

He dismounted and studied the area.

They had camped here. Someone had done a half-assed job of hiding their sign, but that was the best Hunter could say for their efforts.

What he saw in the dirt near Bess's hat froze his blood. Scattered around the clearing, the signs left by four separate bedrolls were plain. But here, at his feet, there had been a struggle. Bess had been on the ground. There had been a heavy weight on top of her. A man, wearing boots.

A violent trembling started in Hunter's knees and vibrated upward. He clenched his fists at his sides and fought to maintain control, of his mind, his body. He would do Bess no good if he ran through the forest bellowing his rage and fear for her. Slowly, after several deep breaths, and imagining each member of the Rawlins gang spitted to the hilt on his knife, Hunter was able to rein in his seething emotions. He had to stay calm, for Bess.

Raising his face to the eastern sky, Hunter of Men spoke in the language of his mother's people. "Man-Above, Great Father of the Inuna-ina, grant me power over these enemies who would dishonor someone whose heart is so pure and innocent as my Blue Eyes. Grant me the eyes of the eagle, the cunning of the fox, the swiftness of the deer, the strength of the bear, with which to tear these men limb from limb."

Then, in the odd mingling of languages, religions, and cultures in which he'd been raised, Hunter finished the prayer in English. "Amen."

For long moments, he held Bess's ruined hat in his hands, bitterly regretting the hurt he'd caused her yesterday when she came to see him. If the unthinkable happened and he did not get her back alive, he would forever damn himself that their final conversation had been an argument. If he got her back—

No. Not if. *When* he got her back . . .

Carefully he placed her hat, bedraggled flowers and all, in his saddlebag.

Something metal flashed in the sun. He stooped and sifted the dirt aside with his fingers.

A hat pin. Bess's. With a trace of blood on the pointed tip.

She was fighting them. It was the only thing that made sense. If they wanted to hurt her, they had ample means. Hunter doubted it would ever occur to a rough bunch of outlaws that hatpins even existed, let alone that one could be used as a weapon.

No, that wasn't Bess's blood. She had used it to stab one of them.

A deep shudder ran through him. He didn't know whether to be fiercely proud of her courage and ingenuity, or even more afraid for her safety. No one in the Rawlins gang struck him as particularly tolerant of a woman's attempts to defend herself. She might very well have only angered them more.

Hunter turned and looked up the mountain in the direction they had taken her.

"Hold on, Blue Eyes. I'm coming."

CHAPTER FIVE

The afternoon sun was in her eyes, making Bess's battle against tears that much more difficult. Bitterly she regretted having sat up all night. She doubted she could have slept, but stretching out, even on the cold ground, might have eased her muscles somewhat. Her legs hurt so badly now—not only from straddling the horse, but also because the stirrups were still set to accommodate Hunter's longer legs and she couldn't reach them—that it was all she could do to keep from weeping openly. Her hands, tied once more to the saddle horn, had gone numb hours ago. Her shoulders ached something fierce, and her backside, she was certain, was one big bruise. Her bladder was full to bursting, while her mouth was too dry for words. And now the sun was in her eyes.

But she fought her tears, fought them from sheer stubbornness. She would not give these outlaws the satisfaction of knowing how close she was to breaking.

Suddenly Ned Rawlins called a halt, the first in hours. As they had before, the men made no pretense at decency, opening their pants and relieving themselves in front of her. Billy seemed to take special delight in facing her while he did it. She had stopped being shocked, but a fierce blush stung her cheeks. She closed her eyes and turned her face away, her stomach tightening in panic.

Would Ned go back on his word to Cecil not to bother her? Would they come at her this time? Would one or two of them hold her down and let Billy pull up her skirts?

God, please, no.

She opened her eyes in time to see Ned Rawlins striding toward her, his face set in hard lines. Without words, he untied her hands and stepped back.

"If you gotta go, do it now."

Heat suffused her face as another blush stung her cheeks.

Ned glared at her through narrowed eyes. "Girl, you've got 'til the count of three to get down off that horse before I tie your hands again."

If she didn't get down and get to the privacy of the nearest bushes immediately, Bess knew she would soon humiliate herself right there in the saddle. She needed, desperately, to dismount. She just didn't think she was capable of swinging her leg over the back of the horse.

"One."

She slid sideways and felt for the left stirrup with her foot.

"Two."

Her foot found the stirrup, but her knee refused to bear her weight. She pitched out of the saddle and straight into Ned Rawlins's chest.

He wasn't expecting it. They tumbled to the ground together. Rawlins bore the brunt of the impact. Not only did he have Bess's unexpected weight to contend with, but the sharp point of her elbow jabbed directly into his diaphragm. His breath left him in an audible *woof.*

Having landed on top of him, Bess fared better. Fear of his reaction had her ignoring the pain and stiffness of her muscles and the numbness of her hands. She scrambled to her feet and dashed through the undergrowth beside the trail, disregarding the sound of rending fabric as her skirt caught on twigs and brambles. She jerked it free without slowing her pace and kept running.

Behind her, she heard the distinct sound of a gun being cocked. Billy's voice rang out sharply. "You get out of sight, girl, I'm coming after you."

Bess bit back a scream of pure rage and forced herself to stop her headlong flight. Running would do her no good. Already the rush of adrenalin was fading, letting her numerous pains be felt. In any case, she would not get far, trussed up as she was in a corset, and with her voluminous petticoats to catch on every twig and bramble.

She would have to bide her time and take care not to arouse the men's anger. Or anything else, she thought with a shudder.

Never before had Bess truly hated anyone, not even the Arapaho dog soldiers who had captured her and her family years ago. She had feared them, been terrified of them, but that terror had not left room for hatred.

There were people she disliked, but none she could truly say she despised. Until now. For the first time in her life, she felt the hot flood of hatred fill her veins. It gave her the strength and determination to take care of her business, straighten her skirt with a jerk, and march back out to the horses with her head high. Let them think the flames in her cheeks were from embarrassment.

The heat deserted her a moment later, however, and left her shaken when Ned Rawlins blindfolded her after tying her hands again.

"But—but why?" she protested.

"Shut up." He checked the blindfold and made sure it was tight. "Can you see anything?"

"Through closed eyes and your filthy bandanna?" she asked hotly.

Ned grunted and gave the knot at the back of her head one final tug, chuckling when she winced.

He took a minute to glance up the mountain. He couldn't see the cabin from here, but it was only a few hundred yards up, as the crow flies. Couldn't get there that way, of course. The trail zigzagged back and forth up the steep side to the shoulder of the mountain.

No, he couldn't see the cabin, but if he looked hard enough, he could see an occasional whiff of smoke drifting up from the trees up there. That meant the boss was waiting for them. Warming his lazy ass before a fire. Ned was about ready to be shed of the man, and that was a fact.

They had hooked up with J.T. two years ago this past winter.

Well, that wasn't exactly right. It had been J.T. who found them.

It had been just Ned and Cecil back in those days. Hellfire, what fun they'd had. They weren't out to get rich, just kick up their heels a little, have a good time, with nobody to tell them what to do. They eventually wanted to have enough money to live like respectable citizens. But first they wanted some fun.

Somehow their robberies had drawn the attention of the man who, according to him, was in the position to help them take bigger and bigger hauls, to really make a name for themselves. All they had to do, J.T. swore, was bring in a couple of more men and hit the places that he knew had enough money to make it worth their while.

Ned and Cecil had balked at first. They knew they could get two other men to ride with them, but they didn't feel like putting up with any wisecracks, and most men wouldn't have anything to do with men like Ned and Cecil. Men who preferred each other over women.

Then they thought of their own brothers, who already knew about their particular tastes and didn't give a damn. So they'd brought Woody and Billy out from Missouri and started making

a name for themselves. The Rawlins gang. Ned smiled. It had
a nice ring to it.

But then, he figured they coulda done the same thing without
J.T., if they'd wanted. These days he was wishin' they had.
Wishin' like hell they'd never met that uppity bastard.

So what if their takes had been on the small side back then,
compared to what they were now? At least they'd had no one
to answer to but themselves. It had been more fun then. No
one to come along and take a cut off the top before they divvied
up their haul.

Still, the bastard's information was good. He seemed to know
where the money was. Hadn't steered them wrong yet. Which
didn't mean they wouldn't be doing a little of their own skim-
ming off the top. Now that the girl was blindfolded, Ned
motioned for Woody to start digging. The man up the mountain
would never know the difference if a few thousand dollars
didn't make it to the cabin, now would he?

Ned chuckled at his own wit. The man thought he was smart,
but Ned Rawlins was smarter, by God. He would get the gang
out from under J.T.'s thumb. They had one more job lined up
after this one. They would go their own way right now, but a
U.S. Army payroll was too damn good to pass up. Besides,
they had to give the boss his share of this take, because Ned
wasn't ready to leave the territory yet, and J.T. knew too much
about them, knew all their hideouts, their friends.

They had Billy to thank for the latter. Billy liked to hear
himself talk too damn much, and he didn't worry none about
who might be listening.

Ned sighed. Some days, he wished he'd left his little brother
back home in Missouri. The kid was twenty years old and acted
twelve most of the time. Except when it came to women. He
was man enough then; he was a crazy man with women.

Yeah, things had sure been better before Ned and Cecil had
brought their little brothers in with them, before they'd hooked
up with J.T. Now Cecil was dyin'. Damn shame about that,

but there didn't seem to be anything anybody could do about
it. The girl could change that damn bandage every five minutes
from here to Sunday, and Cecil was still gonna die.

It was time, Ned thought, to think about making a few
changes in the way things ran around here. Maybe, after the
Army payroll, it would be time to become respectable.

When Woody finished digging the hole, Ned dropped in
three bank bags of twenty-dollar gold pieces. Billy then took
over and refilled the holes.

At least those two were good for something. They had strong
backs. Too bad their minds weren't much use.

Again Ned hoped that this little filly they'd dragged along
with them would be able to take the edge off Billy's appetite
for a few days. But even Billy drew the line at screwing a
corpse, which was why Ned had blindfolded the girl just now.
The boss man was going to pitch a fit when he saw they'd
brought her along, but Ned would be able to talk his way around
that, as long as the girl never got a look at the man.

Hell, she wasn't gonna get the chance to tell anybody anything anyway, so it didn't make any difference to Ned if she
was blindfolded or not. But J.T. was as careful as a long-tailed
cat in a room full of rocking chairs. If the girl saw his face,
the man would kill her right then and there, then Billy wouldn't
have her to play with, and he'd get all itchy. Billy was easier
to control when he wasn't all itchy.

By the time Bess realized they had stopped again, someone
was untying her hands and pulling her from the saddle. It took
a moment for her legs to steady. It was one thing to ride astride,
without benefit of stirrups, when she wasn't used to riding
astride at all. But the added disadvantage of being blindfolded
had nearly been more than Bess could deal with. If it wasn't
for the thin strip at the bottom edge of the blindfold that she
could see out of, she would have long since lost her balance

and fallen from the saddle. With her hands tied, she would have been dragged, and would quite likely have broken her wrists.

"Hello in the house," Billy called out.

House? They were at a house? She didn't know whether to be grateful or terrified.

"Shut up, Billy," Ned growled. "You know he likes to pretend he's not even here."

"Yeah, well, then he shouldn't build a fire and send all that smoke out all over creation. He's a damn peculiar son of a bitch, I'll say that for him. We oughta be shed of him, Ned. We don't need him bossin' this outfit. You're smarter than he is. You oughta take over as boss."

"I'm *your* boss, and don't you forget it." Then Ned said, "Cecil? You still with us?"

"That's a damn mean thing to say, Ned," Woody complained. "He's bad off. Real bad off. If the girl don't fix him, he's gonna die. He dies, I'll kill her. You hear that, girl? You gotta fix my brother."

Bess tried to swallow, but her mouth was too dry.

"Get him on inside," Ned said. Then, "Billy, you bring the girl. And check that blindfold. If she sees J.T., he'll kill her on the spot and you won't get your fun."

Fervently Bess prayed for her hatred and rage to return, for her fear was making her weak. Her knees were turning to jelly. When Billy grasped her arm and jerked her forward, she didn't have to pretend that she couldn't see, then fake a stumble. She could see only a narrow strip below each eye. To be sure of her steps, she would have to move forward mere inches at a time. Billy's stride was long and hurried. In his rushed wake, she faltered and fell to her knees in the dirt. By the time Billy dragged her indoors, she had skinned her knees and palms, hit her head on the door jamb, and rammed her shin into something unforgivably hard.

Still gasping for breath, she heard a new voice speak.

"What is all of this?" a man demanded.

The boss, Bess thought. The one Rawlins had spoken of, the one called J.T. Through the slit between her cheeks and the bandanna, she saw his boots. Spotless and gleaming, with not a speck of dust on them, as though shined only moments ago, they were black leather and looked expensive. By tilting her head slightly, Bess could see his trousers, and again she thought, *expensive.*

"What is she doing here, and what happened to him?"

Over the sound of grunts and shuffling, which Bess assumed was Woody helping Cecil in, Ned Rawlins said, "Cecil got himself shot. The girl's taking care of him. Then she's gonna take care of us, if you know what I mean."

Someone—Billy, she thought—bumped into Bess and knocked her off balance. While she staggered to regain her footing, she caught a glimpse of a man's hand. She knew at once that it belonged to the new man, for it was clean and well cared for, the nails neat and trimmed. In it he gripped a fine-grained black leather glove. A two-inch scar marked the outside edge of his palm just above his little finger.

"You kidnapped a girl," the man bellowed, "right from the middle of town? Good God, man, have you no sense at all? Robbing the bank surely angered the townsfolk enough. Now they'll be out for blood. They'll hang you on sight for stealing one of their women. Of all the *stupid—*"

Ned Rawlins stepped into Bess's narrow line of vision. "Before you go saying something I'm going to have to ram back down your throat, *Colonel—*"

"I told you not to call me that," the man hissed.

Ned went on as though the man hadn't spoken. "You told us this job would be a cinch."

"It should have been. Would have been, if you'd been thinking with your brains instead of with what's between your legs, you fool."

"I guess you think three armed guards is a cinch."

"What armed guards?"

"The ones you forgot to mention, *Colonel.* The ones at the bank. One of them got off a lucky shot at Cecil here. If you'd bothered to warn us—"

"I didn't know about any guards."

"You're supposed to know, damn you. That's what your cut's for."

"If it wasn't for me, you wouldn't have known that two-bit bank had any money worth stealing. Now you've brought back a girl who can identify all of you, and probably a dozen witnesses saw you take her."

"Nobody saw us take her," Ned bit back.

"In the entire town, no one saw you take her?" the other man demanded.

"We didn't take her from town. We took her from a homestead up a canyon. There's not a man alive who saw us."

The words rang in Bess's ears. *Not a man alive.*

Oh, God. Hunter!

"She can identify you," the fifth man said.

"You really must take me for a fool," Rawlins said with disgust. "When we get finished with her, she won't be telling anybody anything."

Afraid to so much as breathe lest she draw attention to herself, Bess stood frozen to the spot. She had understood from the beginning that they would have to kill her, but a tiny seed of hope had still lived, hope that they might let her go. That hope died a brutal death as the men spoke so plainly of killing her.

Oh, God, to die here in this miserable place, at the hands of these outlaws. It was too cruel to contemplate.

At first she hadn't wanted to live without Hunter. She still would not choose to be without him, without the life they could have had, the love they could have shared. But she still had her family. She could live for them, couldn't she? Didn't she want desperately to see her nieces and nephew grow to adulthood on the Double D? Didn't she want to be there for Aunt Gussie when old age finally claimed her?

Now these men, who had already taken Hunter and destroyed her future with him, would take the rest of her life as well, and leave her family to mourn. The thought was almost more than she could bear. Where was her anger? She wished desperately for its return, for terror and sadness threatened to send her to her knees.

"You're going to kill her?"

Bess's blood chilled.

"What do you think?"

"I think I don't wish to know about any of this. I want no part in murder."

"Then maybe you want no part in the rest of it," Rawlins responded.

"Maybe you're correct. Perhaps it would be best if this is our last association. I will make other arrangements for that Army payroll next month."

"Now, hold on," Billy said, his tone cajoling. It sounded to Bess as though he slapped someone on the back. "No need to get hasty here, fellas. Why, this is just a little misunderstandin', ain't that right, Ned? We didn't mean no harm in bringin' the girl up here, J.T. When we're finished with her, we'll take care of her so's she won't be talkin' to nobody. Besides which, she couldn't name you anyhow, right? Hell, why don't you take a turn on her yourself afore you go? You can be first."

"I'm afraid I shall have to decline your generous offer." The man's voice dripped with sarcasm. "I believe we have business to conduct? Let's get on with it. I have a need to be away from this place."

After a moment, Bess realized the thumps and shuffling she was hearing were the sounds of the men counting out and dividing up the money they'd stolen. She toyed fleetingly with the idea of telling the fifth man about the money the others had hidden before reaching the cabin, but then discarded the idea. Making such a claim would undoubtedly only serve to get her killed that much sooner, and she was in no hurry to die. If a chance came during the night for escape, she would take the wild, untamed mountains over these evil men in a heartbeat.

When they finished dividing up the money, the fifth man, J.T., made ready to leave.

"Don't forget to make sure this girl can't talk."

"It's not something we're likely to forget," Ned bit out. "It's our necks, after all. She hasn't seen you."

The man did not answer. The rhythmic sound of his footsteps crossed the room. The door opened, letting a gust of fresh air into the close atmosphere of the cabin.

"I'll have that payroll information for you when I come back through this area. Be in Walsenburg July Fourth or I'll find a new gang to handle it." He did not wait for an answer, but stepped outside and slammed the door behind him.

"I swear to God, Ned," Billy said heatedly, "I'd just as soon shoot that son of a bitch as look at him."

"You might just get your chance, little brother. But not before we hit that Army payroll. We need him for that. After that—well, we'll see. Now get that girl over there to see about Cecil."

Footsteps came toward her. Hands gripped her shoulders and spun her around so fast that she nearly fell. A tug at the knot in the bandanna, a painful pull on her hair. Then, praise God, the foul-smelling blindfold fell away.

Bess had to blink several times to clear her vision. The room was dim, the only light coming from the small fire in the fireplace. The only window in the room was shuttered; a thin stream of light seeped in around the edges.

There was no furniture. None. Not even a shelf on the wall.

Cecil lay unconscious in the corner opposite the door. His face was bathed in sweat and grime. He smelled of death.

Woody shoved her toward his brother. "Fix him." The plead-ing she had once seen in his eyes had been replaced with impatience and anger. "Fix him!"

It was impossible, Bess discovered, to take a deep breath and not also take in the smells of sweat and blood and death surrounding her. Not wanting to show any more weakness to these men than she already had, she managed to cover her gag with a cough.

"I'll need light," she said, trying to keep her voice even, her tone practical. "And water, preferably hot. And more band-aging."

"You don't need any of that stuff," Woody bellowed, advancing on her. "Just *fix* him, damn you."

"I—I can't d-do anything for him without—"

"I said *fix* him!" Tugging her down to Cecil's side, Woody slapped Bess's hand flat onto the bloodiest part of the bandage on Cecil's chest.

Cecil groaned and tried instinctively to move away from the pain.

Bess cringed, at both the pain she knew they were causing the man and at the bloody gore beneath her palm. The harder she tried to pull away, the harder Woody squeezed her wrist and pressed her hand against Cecil's chest.

"Fix him, damn you!"

"This isn't going to fix him," she cried. "You're hurting him."

"Touch him," Woody raved. "You touch him, and his wound goes away. That's what Gonzales said. He saw it with his own eyes. He wouldn't lie. Just do it, damn you, do it!"

His grip was so tight, Bess felt the bones of her wrist grind together. She cried out. "I can't! I don't know what you're talking about!"

"Liar!" With the back of his free hand, he struck her across the cheek. She would have been knocked several feet across the floor by the force of the blow, except he still had her by the wrist.

Bess cried out involuntarily and tasted blood.

"You heal him now, or I'll kill you."

She tried to dodge the next blow, but failed. Pain exploded along her jaw.

"For Christ's sake, Wood," Billy said with disgust. "What do you think she is, some goddamn faith healer?"

From the beginning, Bess had thought of Woody as slow-witted. She'd never associated that affliction with meanness before, but pure meanness was in his eyes now. He would kill her, and enjoy it. As if she were a bug on the ground, he would crush her beneath his boot heel and laugh while doing it.

Maybe he wasn't slow-witted and mean. Maybe, she thought as an icy weight settled in the pit of her stomach, he was just plain crazy.

He turned his blazing eyes on Billy. "Gonzales said——"

"I done told ya and told ya, you stupid idiot, Gonzales is nothin' but a drunk ol' greaser who wouldn't know his ass from a hole in the ground if you gave him a map. Kinda like you, in that regard."

Woody shoved Bess aside. With a roar of rage, he flew at Billy. They went down swinging at each other. Dust and curses and the meaty sound of fists striking flesh filled the air.

While Bess crouched in the corner near Cecil's feet, Ned Rawlins threw open the door.

The sudden bright light nearly blinded Bess.

Kicking and cussing, Rawlins waded into the fray. He grabbed each man by the hair and started dragging both of them toward the door. "Take it outside, boys."

He was rewarded with an elbow in the gut and a fist in the eye. He went down with a sharp curse.

Bess stared past the three brawling men at the open door. The gate to freedom. Could she do it? Could she slip past them and escape into the forest?

The truth was, she couldn't afford not to try, and she knew it. She would take the treacherous mountain and wild animals and the dark of night any day over what awaited her here in this cabin. She had no choice.

Easing herself up on trembling legs, Bess braced her back against the wall and inched her way toward the door.

Billy tripped over Ned's outstretched boot and fell backward, straight into Bess, nearly knocking the wind out of her.

"You see that?" Ned roared, pointing at her. "Your little darlin' there was headed for the door, and not a one of us was looking. Goddamn women are more trouble than they're worth. You—" He kicked Woody in the leg. "Go dig up the stash crate and get her a lantern so she can see to work on Cecil. And bring in some water while you're at it."

Woody staggered to his feet and snarled. "How come I gotta do it?"

"Because he's your damn brother."

Billy turned to Bess and tried to pull her close to him. She struggled to free herself.

"Billy, unhand her and get out there and haul in our supplies. I'm hungry, and my stomach comes before your pecker. When she's finished with Cecil, she can cook."

Bess sagged against the wall. When Woody and Billy left, she looked up and found Ned Rawlins staring at her with a brooding look.

"Thank you," she managed.

Rawlins snorted. "For what?"

She made a half-hearted gesture toward the door. "For calling him off me."

"Don't thank me yet, girl. It ain't even dark. Gonna be a hell of a long night."

Bess's throat closed in terror.

CHAPTER SIX

It was late afternoon when Hunter came upon another place on the trail where the outlaws had stopped. They were still letting Bess go into the bushes alone. They probably figured she couldn't run far before they could catch her. And they would be right. A woman on foot, trussed up in a corset, with no telling how many petticoats under her full skirt, was no match in a race against a man on horseback.

There was something about this spot, though, that was different from the other places they'd stopped. Rawlins had taken them along well-traveled tracks at the lower elevations; then he'd followed game trails. Only occasionally had he cut directly through the forest or across a small meadow to pick up another game trail. They had stopped twice before. The signs had been plain enough. As if Rawlins wasn't particularly worried about anyone following.

"Well, I'm following, ye bloody bastard," Hunter muttered.

He studied the place that was little more than a wide spot

along a well-traveled game trail. Something wasn't right. He wasn't sure what, but something about the site nagged at him.

Just inside the brush, along the path of Bess's footprints where she'd gone for a moment of privacy, sat a small boulder, no higher than Hunter's knee. It was surrounded by brush, looking as though it had been there for years. Yet something . . .

He walked around the boulder, studying it. He'd made one complete trip before he realized that the top of the boulder held loose dirt and a stain. The kind of stain that happened when a rock sat on damp earth for a long, long time. This rock had been moved. Rolled bottom up. Recently.

Then he noticed several disturbances in the ground a couple of yards away from the boulder—scrub had been pulled up. And stuck around the boulder?

Yes, he found when he kicked at a bush next to the boulder. The bush fell over; its roots had not been in the ground. Beneath it, the earth was freshly turned.

A chill crept down Hunter's spine. Someone had buried something here, no more than a few hours past, and concealed the spot with a big rock and scrub pulled up and tucked around it.

He pulled the rest of the loose brush aside. With his hands clenched into fists at his sides and fear lodged in his heart, he prayed for strength, for courage, as he stared at the marks of boot heels used to tamp down the freshly turned earth.

It couldn't be Bess. They couldn't have— He would know. Somehow he would sense it in the air, feel it in his heart if Bess no longer walked the earth. She couldn't be here. Man-Above, she could not be.

Too small, came the thought.

Relief nearly made him giddy. The spot that had been dug up was too small for anyone to have buried a person, except perhaps a small child. If he'd been thinking straight, he would have realized that immediately and saved himself considerable anguish. His fear for Bess was making him stupid. If he couldn't focus any better than this, how the hell did he think he was going to get her back?

Snarling at himself, he bent and put his shoulder to the boulder and rolled it aside. Using the small shovel he had packed automatically—he wasn't a prospector's son for nothing—he attacked the loose dirt.

It took only minutes to uncover the four white canvas bags marked "Wells Fargo." Hunter let out a soundless whistle. They were filled with twenty-dollar gold pieces.

Hurrying now, because the day was passing, he loaded one bag—all the extra weight he was willing to burden his horse with—into his saddlebag. He wouldn't bother taking it at all, but it could be useful in getting Bess back. That is, if something forced him to deal with the gang, instead of killing them. The other bags he reburied in a new location.

He was gaining on them. Judging by the horse droppings, they were now only a couple of hours ahead.

An hour ago, at the place where they'd left the trail and cut through the pines, he'd thought he'd known where they were headed. Hunter had hunted this area of Greenhorn Mountain several times with his father.

He usually smiled when he thought of the name of the mountain. Newcomers thought it was named for previous newcomers. Instead it was named for the Comanche chief Cuerno Verde, Green Horn.

Of course, Cuerno Verde had been given the honor of having the mountain named after him by getting himself killed there by the Spanish back in 1779. An honor the Comanche would probably rather have done without.

But Hunter found nothing to smile about today on Greenhorn Mountain. A few miles east of this trail the granite mountain was honeycombed with caves. More than once, Hunter had thought perhaps that was where Rawlins was headed. But the tracks left by the outlaw and his gang had veered west again and rejoined the game trail.

Hunter didn't know where he was headed now, only that he was following Ned Rawlins, and he wasn't going to stop.

"Hold on, Blue Eyes, I'm coming."

Tonight, with the help of Man-Above, he would have Bess back in his arms, and he would never, ever let her go.

And four men would die.

When Woody and Billy returned to the cabin from the errands Ned had sent them on, Bess tended Cecil then fell upon the chore of cooking as if her life depended on it. In some ways, perhaps it did. As long as she was cooking, they would leave her alone. She took as long as she possibly could to fry the bacon, then made pan biscuits.

Ned unwittingly aided her in her effort to take as long as possible by his reaction to her request for a knife.

"Give you a what?"

"A knife. I need a knife. For the bacon."

"Oh, that's funny, girl, real funny. So you can use it on me?"

"As much pleasure as that might give me," she said without thinking, "I'm sure these two"—she motioned toward Billy and Woody—"would come to your aid should I try to overpower you."

Billy hooted with laughter. "Now, ain't that a picture. A little bitty mite like her, overpowering the big, bad outlaw Ned Rawlins." He hauled a whiskey bottle from his saddlebags and took a long pull. "Yessiree, I can see the newspapers now. The girl who done in Ned Rawlins. With his own knife." He snickered some more, then took another drink.

The ensuing argument between Ned and Billy went on for several minutes, while Bess did her best to become invisible beside the fireplace. But finally Ned turned back to her and

sliced the bacon himself rather than hand her the knife from
his belt.

Throughout it all, Woody sat beside Cecil and guzzled from
his own bottle like a man dying of thirst.

The bacon cooked much too quickly for Bess's peace of
mind, as did the biscuits that followed. The smells made her
mouth water. The only thing she'd eaten all day was a piece
of hardtack at noon, and suddenly she was starving. Until she
looked up and saw the way Billy was watching her, his mouth
open, his tongue sliding back and forth along his lower lip.
Bess's stomach heaved.

When she served up the meal on tin plates, she had to force
herself to eat. She wouldn't have bothered, but she needed the
food to keep up her strength. If the chance to escape presented
itself, she was determined to take it. It would be too terrible
if she were to fail due to lack of nourishment when food was
at hand.

She picked up her plate, and as she took her first bite, she
stared in amazement as the men seemed to inhale the food from
their plates. It was gone, every morsel she had cooked, except
that which remained on her own plate. Gone before she took
her second bite.

Billy tossed his plate toward the corner near the window. It
landed face down in the dirt. Leaning back and bracing himself
on his elbows, he grinned at her and belched.

"I say to hell with J.T.," Billy said, his words slurring. "I
think we oughta keep her."

"An' I think," Woody said, his eyes narrowed at Bess as
he drank from his own bottle, "we oughta just kill her now."

Billy gave him a half-hearted shove. "You don't wanna do
that. Hell, we ain't fucked her yet. 'Sides, she's takin' care o'
Cecil."

"She's lettin' him die, is what she's doin'," Woody said
with a snarl, his freckles standing out in sharp relief. "I ain't
dippin' my wick in the bitch that's killin' my brother. He dies,

she dies. You wanna piece of her, you better get it now, Billy Boy.''

"Hot damn." Billy staggered to his feet. "Hear that, Ned? Woody says I can have her now."

A visible trembling shook Bess's hands.

"Blood runs real thick in the Smith clan," Ned said sarcastically.

"What do you mean by that?" Woody demanded.

Ned leaned back against the wall and stretched out his legs. "Never mind, Wood. Let's just say that this ain't the Woody Smith gang. I make the decisions around here, and I'll say what happens to the girl, and when. Right now, she's Cecil's."

"Hell, Ned," Billy whined. "I won't use her for long. She can take care of Cecil after."

Ned set his bottle down and gave his little brother a hard look. "You can wait, Billy."

"How come I have to wait?" Billy demanded. "How come you take Cecil's side over your own flesh and blood, goddammit? He's as good as dead, anyway."

Ned moved so fast that Bess flinched. He jumped up and had Billy by the front of his shirt in an instant. Billy's whiskey left a trail in the dirt when the bottle landed on its side and rolled. When it stopped, a puddle formed.

"If he's as good as dead," Ned snarled into Billy's face, "it's because he got between me and that bullet—on purpose— while my own *flesh and blood* hightailed his yellow ass out the door the minute the lead started flying."

Anger exploded in the air. Bess swore she could smell it, feel it suddenly coating her skin.

Billy's face turned purple with rage. "Who you callin' yellow? Goddammit, I ain't yellow, and you got no call sayin' so. Hellfire. If Woody wasn't so stupid—"

Woody leaped to his feet. "Who you callin' stupid?"

"—he'd a had the horses there on time and we woulda been halfway outa the county afore the first shot was fired."

Woody shoved hard at Billy's shoulder. "I asked you a question, damn you. Who you callin' stupid?"

"You, Wood Head."

Woody roared. Lowering his head like an angry bull, he charged and rammed Billy in the gut. Unlike during the previous fight, this time Ned was able to sidestep the two and avoid going down with them. They rolled across the floor, cussing and pounding each other and gouging at each other's eyes. They rolled over tin plates and the puddle of spilled whiskey.

Woody being of a more beefy build, he had the advantage. He got both arms around Billy's chest and squeezed. But Billy wedged his forearm beneath Woody's chin and pried Woody's head back until Woody was forced to let go or have his neck broken. Billy shoved hard and Woody tumbled straight into the fire. Sparks and ashes belched out into the room, and his shirt sleeve began to smolder.

Woody didn't notice. He roared up from the hearth and lunged at Billy, catching him in another bear hug. More smoke rose from his sleeve, and now from Billy's back.

"Ah, hell," Ned complained. He grabbed the water bucket from where Bess had left it next to Cecil. It was still nearly full, and the water in it was liberally laced with Cecil's blood. Ned tossed it onto the two younger men where Woody's arm encircled Billy's back. It splashed onto Billy's head, into Woody's face, and over his shoulder to douse half the fire in the hearth.

Woody spat and coughed and jumped back from Billy.

"Shit," Billy hollered, whirling on Ned. "What the hell'd you do that for?"

"So you wouldn't burn the goddamn cabin down around our heads."

"Huh?"

Woody gaped down at the black holes burned in his sleeve. "I was on fire! Damn you, Billy, was you tryin' to burn me alive, knockin' me into the fire that way?"

"Don't be stupid."

"Don't call me stupid."

"Boys." Ned's deadly quiet voice seemed to roar like thunder through the small cabin. "You're starting to really piss me off."

"You just stay outta this," Billy snarled. "This is between me and Wood."

"You keep on pissing me off," Ned continued in that same quiet voice while rubbing his palm over the butt of the pistol in his holster, "I'm gonna have to kill you."

Woody looked startled. His Adam's apple bounced quickly up and down on a swallow. He took a step back.

Billy laughed, boisterously at first, his tongue poking out around his broken tooth. When Ned didn't so much as crack a smile, Billy's laughter turned nervous. "Ah, come on, big brother, you don't mean that."

"Don't I?"

Bess felt a new shiver of fear trace her spine. He did mean it, she realized. It was there in his eyes. Ned Rawlins would kill his own brother, and would lose no sleep over it.

God in heaven, what kind of man was this? That morning he had honored his dying partner's wish and saved Bess from rape, and now, with the sun not yet down on the same day, he threatened to kill his own brother. If he would kill Billy, what in God's name would he do to her?

"Jesus, Ned." Billy laughed nervously again and ran a hand over the top of his head. "A body didn't know you better, they'd think you was serious."

Ned's beard moved as though he might be smiling, but his eyes were hard and cold. "Get on out there and bring in some more wood. I don't fancy freezing my ass off tonight."

"Sure." Billy scooted around Ned and sidled toward the door. "Sure thing, Ned. I'll get plenty of wood. I'll even chop some more so we'll have plenty tomorrow."

"You do that, Billy Boy. You do that."

Billy all but ran out the door. A few minutes later, the sound of an ax biting wood rang out hollowly.

A quarter mile down the mountain—as the crow flies, but a good hour's ride following the trail—Hunter drew his horse to a sharp halt and listened.

There it was again, an ax striking wood. The unmistakable sound of man.

Hunter had to caution himself against charging up the mountain. He had hunted in this area, but not in a few years. For all he knew, someone could be homesteading up there somewhere. The fact that someone was up ahead of him didn't mean it was Rawlins.

But it had to be. Man-Above, it had to be. He dismounted and led his horse deep into the forest. "Quiet, my brother," he whispered in Arapaho. "We do not want anyone to know we are here."

Instead of tying his horse, he looped the reins over the saddle horn so the animal would not be at the total mercy of a bear or wildcat should one happen along.

"My brother," he said softly in Arapaho, "stay here if you can, so I can find you when I return."

Hunter then tugged off his boots and reached into his saddle-bag for his moccasins. They would allow him to move more quietly up the mountain.

A moment later he took quick inventory. Revolver and extra bullets, two belt knives, and a coil of rope. He would leave his repeating rifle, as it would only hamper him. He planned on being within pistol range of those bastards.

As eager as he was to head out, he took precious seconds to pray to Man-Above for strength and cunning, for the skill to defeat his enemies and bring Bess safely home. Then he turned and, ignoring the trail, took the mountain on foot.

"Hold on, Blue Eyes, I'm coming."

* * *

Since Billy had gone outside a few minutes earlier, Woody
sat in a corner and watched every move Ned made. Bess got
the impression that he was, just then, as afraid of Ned as she
was.

And she was afraid. Deeply afraid. She closed her eyes and
tried to bring Hunter's face to mind, but the picture behind
her closed lids was of that instant when Ned Rawlins's bullet
slammed into him and halted him as though he'd run into an
invisible wall. Bess couldn't get it out of her mind, the way
his roar of rage was cut off so abruptly. The look of shock in
his eyes.

*Don't! Don't remember him that way. Think of something
else. Think of when you met.*

She'd been as terrified the day they met as she was today.
Not of Hunter, never of Hunter. He had saved her life.

To be fair, she thought with a hidden smile, his sister and
father had helped, and it hadn't been just her whom they had
saved, but Carson and Megan, as well.

Carson had brought Megan and Bess to Colorado Territory
after the war to rebuild the ranch their late father had started
before the fighting between the North and South broke out.
Innes MacDougall had been a friend of their father's and had
met them in Pueblo. The four of them—Mr. Mac, Carson, six-
year-old Megan, and Bess—had left Pueblo in their new wagon
loaded with supplies and headed for the ranch. A half day south
of Pueblo they'd been attacked by Arapaho dog soldiers and
taken to their winter village in the foothills of the Sierra
Mojada—the Wet Mountains. The same mountains, Bess
thought with a wrench in her heart, where she might very well
die this time.

But she hadn't died in the Arapaho village. Hunter, his sister,
Winter Fawn, and their father, Mr. Mac, had spirited them

away in the dark of night. They had fled for their lives, with Hunter leading the way through a long, terrifying night.

Oh, God, she remembered so clearly riding astride that bare-backed horse and clinging to Hunter as if her life had depended on it. It had. His strong, steady presence and the warmth of his body had comforted her, kept her calm. She'd been barely thirteen and hadn't been around boys much. There had been few boys in Atlanta during the war. Leaning against Hunter's bare, muscular back, feeling the steely strength in his legs pressed against hers, had brought new sensations to her. Her heart had raced all night. She'd known even then that the danger surrounding them had been only part of the cause.

When they had finally reached the safety of the ranch a few days later, Hunter and his family had stayed. Aunt Gussie had arrived from Atlanta, and Bess's family had been complete. Winter Fawn had married Carson, and within a couple of years, Aunt Gussie had married Mr. Mac.

By the time Bess was fourteen—before Aunt Gussie and Mr. Mac were married—Bess knew that Hunter was the only man she would ever love.

She had a flash of Hunter smiling down at her in the dappled moonlight beneath the cottonwoods along the banks of the river behind the ranch house. How many times had she sneaked out of her room over the years to meet him after everyone else was in bed? Dozens. Countless.

Oh, the plans they had made, there along the banks of the Huerfano. They wanted a ranch of their own. Hunter would raise and train horses. They would have a dozen black-haired children. Boys with his gray eyes, girls with her blue. She would have a huge kitchen garden. Their children would grow straight and tall, and would be raised to honor both sides of their heritage, the white and the Arapaho. Night after night, whenever the weather permitted, she and Hunter would walk or sit beside the river and share their dreams.

Then they started sharing other things. Touches, casual at

first, then less so. And kisses. Innocent at first, then not so innocent. Her heart twisted at the memory.

But a couple of years ago, Hunter had started putting distance between them. No longer did she lie in her bed at night and hear the soft, warbling whistle of the mountain bluebird calling her to walk among the shadows and hold hands with the man she loved. The mountain bluebird sang only at dawn now, as was its nature. Hunter no longer imitated the bird to let her know he was waiting.

For as long as she lived, Bess would never forgive herself for riding to Hunter's yesterday—God, had it been only yesterday?—and baiting him, trying to make him jealous. How petty of her. How dishonest and shameful. She should have told him directly how she felt, how much she loved him, and asked if there was any hope that he would ever love her again.

Instead of exposing her honest feelings, she had held back and tried to manipulate him. May God forgive her.

From the depths of her sweetest memories, she could almost swear that even now she could hear that soft, warbling whistle.

"It's awful quiet out there."

Woody's voice pulled her rudely from her memories. Only then did she realize that Billy's ax had been silent for several minutes. Outside the open door, shadows stretched deep as the sun set behind the mountain. Inside, with barely a flicker left in the damp hearth, it was gloomy.

"What do you suppose is takin' Billy so long?" Woody asked.

Ned's beard bunched up around his mouth. "He probably got his ass lost."

Woody snorted with nervous laughter. "Atween here and the woodpile?"

Beside Bess, Cecil groaned and rolled his head back and forth on the ground. Thick layers of sweat and grime coated his face and neck.

"Is he comin' 'round?" Woody asked, his tone hovering somewhere between hope and irritation.

"No," Bess answered. "He's burning up with fever. I . . . I could use some more water."

Woody merely stared at her broodingly.

Ned crossed the room and nudged Woody with the toe of his boot. "Go refill that bucket. And while you're out there, see if you can find that no-good brother of mine."

"Aw, Ned, you know Billy's not a no-good."

Ned grunted. "Just get out there and see what's happened to him. Hell, he's probably chopped off his own foot with the damn ax and is sitting out there crying like the baby he is."

Ned's callousness toward his own brother continued to appall Bess. It gave her a sick feeling in the pit of her stomach.

Woody climbed to his feet and ambled toward the door.

"Woody," Ned said tiredly. "Take the goddamn bucket."

"Oh. I forgot."

Woody snagged the bucket by the bail and hightailed it out the door, slamming it shut behind him before Ned could say anything else. Woody figured the less chance he gave Ned to yell at him, the better. He was getting tired of Ned yelling at him all the damn time. Ned didn't used to yell at him near so much before Cecil got shot.

It was the girl, Woody figured, heading for the stream. Ned didn't like girls. Woody didn't understand that, but there it was. Ned and Cecil liked each other. It was a sin, Mama said, but Ned and Cecil didn't seem to care that they was goin' to hell.

Cecil had better hurry up and get well. 'Cept Woody didn't see how that was gonna happen, Cecil bein' gut shot, an' all. It was that girl's fault. Miss Bess. Ol' Gonzales said all she had to do was put her hand over a wound, and the wound healed. Like magic. Like that fella at the carnival back home who pulled a silver dollar outa Woody's ear that time.

But the damn girl wasn't cooperating. Woody figured he'd

just have to up and kill her for that. Wring her neck, just like a chicken. And that was too damn bad, 'cause she sure had a pretty neck.

Maybe Cecil would get well. If he did, Woody thought maybe he'd ask Cec to take him home. He was tired of hiding out all the time, tired of taking orders from Ned. Tired of Billy picking on him all the damn time.

Where had Billy got off to, anyhow? There was the stump, and there was the ax, but no Billy.

"Billy? Hey, Billy!" he shouted. "Where the damn hell'd ya go?"

At a slight rustling in the brush behind him, Woody turned. Nothing. Probably just a damn rabbit.

"Oh, Billl-lee, where arrre you?"

From across the stream, a bird called, a soft, warbling whistle, kinda pretty-like. But no Billy.

Woody frowned and went to the stream to fill the bucket. If that damn Billy was hiding from him, Woody didn't want to play. Billy liked to make him look stupid, and Woody was tired of it.

Yep, the more he thought about it, the more he wanted to go home.

But Ned had said to find Billy. Woody shuddered at the thought of going back to the cabin and confessing that Billy wasn't around.

"Come on, Billy, Ned wants ya." When he got no answer, he pushed himself to his feet and hauled up the bucket. "Goddammit, Billy," he yelled. "Get your ass—*umph.*" One minute he'd been hollering, the next, pain exploded in the back of his head, his breath left him. He saw bright lights flash before his eyes, and heard the bird call again. Then he saw blackness and heard nothing.

CHAPTER SEVEN

In the cabin, they heard Woody outside calling for Billy. Heard him cussing when Billy didn't answer. Heard him splash the bucket into the stream.

And Bess heard the gentle call of the mountain bluebird. Her heart missed one beat, two. There was no denying she'd heard it this time. It was not her imagination.

Yet it could not have been a real mountain bluebird; they called only at dawn.

Hunter!

She squeezed her eyes shut against the sting of tears. It couldn't be Hunter, she knew that. But her heart soared anyway.

When Woody's words were cut off abruptly in a grunt, Bess tensed. Across the small room, Ned was leaning against the wall next to the shuttered window, using a knife to clean under his nails. He paused with the point of the knife blade under the nail of his middle finger. He narrowed his eyes and cocked his head.

Outside, the bird called again.

Bess sucked in a sharp breath. It *was* Hunter. She didn't know how it could be, but the knowledge was a certainty inside her. Maybe Winter Fawn had followed Bess to Hunter's cabin for some reason, and was able to heal his wound. Or maybe—

What difference did it make? He was alive! He was here. He had come for her.

Ned pushed open one side of the shutters just enough to allow him to peer out. "Woody?" he called sharply.

The only answer was the soft call of the mountain bluebird.

Bess pushed herself to her feet.

At her movement, Ned gave her a sharp look, then turned back toward the window. "Woody? Billy? Answer me, damn you."

Bess knew she had to do something, and quickly. Wherever Hunter was out there, he would have to step into the open to get to the cabin. Ned would see him and shoot him again. Even now, the outlaw was reaching for the revolver at his hip.

Frantically she looked around the room for something to use as a weapon. There were three rifles, but she would have to pass Ned to get to them.

The fireplace! A poker—

There was no poker. There were no tools at all for the fireplace.

"Somebody's out there," Ned murmured.

Bess grabbed the handle of the cast-iron skillet in both hands. In a rush, she flew across the room and whacked Ned Rawlins on the back of his head with all her strength.

Ned staggered against the wall, then went down.

With a choked cry, Bess dropped the skillet and fled the cabin.

Hunter was inside the tree line, working his way past the brush corral that held the outlaws' four horses and Bess's mare, making his way carefully, quietly, toward the back of the cabin, which was still a dozen yards away. He heard a dull clang from inside the cabin, followed by Bess's cry. His heart nearly stopped.

Then he saw her burst from the cabin door into the open. "Bess!" He broke from the trees and ran for her.

Crying his name, she ran toward him, but her skirt hampered her. When he reached her, they were nearly to the stream he'd left only moments earlier where he'd caught the second outlaw.

There was now no need to sneak up on the rear of the cabin, so instead of turning back the way he'd come, Hunter grabbed Bess by the hand and, without slowing, gave her a sharp command to run as he pulled her toward the stream and the dense stand of pines on the other side.

He couldn't let himself think about how pale she was, how dark and haunted her eyes. The bruises on her face, if he thought about them, would cripple him. He didn't know how she'd gotten away from Ned Rawlins, but Hunter had to assume the man would try to stop them. They had to make the safety of the trees.

Behind them, the cabin door slammed open.

Bess slowed and looked back with terrified eyes.

"No!" Hunter warned, jerking her forward. "Run!" Drawing his gun, Hunter glanced over his shoulder to see Ned Rawlins stagger into the open doorway clutching his head.

Even from thirty yards away, Hunter read the shock on the man's face when he spotted him.

"You're dead!" Rawlins thundered, raising his gun. "I killed you myself!"

Hunter didn't waste his breath replying. He fired. But hitting a target behind him while running over rough ground was nigh on to impossible. He wasn't surprised to see a chip of wood fly from the front of the cabin a good two feet from the door.

Rawlins returned fire.

Bess stumbled and went down, collapsing into the stream, a hideous streak of blood across her temple.

She'd been hit!

"No!" Hunter roared in protest. With his gun still in his right hand, he scooped Bess up in his left arm and kept running. He fired back toward the cabin again, and this time Rawlins ducked back inside.

Clutching Bess tightly to his chest, Hunter sprinted into the trees and kept going. He couldn't let himself think about how badly she might be hurt. Stopping now would only put her in more danger. He crashed past the two men he had left tied up. Both were still out cold.

Ahead the ground dropped off sharply. Hunter holstered his revolver in order to hold Bess more securely while he skidded down the slope. Still he kept going, until a huge boulder loomed ahead. Once behind it, he stopped, his chest heaving, his fear for Bess turning his knees to water.

He couldn't make himself let go of her, so he braced his back against the rock and slid down until he cradled her in his lap. Man-Above, was she even still breathing? The wound didn't look bad; the bullet just grazed her, taking with it a narrow strip of skin at her right temple.

"Bess? Blue Eyes, talk to me." He felt for a pulse in her neck, but his own heart was pounding so hard that that was all he could feel. Her head rolled limply against his arm. Her face was nearly as white as the thin paper in his father's Bible. She was dirty, she was bruised, and she was bloody. She was also soaking wet from having fallen into the stream. That water came straight from the snowfield higher up the mountain, and it left her skin feeling as cold as ice.

But she was breathing. Thank God she was breathing. "Come on, Bess, come back to me."

From back up the slope came the sound of bellowing, followed by a gunshot. That would be Rawlins, trying to call in his men.

The men wouldn't be able to answer. When Hunter tied them each to a tree, he had also gagged them.

He had to get Bess out of there. He had to get her dry and

warm. The light was fading. He didn't have much time to get her back to his horse and find a safe place for the night. Getting her to safety was more important than going back up the mountain to kill a nest of snakes.

Another gunshot rang out.

Hunter had to move, and had to move now.

The trip down the mountain was a nightmare for Hunter. With every step, the light faded. Bess was a small woman, but unconscious she was boneless and nearly slipped through his arms several times. And he was trying to take care to pass quietly through the forest, in case Rawlins was already after them.

Hunter paused from time to time and listened, but heard no pursuit. The quiet only made him want to hurry more. It shouldn't be so quiet. Rawlins should be after them. Why wasn't he?

Twice Hunter, with Bess cradled in his arms, crossed the game trail that wound back and forth up the side of the mountain until it led up onto the shoulder and into the clearing where the hideout cabin sat. The same trail Rawlins and his men— and Bess—had ridden earlier that afternoon.

Bess. He looked down at her. She was so still and pale that his heart clenched in fear. No matter how closely he held her, she wasn't warming; her skin still felt like ice beneath his hands. The air was turning chilly. Her clothes would never dry without a fire. He had to get her to shelter.

It was almost full dark when he finally reached the horse. With Bess in his arms, he climbed into the saddle and guided the horse away from the trail and deeper into the pines. It would be the caves for them tonight. There he would be able to build a fire behind a screening shelter of scrub and get Bess warm.

"Hold on, Blue Eyes, I've got you now."

* * *

The horse was hidden as well as possible in the thick brush, scrub, and cedars that clustered together a few yards from the cave. Uprooted scrub and cut cedar limbs concealed the mouth, and a small fire made progress toward warming the chilled air inside the granite cavern.

Bess lay on Hunter's bedroll next to the fire. It was time to get her out of those cold, wet clothes before she froze to death, and before her clothes turned the blankets too damp for her to sleep beneath.

Carefully he rolled her to her side so he could reach the row of tiny buttons down her back. He wasn't terribly surprised to find his hands shaking—he'd nearly lost her, she was hurt, and she should have come around by now. Dammit, she should have come around.

No, the shaking didn't surprise him, but it made dealing with those tiny buttons an exercise in frustration.

She hadn't made a sound, even with all his rough handling, hauling her through the trees, on and off the horse. She should have made a sound. A moan. A groan. Something.

Anything.

"Come on, Blue Eyes," he pleaded as he worked the dress off, only to be confronted with petticoats, corset cover, corset, and more. She was wet clear through her camisole and drawers, all the way to her pale, icy skin.

Hunter had undressed a woman a time or two, but never Bess, regardless of how badly he'd wanted to over the years. That was one of the reasons he'd tried like hell to put distance between them lately, because he'd wanted her so damn bad. Those walks along the river at night ... They—she—had turned into too much of a temptation for a young man whose blood ran hot. She'd been too sweet, too willing.

It would have been too easy, there beneath the cottonwoods along the banks of the river, to forget his vow not to take advantage of her innocence. Not to dishonor her. Then there had been that night he had come too close to the edge. So close that he'd almost taken her.

In his eyes, she would not have been dishonored by letting him make love to her, but he knew the rest of the world would see things differently. It wasn't something he could even talk to her about. She had a way of arguing, Bess did, without raising her voice, that always got to him. Like yesterday, at his cabin, when he'd let his pride come between them once again.

Had it been only yesterday? Only a day since their lives had been ripped apart? Since she had been torn from his side and forced to endure the pain and terror she must have known at the hands of those bastards?

Damn his hide, he thought in a rush of insanity. He should have made love to her when he'd had the chance. He should have taken her there beneath the cottonwoods along the river and lost himself in her, claimed her once and for all as his.

But to have his first time to undress her, to see her beautiful skin bared, be like this—it wasn't right. It wasn't fair to either of them. When she came to, she wouldn't like it, not one damn little bit. But it was necessary, and she would realize that and forgive him. He hoped.

As he peeled away the last layer of cloth, he ground his teeth to keep from cursing and ramming his fist into the stone wall of the cave. Or crying.

Man-Above, the bruises. Not just the one on her cheek, which he'd almost grown used to seeing, but on her arms, her legs. The insides of her thighs, which were rubbed raw and darkly bruised. Her breasts. Five dark marks in the shape of a man's fingers, encircling one pale, perfect breast. Rope burns on her wrists.

"Blue Eyes," he whispered around the painful lump that rose in his throat. "I'm sorry. So damn sorry I let this happen to you."

After cleansing the wound at her temple and getting as much

blood out of her hair as possible with only a damp rag, he swallowed hard and struggled to get her into the clean skirt and blouse he'd brought for her. Megan had gotten them for him before he'd left the ranch. The simple gray skirt and white blouse were some of Bess's favorite clothes. Quickly, before he could give in to the need to touch her in other ways, to somehow wipe away the marks of her ordeal as he had wiped away the blood of her wound, he got her dressed and wrapped her in his blankets.

Nothing he could do, he feared, would make her forget what she'd been through. He lay down beside her and took her into his arms and held her as tightly as he dared, knowing it might be the last time for a long while. When she came to and remembered that those bastards had had their hands all over her, had undoubtedly raped her, she wasn't likely to want a man touching her at all.

"Especially not the stupid son of a bitch who let them take her right out from under his own roof."

There was a darkness in her mind, terrifying with its leering faces, its guns and blood, pain and threats. A hopeless, helpless fear. It paralyzed her. She tried to shrink away from it, but there was nowhere to go, nowhere safe. Except beyond the dark walls of her prison. Out there, somewhere, there was hope. There was safety. There was exquisite joy. Wrenching herself away from the leering demons, she flung herself beyond the walls. And it was all there, the hope, the joy, the safety.

And then it was gone.

But she could still see it, couldn't she? That safety? That hope? As she came slowly awake, she thought surely the light dancing beyond her closed eyelids was the light beyond her prison, beckoning her with fragile fingers to step forth and be safe.

Slowly, as sense returned, she realized that she was enveloped in warmth. Oh, but it felt heavenly. Yet in the back of her mind, the fear lingered. Fear of what? She couldn't remember. There was only this nagging sense of terror that she fought to escape.

And there was pain. She pressed her fingers to her temple. "Bloody hell, my head hurts."

Feeling her move, hearing her voice, Hunter was swamped with relief. Then her words penetrated, and he couldn't help but chuckle, despite her pain. It wasn't the slight Scottish burr— a perfect imitation of the accent that crept into his own voice now and then, and his sister's, and was always prevalent in his father's—that had him laughing. It was the words she'd used. His Bess *never* swore.

"It's not funny, dammit."

Hunter squeezed her shoulder gently. "I'm sorry, Blue Eyes. I know your head hurts. I laughed because I was just so glad to hear your voice."

"I'm glad you're amused," she said with irritation. With one hand clutching her head, she slowly sat up. Looking down at him over her shoulder, she frowned like a cranky child awakened too early from a nap.

Hunter smiled and brushed a long strand of her hair back over her shoulder. "Hi," he said softly.

Her frown deepened. "Hi, yourself. Why'd you call me that?"

Now it was Hunter's turn to frown. "What, Blue Eyes? I've always called you that."

Tentatively fingering her head, she stared down at her skirt as if fascinated by it. "It's not my name."

Something was wrong. Hunter used one finger on her chin to turn her back to him. There was something in her eyes . . .

"Bess?"

One corner of her mouth quirked down farther. The crease between her eyes deepened. "That's not my name, either."

Something cold and clammy skittered down Hunter's spine.

Slowly, his eyes never leaving hers, he sat up. "Man-Above, Bess, what—"

"Don't call me that. And who's this Man-Above?"

An unnamed fear made him snap at her. "God. Do you recognize *that* name?"

"Yes," she bit back. "I know who God is. What I don't know," she said, scooting away from him and dangerously close to the fire, "is who the hell you are."

Hunter started to laugh, although he didn't appreciate the joke. But that look in her eyes . . . "Bess?"

"I told you not to call me that. My name is . . ." How odd, she thought. One instant, her name was there, right on her tongue. Then she'd looked into his eyes, and it was gone. "This is silly. My name is . . ." Panic came swiftly and gripped her by the throat. "Dear God, what is my name?"

Hunter saw the panic in her eyes and felt it in his gut. He'd known a warrior once who'd lost his memory after being clubbed on the head. The man had eventually died, never having remembered the first thirty years of his life. *Man-Above, don't let that happen to Bess.*

"Easy, Bess," he offered quietly, trying to control his voice and keep it even. Slowly, so as not to startle her, he reached for her. "You've been injured—"

"Stay away from me," she warned, backing out of the blanket and farther away from him.

"Watch out!"

But his warning came too late. She cried out as she brushed the side of her hand against a glowing coal.

"Please," he said earnestly. "I won't hurt you. I would never hurt you. Here." He held out the blanket she'd been sleeping in. "Wrap up in this before you get cold."

Hesitantly, she reached for the blanket with a hand that trembled. "Do I . . . know you?"

"For a long time," he said quietly, trying to reassure her with his voice.

"What's—" She paused to moisten her lips with the tip of her tongue. "What's your name?"

"Hunter."

"It's . . . an unusual name. You look Indian. Except you have gray eyes."

He smiled slowly. "If it gives you a clue, my full name is Hunter MacDougall."

"You're kidding." She looked as though she were trying not to smile.

"I wouldn't joke about it. A person's name is serious business."

She glanced down at the blanket and pulled it across her lap. She studied it for a long while before looking back up at him. "What's mine?" she asked in a voice that shook.

"Elizabeth Dulaney. Everyone calls you Bess."

"You called me something else."

"Blue Eyes. Your eyes are the deep blue of a mountain lake under a clear sky."

She cocked her head. "Are you a poet, Mr. MacDougall? Or merely a flatterer?"

Although her barb was unintentional, Hunter found that it hurt, bad, to hear her call him Mr. MacDougall. For that matter, it hurt that she couldn't remember him. Hurt like hell. If it hurt him this much, he could only imagine how much it must be scaring her. "I'm a rancher. A horse trainer."

"Are you good at it?"

"I am. Bess—"

She shook her head and frowned again. "If that's my name," she murmured, "why does it mean nothing to me? Why can't I remember?"

"Take it easy," he offered. "It'll come. You've been injured."

She put a hand to her head again. "Here?" She winced. "It hurts. What happened?"

"You don't remember?"

"Remember what?"

Hunter debated with himself over what to tell her. If he had his way, she would never remember what she had been through at the hands of Ned Rawlins and his gang. But to not tell her something that so directly affected her wasn't right.

"What is it that you don't want to tell me? Did you do this to me?"

"No," he protested. Then he closed his eyes for a moment and tasted guilt. "But I let it happen."

"Let what happen?"

He looked at her steadily. Were it him, he would hate being kept in the dark. "You were kidnapped."

"By you?" she demanded sharply.

"No." He shook his head. "Do you remember riding out to my place yesterday morning?"

Her brow furrowed in concentration. After a moment, she gave up and shook her head. "No. Why would I come to see you?"

"Like I said, we've known each other for years." He wouldn't tell her she had come to dangle Virgil Horton under his nose to make him jealous. That she could find out on her own. If she never remembered Virgil Horton again, that was just fine with him. "Do you remember Ned Rawlins and his gang?"

She raised a hand to her forehead. Her eyes turned dark with pain. "Aren't they those bank robbers?"

"There, see? You do remember something."

"Why do I know who Ned Rawlins is, but I can't remember my own damn name?" she said in frustration. "Do I know him?" When he didn't answer right away, she glared at him. "Tell me."

Hunter let out a long, slow breath. "You met him and his gang yesterday, when they kidnapped you."

Wariness stole into her eyes. She straightened, seemed to

grow taller before his eyes. "When *they* kidnapped me, or when *you* did?"

"Bess . . ." Her suspicion felt like a knife to his heart. But why shouldn't she be suspicious? Why should she believe him? He went on as though she hadn't spoken. "They had apparently pulled off a robbery somewhere in the area yesterday morning before the storm hit. One of their men was shot. They saw the smoke from my cabin and barged in on us while you were there. They took you with them to take care of their wounded man."

He watched her struggle with the information, saw her throat work on a swallow, her hands fist in the blanket.

"What—" She swallowed again. "What happened after that? How did I end up here with you?"

"I came after you. They brought you up into the mountains, to a cabin. I followed."

"You rescued me?" she asked cautiously.

"I helped. You apparently did a little of your own rescuing."

"What do you mean?"

Hunter shrugged and gave her a half grin. "I'm not sure. I'd whistled, so you must have known I was outside. I'd already taken care of two of the gang. That left you inside with the wounded man—if he was still alive—and Rawlins." His smile widened. "You must have whacked him with something. I heard the impact. Then you ran outside."

She blinked. "I whacked a man?"

"Seems so."

She thought a moment, then nodded. "Yes, I think I could whack someone."

Hunter threw back his head and laughed.

Oh, she thought, he had a wonderful laugh. Suddenly he looked years younger, and not nearly so grim. He was a handsome man, with that dark skin, those strong, chiseled features, and that long black hair that hung past his shoulders and made her want to plunge her fingers into it.

Gracious! Was she the type of woman who went around plunging her fingers into men's hair?

But more important right now, was he telling the truth? Or was he merely trying to get her to trust him so she wouldn't be any trouble?

How was she to know?

"Why can't I remember?" she cried in frustration.

His smile disappeared as if it had never been. "Because the bastard shot you."

Fear sent a shudder up her spine. "Shot me?"

"The bullet grazed your temple. That's why your head hurts. And I suspect that's why you can't remember. You fell in the stream," he added, glad now that her clothes had dried during the night and, except for her shoes and stockings, were already folded and stuffed into his saddlebags. He didn't think she was ready to learn that he had undressed her. "You were out for several hours."

She shook her head. "I just . . . can't remember."

"It'll come. Give it time, Bess."

Bess. Was that her name? It meant nothing to her. She would have thought her own name would sound familiar, that she would instinctively know it was hers.

God, what was she supposed to do? Was she to believe this man with the gray eyes and chiseled cheekbones? He seemed nice enough, except when he spoke of Ned Rawlins and his face turned hard, his voice cold. At those times, he looked capable of anything. Even murder.

Icy fingers of fear skidded across her shoulders. What was she going to do? Something about this man made her want to trust him, but her willingness to do so made her question herself. How could she trust her own judgment when she couldn't even remember her own name?

Oh, God, why was this happening to her?

"You could do with some more rest," he offered quietly.

The very quietness of his voice, the smooth, even tone, made her wary. She heard restraint in his voice. He wasn't saying what he really wanted to say.

Now, how did she know such a thing?

She didn't know. Instinct, maybe. Instinct, it seemed, was all she had.

"Bess?"

With a sigh, she supposed she would have to get used to answering to that name, at least until she remembered if it truly was her name.

"No, thank you," she answered. "I feel as though I've been asleep my entire life."

He was silent for a moment, then gave a slight nod. "It'll be light soon, anyway. I'll fix us something to eat. You must be hungry."

She wasn't, she thought. But whatever the day brought, she would need her strength to face it. Therefore, she would eat.

Why did that thought seem familiar, as if she'd thought the same thing only recently? Was it a memory?

Concentrate, she told herself. If only she could concentrate hard enough, surely she would be able to remember.

But with concentration came a sharp pain in her head, so sharp that her vision grayed. She squeezed her eyes shut and tried to ignore it.

Hunter watched her face tighten with pain and had to force himself not to reach out and pull her into his arms. "Don't," he pleaded. "Don't try to force it. It'll come in its own time, Blue Eyes."

His voice relaxed her. How odd, she thought, that a man's voice—a stranger's voice—should ease the pain in her head and the tension in her shoulders.

He might be a stranger, but it suddenly occurred to her that, at least for now, he was the only person in the world whom she knew.

Now *that* was a sobering thought.

CHAPTER EIGHT

Hunter paced outside the cave, waiting for Bess to return from a trip to the bushes.

The horse was saddled, everything but the bedroll was packed and loaded, and Hunter had changed from his moccasins to his boots. Now it was light enough for them to head out. He was more than anxious to get Bess down the mountain and to the Double D. Winter Fawn could take care of her head wound, and hopefully that would restore her memory.

And while his sister did that, she could also heal the bruises that marred Bess's flesh and weighed like lead on his soul.

She had said she wasn't hungry. Smiling, he remembered the way she had picked at the beans and bacon he'd fixed. After about two bites, she had started shoveling the food in as if she hadn't eaten in a week.

His smile faded. Maybe Rawlins hadn't fed her.

Damn, he couldn't believe he'd left that bastard and his men alive. Alive, and with horses. Which meant they could easily come after him and Bess.

They would have reason to come after them. They thought they had killed him, but now Rawlins knew better.

Being wanted for bank robbery was one thing. Murder and kidnapping was something else entirely. If they made sure that Bess and Hunter couldn't tell what had happened, there would be no witnesses to their latest crimes.

On the other hand, Rawlins might decide to cut his losses and take his gang elsewhere.

Hunter just couldn't be sure what the man would do, and he wasn't willing to risk Bess's safety on a guess. He had to get her home. Then, by damn, he could go back and take care of Rawlins.

The sky was getting lighter. What was taking her so long out there? He paused next to the horse and clamped down on his impatience. He didn't like having her out of his sight. Out of his reach.

She was being awfully quiet out there, and she'd been gone more than long enough to take care of business.

"Bess?" he called.

Twenty yards away, behind a barn-sized boulder, she heard him call her name. If that was really her name. For now, she guessed it would have to do.

She cursed the fact that he was close enough that she could hear him call. She'd been moving as quietly as she could so as not to alert him of her whereabouts, but evidently she hadn't been moving fast enough.

Now what? She had to get away from him. She had to find someone she knew, someone she recognized.

She hadn't planned to run away from him when she started into the bushes. He was, after all, the only person she knew just then in the entire world, it seemed. But while going about her business, the cuffs of her sleeves had chafed painfully against her wrists. She had pulled the sleeves up to reveal horrible, ugly marks on both wrists. Marks left by a rope. She didn't know how she knew that, since she couldn't remember being tied up, but she knew it. Her wrists had been bound, tightly and for a long time.

The question arose then—bound by whom? Some outlaw named Ned Rawlins? Or another man, named Hunter MacDougall? She would be a fool to simply take his word as truth. If a man would rob banks and kidnap innocent women, lying would prove no hardship at all.

Was she an innocent woman?

God, the questions went around and around inside her head until she couldn't think at all, let alone remember anything.

Fear made her heart pound loudly enough that it was a wonder he couldn't hear it back there in the clearing.

She had to get away from him.

"Bess?" He called louder this time. "Answer me, or I'm coming after you."

She held her breath and pressed her back against the boulder. Would he really come after her?

An instant later, she heard a crashing in the brush and had her answer.

It was too late to run now. He would only catch her. She would have to wait for a better time. For now she would do her best to put him at ease. If he thought she would meekly go along with him, her next escape attempt might prove more successful.

But no, she couldn't act meek. She hadn't up until now. An abrupt change in her behavior might make him suspicious, put him more on guard.

"Bess?"

She took a deep breath and stepped from behind the boulder. "I'm coming, dammit."

Hunter hadn't realized how worried he'd been until he heard her voice, and an instant later, saw her. She emerged through the trees, yanking her skirt free of each bush and bramble that grabbed it along the way. "There you are."

"Bloody hell, you'd think a man would give a woman more

than a second or two of privacy before he started hollering at her.'' With a final flick of her skirt as she stepped beyond the brush and into the clearing, she glared at him. ''You'd think that wouldn't be too much to ask, wouldn't you. You're as bad as—'' She stopped a half dozen yards away. Stopped walking, stopped talking.

''As bad as who?'' Hunter asked cautiously, wondering if she suddenly remembered something. ''Someone who didn't want to give you enough privacy?'' Damn them, had they watched while she took care of intimate business? But no, he'd studied the signs himself. They had let her go, and hadn't followed. ''As bad as who, Bess?''

''Damn.'' She pressed her fingers to her brow. ''It was right there, like turning a corner and finding nothing more than what should have been there. Then it was gone. Just . . . gone.''

Hunter crossed to her and held out his hand. ''It'll come back.''

She ignored his outstretched hand. Lines of what could only be called irritation marked her face. ''You keep saying that.''

''Because it will,'' he insisted, stepping closer, hoping, praying that he spoke the truth.

''Don't touch me.'' She backed up rapidly.

''Okay, okay.'' He retreated and held his hands up, palms out, as though surrendering.

''You might be the only person I know right now, but that doesn't mean I believe everything you've said. It doesn't mean I trust you.''

''I guess I can understand that.''

''Oh, stop being so damn agreeable,'' she said irritably.

''Yes, ma'am.'' Hunter bit the inside of his cheek to keep from grinning. Strip away the outer layers, and his Bess was a surprising woman. She was going to be appalled at herself when she remembered all those polite Southern lady teachings her Aunt Gussie had been drilling into her all her life, and how she had forgotten them.

"And so polite," she snapped. "Don't you ever get irritated?"

"Oh, I think I could manage it if I thought about it long enough. Come on. It's time to go." He'd already decided to take the easier, if longer, route down the mountain. It would add a couple of hours to their trip, but she'd had a rough couple of days. The other trail down—the one he had followed to reach her—was as steep as all get-out most of the way. It would be harder on her, harder on the horse, and might lead them right smack into Ned Rawlins, if he was on his way down the mountain.

Not that Hunter didn't want to get his hands on that bastard, but not with Bess along. He would gladly add a couple of hours to the trip to keep her as far away from Rawlins as possible.

He led the horse to the middle of the clearing, then turned to wait for Bess. "You can ride in front and sit sideways—"

"Sit on your lap, you mean," she said, eyes narrowed with suspicion.

Hunter nodded. "Basically, yes. Or you can ride astride behind, but I suspect you've spent most of the past two days straddling the back of a horse. I doubt you're in any shape to do it again. You're used to a sidesaddle."

To avoid those piercing gray eyes, she forced herself to look at the horse. There was no way she could sit on this stranger's lap, no matter how badly her thighs ached with every step she took.

"I can walk."

"We might need to do just that now and then to give the horse a rest. But until then, we both ride."

So, she thought. He's not always so agreeable. There was steel in his voice now. Would he force her to ride with him? "I'd rather not," she said, hoping her voice sounded more firm to him than it did to her. "In fact, I'm feeling much better now. You can go on without me."

''And leave you here?'' he said, incredulous. ''Not on your life.''

''I don't see why—''

''Where would you go?''

''Downhill, for starters.''

''Downhill. Great. And then what? What are you going to do when you get hungry? What are you going to do if you run into Ned Rawlins? You won't know who he is, but he's not going to have any trouble recognizing you. Dammit, Bess, he'll kill you.''

Obviously she hadn't thought her plan through very well. It hadn't even been a plan, really, just a desperate bid to put some distance between herself and this man she refused to let herself trust. But if he told the truth, and there was a man out there who wanted to kill her . . . ''I'll ride behind.''

''Good.'' He settled his hat on his head and reached for the saddle horn. ''I'll mount up first, then pull you up behind me.''

She knew she was going to regret this, but she wasn't ready to sit on his lap and have his arms around her. She gave him a nod that she hoped spoke of agreement rather than reluctance.

A moment later, when she placed her foot on his and let him pull her up onto the broad back of the horse, her inner thighs screamed in protest. She bit back a groan of pain, reminding herself that this way, she didn't have to completely entrust herself to his keeping.

Instinct told her again that this was a man she could trust, but she was afraid to listen. Looking into his eyes made her breath catch. Sitting this close and feeling the warmth of his body made her heart pound, made her long for a strong pair of arms to wrap around her. She didn't understand what any of it meant; she only knew that whatever it was that stirred to life inside her when she got near him confused and frightened her.

She was never going to be able to think straight and remember anything as long as she was around him.

They rode for what seemed like hours. Her thighs ached, her head pounded, and her hands cramped from holding on to the back of the saddle. He had invited her to hold on to him. She had declined. It disturbed her how difficult it had been to keep from reaching for him, from leaning against his broad, strong back and resting her head on his shoulder. It seemed to her that she had done that before, with this man, but still, she didn't trust him. Didn't trust that look of guilt that came into his eyes whenever he spoke of her kidnapping.

She didn't trust him. That was natural, Hunter kept telling himself. It stung, but it was no more than he deserved. Even if she hadn't lost her memory, he wouldn't blame her for not trusting him. Not after he let them take her. Man-Above, he couldn't believe he'd let them take her.

But no matter how little she trusted him, he hoped she had put that stupid idea of taking off on her own out of her mind. She surely couldn't have lost her common sense along with her memory.

There was no real trail on this part of the mountain, but Hunter didn't need one. He knew the creek they followed would empty into the stream that would lead them to the Huerfano. He deliberately kept that knowledge to himself so she wouldn't get it into her head that she could find her own way back to civilization.

He wished she would touch him. He needed her to touch him. But she was expending a great deal of energy to make sure she didn't.

It served him right. For months—two years now—he'd done everything possible to avoid her touch, because he knew she could weaken him, make him want her even more than he already did. She'd had no idea how much he wanted her, how he ached to hold her, kiss her, make love to her.

Why had he thought he had to provide her with a nice house

instead of his cabin before he married her? Damn his hide, he should have married her months ago. Other couples started out with less. What had he been trying to prove? She should already be big and round with his child.

How would she have survived Ned Rawlins in that condition, you fool?

Man-Above, he had to stop thinking about what he should have done and pay attention to what he was doing now, before he let Ned Rawlins ride right up to them.

He didn't think the outlaw would come this way, but he couldn't afford to let down his guard.

They stopped around mid-morning to rest the horse and stretch their legs. Hunter figured she had to be stiff and sore. Maybe that was why she'd been so quiet all morning.

He sat still a moment, then spoke to her over his shoulder. "We'll rest here a while."

He wasn't sure, but he thought he heard a small sigh of relief.

"Do you want to get down first, the same way you got up, or do you want me to get down and lift you to the ground?"

Bess bit the inside of her mouth. This was her chance. She did need, desperately, to get down. Her bladder was about to burst, and her legs hurt to the point of drawing tears. But he was offering to dismount and leave her, albeit for only a few seconds, on the horse alone.

Was she a good rider? Good enough to ride out of these mountains alone?

She was about to find out.

"I don't think I can swing my leg over this beast," she said, and it wasn't a lie. "I guess you'll have to get down first."

She had noted before that the ends of the reins were tied together. She watched over his shoulder as he draped them loosely over the saddle horn. They would be easy enough to grab, if she could move up into the saddle fast enough.

He kicked both feet free of the stirrups, threw his right leg up over the horse's neck, and slid to the ground, his back to the horse, and to her.

There was no time for her to think. She'd made up her mind to get away from him, and this was her chance. There were oak trees here. Didn't that mean they were getting closer to being out of the mountains?

Yes, she thought it did.

The instant his boots hit the ground, while his back was still turned, she braced her hands in the middle of the saddle and levered herself up over the cantle and into the seat, biting back a groan of pain and effort.

"What the—" He was turning to see what she was doing.

She didn't give him the chance. She grabbed the reins with both hands. Putting her left foot on the back of Hunter's shoulder, she shoved with all her might, then kicked the horse's sides.

Hunter was taken completely by surprise. Her shove knocked him forward. He staggered to keep his balance. He straightened and turned in time to see Bess clinging to the saddle horn with both hands as the horse carried her out of the clearing.

"Bess! Goddammit." He yanked off his hat and slammed it to the ground in frustration. "What the hell's the matter with you?" he called.

But of course, she did not answer.

"Well, hell." She must want to get away from him worse than he'd thought. He couldn't let her, of course. She didn't know where she was going, wouldn't recognize any place or anyone until she got her memory back.

Disgusted with himself for lowering his guard, he let out a sharp, shrill whistle, grateful he'd ridden one of his own trained horses rather than one from the Double D's remuda.

Just as he'd been trained, the gelding came to an abrupt halt thirty yards away, nearly sending Bess tumbling to the ground.

Hunter stood where Bess had left him and folded his arms

across his chest, watching through narrowed eyes as she kicked and clucked and yelled, trying to make the horse go.

He gave a low, two-note whistle.

The gelding's ears twitched.

As if connected, the horse's ears and Bess's head turned as one. The horse listened for Hunter's next command, and Bess looked back over her shoulder at him, her face contorted in fear.

That look nearly sent Hunter to his knees. The *last* thing he wanted was for her to be afraid of him. Dammit. He was going to have to do something to gain her trust before she did something foolish and actually got away from him the next time.

He whistled again, three notes this time. The horse, still ignoring the demands of its rider, turned around and ambled back up the creek until it stood with its muzzle barely a foot from Hunter's chest.

"I'm sorry," Hunter said to Bess. "But I can't let you ride off alone." He looked away, unable to face the fear in her eyes. Man-Above, she looked as wary and skittish as a wild mustang.

And that, he thought suddenly, was exactly how he would treat her. A wild horse was an animal always ready to flee at the first sign of danger. But it was a herd animal, too, and didn't like being left alone. Feared it, avoided it, unless it was run off by a stronger, more aggressive member of the herd. He'd seen young horses run off for acting up, biting another horse, or generally irritating the lead mare, who usually meted out the discipline.

Hunter would play the lead mare in this little herd of theirs. While he wouldn't run Bess off, he could ignore her. With any luck, like the young upstart colt or filly, she would soon realize she didn't want to be alone and would try to return to the herd.

And if she ever found out he was comparing her to a horse, she would chew him up and spit him out.

At least, the old Bess, from years ago, would have. The Bess who used to yell at him, laugh with him, love him.

Hunter stepped past her and removed the saddlebags. Saying nothing, confident the horse would not leave no matter what she did, he left her sitting there on the animal's back and set about building a small fire to make coffee. He hadn't planned on stopping for that long, but he needed a little time to win if not her trust, at least her cooperation.

Bess watched, amazed and confused. Wasn't he going to yell at her or something? Or at least help her off the horse?

Apparently not, she decided. He was taking his own sweet time gathering twigs and branches and dried leaves. Obviously, he was about to build a fire, but at the rate he was going, it would be sundown before the first flame lit.

He was ignoring her.

Well, she could just ignore him right back.

He'd said he was a horse trainer. He was apparently very good at it. When she tried again to get the horse to move and its only movement was to turn its head and stare at her with a bored expression, she realized that she would not be riding away on this animal.

Since that was the case, she needed to get down and pay a visit to the nearest privacy before she humiliated herself. To hell with his horse. She would walk if she had to, to get away from this man. She could feel the sharp edge of panic getting closer. She had to get away.

A little voice in the back of her head warned her she was being foolish. She wondered if she should heed it. He was right—she had no idea where to go, whom to trust. Was she in the habit of making things more difficult for herself with rash decisions? Sooner or later, if she stayed with Hunter, they were bound to run into people.

But her first problem was to get down from the horse. Her feet did not reach the stirrups, which were adjusted to accommodate Hunter's long legs. She thought maybe she could slide down to her left until she was able to reach that stirrup, then swing her right leg over the back of the horse.

The mere thought of such a movement made her thighs scream with pain. She would do better to dismount the way he had a few minutes earlier, by bringing her right leg over the horse's neck and dangling both feet down the left side of the animal. Then she could slide to the ground.

She leaned over as far as she dared and looked. The ground, she noticed with dread, was a long way down.

She looked back over at Hunter. She didn't want to ask for his help. A man who looked guilty when he spoke of her kidnapping wasn't to be trusted. A man who could stop a horse with a whistle—*his* horse, which she had been stealing at the time—couldn't be expected to be helpful.

"If you were any kind of gentleman," she muttered, "you'd help me off this beast."

From the corner of his eye, Hunter had been watching her try to figure out how to dismount without killing herself. He'd had to fight himself to keep from helping, vowing that if she wanted his help, she would have to ask for it.

Well, she was asking. Sort of, he thought, fighting a grim smile. But just so that she understood the rules he was establishing, he glanced over at her. "You mean *my* beast? The one you were stealing, along with all my personal belongings, when you left me here on foot?"

She heaved a sigh and looked up at the sky. "That's the only beast around here."

"I'll be glad to help you down," he offered, dusting bits of dead leaves from his fingers. "All you have to do is ask."

No sigh this time, but a quick, wary glance before she looked off into the trees. "Would you . . . help me down? Please?"

"Certainly." He crossed the ground toward her with slow, deliberate steps. Standing beside the horse, he looked up at her for a long moment.

She refused to meet his gaze.

Hunter wanted to ask her again to trust him, but he realized that he would have to earn her trust. As wary as she looked, that could take a while. He reached for her waist. "Put your hands on my shoulders."

Despite her vow not to look at him, Bess found herself doing just that. It was hard to admit how much his looks appealed to her. He was a handsome man, but it was more than that. More than the dark, hard features. It was the way those perfectly shaped lips clamped down over whatever it was he wanted to say to her while his jaw ticked in irritation. It was his constant patience in the face of her rudeness. It was the gentle strength in his hands, the solid width of his shoulders. It was a dozen things, and they all combined to make her feel things she didn't understand, things she didn't trust.

Yet when his hands fitted themselves around her waist, she did not pull back. She could not. As if they had a will of their own, her hands reached out for his shoulders. Oh, they were strong shoulders, and hard. Solid. Dependable. They felt as though they could carry the weight of the world, or shelter a frightened woman.

He lifted her from the saddle with an ease that amazed her. When her feet touched the ground, she felt the sudden, fierce need to step away from him, out from under whatever spell his touch, his mere nearness, seemed to weave.

Her legs, however, had other ideas. They refused to hold her weight. She felt her knees buckle. She gasped and gripped his shoulders tighter.

"Steady," he said, his voice low and intimate while his hands, still at her waist, steadied her.

"I'm sorry," she said hurriedly. "My legs . . ."

"I know. Just give yourself a minute."

There he went again, she noticed, looking guilty, as though the pain and weakness in her legs were his fault.

Maybe, said a darker voice in her mind, *they are. Maybe he did this to you.*

With a cry of frustration, she wrenched herself away from him and forced her legs to carry her across the clearing and into the bushes.

Hunter let his hands fall to his sides and fought the urge to go after her, to call her name. To warn her that if she tried to flee he would come after her. But no, he was trying to earn her trust. To do that, he had to offer his.

She had touched him. Not necessarily willingly, but she had touched him. He had thought that when she did, this burning ache deep in his gut would ease. He'd been wrong. It was worse. He wanted much, much more than a mere touch grudgingly given.

Ach, ma blue-eyed lass, be there aught I can do to make ye love me again?

When he realized the words that were in his heart, he snorted with disgust at himself. He was a stranger to her. She wasn't about to give him what he wanted, what he needed. What he'd had in the palm of his hand for so long and had taken for granted, as though it—she—would always be his.

Even if—when—she regained her memory, she wasn't likely to think too kindly of him for letting this happen to her. He damn sure didn't think too kindly of himself.

After Bess had relieved herself in the privacy of the wooded brush, she turned back for the clearing. She was going to be sensible about this. As Hunter had said and she'd told herself, if she took off on her own, she wouldn't know where to go.

If only she felt more comfortable trusting him, she thought in frustration. He was hiding something from her. She could see it in his eyes, when he wasn't looking guilty.

When she broke through the trees and into the clearing, the horse was munching on the sparse grass and Hunter was sitting on the ground before a small fire. His back was to her, and he was staring at the small coffee pot blackened with use.

She didn't know how to approach him, how to find out what she needed to know.

All you have to do is ask, he'd said.

All right, she would ask. "Is that coffee?"

The instant the words were out, she cursed herself. That was not what she meant to ask.

Without turning to look at her, he answered, "Aye."

Aye, she thought, *not yes.* Another piece of the puzzle that was Hunter MacDougall. Now, if only she knew where that piece belonged, and how many pieces still were missing.

"Is there enough for two?" she asked tentatively.

"Aye."

Bess ground her teeth. If there was anything more frustrating than someone who answered every question with no more than a single word, she didn't know what it was.

A sudden stillness came over her. She waited, feeling as if a piece of herself were about to fall into place. She didn't like one-word answers. Had never liked them.

How did she know that?

Her heart started pounding; her head throbbed. She gasped against the sudden pain.

With his back to her, Hunter heard her stop some distance away. He'd been thinking—brooding was more like it—about Ned Rawlins, and how he should have gone back and killed the bastard. Then he heard a small, pain-filled gasp. Jumping to his feet, he whirled and drew his revolver, half expecting to see the outlaw riding down on them.

Bess's eyes flew open wide. She cried out.

Realizing instantly that he had overreacted, Hunter jerked the barrel of his gun toward the sky, then holstered the weapon. "I'm sorry."

"Sorry!" she croaked. "You scare ten years off my life and you're *sorry?*" With each word, her voice rose in pitch and volume. "What the hell did you do that for? Who were you going to shoot? Me? Are you sure *you're* not the outlaw who kidnapped me?'' By now she was screaming at him, a touch of hysteria in her eyes.

Hysteria, and more, Hunter realized. He saw in those blue depths the source of her fear. "That's what you think, isn't it? That everything I've told you is a lie, and that I'm the one who kidnapped you."

He saw her swallow and wouldn't have been surprised if she backed away, even though there were at least three yards of bare ground between them. But she stood her ground, and he was unaccountably proud of her for that.

"Give me one good reason why I shouldn't think that very thing," she demanded. "I have rope burns on my wrists."

Hunter flinched as though she had slapped him. If he closed his eyes, he could clearly see those marks, and others, that marred her fair skin. He would see them in his sleep for years. He forced himself to keep his eyes open, and directly on hers. "I know. I'm sorry."

"You tied me up?" she demanded, her face a mixture of outrage and wariness.

"No," he protested. "Man-Above, no, Bess."

"Then tell me," she hissed, crouching slightly as she began circling around him toward the fire, "why you look so damn guilty every time you mention my kidnapping. Why you keep apologizing for what you say happened to me."

"Because it's my fault," he bit out. "Dammit, Bess, you were on my land, standing in my house. You should have been safe!" He ran his splayed fingers across the top of his head. "I should have been paying attention. There's no way in hell they should have been able to take us by surprise that way, and when they did, I should have been able to keep them from taking you."

Bess stood still and slowly straightened. "You feel responsible?"

"Bloody hell, of course I feel responsible," he bellowed. "I let them take you right out from under my nose!"

She believed him. She wasn't sure why—maybe it was the anguish, the self-directed anger in his eyes—but she believed him. "How many of them were there?"

He ran his fingers through his hair again and turned half away from her. "Four."

"And you think you should have been able to deal with four men against one?"

"One of them was wounded. I only needed to handle three of them."

She folded her arms across her chest and cocked her head. "Oh, well, I see your point, then. Certainly. I mean, three desperate outlaws, who probably had their guns drawn when they surprised us. On the run from the law, prices on their heads, no scruples, not afraid to kill anyone who got in their way. Of course you should have been able to handle them."

Hunter eyed her over his shoulder. "You're making sport of me."

"Yes," she said, her lips pursed. "I am. Is that coffee about ready?"

"Does this mean you believe me? That I'm not the one who hurt you?"

Bess paused before answering. By saying yes, she could be giving him a weapon to use against her. On the other hand, her life was already in his hands. She had to trust someone. And there was just something about this man, with his troubled gray eyes and his long black hair, that she wanted to trust.

"Yes," she said finally. "I guess I do."

"If I trust you not to take off on your own, will you trust me to get you home?"

"All right."

"Fair enough," he said with a nod. "Now, how about that coffee?"

She offered a small smile. "I'd like that. Thank you. But first I want to wash up at the stream." She looked down at her hands, which were less than clean, and made a face.

"There's soap in the saddlebag," he offered.

"Oh, thank you," she said with feeling. She lifted a thick strand of her snarled hair. "I don't suppose you have a comb or brush I could borrow."

He smiled. "I think we can come up with something."

She followed him to the saddlebags, which he'd left near the fire. He knelt and unbuckled one of the bags and pulled out a small drawstring bag made of calico.

"Why, Mr. MacDougall, how . . . feminine," she teased.

"Very funny, Blue Eyes. It so happens, it's yours."

"Mine?" Tentatively she reached for it, wondering if it would feel more familiar than it looked.

"I had to go by the ranch and let them know what happened before I came after you. I, uh, picked up a few of your things to bring along."

"Are you always so thoughtful?"

"No," he said, looking away. "No, I'm not."

Bess wondered what he meant by that. She might have asked, but as her gaze slid past the saddlebag again, something caught her eye. "What's that?"

"What?"

"It looks like you brought along something else of mine, unless you're in the habit of wearing pink striped shirts. Is that a dress?" She bent down and reached for the fabric barely showing in the open flap of the bag.

"You don't—" But he was too late to stop her from pulling the skirt free. Hunter hung his head and closed his eyes. Now he was going to have to explain things he'd rather not explain. He'd only just gained a modicum of her trust. This was bound to destroy it. The old Bess would have been embarrassed, but she would, in the end, have taken it in stride. This Bess—he feared she wouldn't take the news so well.

Resigned, he opened his eyes in time to see her raise the ruined dress. Her underthings—corset, drawers, and all—fell out on the ground.

"Oh," she cried, her face flushing as she grabbed for the intimate articles. She wadded them in a ball and stuffed them back into the saddlebag, leaving the dress draped across her knees. Then she looked again at the dress and frowned. "I don't understand. This dress is soiled. And look here. It's torn in two, three places at least. Why would you bring this?"

To stall, Hunter cleared his throat. Twice.

"You've got that guilty look again, MacDougall. Why would you bring ruined clothes for me to wear?"

He cleared his throat again. "I, uh, didn't bring them."

"What do you mean, you didn't bring them? They were in your saddlebag, weren't they? Oh. They're someone else's?"

"Nae," he cried, appalled. "Ye canna believe I be in the habit of carryin' around some other lassie's clothes. I wouldna do such a thing."

His protest momentarily distracted Bess from the question of the clothes. She couldn't help but grin. "Ach, it seems the lad comes by the name MacDougall honestly."

Hunter stilled and searched her face. "Ah, lassie," he said softly, " 'tis good it is to hear ye mock ma speech again, the way ye always did."

It hurts him, she realized with wonder. It hurt him that she couldn't remember him, that she treated him as a stranger. She hadn't considered that a man such as he, strong in every way imaginable, could be hurt. "I'm sorry."

He shook his head. "Don't be. You've always teased me that way when I let that accent creep into my speech."

"I wish I could say that I remembered and that that's why I did it just now." A heavy sadness settled over her shoulders. "The truth is, I didn't think about it. I just opened my mouth, and out it came."

"Don't you see what that means?"

"Not really, except that I should remember to think before I open my mouth."

"No, it means that you haven't lost yourself."

She sucked in a sharp breath. "How did you know . . ."

"Ach, lassie, 'tis all over your face, it is." Then the burr slipped out of his voice. "How could you not be thinking that, when you can't remember anything about yourself? But the woman who knows herself as Bess Dulaney is still there. It will all come back to you. Just be patient."

"Is Bess Dulaney a patient person?" she asked.

"Sometimes. Most of the time," he corrected with a smile. "As long as you know you'll get your way in the end."

"Since you said that with a smile on your face, I'm going to assume you're teasing me." She looked down at the pink stripes in her hands. "So, just why did you bring my laundry and mending in your saddlebag?"

She stood and held the dress up, using one hand to hold the neck against her throat, the other to hold the waist in place. "It's a shame it's in such sad shape. It looks like it was so pretty. But what's this?" She peered down at the dark stain on the right shoulder. "It looks like . . . blood." She raised her right hand to touch the wound on her temple.

"Bess . . ."

"It's my blood," she said. Then, "I was wearing this when I was shot?"

"Bess—"

"Oh, stop. Unless you've been lying to me all along, it was not your fault I got shot."

"I haven't been lying," he bit out. "But I should have—"

"Been able to protect me. I've known you less than a day, and I'm already tired of hearing that. Don't I ever take care of myself?"

"Of course you do."

"I'm glad to hear it. So now you can stop feeling guilty over every little thing."

The muscle along his jaw flexed. "I don't consider your getting shot in the head a 'little thing'."

"Well, thank you very much. Neither do I." She frowned

down at the dress, looked back at him, then at the dress again. "But I wasn't wearing this when I woke up this morning."

Hunter's face darkened as he looked away. "Uh, no, you— uh, weren't."

Her eyes widened. She clutched the dress to her bosom and took a step back. "You undressed me?" she demanded, her voice rising. "You took off my clothes—" She glanced down to the saddlebag, which held her corset and drawers and other underthings. "—*all* of them? While I was unconscious?" The last word ended in a screech that made Hunter flinch.

In his own defense, he rushed to explain. "When you were hit, you fell into the stream—early snowmelt and icy cold. It was late, the air was cooling. By the time I got you to shelter, you were freezing. Your skin was like ice and your clothes were still wet. I had to get you warm, and that meant getting you dry."

Bess fought against embarrassment and lost as heat flamed her cheeks. "Oh. I see. Well."

"I swear to you, Bess, all I did was change your clothes. That's all. That's how I knew about the rope burns on your wrists," he added.

She nodded, then met his gaze squarely. "And was this the first time you've undressed me, or have there been others?"

Meeting her gaze, he said, "It was the first time, Bess. The only time. I changed your clothes because I had to, and that's all I did. I swear it."

For a long moment, neither spoke. The only sounds were the horse munching grass, two birds fussing at each other on a branch overhanging the stream across the clearing, and the rustle of wind in the trees.

"Okay. Well." Bess folded the dress and stuffed it back into the saddlebag. "I guess I'll go wash up." She picked up the drawstring bag. "You say there's soap in here?"

"And a comb and brush. There's a small mirror on the back of the brush."

"Okay. I'll just . . . just go wash up." She stood and started across the clearing toward the stream. Halfway there she stopped and looked back over her shoulder. "Hunter?"

"Aye?" he said warily.

A slow, shy smile curved her lips. Her cheeks were still rosy red with embarrassment. "Thank you for taking care of me."

Hunter swallowed. That was his Bess, pure and simple. "You're welcome." He poured himself a cup of coffee.

"And Hunter?"

"Aye?" He took a sip.

"Thanks for not putting that corset back on me."

While he spewed coffee out his mouth, she dashed the rest of the way to the stream. The Bess he knew would never even have said the word *corset* in front of a man, much less discuss how she came to be without one. And thank him for it.

In all honesty, though, that wasn't true. The old Bess, back before that night at the river, would have said anything she pleased, no matter how outrageous. If that Bess was back now, Hunter was glad. He had missed her.

He watched as she knelt out of sight at the creek, hidden from his view by a shoulder-high stand of willow whips. Without her memory, Bess was a slightly different person. He only hoped he could survive the changes. And he prayed, earnestly, that her memory would return swiftly. For her sake, and his.

From her spot by the creek, he heard a glad cry. "Oh! Hairpins!"

Hunter chuckled. Maybe she hadn't changed all that much. It always had been the small things in life that pleased her.

CHAPTER NINE

After finishing their coffee and eating the two leftover pan biscuits from breakfast, they packed up and rode away from the little clearing by the creek. As Bess rode astride behind Hunter again—with her hair thankfully up off her neck, thanks to the hairpins she'd found—she once more gripped the cantle rather than hold on to him.

His confession of having undressed her kept playing back through her mind. With it came imaginings of what it might be like to feel his large, dark hands on her flesh. She was quite sure she might go to hell for thinking such a thing, but she couldn't seem to help it.

And who, she wondered, deliberately distracting herself, had taught her about going to hell? And why did riding behind him this way seem almost familiar, teasing her with a memory that was just out of her reach?

Then there was that face she'd seen in the mirror. Her face. Bruised and dirty and completely unfamiliar. The face of a stranger. She had been so unsettled when she'd looked in the small mirror on the back of the pretty silver hairbrush that even now, hours later, she shied away from thinking of it.

The afternoon was growing long. It was time for a distraction. It was time, she decided, to ask a few questions.

"You said we've known each other a long time?"

"That's right. About seven years."

"Have we . . . have we ridden this way before?"

It seemed to her as if a stillness came over him. "A time or two, I guess. A long time ago."

She wondered at the sadness in his voice, but was afraid to ask about it. Instead, she asked, "Where are you taking me?"

"Home."

"Whose home. Mine or yours?"

"Yours."

"Are you going to answer every question I ask with a single word?"

He chuckled. "What do you want to know?"

"Where do I live? Tell me about it. Do I have any family?"

"You mean someone else who can verify what I've told you?" he asked, all laughter gone from his voice.

"That wasn't what I was thinking, but now that you mention it . . ."

"Unfortunately, all they know about your kidnapping is what I told Winter Fawn."

"Winter Fawn? What a beautiful name. Who is she?"

"My sister. She's married to your brother."

Bess—it still felt odd to think of herself as Bess—was startled to learn she had a brother. "What's his name? What is he like?"

"His name's Carson Dulaney. He's a rancher, raises cattle on the Double D ranch along the Huerfano River."

"What's he like? Is he nice? Mean? Did he send you after me? Why didn't he come himself?"

Hunter heard the nerves in her voice. He couldn't imagine what it would feel like to have no knowledge of himself, his past, his own family. He didn't want to talk about his own relationship with Bess, but there was plenty of other territory he could cover.

"He's a good man," he told her. "Fair. Capable. He's got black hair and blue eyes, like you."

"Something tells me you don't call him Blue Eyes," she said, surprising a laugh out of him.

"You're right. I don't think the good captain would appreciate it."

"Captain? He's in the Army?"

"Not anymore. He fought for the South in what you whites call the War Between the States."

Bess sucked in a quick breath. "The War of Northern Aggression."

"That's what your Aunt Gussie calls it. Do you remember it?"

She was quiet for a long moment. He could almost feel her straining to remember. Then she said, "I know what it is, that there was fighting, but I—"

"It'll—"

"Come. So you say."

"Just—"

"Give it time. I know," she said with frustration. "I *know* about the war, but I don't *remember* it. You said I have an aunt?"

"Your Aunt Gussie. Augusta Dulaney Winthrop MacDougall."

Bess giggled. "All of that?" Then she said, "Wait a minute. Your name is MacDougall."

"She married my father. His name's Innes MacDougall. You call him Mr. Mac."

"I think I'm confused. My brother is married to your sister, and my aunt is married to your father?"

"You'll get used to it," he said with a chuckle. "Then there's Megan. She's your brother's girl from his first marriage."

"He was married to someone else before he married your sister? What happened?"

"All I know is that his first wife died during the war. Megan's thirteen now, and looks a lot like you. Carson's already talking about building a fence around her to keep the boys away."

"Why, Mr. MacDougall, is that your roundabout way of telling me you think I'm pretty?"

"Aye," he said with an exaggerated Scottish accent. "The lassie's memory might be gone, but her personality's still there."

"What's that supposed to mean?" she asked suspiciously.

"It means, ma bonny lass, that ye've always been fair to middlin' at wheedlin' a compliment oot o' a mon."

"Good for me," she said with a laugh.

"Aye, and Megan is just as bad. And she's already teaching April and Bonnie, the wee lassies, how to work their wiles on the poor, unsuspecting men of the world."

"And just who be these wee lassies ye speak of, laddie?"

Hunter laughed again, delighted with her teasing. "They're Carson and Winter Fawn's girls. April's six, Bonnie's four. They have a three-year-old brother named Innes Edmond, after my father and yours."

"My father's name is Edmond?"

"Aye. But I'm sorry to be the one to tell you," he said quietly, "that he was killed during the war."

Bess had not thought to wonder about her parents, who they were, where they were, until Hunter mentioned her father. She'd been distracted by learning of her brother and his family. To learn now that her father was dead brought an ache to her heart. How could she hurt for a man she couldn't remember?

She had no answer, only knew that she did. "And my mother?" she forced herself to ask.

Hunter's shoulders seemed to sag. "She died when you were a baby, I'm told."

The sadness weighed more heavily on her shoulders. She fell quiet and tried to absorb all that Hunter had told her.

Even without her parents, there were so many people to remember. What would they think when they learned she had no memory of any of them?

"It's a lot to take in," she confessed to Hunter. "I don't remember any of them. I don't remember anything. I've been around you all day. Shouldn't I be remembering something about you by now? You said we knew each other. Were we . . . close?"

For a long moment, she was afraid he wasn't going to answer. Then, finally, he said, "Once. A long time ago."

"How close were we?"

He shrugged. "Does it matter?"

"It must matter to you, or you'd tell me."

"We were friends."

"Friends?"

"Best friends."

She didn't know why she was pushing him this way, but she couldn't seem to stop. Maybe it had something to do with the way the muscles of his back had suddenly tightened, as if he expected a blow. "Nothing more than that?" When he didn't answer, she said, "You're not going to tell me, are you."

"Maybe I don't want to prejudice you. Maybe you should form your own opinion about me, until you remember. Then you can decide for yourself what we are—were—to each other."

"Gracious. You sound so serious."

He chuckled, but it didn't sound to Bess as though he was amused. "What's so funny?"

"Gracious is what you always say when you get flustered."

"I am not flustered."

"You always deny it." This time there was a smile in his voice.

* * *

As the sun set, it was more than apparent to Hunter that they weren't going to make the Double D that day. Bess hadn't complained, but the last time they had dismounted to walk a while and give the horse a rest, she'd been so pale, he'd feared she was going to faint. Now he suspected, from how quiet she'd grown in the hour since, that her head was hurting again.

"I hope you won't be too disappointed," he told her, "but I'm not going to be able to get you home tonight like I promised."

"Why not? How much farther is it?"

She might not admit to being tired, but her voice was filled with exhaustion. Considering the commotion her return was bound to cause at the ranch, he didn't want her to go through that when she was near the end of her strength.

"It's only a couple more hours, but the horse has had about all he can take for one day, and it'll be dark before we could get there. We'll stop in town for the night, get you a room at the hotel."

Bess sagged in relief. If the truth be known, she was not all that eager to be presented—in her exhausted, bedraggled, filthy state—to a group of strangers who in all likelihood would expect her to behave as she normally did, to smile and laugh and love them the way their sister, aunt, and niece always had. The problem was that Bess could not behave the way they would expect her to.

Would they be willing, as Hunter apparently was, to give her the time she needed to form her own opinions, to let her feelings grow, or not, for each of them according to whatever was in her heart? How disappointed would they be when she did not, could not, relate to them the way she had in the past?

"Bess?"

"Oh. I'm sorry. My mind was wandering. A hotel, did you say?"

"It's nothing fancy, but it's solid and clean and has real beds."

"And a bath?" It wasn't just the dust and grime of the trail that she wanted to wash away, but the touch of those unknown men who had taken her from her home and robbed her of her past. She couldn't remember their touch, for which she was, for now, grateful. But she sensed it, felt it as something foul. She had a sudden, overwhelming need to bathe. "Will I be able to get a hot bath?"

"And a decent meal."

Just over an hour later, as true dark settled across the long, narrow valley of the Huerfano River, they rode into the town of Badito. It was a small, dusty town built mostly of adobe. But it was not a quiet town. The main street was busy with traffic—men on horseback, two freight wagons, three buckboards, and a carriage. Men and women hurried along their way on foot while a loose hog rooted in a pile of garbage in the alley between two buildings. Somewhere behind one of the buildings lining the street, children shrieked with laughter and dogs barked. The tinkling of off-key piano music and rough male laughter spilled out through the open door of an establishment whose sign proclaimed it simply The Saloon.

Nothing, absolutely nothing, looked familiar to Bess.

Hunter guided the horse to the hitching rail in front of the Badito Inn, where he dismounted, then lifted Bess down from the saddle. He held on to her waist until she was steady on her feet, then unstrapped his saddlebags and tossed them over his shoulder and slid his rifle from the saddle scabbard.

The hotel was one of the few buildings in town to have a raised boardwalk. Bess stepped up onto it, then paused, frowning. "Do they know me here? Am I supposed to know them?"

Hunter stepped up beside her. With his hat still pulled low over his eyes, his face was barely visible in the waning light. He spoke softly so his voice wouldn't carry. "Jeremy Cotterson is probably working the desk tonight. He and his wife, Sally, moved here from Connecticut a couple of years ago and bought this place. You know them, but not very well. He likes to gossip. She likes to boss the hired help around.''

Bess smiled and placed a hand on Hunter's arm. ''Thank you.''

Saying nothing, Hunter pushed the door open and stepped aside for Bess to enter.

Bess's first thought was that Sally Cotterson was quite good at bossing her hired help. The oak floor was spotless and gleaming. The room ran the width of the building, with a seating area to the left, and the front desk to the right. Behind the desk was a curtained door. A staircase bisected the room, separating the lobby from the desk area. Everything was neat and immaculate, and there wasn't a soul in sight. Bess breathed a sigh of relief.

Hunter strode to the front desk and rang the bell. Almost instantly the curtain behind the desk was shoved aside and a tall, thin man with bushy graying sideburns stepped up behind the desk. He was in his late thirties, with a short, pudgy nose, wire-rimmed spectacles so thick they made his eyes look bugged, and a wide, friendly smile.

''Well, hello there, Hunter. And Miss Bess, what a pleasure to see you here in our establishment. What can I do for you?''

''We need a couple of rooms for the night,'' Hunter told him. ''And Miss Dulaney would like a hot bath brought to her room.''

''Certainly, certainly. We have a bathing chamber at the end of the hall upstairs, of course. But business being light this night, and it being Miss Bess and all, we'll just haul our extra bathtub right straight to your room, Miss Bess.''

''Thank you, Mr. Cotterson. I appreciate the trouble,'' Bess said, grateful that Hunter had told her the man's name, since he seemed to know her so well.

''No trouble, no trouble at all,'' Cotterson said.

Bess pursed her lips to keep from smiling. No trouble indeed, when he'd just deliberately pointed out to her how much trouble it was going to be. But for her, he would do it.

Was her family so influential, then, she wondered, that people were in the habit of going out of their way for them?

But of course, Cotterson would surely charge for the service.

She thought to wonder if Hunter had money enough on him to pay for their rooms. Surely he did, or he wouldn't have brought her here.

Cotterson opened his guest register and turned it toward them. "Just sign in, and we'll take care of everything you need. If you don't mind my saying so, you look like you've ridden pretty hard today."

Hunter gave him a half smile. "You got that right."

Bess ducked her head, hoping that if the man saw the bruise on her face, he might think it was dirt. What he would think in the morning when, after her bath, the mark was still there, was another matter. Perhaps after a good night's sleep she would be better prepared to deal with the questions and speculation she would see in everyone's eyes.

"Would you be wanting the missus to bring you up each a bowl of her hearty beef stew and some of her freshly baked bread?"

"Oh," Bess said with feeling. "Yes. Please. That would be wonderful. I don't know which I want worse—the meal or the bath."

Cotterson beamed at her. "Well, we'll just bring them both at once, and you can decide at the time."

Hunter signed the book for both of them. Cotterson selected two keys from the board on the wall beside the curtained door. He looked at the keys in his hand, then back at Bess and Hunter. With a thoughtful frown, he replaced one of the keys and selected another. With a satisfied nod, he stepped out from behind the desk.

"Right this way, folks. Say," he said as he led them to the stairs, then up. Oil lamps kept the upstairs hallway from being dark. "Did you hear about the robbery over at Walsenburg a couple of days ago?" His voice quivered with excitement, even as he tried to look sober. "The Rawlins gang held up the bank. Folks are saying that because Wells Fargo had just delivered a shipment, that Rawlins character got away with nearly eight thousand dollars."

"That much, huh?" was all Hunter said.

"The county sheriff's got a posse out, and word is that they've raised the reward on Ned Rawlins to a thousand dollars, because this time he shot a man. Rumor has it that if the sheriff doesn't catch that outlaw soon ... well, you know, county elections are coming up this fall." Cotterson shook his head and clucked his tongue. "Could be we'll have a new county sheriff before the dust settles from this robbery."

He stopped at the door to room number one in the front corner. "We'll put you in here, Miss Bess. It's our nicest room, and the largest, too. Plenty of room," he said, unlocking the door and swinging it open, "for the bathtub."

Bess stood in the hall until Cotterson lit the lamp on the bedside table and filled the room with light. There was one window, facing the street and heavily draped, next to the bedside table. The bed was wide, with a brass headboard and light blue coverlet. A spindle-backed rocker stood in the far corner, and across from it stood a full-length mirror on a stand. Next to the door stood a wardrobe, with two drawers in the bottom and a small stove next to it for heat. There was not a speck of dust in sight.

"Thank you, Mr. Cotterson. The room is fine."

Hunter stepped inside. After looking around briefly, he nodded, satisfied that Bess would be comfortable here.

"Your room," Cotterson pointedly said to Hunter, "is down the hall. Miss Bess, we'll have that stew and your bath up here as soon as the water heats."

"Thank you," she said.

"If you need anything else," the man offered, "you just let

me know. When you're finished with your supper and bath, you can just leave everything for the maid to take care of tomorrow, or you can pull the bell cord there in the corner and someone will be right up.''

''Thank you. I'm sure I'll be fine.''

''Very well, then. Hunter? Right this way.''

It wasn't lost on Bess that the man had already told them business was light, yet he put Hunter ''down the hall'' rather than in the room next to hers, or the one directly across the hall. Nor did she miss the fact that Cotterson stood aside and waited for Hunter to leave the room first.

Bess bit back a secret smile. She wondered which was uppermost in the man's mind—protecting her virtue or the reputation of his hotel.

Hunter paused at the doorway and gave her a final look. ''I'm going to go stable the horse. Then I'll be in my room the rest of the night if you need me.''

Bess nodded and offered him a smile. ''Thanks. I'm sure I'll be fine.''

When the door closed behind the two men, she stood beside the bed and looked around. Gradually it occurred to her that this was the first time in her entire memory that she was indoors, that she would take a bath, sleep in a bed.

And it was the first time in her entire memory that she had been alone.

She fought the irrational urge to call out to Hunter, just to make certain he was still nearby.

''Don't be a ninny,'' she told herself. Her voice in the empty room sounded hollow. ''You're a grown woman. You can certainly spend the night in a room on your own. You've probably done it for years.'' Unless, of course, she shared a room with someone else at the ranch. Perhaps with her thirteen-year-old niece.

Which was all beside the point. She was going to get a bath.

Now that was a point worth remembering. And it brought a smile to her lips.

When Hunter returned from stabling his horse at the livery, a steaming bowl of Mrs. Cotterson's stew, along with a thick slice of fresh, warm bread waited for him on a tray beside the bed in his room. It sure beat the hell out of trail food, he acknowledged as he wolfed it down. He could have eaten at least two more servings without getting full, but he let the matter go. He didn't want to go downstairs and put Mrs. Cotterson to the extra trouble. He wanted, instead, to check on Bess.

Did she have enough to eat? Had her bath been delivered? He hated leaving her alone, hated having her out of his sight, even knowing she was only a few yards away, safe in her own room.

His saddlebags, which he'd tossed onto the straight-backed chair in the corner—no rocking chair for him, he thought with a smirk—caught his eye. Well, hell. He'd forgotten to give Bess her comb and brush and other things.

He swore at himself, wondering if he'd forgotten on purpose so he'd have an excuse to knock on her door and check on her. It didn't matter now, he supposed. She would need the things in the saddlebag. And, he realized, she had nothing to sleep in. He would have to take her things to her, along with his extra shirt.

He unbuckled the bags and hefted the one containing her things, then dug out his spare shirt. He started toward the door, his boot steps loud in the silence of the room.

That wouldn't do. Cotterson, the old gossip, was probably downstairs right now listening for creaking floorboards. Wouldn't he just love to have it to spread around town that the half-breed snuck down the hall to Miss Bess's room.

Nae, he'd not be givin' the town crier any dirt to spread around about Bess. He went back to the other saddlebag and pulled out his moccasins. He would still have to step carefully over that squeaky board that ran down the middle of the hall, but at least this way his steps wouldn't echo clear into next week.

He slipped out his door and into the hall, feeling as stupid as hell. He was a grown man; he shouldn't have to sneak anywhere. But he would do it to avoid creating gossip about Bess.

"Pretend you're sneaking up on a quail," he muttered to himself.

Ach, wouldn't the blue-eyed lass love that, bein' referred to as a bird. And one that couldna fly worth a damn, at that. She'd box your ears, lad, and that's a fact.

But that wasn't fair, he told himself. Bess had never boxed anyone's ears in her life. She'd told him she wanted to once, he remembered, biting back a grin, that time when some boy at school had put a garter snake in her lunch pail. But she'd been too much of a lady, even all those years ago, to do anything more than deliver a stinging lecture to the culprit.

Hunter, not having been raised as a gentleman, had threatened to cut off the weasel's ears if he ever bothered Bess again.

He shook his head to dispel the memory. Stepping across the middle floorboard, he made his way quietly to Bess's door. The past, he reminded himself, had no bearing on today. Not as long as Bess couldn't remember it.

At her door, he paused and listened for the splash of water that would tell him she was already in the bath. If she was, he'd have to come back later. But hearing nothing, he tapped lightly. "Bess?" he called in a low voice that he hoped wouldn't carry downstairs. "I brought your comb and brush and things."

There was no response.

"Bess?"

Through the door he heard what sounded like a muffled yelp of pain. "Bess? Are you all right?" When she didn't answer, he knocked again, louder this time, too worried about her, suddenly, to concern himself with whether or not Cotterson heard him. "Bess, if you don't answer me, I'm coming in."

She did not answer.

A host of catastrophes ran through Hunter's mind as he feared the worst. She had fallen and hit her head and was lying unconscious on the floor.

She had been so exhausted that she'd fallen asleep in her bath and drowned.

She'd changed her mind about trusting him and had fled out the window.

Ned Rawlins had followed them and had kidnapped her again.

Anything! Anything could have happened to her! His gut clenched and his hands shook.

"Bess!" Fully prepared to break down the door, he reached for the knob. He was not comforted by the fact that it turned easily beneath his hand. The door swung open at his touch.

The bathtub had been delivered. The water level was low, with steam wafting from it. Four full buckets—presumably of cold water—sat beside it, waiting to be added to make the water temperature comfortable. A tray, containing two heavy towels, a washcloth, several different small bars of soap, and two small bottles filled with what looked like bath oil, sat on the floor at the far end of the tub.

Next to the bed, the lamp put out a bright, steady glow.

In the far corner, the skirt and blouse that he himself had put on Bess that morning lay neatly draped over the back of the rocking chair.

Bess stood, naked, with her back to him, looking at herself in the long oval mirror. With her hair still pinned up in a knot at the back of her head, every bruise and scrape on her body was visible.

Despite that, Hunter's heart nearly stopped, so relieved was he to see that she was safe.

"Aw, Bess." He closed the door behind him. Safe she might

be, but she was not all right. She was using both hands to cover her mouth and muffle the sounds of her weeping. Tears streamed quietly down her face while she looked at the black-and-blue marks all over her body. Marks that were darker and more numerous than they'd been that morning. Marks that told the story of her ordeal at the hands of Ned Rawlins and his gang.

Hunter yanked the coverlet from the bed. When he stepped up behind her and wrapped her in it, she lowered her hands and slowly met his gaze in the mirror. Her eyes, normally so expressive, so full of life, were empty. They slid away from meeting his and stared blankly at something he could not see.

"Bess, Blue Eyes, talk to me."

But she only continued to stare blankly into the mirror.

The room was growing cool now that night had settled. Through the coverlet Hunter felt Bess shiver. "You're getting cold, Bess. Don't you want to take that hot bath now?"

Again she did not answer.

Not knowing what else to do, Hunter picked her up in his arms and sat on the end of the bed, holding her on his lap as though she were a child in need of comfort. She might not be a child, but it was obvious to him that she was in need. He just wasn't certain he knew how to give her what she needed.

A few feet away, steam still rose from the tub.

"Here." He shifted her to sit on the bed. With barely more solidity than a rag doll, she sat exactly as he placed her.

With every second she failed to respond to him, Hunter's worry grew. She'd been fine when he'd left her. She'd been fine all day, except for the loss of her memory, which, of course, was no small loss.

She'd known she had been shot. She'd known she had been bound. But until she had stood before the mirror, she hadn't had any real idea of the extent of the injuries she had suffered at the hands of her captors.

Man-Above, he would have spared her that. He shouldn't have brought her here. He should have taken her on to the ranch, where Winter Fawn, and Gussie if she was there, could help her through this.

But no, he'd been selfish, he admitted as he rolled up his sleeves and poured cold water into the hot in the tub. He hadn't been willing to share her with her family yet. He had thought that perhaps she wasn't quite ready for them, that she needed a good night's rest first, but that could have been his own wants swaying him.

From the corner of his eye, as he added a second bucket of cold water to the tub, he saw her shiver. The coverlet fell from her shoulder, baring her bruised breast. She made no attempt to cover herself. She didn't seem aware that she needed to.

"Hold on, Blue Eyes," he told her. "I'll get you warm."

He should probably go find a woman to help her. Mrs. Cotterson would no doubt know what to do. But Bess knew that he had already seen her in the altogether. He wasn't sure she would appreciate having others see her in this condition and know what she had been through. Unless and until Bess objected, he would care for her himself. For her sake, as well as his own need. If that was selfish of him, so be it. It sure wasn't his only fault.

After satisfying himself that the water was the right temperature, hot enough to warm her, but not enough to scald, he scooped out two bucketsful to use for rinsing, then gently removed the coverlet from her and lifted her in his arms.

"I'm going to put you in the bath now," he said, not knowing if she heard him or not. He didn't know if she even knew what he was doing. When he carefully eased her into the water, she gave no indication that she knew or cared. She merely sat as he placed her and stared straight ahead.

The lamplight hit the rim of the tub and cast the surface of the water in shadow. The water level struck her a few inches above her waist, hiding everything below that from his view. Leaving everything above exposed. Hunter had the almost irresistible urge to lean down and kiss each of those fingerprint bruises encircling her breast, to wipe them away with his lips, make them disappear as though they had never been.

Impossible, of course. And if he were to even try, he feared his kisses would go astray and he would end up taking her beautiful, dark nipple into his mouth and . . . and shaming them both. She was far too vulnerable for him to be having thoughts like that. He pulled his gaze from her breast and smoothed a hand over her shoulder.

"Are you with me, Blue Eyes? Do you want me to wash your hair?" He'd never washed a woman's hair before, but he wanted to wash away, even if only symbolically, every trace of her ordeal. If he could scrub away her bruises, he would. Because that wasn't possible, he would do what little he could.

With fingers that felt suddenly clumsy, he searched out the pins in her hair and removed them, tucking them into the pocket of his denims. Long and thick, her black, wavy hair spilled down into his hands. He had always loved her hair. It felt like the white man's silk against his skin. When she was younger, she had worn it down, sometimes tied at her nape with a pretty ribbon. But during the last few years she had worn it up, either in a simple knot, as she had today, or in fancy curls that bounced when she walked.

He held it now, savoring the weight of it, resisting the urge to bury his face in it and simply breathe its essence. Man-Above, he loved the feel of it. It was so long—it hung past the middle of her back—that the ends trailed in the water, floating there for several seconds before soaking up enough water to fall below the surface and out of his sight.

Some day, when he finally made her his and made love to her, he wanted to feel her hair all over his bare skin. He wondered if he would ever get the chance.

But he was supposed to be washing it, not painting arousing pictures in his mind of her rising above him in bed, with her hair streaming down her back . . .

And wasn't he the jackass for thinking such thoughts at a time like this.

Speaking softly, he said, "Let's scoot you forward, so you can lean back and wet your hair. That's it, I won't dunk you like I did that time in the river." He held her head in one hand and used the other to scoop water up along her hairline, being careful to keep it out of her face. "I know you don't remember, but it was funny. We were swimming in the river behind your house. You were so mad at me for dunking you, but you got even when you grabbed my foot and pulled me under. Then Megan joined in. I told you about Megan, your niece? Sit up now, nice and easy. That's it. Then the two of you nearly drowned me."

He kept talking, about anything and everything he could think of, while checking out the soap. "Sandalwood. That won't do. Doesn't smell like you at all. Ah, roses. That's you. We'll use this one." He gently rubbed the small bar into her hair. He worked up a thick lather, then continued for several minutes to work it through her hair and rub gently against her scalp. The soft scent of roses teased the air.

He wished he knew if she was enjoying this at all, if she was even aware that he was washing her hair. He had to assume she wasn't, for she didn't even wince when his fingers brushed across the wound at her temple.

He took his time, wondering why he had never done something so pleasurable before. Pleasurable, that is, as long as he didn't look too deeply into her eyes. Every time he saw that blank, inward stare, he was torn between raging at fate and Ned Rawlins, and weeping.

Gently he eased her down again until the water lapped around her face. It took him several minutes to get the soap out of her hair. When he'd gotten out as much as he could, he pulled her up and tilted her head back. Then he poured clear water through her hair from the bucket of warm he had set aside. After that, he wrung as much water as possible out of the long mass, then placed one of the towels over the back edge of the tub and pulled Bess back until her head rested on the towel, with her hair draped out onto the floor. He didn't know what else to do with that much hair.

Damn, he'd forgotten the bath oil. He found the decanter that smelled of roses and poured a small amount into the tub. The scent rose on the steam and filled the room. Filled his head, reminding him of two days ago when she'd come to him in the canyon, and countless other times when he'd stood next to her and tried not to let her scent go to his head.

"I'm going to wash your face now." He dipped the washrag into the water, then rubbed it with the perfumed soap. "Close your eyes, Bess," he asked softly, "so I won't get soap in them."

She did not shut her eyes, until he leaned down and kissed them. Even then, she gave no other indication that she was aware of him or her surroundings.

As carefully as possible, Hunter used the soapy washcloth to clean and rinse her soiled, sunburned face. Then he did the same with first one arm, then the other, raising each one in turn from the water, then lowering it back down.

Now he had to consider what her reaction was going to be later when she realized that he had washed all of her, head to toe, while she had been unaware. Perhaps he should consider that simply sitting in the water had cleaned her enough.

But he could at least scrub her back before he hauled her out of the tub.

So deciding, he placed a hand behind her neck and pulled her up until she was sitting. He took the hairpins from his pocket to secure her hair up out of the way, but the hair didn't want to be secured. It developed a life of its own, slipping and slithering from his hold. How did women manage?

Then suddenly, she spoke. "You never said ... I never thought to ask ... is there a man I can't remember, who's thinking I'm going to ... to marry him? Do I have a beau?"

In the process of placing the last pin in her hair, Hunter jerked in surprise, letting the hair fall down her back and trail in the water. He shifted position so he could see her face. Awareness was back in her eyes. So was devastation. "Bess—"

"I hope not," she said, still staring straight ahead rather than looking at him. "Maybe you shouldn't tell me just yet. It seems . . . if there is such a man, I'll have to disappoint him."

With one hand on her shoulder for comfort—his as much as hers—Hunter placed a finger to her chin and turned her head until she faced him, but still she refused to meet his gaze. "What are you talking about? Bess, look at me."

She looked at his hand on her shoulder, then finally raised her gaze to his, her expression puzzled. "It doesn't disgust you to touch me?"

"Blue Eyes, no. Never. How can you ask such a thing?"

Her gaze lowered to somewhere around his chin. "You can see for yourself. Look at me. I'm a mess. The marks they left on me. They must have . . . must have . . . raped me."

"You don't know that," he said earnestly.

"Don't I?"

"Do you remember it?"

"No." She shook her head. "I can't remember it, but it's obvious that it's true."

Aye, he thought, struggling to bite back his sudden fury. She didn't need his anger now; she needed his care. It was obvious to him, too. They must have raped her. She'd been with them most of one day, all night, and all the next day. The location of her bruises told their own tale. "I'm glad you can't remember it," he said fiercely, pulling her close and wrapping his arms around her. "If it really happened, I hope you never remember it."

"It must have happened," she said, her voice muffled against his shoulder. A sob broke loose of her control and shook her. "I'm ruined, Hunter. No man will have me now."

Hunter pushed her away and held her by her shoulders. "Look at me." He gave her a small shake. "Look at me, Bess." He waited until she did, then said fiercely, "You don't know that it really happened. And even if it did, any man who would let something like that keep him from marrying you isn't good enough for you. He doesn't deserve you."

She gave him a smile that was so sad, it nearly broke his heart. "You're so sweet, Hunter, to say that."

"I'm not sweet. I said it because it's true."

"I don't believe you." She let her head fall lightly to his shoulder. "But thank you for saying it."

"If I didn't believe it," he told her quietly, "I wouldn't have said it."

They stayed like that for long moments, Hunter on his knees beside the tub, with his arms around her, Bess with her head on his shoulder.

Finally she pushed away and sat up. "I'm getting you all wet."

"It doesn't matter," he told her with a small smile. "Here." He handed her the washcloth and soap. "I washed your hair and your face and arms. You do the rest before your toes wrinkle and the water gets cold." He started to rise.

She grabbed his hand. "Are you going? Leaving me alone?" she asked, a catch in her voice.

"Not if you don't want me to."

"Stay," she said, looking into his eyes. "Don't leave me alone."

Hunter stroked a wet strand of hair away from her face. "I'll stay, Blue Eyes."

CHAPTER TEN

Hunter stayed.

He gave her the hairpins, and she gave her hair a twist and a flip and had it pinned atop her head so fast that it baffled him after his unsuccessful attempts.

He sat on the side of the bed with his back to the tub to give her what privacy he could and still not leave her alone. And tried not to remember the look of her slender neck after she'd pinned up her hair.

Yet even from the distance of several feet, he could still smell the roses in her bathwater. He could hear every tinkle and splash as she washed herself. He could feel the steam in the air. He could imagine . . .

Hell, he could imagine too damn much. Soft lamplight sparkling off drops of water that clung to pale, bare skin. The feel and taste of those drops on his tongue if he were to lick them off. Shadow and light moving and shifting over the surface of the water, first revealing, then hiding the soft curves of her body.

The air in the room might be cooling, but Hunter was about to sweat. He had to get his mind on something else.

That was easy enough to do. All he had to do was remember why and how he had come to be in this room with Bess. What she went through at the hands of Ned Rawlins tore at Hunter's insides in a way that nothing in his life ever had, not even his leaving his mother's people, the Arapaho, in the dead of night never to return.

Behind him, it had grown silent. No more little splashes of water. No more soft swiping of soapy, wet cloth over skin. No more quick intake of breath when she discovered another bruise, another scrape, another sore spot.

"Bess?"

Her answer, when it finally came, was a small, quiet sob that tore a hole in Hunter's heart. He turned and found her with her face buried against her raised knees, her fists knotted around the washcloth.

"Ah, Blue Eyes," he said, aching for her. He rounded the bed and knelt beside the tub. "The water's gone cold. You'll catch a chill if we don't get you out." He lifted her from the tub and stood her between his knees. "You go right on ahead and cry if you want, while I dry you off."

He dried her thoroughly, being as gentle as he could. He had no trouble keeping his mind off wanting her. He hurt too bad for her just then to think of anything other than taking care of her.

"I'm s-sorry," she sobbed.

"For what?" he asked, running the towel down her back one final time.

"I c-can't s-stop crying."

"You don't need to stop. Here. I brought you a shirt of mine to sleep in. Hold your arms up."

Like a child, she obeyed. As if she were that child, he slipped his shirt down over her head and tucked her arms into the sleeves. He had to roll them up three times to find her fingers; the hem reached nearly to her knees.

"You shouldn't hold in your tears, Blue Eyes." He wrapped her again in the coverlet, grabbed the extra towel to use on her hair, and settled against the headboard of the bed with her in his lap.

She cried the entire time.

"If you hold them in, either they will poison you, or you'll choke on them," he said softly. "Just cry all you need to, and let all the pain and confusion flow out with your tears. I'll keep you safe, I promise."

She leaned against him and pressed her face to his shoulder and continued to cry, great, racking sobs.

Hunter kissed her brow and offered whatever words of comfort he could think of, but he did not suggest she quit crying. He believed the words he'd spoken, that tears held back could poison a person. Tears, anger, fear, even happiness. None should be held tight.

Pulling the pins free and tossing them onto the bedside table, he stroked her wet hair with the towel. "That's right, Blue Eyes, let it all out."

"I'm g-getting you all w-wet. Your"—sniff—"poor sh-shirt."

"My shirt and I are honored to receive your tears."

She sobbed again, breaking his heart. "Why are you b-being so n-nice to me?"

"Because you're a very special woman." With the toe of his moccasin, he snared the bag he'd brought for her that contained her brush and comb. After dragging it up until he could grasp it, he fished out her comb and went to work as gently as possible on the snarls in her hair. "And you deserve to be treated nicely."

Another sob choked her. "When you're n-nice, it just makes me want . . . m-more."

Hunter closed his eyes and pressed his cheek against the top of her head. "Whatever you want, if it's within my power, I will give you. Anything, Bess. Everything."

"Oh, H-H-Hunter," she wailed. "It was you. You were my beau, weren't you?"

Hunter took in a slow breath and let it out. "Under the circumstances, that's not a fair question, Blue Eyes."

"Why?"

"Because if I say no, I'm not your beau, I don't love you, it might hurt your feelings, and I never want to hurt you. But if I say yes, I am yours, you won't be able to remember the feelings and return them, and then I'm the one who's hurt. Ask me anything else, Blue Eyes, but don't ask me to hurt one of us tonight."

She was silent for a moment, except for the sound of her weeping as it quieted. Then she said, "Anything?"

"Anything."

"W-would you lie to me, if I asked you to?"

"Why would you want me to lie to you?"

She pushed herself away from him, but only far enough so that she could sit up and look him in the eye. But she couldn't hold his gaze when she brushed a hand across the bruise on her cheek and said, "Tell me I'm not ugly."

"Ah, Bess." Her eyes were red and swollen, her lashes clumped together by tears. Her face was pale and flushed all at once, and bruised, and her lips were puffy. "The bruise is a sacrilege. You're so beautiful, inside and out, you take my breath away."

Another small sob broke loose. She wrapped her arms around his chest and held him tightly.

Hunter reveled in her touch. It had been so long since she'd held him in her arms. Man-Above, what a fool he'd been to push her away so many times in the past, when all he'd really wanted to do was make her his.

"Tell me you love me," she whispered tearfully. "Even if it's not true, tell me you love me, Hunter."

A giant fist squeezed his heart. If he survived this night without falling apart into a hundred million pieces, it would be a miracle. He returned her hug and pressed his lips to her forehead. "I love you." He hoped that her own crying prevented her from hearing the ragged emotion he was unable to control in his voice. "I love you, Bess."

"I don't want to remember what those men did to me," she whispered, fisting her hands in his shirt. "I don't want that to be my only memory. Make love to me, Hunter."

"Ah, Bess." Hunter squeezed his eyes shut and held her as tightly as he dared. She had offered herself to him once before, his Bess had, two years ago. It had been at once the sweetest and most painful moment of his life, and it had been the beginning of the distance Hunter had deliberately placed between himself and this girl—woman—he loved so much.

She had been eighteen and eager. He'd been twenty, and just as eager. They had been meeting along the banks of the river for years, but until that night, Hunter had never done more than kiss her.

Well, he thought now with humor, not much more, anyway. Not enough to get them into serious trouble.

But that one night, when the summer moon waxed full and the breeze blew warm, their kissing and petting and teasing had gotten out of hand. He had been on fire for her and she for him. She had been more than willing; she'd been eager, pulling at his shirt to get at his bare skin.

The mere memory of that night, after two years, still had the power to make him hard.

He never knew where the strength had come from to pull away. At the time he'd been sure that it wasn't strength at all, but stupidity. Cowardice. A beautiful, warm, willing woman who loved him, whom he loved. The hot blood of youth pounding in their veins. He had known years earlier that there would be no other woman for him. He would marry her and make her his forever.

But some nagging little corner of his mind had warned him that if he took her then and there and made her truly his, he'd better be prepared to take her the rest of the way, straight into marriage. To honor and protect her, to provide for her and the children they would make.

It was the latter, the providing, that had hit him in the face like a cold splash from the river. How could he provide for a wife—let alone children—when he lived in a bunkhouse and drew cowboy wages from her brother? How could he make her understand that she was too important to him, that he couldn't, wouldn't, marry her unless and until he could provide her with a nice, comfortable home?

She hadn't understood. He had hurt her so badly that night with his inept explanations. She'd been humiliated, feeling as if she had thrown herself at a man who didn't want her.

Not want her? Man-Above, she had never had any idea just how much he did want her. No idea of the way his body, heart, and soul yearned for her, hummed in her presence. The way his hands sometimes shook with the need to touch her.

It had been like that for him from the day he met her, and he knew it would never change.

That night at the river had shown him that he wasn't to be trusted around Bess. It had been such a close call. She had been so sweet, so willing. So responsive to his every touch. He had very nearly lost control and dishonored them both.

Now, here she was again, offering herself. Asking him to make love to her. But she was too damn vulnerable right now for him to give her what she thought she wanted. There was no way he could let himself take advantage of her when she couldn't even remember who she was, let alone who he was.

"I would give anything to be able to give you what you think you want," he whispered fiercely. "But you would only end up hating yourself, and me."

"Hunter—"

"Ask me again," he said with feeling. "When you get your memory back."

She cried again, quietly this time.

After several long moments, Hunter was able to ease his hold on her and resume combing the tangles from her hair. Such a simple thing, combing a woman's hair. Yet intimate, too. And pleasurable. He loved the feel of the long strands sliding through his fingers.

Maybe Bess found her own pleasure in having him comb her hair, for her tears gradually ceased and her grip on his shirt eased. Long before her hair was dry, she fell asleep.

Ned Rawlins didn't fall asleep so easily. He was spooked, and he didn't mind saying so. He had killed that half-breed two days ago. Shot him square in the chest and watched the blood gush out from the bullet hole. Saw the bastard fall face-down in the mud.

Yet the son of a bitch wasn't dead, because sure as shootin', that wasn't no ghost that got the drop on them at the cabin and took the girl, damn his hide. And damn Billy and Woody, too, for letting themselves get snuck up on like a couple of greenhorns.

Greenhorns. That was rich. A couple of greenhorns got themselves caught up on Greenhorn Mountain. Got themselves killed up there, too, the stupid bastards. They deserved it.

Ned was going to miss Cecil, though. For a little while, at least. They'd had some good times, the two of them, until they'd brought their little brothers in with them. Damn Billy and Woody, anyway. Nothing but screw-ups from the get-go.

Well, he wouldn't have to worry about them anymore. Now their cuts of the loot belonged to him. He wasn't about to lose any sleep over them, as long as he didn't have to go home someday and tell Mama that Billy had just been too stupid to live.

Ned thought to maybe worry a little about J.T., but he couldn't really work up the energy for it. J.T. had given them good information, so they always knew when to hit a place for a big haul, but the man took too big a cut, while Ned and the boys stuck their necks out.

Last time Ned had checked, the reward for him was up to five hundred dollars. He rubbed the front of his neck and wished he could remember if the wanted poster had said "Dead or Alive" on it.

He wouldn't worry much about that, either, though. The drawing of him wasn't very good, and this morning he'd shaved off his beard. Nobody was going to recognize him now. Not even the one person who truly could identify him—the girl. Bess.

Make that two people, he thought, remembering the half-breed.

Somewhere beyond the ring of light cast by his campfire a twig snapped.

Lightning quick, Ned drew his revolver and whirled toward the sound. "Who's there?" he demanded harshly.

The quiet snort of his own horse came back at him.

"Shit." His hand shaking more than he'd have liked to admit, he holstered his gun. "Damn half-breed's got me seeing ghosts and drawing down on my own horse."

But no damn ghost had ever pointed a gun at him before, by God. Now *that* really pissed Ned off.

Maybe it was time to get out of Colorado, Ned allowed reluctantly. He had everybody but J.T.'s share from the last job—except for what they'd buried beneath that boulder on the trail. He wished he hadn't forgotten that money when he took the back trail down the mountain, but seeing that half-breed had spooked the daylights out of him. The man was supposed to be dead, damn his hide.

Maybe the breed wasn't a man after all, Ned thought nervously, looking around at the dark shapes of the trees surrounding him.

They were all trees, weren't they?

Aw, shit, there he went again, thinkin' stupid. Why, if he didn't pull himself together any better than this, he'd soon be as dumb as Woody.

If he swung down toward Walsenburg, he could pick up his secret stash that not even Cecil had known about. That'd make up for the gold left buried under the boulder. After that, Mexico was sounding good. Or hell, maybe he would just stick around Colorado and finally give respectability a try.

After finishing the last of the coffee, he kicked dirt over the fire and stretched out in his bedroll. When he finally fell asleep, he dreamed of dead men rising up and stalking him.

Bess fought her way through the terror of her nightmare. She felt as though she were swimming through a river of molasses, but she knew she had to reach that soft, crooning voice on the other side of her dream. The voice meant safety, respite from the demon that chased through her mind. She tried to scream, but the only thing to emerge from her throat was a harsh gust of breath.

"Bess? Wake up, Bess."

Hunter? He wasn't in her dream, was he?

No, he wasn't there. There was only her, and the man with the cruel hands and the black beard, chasing her, always chasing her. And then he caught her. She tried again to scream, but once more, nothing came out. She tried harder and harder, hoping that if she could only scream, someone would hear, someone . . . strong would help her.

Then the man with the beard reached inside her chest with those hard, cruel hands and ripped out her heart. Laughing, he held it up in his hand while her blood ran down his arm.

Ah, the agony! The pain! Her heart had been ripped out! How could she go on living? Why would she want to?

And then the man with the beard tossed her heart onto the ground and turned to her, grinning.

"Wake up, Blue Eyes."

Yes. Wake up. She had to wake up. The bearded man had friends now, and they were all grabbing at her. Her heart, lying in the dirt on the ground, pounded hard and fast in fear. Bess tried to scream again, and this time managed a small croak. The sound coming from her own throat brought her sharply awake.

"It was just a dream," came Hunter's soothing voice. "Just a dream, Blue Eyes. You're all right, you're safe."

Bess clung to him, trying to catch her breath, feeling her heart race.

Her heart. She'd been dreaming something about her heart, but . . .

"Do you want to talk about it?" Hunter asked, smoothing his callused hand over her sweat-covered brow.

"I can't . . ." She tried to recall the dream, but her head started pounding something fierce. "I can't remember." She let out a harsh bark of bitter laughter. "That figures, doesn't it? I can't remember anything else. Why should I remember my dreams?"

"Let it go, Blue Eyes. It was a bad dream, anyway. No need to remember it."

Bess lay awake then, but it wasn't long before the room began to brighten. Only then did she realize that sometime while she slept, Hunter must have turned the wick down in the lamp.

He had stayed with her, just the way she'd asked him to.

At least he had honored one of her requests, she thought peevishly. He'd turned down all the others she'd made of him.

But when she remembered some of the things she had asked of him, her cheeks flamed with mortification.

* * *

Bess was no less mortified a couple of hours later when they left town, but she had a much more interesting puzzle to work out in her mind, so she set her embarrassment aside. There would be plenty of time, she assumed, to be embarrassed later. Such as the next time she looked into Hunter's eyes and saw in them the knowledge of all that had passed between them last night.

Part of that was what she was thinking about as they left town in the wagon Hunter had rented at the livery. He had tried to rent a buggy, saying it would be more comfortable for her, but there had been no buggy available, only this hard, sturdy buckboard.

They drove west out of Badito. Off to the south across a wide expanse of thick grass, a tree-lined river meandered its way down the valley. To the north lay scrub-covered foothills and stark bluffs. It seemed odd that, while nothing stirred in her memory about this land, neither did it seem unfamiliar to her. It looked, and felt, as though it was the place she should be.

As the wagon rattled its way toward the home she couldn't remember, Bess thought of the things she did recall, the things that had happened since she awoke in a cave with a pain in her head and a man at her side.

His answer last night, when she'd asked if he was her beau, kept playing back through her mind. Or rather, his lack of an answer. She suspected that she'd been close to the mark with her question. And if she was right and there had been something between them, then he was correct—she had the power to hurt him terribly by simply not remembering, not being able to feel for him what she once did.

If she was right.

Glancing at him from the corner of her eye, she could easily see why a woman would be drawn to him. There was something about that chiseled face, those gray eyes, that could hide or reveal at will his thoughts and feelings. His long black hair that hung past his shoulders drew her, too, making her wonder what it might feel like if she ran her fingers through it.

How bold! Again she wondered if she was in the habit of running her fingers through a man's hair. This man's, or some other's?

No, she thought with a growing certainty. This man was surely someone special to her. There was no echo of another in her mind or heart. That must mean something, mustn't it?

But it was more than just his looks that called to her. Since she had come to in that cave, he had been kind, considerate, gentle, solicitous. He had taken tender care of her at every turn, even when she hadn't trusted him and had let her mistrust show in obvious ways. Not once had he turned away from her.

She wondered again what they had been to each other in what she had come to think of as her other life, before, when she had known who she was.

Good God, what would have become of her if she'd awakened with no memory—and been alone?

She shuddered to think of it.

Beside her, Hunter had been sitting with his elbows braced on his knees, the traces running through his fingers. "Are you cold?" he asked, straightening.

"What? Oh, no. I'm fine. How much farther is it?"

"About an hour and a half. Are you nervous?"

"A little." *A lot,* she thought, pressing a hand to the rolling knot of nerves in her stomach. "Am I—was I—close to my family?"

"Yes," he said. "Very."

"Are they . . . I mean, do you think they'll be as . . . patient with me as you've been?"

"You're worried that they're going to expect you to act the way you always have around them."

She nodded. "Yes."

"Don't fash yerself, lass," he said with a thick burr. Then, without the Scottish accent, "I don't think you need to worry. Once they understand, they'll help you every way they can."

"It's not the things I'll be expected to do that concern me so much as the things they'll be expecting me to feel."

"Well," he said, drawing back on the reins. "Here's your chance to find out."

"Wha—" She followed his gaze and saw four riders approaching. One of them let out a shout. "Oh," Bess said. "Is that . . . are they . . . do I know them?"

"Aye. Whoa, there," he called to the wagon team. When the wagon stopped, he set the brake. "The black-haired man in the lead is your brother, Carson. The one with the gray beard is my father. The other two are your brother's men, Beau Rivers and Frank Johansen."

Bess studied the one Hunter said was her brother. He was older than she had expected. She guessed she'd been thinking he was closer to her own age. But then, she didn't know how old she was, she realized with chagrin. But her brother appeared to be more than ten years older than she. Which made sense if he had a daughter who was thirteen.

He looked . . . strong. Like someone a person could count on in times of need.

Yet there was something about him that didn't appear quite right, and she couldn't decide what it was. He was dressed similar to the other men, in denim pants, a red checkered shirt, a brown leather vest. His hat looked similar to the others'.

It was the gun, she thought. Something about the revolver he wore strapped to his thigh. It looked the same as any other revolver, and plenty of men—including Hunter and the ones riding with her brother—wore them. Yet on Carson Dulaney . . .

Bess shook her head at herself. He might be her brother, but she knew nothing about him, not really. Why should it seem odd to her that he wore a gun like other men?

All smiling and talking at once, calling out her name and Hunter's, the riders encircled the wagon.

"Bess!" Carson Dulaney swung down off his horse and reached his arms up to Bess. "Thank God you're safe."

A door in Bess's mind cracked open. Blinding light and deafening noise exploded inside her head. Her vision grayed around the edges, and all she could see were big, gloved hands coming at her, grabbing for her.

With a sharp cry, she scooted swiftly toward Hunter, bumping up against his shoulder and clinging to his arm with both hands.

Startled, Carson froze. "Bess?"

Her action triggered all of Hunter's protective instincts. "Easy, Blue Eyes." He knew there was no danger here for her, but she was afraid. A man she couldn't remember having ever seen before was reaching to grab her. Hunter placed his arm in front of her to shield her from Carson's touch. "Back off a little, Carson," he said matter-of-factly. "Give her a little room. There's a . . . slight complication."

Carson let his arms fall to his sides. Alarmed and bewildered, he looked at Hunter, then at Bess. "What complication?"

Hunter knew there was no easy way to say it, so he just said it straight out. "She doesn't remember you."

"Don't be ridiculous," Carson bit out. "What's going on Hunter? Bess, are you all right?"

Against Hunter's arm, Bess stirred. "I'm sorry," she said to Carson, her voice catching. "Hunter says you're my brother, but I don't remember you. I don't remember me. I don't remember anything."

CHAPTER ELEVEN

"Ye killed the bloody bastards, I hope." Innes MacDougall said to Hunter after hearing what had happened to Bess. Innes's face, what little was visible above his bushy gray beard, was flushed red with fury and indignation on Bess's behalf. His eyes were the same changeable gray as Hunter's. Right now the elder MacDougall's looked like flint layered in ice.

"At the time," Hunter answered, "it was more important to get Bess to safety than to go back and kill them. I suppose I'll have to finish up that little chore, but he'd already shot her once. I wasn't going to stick around and give him another try."

A low growl issued from Mr. MacDougall's throat. "Aye, ye had the right of it, lad. It just sticks in ma craw to think of that bastard gettin' away with harmin' our lass here, the mangy cur."

"Aye," Hunter agreed grimly. "It sticks, all right."

Bess had gotten over her scare the minute Carson had backed away and allowed Hunter to explain about her memory loss.

She looked at her brother now with a wry twist on her lips. "Have they always been this bloodthirsty?"

"My God," Carson said with obvious bewilderment. "It's true, then. You really don't remember, do you?"

Bess blinked and looked away from the hurt in his eyes. "I'm sorry," she whispered.

"No," Carson said instantly. "You have nothing to be sorry for. None of this is your fault. It's just going to take a little getting used to, for all of us. Let's get you home to Winter Fawn. Maybe she can do something about the injury to your head. Maybe that will help."

"My thoughts exactly," Hunter told him.

When they reached the Double D, Bess was overwhelmed by people calling her name, asking after her, eager to see her. The love and affection they felt for her was evident in their faces, their voices, their hands that reached out eagerly to her.

"Praise God she's safe."

"Bess, child, we were so worried."

"Oh, your poor face. And your head! What did those monsters do to you?"

Taken all together at once, they overwhelmed her. Had it not been for Hunter, Bess feared she would have bolted. But once he explained her memory loss to them, as he'd done out on the road to Carson and the other men, they seemed unsure how to act.

Bess knew the feeling only too well. How was she supposed to act? As if she knew and loved them, as they obviously did her? How was she to pretend to belong when her mind was a whirl of confusion?

But as he had every time since she'd awakened in that cave, Hunter came to her aid. He helped her down from the wagon and introduced her family to her one by one.

They were all there, just as he had described them yesterday. But he hadn't done any of them justice.

His sister and Carson's wife, Winter Fawn, was a truly beautiful woman—inside, it seemed, and out. Her skin shone coppery in the morning sunlight, her features even and delicate. She wore her hair coiled at her nape. It was that same lustrous black as Hunter's, as dark and shiny as a raven's wing. She, too, had inherited Innes MacDougall's gray eyes, but hers were soft, like a morning mist.

Watching those eyes settle on her, Bess wondered fleetingly how she knew what a morning mist looked like. Had she seen such a thing in her forgotten past?

"Oh, dear," said the woman who must be Aunt Gussie. "If this is awkward for us, you poor child, I can't begin to imagine how it must feel to you." Her soft, round face was lined with concern and years of living. Her coal-black hair was streaked with gray. When she gripped Bess's hand, Bess returned the grasp, wanting desperately to know this woman. Her soft Southern drawl made Bess realize that she herself spoke with that same accent. So, too, did Carson.

And why, Bess asked herself yet again, could she remember and identify a Southern drawl, but fail to recognize her own family? Or remember what she did last week?

Megan, Carson's daughter by his first wife, gave her a sweet, if confused, smile. She was a softer, petite version of Carson. *Did I look like that at her age?* Bess wondered.

Then there were the little ones, six-year-old April, four-year-old Bonnie, and young Innes Edmond, age three. All of them with thick, black hair and adorable grins.

"Aunt Bess, Aunt Bess!" they cried. They did not understand that she didn't know them, that she couldn't remember their little baby kisses, the hugs she must have received and given. They rushed her and wrapped their arms around her legs.

"Where you been, Aunt Bess?" April, the oldest of the three, wanted to know.

"Hold me," little Innes demanded, his arms reaching up for her.

For Bess, it didn't matter that she had no recollection of them. She lifted Innes up in her arms and fell in love right then and there, with all three of them.

Hunter watched it all with mixed emotions. For barely more than twenty-four hours, he had been the only person Bess had known. As much as he ached for her loss of memory, there was a headiness in being the center of a woman's world, being the one to supply all her needs, answer all her questions, chase away her bad dreams at night.

Now there were others to care for her, and for her to care about. That was as it should be, and he was glad she was finally home safely. Yet he could not help the sense of loss that touched him as he watched her take the first tentative steps toward building a new life with her family.

But maybe, he thought, not for the first time, it wouldn't be necessary for her to go through the trauma of starting over. "Winter Fawn," he said to his sister. "Will you see about the wound on her head? The bullet grazed her," he explained. "She was out for several hours, and when she came to, she had no memory."

"Of course I'll see to it, although I don't know . . ." Winter Fawn frowned and bit her lower lip.

She didn't have to finish for Hunter to know what she meant. She could heal the flesh, but she wasn't certain that would bring back Bess's memory. Neither was Hunter, but it was all they had.

"Goodness, please forgive us," Winter Fawn told Bess, lifting her son from Bess and handing him to Megan. "Gussie is right—this is all so much to take in. How much more so for you, and here we are, keeping you standing out in the sun and the dust. Come inside where we can take care of you."

Bess started toward the two-story log house with Winter

Fawn, then stopped and looked back at Hunter with slight panic
in her eyes. "Are you . . . are you staying?" she asked him.

Hunter made himself stand where he stood, when what he
wanted to do most in that moment was wrap his arms around
her and pull her to his chest. She looked so lost just now,
overwhelmed by all these strangers. "I won't leave you, Blue
Eyes."

Bess hadn't realized she'd been holding her breath waiting
for his answer, until he gave it. Her lungs filled with air and
her shoulders sagged with relief. He wasn't leaving her here
alone with all these people. They seemed like nice people, and
they were her family, but there were so *many* of them, and she
didn't know them. Knowing Hunter would be nearby helped
ease her tension.

On the porch, Winter Fawn stopped and smiled. "Megan
will keep the children outside for a while, and the men will go
about their work. That way you won't have to try to absorb all
of us at once."

"Thank you," Bess said. "You're being very kind."

Winter Fawn opened the door and led Bess into the house.
"It's very odd to hear you speak to me like that. It's as if
we've just met, which is how it feels to you, I would guess."

"Yes, it is."

The room they stepped into was large, the left half taken up
with a long table surrounded by ten straight-backed chairs.
Beyond the dining area was the kitchen, open to the rest of the
room. To the right of the front door was the parlor area, with
a horsehide sofa, a wooden rocker, a Queen Anne chair, and
a large fireplace. There was a homey quality to the house that
made Bess feel welcome.

"I'll put on some water for tea," Gussie said, "while Winter
Fawn takes care of your wound, dear."

"Aye, thank you, Gussie," Winter Fawn said. She led Bess
to the sofa. "Gussie and Innes live a few miles west of here.
They came early this morning so they could be here when you

came back to us. We've been so worried about you. Does the wound on your head give you pain?''

"Sometimes," Bess confessed. "Are you a healer?''

"Aye." Winter Fawn's smile was wry. "Tell me, is there anything you remember about your past? Anything at all?''

Bess folded her hands in her lap and looked down at them. "Nothing. Sometimes . . .''

"Sometimes?" Winter Fawn prompted.

"Sometimes I feel like it's all there, inside my head. I get a feeling, or a glimpse of something, and it just seems that if I concentrate, it will all come back to me. But when I concentrate, the pain in my head nearly blinds me, and whatever it was I thought I was about to grasp just slips away.''

"Oh, Bess, I am so sorry this terrible thing has happened to you. I don't know if I can do anything about your loss of memory, but I can at least take care of that nasty bullet graze.''

"Perhaps," Gussie said as she came and joined them, "you should explain to Bess, dear. She has surely had enough surprises for one day, what with meeting all of us.''

"Explain what?" Bess wanted to know.

"It's nothing," Winter Fawn assured her. "Only that I'm going to place my hand over the wound at your temple. It will feel warm, but it willna hurt.'' The last was said with that same Scottish burr that was so evident in Innes's speech and that slipped into Hunter's voice now and then.

Then, before Bess thought to question what Winter Fawn said, the woman pressed her hand gently to Bess's temple. The heat was instant and soothing. Bess hadn't noticed the constant ache until now, when it was relieved.

But how could that be? She started to ask, but the words dried on her tongue. Right before her very eyes, the skin along the hairline at Winter Fawn's temple split open. Blood oozed in the inch-long furrow that appeared. It looked, to Bess's shocked gaze, exactly like the wound on her own head, which she'd seen last night in the mirror. "I don't . . . I don't understand," she managed.

Gussie patted her arm in comfort, but said nothing.

Winter Fawn's eyes darkened with what looked to Bess like pain. Then, even more astounding, the wound on Winter Fawn's temple began to fade. It narrowed and shortened until there was nothing left but smooth skin, with a trace of dried blood as a reminder of what had once been. At the same time, the heat of her touch on Bess faded.

"There," Winter Fawn said, taking her hand from Bess's head. "I had no trouble finding the pain, but I'm sorry, Bess— I could not feel any deeper injury. You still have no memory, do you?"

Bess swallowed and shook her head.

From the kitchen came a sharp, shrill whistle.

"That'll be the tea." Gussie rose. "I'll bring it in here so we can relax and enjoy it."

Bess barely registered Gussie's leaving. She could not take her gaze from her brother's wife. "What . . . what just happened?"

Winter Fawn brushed her fingers along her own temple, then looked at the flakes of dried blood on them. "Exactly what it looked like." Some of the warmth was gone from her voice. "Here. Feel." She took Bess's hand and had her feel of her own wound.

Or, Bess thought in shock, where her wound used to be. "I—I don't understand."

Winter Fawn shook her head. "Neither do I. It is a gift I was born with." Her voice tightened. Her expression turned wary. "I do not question the how or why of it, I only use it to help others."

"Did I know about this?" Bess asked, awestruck.

"Aye, you did."

"Jesus, Mary, and Joseph," Bess exclaimed. "How could I have forgotten something like that?"

"Young lady!" The tea tray rattled in Gussie's hands as she carried it to them at the sofa. "You have apparently lost more than your memory. You manners have taken a decided turn for the worse. Jesus, Mary, and Joseph, indeed."

Bess blushed to the roots of her hair at the scolding. "I'm sorry. Hunter tells me that I never swear, yet it seems since yesterday, I've—ah, lapsed in that area."

"Never mind, dear," Gussie relented as she placed the tray on the table before the sofa. "I suppose you've earned the right to a few choice words now and then, what with all you've been through in the past few days. I shouldn't have scolded you like that."

"Please," Bess said earnestly. "I hope you'll understand that I can't behave exactly as I have in the past, because I don't remember how that was."

"Of course you can't, dear," Gussie told her, handing her a cup of tea. "Perhaps at least part of your memory loss is more of a blessing than a curse. I can't begin to imagine how terrified you must have been at the hands of those horrible outlaws." Then her eyes widened, as though she had in that moment thought of something. As if it were too horrible for words, she lowered her gaze and covered her mouth with her fingers.

Bess didn't need to be told that Gussie had just realized that Bess might possibly have been raped. This was her aunt, Bess reminded herself. But that didn't help. While she could not control the heat of another blush, she could not bring herself to broach the subject aloud.

Thankfully it was not necessary. Hunter chose that moment to open the door and come in. "I brought your things, Bess." In one hand he held the bag with her comb and brush. In the other, her folded dress, with her underthings hidden inside the bundle.

"Thank you," she told him. It seemed he was always coming to her rescue just when she needed him.

* * *

Hunter stayed on at the Double D. There was no way he could ride off and leave Bess there. He would ride to his cabin every few days to check on his horses. He could not bring himself to consider staying that far away from Bess for more than the few hours it would take to ride there and back.

As he tossed his gear into the barn, the men gave him an odd look now and then, but no one said anything. Not even his father or Carson, which was just as well, because Hunter was in no mood for more of their talk about Bess being too young to get married, or how Hunter ought to step aside and let her get to know other fellows.

To be fair, neither Hunter's father nor Carson had said anything of the kind in the past year or two, but they'd said enough of it up until then that sometimes, when he looked at Bess, their words rang in his head.

Seven years ago they had come here together, the Dulaneys and the MacDougalls, after the MacDougalls helped the Dulaneys escape from the Arapaho Dogmen who had captured them. That ordeal had bound them closely, tie upon tie. The escape from the Arapaho village, the shared terror of running through the night for their very lives. The struggle to build the ranch. Carson and Winter Fawn's struggle to understand and trust each other. The shared joy in their marriage. The surprise romance between Gussie and Hunter's father, and their marriage.

Tie upon tie. They were close. All of them.

Through it all, Hunter and Bess had grown to adulthood together, sharing their dreams, their secrets. No one knew Hunter better than Bess. No one knew her better than he did. It would have been impossible for them not to fall in love. It was their destiny, it seemed.

But Carson had feared that the two of them were only infatuated with each other because they didn't know anyone else well, had never let anyone else into their friendship. Bess knew no other boys, Hunter no other girls. Innes had agreed with Carson that they should get to know people their own age from town and the other ranches.

Looking back now on all of it, up to and including Bess's kidnapping, it seemed to Hunter that the real danger had been in he and Bess being so used to each other that they would take each other for granted. It shamed him to admit he'd been guilty of that. But so, he thought, had Bess, to some degree.

In any case, Carson and Innes had their way when Bess had started going to school in Badito. She'd met other people her own age and made friends. Hunter had been fifteen that year, Bess thirteen. He'd been too old to start white man's school for the first time. No way was he going to let a bunch of white kids make fun of him because he couldn't read. He'd since learned to read, thanks to Bess and Gussie, but it was something he still struggled with.

There were times he'd wondered if he shouldn't have simply taken Bess and run off to rejoin the tribe a long time ago. There a man didn't need to know how to read. A man didn't need white man's money to provide for his wife and their children. He only needed his skill as a hunter and, sometimes, as a warrior. Those skills he had.

He tried to picture Bess living out her life in a skin lodge on the plains, as she had mentioned that day of the kidnapping, and couldn't. The one time he'd seen her among his people, the day she and Carson and Megan had been captured by the Dogmen, her eyes had been wide and blank with terror.

No, no matter what she said, Bess was not meant to live such a rough life. She was used to solid walls, a sturdy roof. Pots and pans and a cookstove. A different dress to wear each day. Hot baths, he added with a slight smile.

No, he could not have taken Bess back to his mother's people. But he should have married her. He should have married her two years ago when they discovered they were so hot for each other that he'd had to distance himself from her to keep from giving in to his need and hers.

If he'd married her then, he would still be working for her brother. There would be no cabin in the canyon to the east. They might have their own small cabin here at the ranch headquarters. She wouldn't have the home he wanted for her, but they would have been together. There might even have been a child by now. And she would not have been kidnapped.

Regret tasted bitter on his tongue.

Now she looked at him as a stranger. Would she ever get her memory back? And if she did, would she be able to forgive him that their last words to each other before the Rawlins gang took her were hurtful?

Damn Ned Rawlins. Hunter rammed his fist into the stall he'd chosen to bed down in. *And damn me.* He hit the side of the stall again.

"The wall offends my son?"

Hunter whirled at the sound of his father's voice. Not only was he surprised that he hadn't heard him enter the barn, he was also surprised by the language. It was seldom that his father spoke the Arapaho tongue these days.

"A great number of things offend me," Hunter replied in the same language. Then, in English, because he had learned to think in English, he added harshly, "Mostly I offend myself."

"Aye." Rocking back on his heels and stroking his beard, Innes, too, switched to English, although his was thickly flavored with the accent of Scottish Highlands where he'd been born. " 'Twas right offensive of ye to be savin' the lass from them wot took her. I canna ken what ye was thinkin' to do such a dastardly thing."

In no mood to be humored, Hunter bit back a growl of frustration and turned away.

"Son," Innes said quietly. "Ye saved her life, ye did. Them bloody bastards woulda killed her rather than let her go. Ye know that."

Hunter picked up his bedroll and tossed it into the far corner of the stall.

"Did they hurt her bad?" Innes asked.

"Man-Above smiles on her. She canna remember."

"Maybe 'tis a blessing, that. Do ye still love her, then?"

Hunter whirled on his father. "What kind of question is that? Of course I love her."

"Aye." Innes nodded and smiled. "Aye, that ye do. If ye ask ma advice—which ye didna, but I'm yer faither, so I'll be givin' it anyway—don't fash yerself over what happened or what didna. Just be glad ye got her back, lad. Ye did right good with that, ye did, and I'm proud of ye."

With that, Innes turned and left the barn.

Hunter stood in the stall, grateful for his father's words. They helped. Some. A little.

Yes, he still loved Bess. But she no longer knew him. If she never regained her memory, could she learn to love him again?

And what if she did remember? Did he dare try to win her love and bind her to him before she remembered what she'd been through? Before she could remember that she had given up on him and was turning to that rich damn Horton?

If Hunter won her love again, and then her memory returned, would she grow to hate him for taking advantage of her vulnerability?

The questions haunted. Answers eluded.

When Hunter came in with the other men for supper, Bess was both relieved—enormously—and apprehensive. Relieved because she had secretly feared he would leave her here with this family—her family—and return to his home, regardless of what he'd said. Apprehensive because she could not recall ever being around him in this close-knit family setting. Would he treat her differently? Would she become simply one of the family to him, rather than the sole recipient of his attention, as she had been before he'd brought her here?

He had cleaned up before coming in. He had shaved, the hair around his face was damp from washing, and he wore clean clothes. The sight of him made her heart pound. When those piercing gray eyes settled on her, her mouth went dry and her palms turned damp.

She wanted to run to him, throw her arms around him. But she forced herself to stand back, certain that such forward behavior would be frowned upon by everyone. Aunt Gussie in particular seemed a stickler for observing the proprieties.

Hunter didn't give a damn about propriety. Her eyes were so expressive of her feelings that he had no trouble reading the apprehension in them, and something else that looked like welcome. He hoped it was a welcome for him. He stepped around the table and stood before her. "How are you doing?"

The intimate tone in his voice had Bess struggling to draw a breath. She wondered frantically if he had always had this effect on her. The house was crowded with people, everyone talking, laughing, moving around the table. Yet she felt as if she and Hunter were the only two people there. Maybe the only two people in the world.

"Something's different," he said.

Bess smiled, her nervousness fading. "Clean clothes and a comb and brush will do wonders."

"You look pretty."

One of the children giggled. Bess didn't notice which one, didn't care. "Thank you."

His gaze as he studied her felt like a warm touch. Then his eyes widened. "Your head." He stroked the tips of his fingers along her temple. "It's healed."

Bess reached up and touched the smooth skin where only hours ago it was torn. Her fingers collided with his. A hot, tingling sensation raced from her fingers up her arm and clear down to her heels. "Yes," she said with a slight gasp. "Your sister . . . is an amazing woman."

His eyes darkened. "Your memory?"

"No," she said, lowering her gaze. "Nothing."

Hunter placed a finger beneath her chin and raised her head until she looked at him. "Give it time, Blue Eyes."

One corner of her mouth obeyed her command to smile. "I don't have much choice, do I?" Then she remembered what had happened earlier in the kitchen, and her smile widened. "I can cook."

His gaze sharpened. "You remembered how to cook?"

"I wouldn't say I remembered," she said with a small laugh. "Not consciously. It just . . . happened. I peeled and sliced potatoes for Winter Fawn, and without thinking, I heated the skillet on the stove, melted some lard in it, and threw in the potatoes. I added sliced onions, but didn't realize I'd even done it until later."

Hunter grinned at her enthusiasm over the everyday chore she'd accomplished. "What else can you cook?"

She flipped her hands in the air, palms up. "I have no idea. I don't even know what fried potatoes taste like. But Winter Fawn and Gussie assure me that I like them."

"We all like them," Winter Fawn said. "Especially when you cook them."

"I cooked—cook—them often?"

"You taught me how to cook when you were barely older than Megan," Winter Fawn explained as everyone sat down at the table.

Bess started to ask Winter Fawn a question, but first she was distracted by realizing that Hunter was seated directly across from her, then by Gussie loudly clearing her throat.

"Carson, Winter Fawn, I hope you won't think I'm usurping your place in your own home if I say I would like to give the grace."

"We'd be honored, Aunt Gussie," Carson said.

"Thank you, dear," Gussie said. She bowed her head and waited for the others to follow suit. "Our dear Heavenly Father, we give joyous thanks this day for the safe return of our Bess. We thank Thee for Hunter's skill in finding her and bringing her back to us. We ask your blessing, Dear Lord, on this food that will nourish our bodies, and on the grass that feeds the cattle, and we thank Thee for its abundance. Amen."

During the round of amens that followed, Bess heard Carson chuckle. She didn't get the joke until he explained.

"Gussie, if anyone back in Atlanta had told you you would one day be thanking God for the grass, you'd have called them a liar."

"In Atlanta," Gussie stated primly, with a twinkle in her Dulaney-blue eyes, "I was too busy thanking God that those devil-spawned Yankee shells managed to miss our house."

"Amen to that," Carson said with feeling.

A sharp pain shot through Bess's head. She clutched at it and moaned. In her mind she heard loud explosions, one after the other after the other. Terror swamped her. It was dark but for the thin glow of one small candle. The smell of onions and lavender was strong. There was weeping, and the damp ground beneath her shook.

A fork clattered against a plate.

"Bess?"

Hunter's voice. What was Hunter doing here? That wasn't right. He didn't belong—

That fast, the pictures abruptly disappeared. The pain in her head began to fade.

"Bess," Hunter repeated urgently. "What's wrong?"

She blinked, and somehow Hunter was kneeling beside her chair. She hadn't been aware of his getting up and rounding the table. "Hunter?" Then, as her mind rearranged the pictures she'd just seen, the smells, the sounds, she gasped. "The cellar." Her gaze shot to Gussie. "The root cellar. The ground shook. Someone was crying."

"A memory?" Hunter asked. "You remember something?" His voice was calm now, soothing.

"I . . . think so."

Gussie had been blotting her lips with her napkin. Slowly she lowered it to her lap. "You're right, dear. During the shelling we hid in the root cellar. You couldn't have been more than ten or eleven years old."

"Yes," Bess said. The memory was like an old sweater coming unraveled. She struggled to make sense of it. "I was there, and you, and . . . and . . ." Pain stabbed through her temples. She pressed her fingers against them to hold it in, lest her head explode.

"Easy," Hunter crooned.

"I can't . . ."

"Don't try to force it," Hunter said. "Just relax, Blue Eyes."

"It's right there, but I just can't see it all."

"But you remembered," Gussie exclaimed, delighted. "You remembered something."

Bess shook her head in frustration. "Just bits and pieces that don't make sense."

"It'll come, Bess," Hunter told her. "This is a good sign. It means you will remember everything, in time."

"Do you think so?" Bess asked anxiously.

"I do," he said.

Cautiously, Bess steered her mind away from the memory, then tried to recall it. And there it was, waiting for her, still fragmented and incomplete, but it was there. It hadn't gotten lost in the dark emptiness of her past. Slowly she smiled at Hunter. "It's still there. I can remember it. I didn't lose it. Oh, Hunter." She leaned into him and pressed her face against his neck.

Hunter felt the others staring at them, but didn't care. He knew as well as they that he and Bess weren't in the habit of hugging, or even touching much, in front of others. He was through with that. If Bess wanted to touch him, wanted him to touch her, he didn't care who watched or what they thought. He'd come too close to losing her to care anymore about proper behavior.

"It's good, Blue Eyes." He stroked her cheek and brushed his lips across her forehead.

"But it's so little," she protested, tilting her head to look up at him.

"The rest will come, you'll see."

"But what if it doesn't?" she asked, her voice shaking. "All I've got right now are those few tiny bits and pieces that don't fit together. What if that's all I ever remember?"

He held her close and wrapped both arms around her. "Then I suppose we'll cry a little, then we'll give you new memories, all of us, I promise."

Seated at the head of the table next to Bess, Carson felt his throat tighten. He would give anything to help his sister, to make sure she was happy. But he knew now with more certainty than he'd ever known that Hunter was the man she would always turn to. She had no memory of what she felt for him, yet there she was, willingly in his arms, oblivious to anyone else in the room.

Carson had worried over the years that Bess and Hunter had drifted toward each other out of habit and proximity. That was why he'd kept insisting to Hunter that Bess needed to make other friends, that she was too young for marriage, that Hunter shouldn't try to claim all of her attention.

As he raised his gaze to his wife at the foot of the table, Carson knew those old arguments were no longer valid. It didn't matter who Bess knew or what her age. She belonged with Hunter. When Winter Fawn met his gaze, he read the same knowledge in her eyes.

Carson took one long breath, then let it out. No longer would he throw obstacles in their path.

Except . . .

Hell. How fair was it to allow Bess to invest her feelings in Hunter when she had no memory of anyone else?

And Hunter. Would he give Bess enough time to regain her memory—please God, that she regain her memory? Or was Carson going to have to play the heavy-handed big brother again and do what he could to keep them apart until she had a chance to get her feet under herself?

CHAPTER TWELVE

Aside from the hour or so at the hotel in town when Hunter had left her in her room to await her dinner and bath, this was the first time—in Bess's memory—that she had been completely alone. She was relieved to be away from the crush of people downstairs and their expectations of her, yet she felt herself adrift without Hunter's presence.

The latter gave her pause. Yes, his had been the first face she'd seen upon awakening with no memory of who she was. In the short time since, she had learned to trust him, had come to rely upon him for . . . well, for everything.

Oh, he was a man to rely on, there was no mistake about that. He had taken care of her at every turn. He was strong and kind and gentle. When she had thrown herself at him at the hotel, he had been so gallant in his refusal of her request that he make love to her. She was grateful for that—both the gallantry and the refusal.

He'd bathed her and washed her hair and dressed her in his own shirt, all with the greatest care. He'd held her through the night, calming her when a nightmare she couldn't remember had sent her running from her own sleep.

When they'd met Carson and the others on the road and she'd been frightened by Carson reaching for her, Hunter had shielded her and explained her reaction as perfectly normal under the circumstances, when her brother must have thought her demented.

Hunter had eased her through the introductions there and at the ranch, again explaining her memory loss so that she wouldn't be left to do so herself.

At every turn, he was there, helping her, easing her way.

He'd smiled with her over her discovery that she knew how to cook. When that one dark memory of being in a cellar had taken her by surprise, he had been right beside her, easing her through it, past it, holding her when she turned to him.

When the family pressed too closely later during dinner and afterward, telling her things from her past—her birthday was August 22; she would be twenty-one in two-and-a-half months; the day Aunt Gussie arrived with an Army escort; her friends from town; swimming in the river with her nieces; that time her mare got spooked by a rabbit and bucked her off. On and on they went, hoping she would remember. It had been Hunter who had forced them to ease up.

Always there, taking care of her. He was her bulwark against a world that to her had gone a little crazy.

Or maybe it was she who had gone crazy. Was that what this out-of-control feeling meant? Was that why everything before yesterday morning was a blank in her mind, a gaping black hole where her life used to be?

But as long as she had Hunter, she could cope.

That thought made her wonder . . . Had she always needed a man to stand between her and trouble? A man to take care of her? If not Hunter, then her brother, perhaps? The idea disappointed her. She would very much like to think she was capable of standing on her own.

Looking around now at this upstairs bedroom they said was hers, Bess wondered again what kind of woman she was. Was she really this neat and tidy, or had someone straightened up in her absence?

It was a pretty room, one any girl would love. A beautiful four-poster bed with matching bedside table, wardrobe, dresser, and occasional table, all polished to a high sheen and smelling of beeswax. Pink-and-white curtains and comforter. A dark rose-and-green braided rug beside the bed.

On the bedside table stood a lamp whose globe was painted with pink rosebuds. Those same flowers graced the bowl and water pitcher on the occasional table in the corner.

Bess crossed to the window and pushed aside the curtains. It was too dark to see much, but beyond the big tree just outside, whose thick branches she could reach if she opened the window and leaned out, there appeared to be a large vegetable garden. Farther out stood the dark line of trees that followed the river as it meandered its way down the valley. She was anxious to see the view in the daylight.

Turning away, she crossed to the dresser. The comb and mirror-backed brush that Hunter had carried in his saddlebag now lay side by side at a slight angle on the starched white lace runner, as if they had always been there.

At one corner, next to the mirror, sat a pink porcelain box with tiny blue roses painted on it. Inside was a collection of hairpins. At the other corner lay a small bouquet of dried wildflowers. Had she picked them herself, or had someone given them to her?

Since she had chosen to keep them, it made more sense to believe they had been a gift from someone. From Hunter?

Once more her mind circled back to him. She still didn't know what they had been to each other in the past, she and Hunter. Had she loved him? Had he loved her? If he had, did he still love her? If so, her inability to return his feelings must surely hurt, no matter how well he understood that she couldn't help her memory loss.

And if they had not loved each other in the past, what was she supposed to do about these deep feelings for him that she felt bubbling up inside her? She might not remember ever being in love, but she suspected she was falling for Hunter MacDougall. He was a man a woman would be hard pressed not to love.

Hunter might not welcome such feelings from her. Maybe they were only good friends, and that was all he wanted. Maybe he was just being nice to her because he was a nice man. What would he want, really, with a woman who constantly clung to him, depended upon him for every little thing? A man like Hunter needed a strong woman, one who could stand beside him, rather than a weakling he must always protect.

And maybe, she thought, she really was crazy. How could she be falling in love with a man whom, for all practical purposes, she'd known for only two days? Why, the idea was absurd.

She got ready for bed, donning the long white nightgown someone had laid out for her. The bed wasn't large, but she felt lonely when she crawled beneath the covers and turned out the lamp on the bedside table.

As absurd as it sounded, this was the first night in her entire memory that she had slept alone, without Hunter. She made up for it by dreaming of him. And it was most definitely not a nightmare.

The next morning, Bess came awake slowly with a smile on her face. After a long, luxurious stretch, she opened her eyes. And frowned for a long moment while trying to remember where she was. It was still dark, but a faint line of light marked the bottom of the door that didn't quite meet the floor. Beneath her the sheets were crisp and clean, the mattress firm but not hard. Where . . .

Then it came back to her. Not that vast portion of her memory that she'd lost, but the past two days. She was in her room in her brother's house at the Double D Ranch.

The clank of a pan being set on the stove. That was what had awakened her. Now she heard a low voice. Carson. Then the front door opened and closed. He was going out to do chores while Winter Fawn cooked breakfast.

Aunt Gussie and Mr. Mac had gone home before dark yesterday. That left two fewer people to cook for, but without Aunt Gussie, it also left one less pair of hands to do the cooking. Bess should be down there helping.

She felt along the bedside table for a match and, after finding one, lit the lamp. When she stepped out of bed onto the braided rug, she was startled by the familiarity of the texture of it against her bare feet. She stared at the rug, willing a memory to surface through the emptiness of her past, but there was only a dull throb inside her head.

Bess forced a deep breath, then let it out. How could the feel be familiar when the rug itself was not? Had she made it? Were her fingers that talented?

Another clank of the stove jarred her from her introspection and had her hurrying to get dressed. After splashing water on her face—it was cold!—she found in the dresser a pretty linen chemise trimmed in lace, and matching drawers. A drawer in the bottom of the wardrobe revealed a petticoat. She slipped on the undergarments, then chose a gray skirt like the one she had worn yesterday, and a pink blouse. She gave her hair a quick brushing, then twisted it into a knot at her nape and secured it with pins from the porcelain box on the dresser.

The woman in the mirror, although unfamiliar, would have been pretty but for the ugly bruise marring one cheek. Bess turned away from the face she didn't recognize and rushed downstairs to help Winter Fawn get breakfast cooked and on the table.

"You didn't need to get up so early," Winter Fawn told her.

Bess gave her a level look. "Did I used to get up early and help with breakfast?"

"Well, yes, but—"

"Then that's what I prefer to do now, unless you don't want my help."

"If you're sure you're up to it, I would appreciate the help." But instead of giving Bess something to do or turning back to the stove herself, Winter Fawn smiled slightly and studied Bess.

"What?" Self-consciously she covered her bruised cheek with one hand.

Winter Fawn *tsked* in irritation. Wiping her hands on a towel, she said, "I meant to take care of that last night. Here." Reaching out, she nudged Bess's hand aside and placed her own palm over the bruise.

The heat of her touch, while not uncomfortable, startled Bess. "Wha—" But she swallowed her own question as she saw a bruise appear on Winter Fawn's cheek, then fade away. "Oh," she said softly in wonder.

"There." Winter Fawn nodded in satisfaction.

"Thank you," Bess murmured on a breath. "That's a handy little miracle you've got in your hand."

Winter Fawn had been wary yesterday of how Bess would react to her gift of healing, since the poor girl had no memory of ever having seen it before, although Bess had witnessed it many times. Few people, in fact, knew of the magic of Winter Fawn's touch. Those who did were sometimes startled and wary of it at first. But Bess had accepted the gift gratefully and with awe. Winter Fawn's wariness had been for naught.

But her healing was not usually associated with humor. Bess's comment startled a laugh out of her. "You are different," she told her husband's sister.

Bess took an apron from a peg on the wall and slipped it on. "Different?" The thought made her nervous. She wasn't sure she wanted to know what Winter Fawn meant, but she hadn't been able to keep from asking.

Again Winter Fawn studied her with a slight smile, this time with her head tilted, as if to help her concentrate. "I'm not sure I can put it into words. You've always been honest and polite, and never minded speaking your mind. But . . ." She gave up and shook her head and smiled. "I don't know what it is, but if I figure it out, I'll be sure and tell you."

"Thank you." *I think,* Bess added silently.

The two women worked well together. It felt natural to Bess to turn the flapjacks and stack them on a warm plate, to move the coffeepot to the back of the stove when it finished brewing, to share the small kitchen space with Winter Fawn. It felt as though they had performed this dance a million times, reaching around each other, bending here, stretching there, like a team of well-matched horses.

The thought made Bess laugh.

"What's funny?" Winter Fawn wanted to know.

Bess chuckled. "I was just thinking that we work together like a team of well-matched horses, but I daresay I don't much like the idea of comparing myself, or you, to a horse."

Laughing with her, Winter Fawn agreed.

"Now that's a sound to warm a man's heart," Carson said as he opened the front door and stepped inside.

Winter Fawn paused in the act of turning the bacon and angled her cheek toward him. "And what sound would that be, husband?"

Carson kissed the proffered cheek and winked at Bess. "The sound of two women laughing while fixing my breakfast."

Winter Fawn raised her eyebrows. "Two women, is it?" Her father's Scottish burr crept into her speech. "Ach, and how long hae ye been thinkin' ye want yerself two women, when 'tis all ye can do to handle one?"

"One, is it?" Carson turned to Bess. "You might want to look the other way so you won't get embarrassed." Then, to his wife, he said, "I'll show you how I handle *one.*"

Either he was too fast, or Bess was too slow in turning away. She was still looking at him, smiling at their play and their obvious love for each other, when he turned back to Winter Fawn and pulled her into his arms. The kiss he gave her brought a heated blush to Bess's cheeks. She didn't mean to stare; she meant to turn away. But she could only watch in stunned fascination as her brother practically devoured his wife right before Bess's eyes, so amorous was the kiss he gave her.

Oh, to be held like that, kissed and loved like that. A fierce longing surged within Bess to experience such grand passion for herself.

The front door opened again, and this time it was Hunter who stepped inside.

Carson and Winter Fawn, now standing between Bess and Hunter, seemed not to notice. They clung to each other, their kiss growing deeper.

Hunter's gaze slid over the embracing couple and came to rest on Bess. She stared into his eyes, unable to look away, heat still stinging her cheeks.

Yes, she wanted to experience such a grand passion for herself. With Hunter.

Mortified that he might read her thoughts in her eyes, Bess whirled away and busied herself at the stove.

Hunter tried to breathe past the sudden knot of wanting in his belly. He wanted the right to grab Bess and kiss her the way Carson was kissing Winter Fawn. He wanted the right not to care who might be watching.

He forced a deep breath, then tossed his hat on a peg on the wall beside the door. "Unhand my sister, you mangy dog. A man could starve to death around this place while you distract the cook."

* * *

During breakfast Hunter mentioned that he would be riding to his place in the canyon at sunup to check on his horses and the cabin. If everything was all right, he'd be back for dinner at noon. When breakfast was over and Hunter left the house, Bess excused herself, saying she'd be right back to help wash the dishes, and followed him.

Hunter heard her come out and stopped just beyond the porch, waiting for her. "Is something wrong?" he asked.

"No." She hugged herself to ward off the early morning chill that stung the air. "I just wanted to ask you something."

"You couldn't have asked me inside, where it's warm?" he asked, smiling.

She could have, she admitted to herself, but she had wanted to talk to him alone. "I'd like to go with you this morning."

His answer was flat, swift, and emphatic. "No."

Bess stiffened. She hadn't expected him to refuse. "No? Just like that? Without hearing why I want to go?"

"I don't care how good a reason you've got." His voice rang with steel. "You're not going anywhere near that place as long as Ned Rawlins is running loose."

Bess propped her hands on her hips. "On the outside chance that you're in the habit of telling me what to do, and on the even more remote possibility that I actually *do* what you tell me, I think it only fair to remind you that I have no memory of such high-handedness on your part or any habit of blind obedience on mine; therefore, I don't intend to indulge either of them. Ned Rawlins is probably halfway to Mexico by now. What the hell would he be doing at your cabin?"

Hunter blinked, not only at her swearing, but at her forceful manner in general. Bess might not always agree with him, but she always disagreed gently. At least during the past two years. She had developed a tendency to get her feelings hurt rather than to get angry. Just now there didn't seem to be any hurt in her. She was downright mad. He figured the best way to handle her was with calm reason. Bess always responded well to reason.

"If Rawlins wants to make sure you can't tell anyone he kidnapped you," he offered in a steady voice, "the only place he knows to look for you is at the cabin where he found you in the first place. If he's ever caught, he'll do time for robbery. For kidnapping, he'd probably hang. He's not going to want any witnesses. It's not safe for you to go there."

"If it's not safe for me," she said in an even tone, "it seems to me that it's not safe for you, either. He has seen you, hasn't he? He's aware that you know he kidnapped me?"

She didn't know that Rawlins had shot him, and Hunter wasn't about to tell her. He hoped the bastard did come to the cabin looking for him. "I can take care of myself."

"I'm sure you can. You've also demonstrated that you can take care of me, too."

"I didn't do so good a job of it the last time you came to my place," he bit out.

"We've already had that conversation. I thought we agreed that my getting kidnapped was not your fault."

"We'll see how you feel about that when you get your memory back," he said bitterly.

"What's that supposed to mean?" she demanded, alarmed. What could possibly have happened that would make her think it was Hunter's fault that she'd been kidnapped?

"Never mind," he said tersely. "You're not going with me today, and that's that."

Bess's stomach tightened. "I need to go, Hunter. Maybe if I go back to where it all started, I'll be able to remember."

Hunter hung his head. He took his hat off and ran his fingers through his long hair. "I know you want to get your memory back, Bess, but—"

"There's one thing you're overlooking," she told him.

"What's that?"

"I wasn't asking if I could go with you. I was announcing my intention to do so."

"Dammit, Bess."

"Don't dammit me," she fired back. "This is too important to me, Hunter. Or maybe you don't want me to remember. Is that it? What is it you haven't told me about what happened? What happened that makes you feel so guilty?"

Hunter slapped his hat back on his head. "I only want to keep you safe," he bit out. "Now I've managed to make you suspicious of me."

Bess heaved a sigh. "I'm not suspicious. I may not remember you, Hunter, but I know you. I know the kind of man you are. I know that the only thing making you feel guilty is your overdeveloped sense of responsibility, your protectiveness. You couldn't have done anything to cause that outlaw to kidnap me. I know that, even if you don't. But I want to remember. Coming here, where I've lived for years, didn't help that. Maybe going back to your cabin will."

"Give it a few more days, Bess. Give Rawlins time to get out of the territory. If you still want to go next week, I promise I'll take you. All right?"

She read the sincerity in his eyes and gave in. For now. "All right. Next week. I'll hold you to that."

She looked, Hunter thought, as though she meant it. Remembering how stubborn she could be, his relief was tinged with caution. Before he left, he cornered Carson and told him to make sure no one saddled a horse for her. He wouldn't put it past her to change her mind and come after him.

"It's too dangerous," he told Carson.

"I agree. You keep a sharp eye out," Carson warned. "Rawlins would be wanting you dead, too, if he could find you."

"I damn well hope he does find me," Hunter said grimly.

* * *

The sky was barely light and Bess was still washing the first round of breakfast dishes—there would be more when the little ones woke later—when she heard Hunter ride out of the yard. Her thoughts were in turmoil. Last night she'd been thinking she could love a man like him. This morning his attitude had been positively prehistoric.

"What's prehistoric?"

At the unexpected sound of Megan's voice, Bess jumped, startled. The coffee mug she'd been about to dunk into the dishpan slipped from her grip and landed with a splash that covered one cheek with soapy water.

"I'm sorry," Megan said with a giggle. "I didn't mean to startle you." She set a basket of eggs on the table and sucked on the back of her hand. "You must have been daydreaming pretty good not to hear me come in."

Bess smiled at her thirteen-year-old niece and used the skirt of her apron to wipe the soapy water from her cheek. "I guess I was. What happened to your hand?"

Megan grimaced and held it out. Two small red wounds marred the back of it. "One of the hens didn't like it when I snatched the egg she'd just laid."

Bess shook her head. "Let me guess. The red one with the white tail feathers.

Megan laughed. "How did you know?"

"If she wasn't such a good layer," Bess said, turning back to the dishpan, "I'd say it was past time that mean ol' biddy met the stew pot."

"Aunt Bess!"

At Megan's startled tone, Bess turned quickly. "What?"

"You remembered!"

Startled, Bess gripped the rim of the dishpan. "I—" Her heart pounded with excitement. She closed her eyes and struggled to picture an old red hen with white tail feathers. She was able to visualize such a creature, but it didn't feel as though she actually remembered it. Her knuckles turned white as her grip tightened. If she could remember the hen . . . surely there was more. Surely!

But after concentrating for a long moment, ignoring the dull throb in her head, Bess swore beneath her breath. "I remember the words," she said. "The words make sense. But I don't remember the damn bird," she cried in frustration. "I just—can't—remember. I can say it's a red hen with white tail feathers, and that she's old and mean. But it's like saying the ocean is blue. I know it's true, but I don't remember ever having seen it."

Megan gnawed on her bottom lip. "I could show you. Not the ocean, but the hen."

"Yes," Bess said eagerly. If she couldn't return to the scene of her kidnapping, she could at least try to jar her memory by seeing other things from her past. "Yes!"

Wiping her hands on her apron, Bess followed Megan outside. They passed the barn and corrals, the cook shack, and the bunkhouse before reaching the henhouse. More than two dozen chickens, some red, some white, some a mixture of both, pecked industriously at the dirt and the scant grain scattered in the chicken yard. A hapless beetle wandered too close, and with a squawk of discovery, one hen snatched it up and ran. The others immediately gave chase, trying to take her prize away.

Bess stood outside the small wooden henhouse and willed her mind to remember it. All she got for her effort was another headache.

"Anything?" Megan asked anxiously.

"Nothing," Bess admitted in defeat, her shoulders slumping.

"Come inside." Megan took her by the hand and tugged her into the henhouse.

The air was filled with chaff and dust. Two walls were lined with a double row of straw-filled nest boxes. Small tree limbs, for roosts, angled out from the third wall. Bess recognized what everything was, but could not recall ever actually being there before, seeing it firsthand. She couldn't remember reaching into a nest and lifting out an egg. As far as she could recall, the only time she'd ever even held an egg was that morning when she had cracked open a dozen of them to scramble for breakfast.

"Anything?" Megan asked tentatively.

Bess would have shaken her head no, but it was throbbing too much. "Nothing."

"Well—well . . . *dang.* I was hoping . . ."

"So was I." Bess stepped back out into the morning light and waited for the pain in her head, and the frustration, to ebb.

The argument with Hunter, and what she thought of as a near-miss with her memory, left Bess feeling unsettled. Staying busy seemed to help keep her mind off her problems, so she eagerly took on anything and everything Winter Fawn gave her to do. Bess feared that she was in danger of feeling sorry for herself, and the idea did not sit well. Changing bed linens was much more productive than self-pity, even if every move did remind her of all her bruises.

She liked the house. Downstairs, in addition to the kitchen, dining, and parlor areas, there were two bedrooms. One belonged to Carson and Winter Fawn, the other to their three little ones. The former room held a huge bed, but it would have to, for a man of Carson's size.

Bess wondered if Hunter's bed was big enough to accommodate his tall, muscular frame, and blushed at the thought.

In the children's room there were three narrow beds, two chests, and numerous toys.

Upstairs was Bess's room and, across from it, Megan's. It appeared that the Dulaneys were in imminent need of more room in their home. But surely no one planned for Bess to live there forever. She was nearly twenty-one. Wasn't it time for her to be considering marriage and a family of her own?

Hunter's face, his gray eyes soft and warm, flashed into her mind. She blushed again.

She should ask someone. Winter Fawn would know if Bess had a beau, if she was talking about getting married. If that beau might be Hunter.

Yet Bess held back, wary of asking. What if she had a beau, but it wasn't Hunter?

No, she wasn't ready to hear that. And really, as long as she couldn't remember, it didn't matter. Did it?

Hunter proved to be as good as his word, returning to the ranch just as the women put the noon meal on the table. By the time he washed up outside and made it into the house, everyone else was already seated.

Bess busied herself filling her plate, unsure how to greet him. After all the things he'd done for her, she felt terrible about her behavior that morning. She could at least have been polite.

"Everything okay over at your place?" Carson asked him.

As if by the sheer force of Hunter's will, her gaze rose until it met his.

"Aye," he said. "I brought back Bess's sidesaddle."

"What do you mean?" Carson asked. "I thought Rawlins took her horse when he took her."

"He did, but he left the sidesaddle in my barn and took one of mine instead."

Carson eyed her a moment. "That must have been a rough trip, Bess."

"Undoubtedly," she said, her gaze still locked on Hunter's. She couldn't seem to look away. "But I don't remember it."

"But you will," Megan said with confidence. "You almost remembered the hen."

That comment brought a round of questions that Bess let

Megan answer. Gratefully, Megan drew Hunter's gaze and Bess was finally able to look down at her plate and finish eating.

But as soon as everyone finished and rose from the table, Hunter came and stood before her. "Are you still mad?"

Bess fought a blush and lost. "No. It occurs to me that I was incredibly rude, especially considering all you've done for me. I apologize for that. But I don't care for having anyone make my decisions for me. As it turns out, I could have gone with you. There wouldn't have been a problem, and something there might have triggered my memory."

"You're right. But we didn't know it would be safe. I won't take chances with your life, Bess."

She met his gaze steadily. "I appreciate that, but it's my life, my decision." Then she smiled slightly. "A bigger concern I hadn't thought of would have been riding horseback. I'm not sure I'm quite ready for that this soon."

Hunter's smile was tinged with sympathy. "Still sore?"

She blushed again and nodded.

"No need to rush it. I'd like to give Rawlins a few more days to get wherever he's going before I take you back to the one place he might go looking for you."

"You know," she said, pursing her lips. "If you had put it that way this morning, instead of simply ordering me to stay home, I might not have gotten mad at all."

His smile widened. "I'll remember that next time."

"Aunt Bess," little Bonnie wailed. "My ribbon comed undone."

With a final smile, Bess turned from Hunter to see about her four-year-old niece. *"Came* undone, sweetheart."

"Dat's what I said."

"Here, then, let's retie it, shall we?"

Hunter couldn't work with Carson's horses. Not today. He needed to be calm to work with a horse, and he was anything but calm. A dozen different emotions were boiling up inside of him, any one of which could erupt at the slightest provocation.

Chopping wood seemed appropriate. He grabbed the ax and headed for the woodpile.

He was furious all over again over Bess being kidnapped. Sick with regret for what she'd gone through. Livid because it really wasn't safe, in his opinion, for her to ride out, even with an escort. Dammit, this valley ought to be safe enough for anyone to ride through.

He was still confused over the way she'd reacted this morning to his refusal to take her with him. Granted, he'd been a little heavy-handed, but she sure hadn't wasted any time jumping down his throat. It had been years since she'd done that. The hell of it was, he'd liked it.

Now how was that for crazy?

All these subtle little changes in her personality since she'd lost her memory intrigued him. Not that he particularly cared for her swearing and jumping down his throat. Not exactly, anyway. It was just that there was such fire in her at those times. A fire like she used to carry inside her years ago, and it made him want to get close enough to get singed.

It made him feel disloyal, and that was probably crazy, too. Disloyal to the Bess she had become in recent years, because he liked this new one, who was more like the younger Bess, better?

No, he thought honestly. Not . . . better. In addition to. That was it. Or was he merely trying to justify his feelings to himself?

Either way, he knew he was in trouble. She'd been as mad as a wet hen this morning, and he'd gotten hard. He'd been telling her it wasn't safe for her to go with him, when he'd wanted, desperately, to take her exactly where she wanted to go. But not for anything so selfless as helping her regain her memory. Oh, no, he wasn't that noble by a long shot.

Hunter had wanted Bess for years, but now there was a new urgency inside him to make her his. Now, instead of building walls between them to keep himself from being too tempted, he wanted to build walls around them, enclosing them together and shutting out the rest of the world.

He wanted her.

He wanted to carry her off to his cabin and bar the door. He wanted to peel off her clothes and see how well the two of them fit in his bed. He wanted to see and touch and taste every soft inch of her, bury himself inside her and never come out.

Knowing none of that was possible, he at least wanted to tell her he loved her. But he couldn't put that kind of pressure on her. At least, not so soon. His head and his sense of honor told him that his words, and his wanting, would have to wait until her memory returned.

His heart and the rest of his body urged him to bury the ax in the chopping block and leave it there, to go to the house right now and carry her away. Because no matter how all of them, himself included, avoided saying so, the truth was, she might never get her memory back.

CHAPTER THIRTEEN

It wasn't possible to live with a family that was so loving and close, Bess learned, and not discover the truth of her past relationship with Hunter. It was Megan who eventually revealed it, on Bess's fourth afternoon at the ranch.

To give Winter Fawn a chance to catch her breath, Bess and Megan took the three children down to the river to look for turtles. Hunter, Carson, and another man, whom Bess had yet to meet—one of Carson's men, Bess assumed, since she'd seen him around at a distance—were working with a horse in one of the corrals.

"He's so handsome, don't you think?" Megan asked.

Bess's gaze was centered on Hunter, on the way the afternoon sun gleamed across his bronze skin and long black hair. "Yes," she said, feeling her heart race. "Yes, he is."

Megan laughed. "I was talking about Jeff."

"Hmm?" Bess said, barely listening. She couldn't listen, not when Hunter looked up and caught her gaze. There was an intensity in his eyes and a firmness to his lips that made her breath catch. Then Hunter looked away, and Megan's words registered. "Who?"

Megan laughed again. "Never mind. I can see there's still only one man you care anything about. Losing your memory doesn't seem to have changed that any."

Now the girl had Bess's full attention. "What do you mean?"

Megan skipped ahead a few paces, then turned and hopped backward to face Bess. "Only that you've been in love with Hunter practically your whole life."

There, Bess thought. There was the answer to half of the question that had been humming in her mind for days, and it felt right to her. Her hands started shaking. She hid them in the folds of her skirt. It was the other half of the question that had yet to be answered. "And Hunter? How did he feel about that?"

"Oh," Megan said with a lofty wave of her hand. "You know how men are, never admitting how they feel. But everybody knew you were the only girl for him. April!" she yelled as the little ones broke into a run for the river. "Keep them away from the bank!"

Bess gathered her skirt in her hands and started to run. There were places in the riverbank that would crumble beneath the slightest pressure, toppling an unwary toddler right into the icy water.

Megan reached the children first and quickly had them under control. Bess, still a few yards out, slowed to a walk. She knew the riverbank was crumbly. She didn't *remember* it; the fact was just there, in her mind.

And now she knew she had been in love with Hunter. But she wasn't certain at all, from Megan's description, how he had felt about her.

Oh, how utterly frustrating and unfair! That she should know about a crumbling bank and a red hen, but not remember loving Hunter.

* * *

Word of Bess Dulaney's kidnapping by the Rawlins gang spread up and down the Huerfano Valley like wildfire before a stiff wind. It had no trouble at all reaching the county seat of Walsenburg. Or, more specifically, the Walsenburg Territorial Bank and Trust Company. Bank vice president Virgil Horton, whose daddy owned the bank, was stunned by the news. Miss Dulaney, kidnapped by that damn Rawlins gang who had just robbed his depositors? Bess? Rescued by that damned half-breed?

Immediately Virgil went to his father's office and closed the door. Cigar smoke hung thick and pungent in the air. "It looks as if our plans to regain the Dulaney accounts have hit a snag."

Benjamin Horton did not like snags. He puffed on his cigar and frowned. "What now?"

Virgil told his father the news of Bess's kidnapping. "It's all everyone's talking about."

Benjamin raised his bushy gray brows. "After the kind of rough handling she must have been subjected to, she should be all the more amenable to your courtship. I don't see that as a snag."

"But father, she must have been with those outlaws for a couple of days, at least. That's what everyone's saying. They're saying she's ruined. I can't bring a woman like that into our family. Why, we'd be ostracized."

Benjamin leaned back in his chair and glared at his son with narrowed eyes. "First of all, you underestimate our position and the power and influence of the name Horton in this community. In this entire territory, for that matter. If she is seen on your arm as though nothing is amiss, the talk will stop instantly. There is not a person in this town who would dare criticize my son. If we act as though nothing is wrong, everyone will assume nothing is wrong. After this damn robbery, we need Dulaney's money."

Benjamin knocked the ashes off the end of his cigar, then looked at his only son again. "And secondly, I never said you had to marry the girl. All you have to do is get in good enough with her family to get them to move their money back to our bank. Who would have thought," he muttered half to himself, "that a man who would marry a squaw would end up with so damn much money? Let this be a lesson to you, boy. Never offend anyone. Not if you want to make a success of yourself."

"But sir—"

"Just get that account back for us, son, and I'll make you a full partner."

Virgil felt a smile coming. *A full partner!* "Yes, sir!"

When Bess, Megan, and the children returned to the house from the river, it was time for the little ones' naps. While Winter Fawn and Megan were settling them down and putting them to bed, Bess took a broom outside and began sweeping the dust and grit from the wide, covered porch that ran the length of the house.

From the porch she could see the barn and three corrals, including the one where Hunter and the others had been working. But none of the men were in sight now, she noticed with disappointment. Perhaps they had to ride out and check on some of the cattle.

Gradually she became aware of the quiet. Generally, during the day, the air was filled with sounds. Voices, the jingle of spurs, the neigh of a horse, the bawl of a calf. The rooster enjoyed a good crow now and then, no matter the time of day. But just now there was only the swish of her broom across the planks of the porch.

Then she heard hoofbeats, and her heart raced. Was it Hunter? She looked around and discovered a rider coming from the direction of the road that had brought her from town only days before. Instantly she knew it wasn't Hunter. The man's hair was too short, his shoulders too narrow, his clothes too fancy.

Friend, or foe, she wondered. How was she to know?

Whoever he was, Bess felt no fear. That was perhaps foolish of her, since she wouldn't even recognize the outlaw Ned Rawlins if he rode boldly up to the house, but she had to assume this was not him. Hunter believed she was safe here. That was good enough for her.

The visitor slowed his horse from a trot to a walk as he neared the yard. He was a nice-looking man, with a long, narrow face and hollow cheekbones. His nose was a little too long, even for that face, and his mouth a little too wide. But altogether, with his brown eyes and sandy hair showing beneath his hat brim, he was pleasant enough to look at.

Bess propped her broom against the front of the house and brushed her hands against her apron. "Good afternoon."

"Miss Dulaney," he cried as he dismounted. "Bess." Carelessly he tossed his reins over the hitching rail in front of the porch and rushed to her, taking her hands in his.

Startled by his familiarity, Bess tugged her hands from his grasp and stepped back.

"Bess, I've been so worried about you ever since I heard. I just had to come in person and see for myself that you were all right."

"How kind of you," Bess managed to interject into his rapid speech. "I'm fine, really."

"Should you be up and about so soon? Shouldn't you be resting? Ah," he said, not giving her time to answer, "but look at you. You look as pretty as ever, not at all as if you've just been through such a terrible ordeal. I just want you to know that this changes nothing as far as I'm concerned. Once you're seen on my arm at the Independence Day celebration, no one will dare talk about you any longer."

"Talk about me?"

"Forgive me if I'm being indelicate." He swept his hat from

his head. "It was a long ride. May I sit?" He indicated the swing on the porch.

Bess started to apologize for her lack of manners, but since he was going to be indelicate, as he put it, she refrained. "Of course. Please have a seat." She chose the rocker situated five feet from the swing.

A look of disappointment flashed across the man's face, then disappeared.

Bess knew she really should explain to him that she had no idea who he was, before he rattled on much more. He seemed like a decent fellow; there was no need to let him embarrass himself. "I'm sorry," she began.

"There's no need to apologize," he stated, the cadence of his speech slowing and taking on a condescending tone. "You certainly cannot help that those outlaws kidnapped you, or what they might have done to you while they had you with them."

Bess felt a chill settle into her blood. "What they might have done?"

"It's merely talk, Bess. No one can prove anything, can they? And as I've said, the talk will die once you're seen on my arm. My family is important in Walsenburg, you know that."

"No, actually, I don't."

He had opened his mouth to say something else, but at Bess's words, his teeth clicked and his mouth shut. He blinked. Three times, slowly. Then he smiled. "Oh, you're joking, right?"

"I'm afraid not. You see, I took a knock on the head, and as a result I'm having a little trouble with my memory."

"Oh, my dear Miss Dulaney," he cried. "Bess, how dreadful for you. You don't remember my family?"

Bess covered the impulse to laugh by coughing into her hand. Yes, poor Bess that she couldn't remember his family! "In truth, sir, the trouble with my memory is much broader than that. I don't remember anything before a few days ago. I'm sorry, but I have no idea who you are."

Just then the door of the house opened and Megan stepped out. "Oh! I'm sorry. I heard you talking, Bess, but I didn' know anyone was here. Hello, Mr. Horton. What brings you all the way out here?" There was a glint in her eyes that told Bess Megan didn't care for this man.

He rose to his feet. "Miss Megan, what a pleasure. You grow more lovely each time I see you," he said smoothly. " rode out to pay my respects to your aunt."

"How gallant of you," Megan said coyly. "A four-hour ride, just to pay your respects."

"Yes," he said, his smile forced. "And to settle our arrange ments for Independence Day." He paused with a look of expec tancy, perhaps waiting for Megan to go back inside, since the conversation did not concern her, or for Bess to comment.

"As I was explaining," Bess began.

"Yes," he interrupted. "Your memory loss. How terrible for you. Of course, you must know that makes no difference to me, Bess. I would still very much like to take you to the festivities, if you're feeling up to it."

"I'm sorry . . . Mr. Horton, is it?"

He stared at her, plainly shocked. "You really don't know who I am?"

"I'm afraid not," Bess answered ruefully.

"His name's Virgil Horton," Megan supplied, her eyes nar rowing. "He works in his daddy's bank in Walsenburg. The bank where Daddy used to keep his money until they decided Mama wasn't good enough to step foot in their bank because she's part Indian."

For one shocked instant, no one spoke.

Questions raced through Bess's mind. Was what Megan said true? If so, what had she herself done to make this man think she would welcome his attentions, much less accompany him to the celebration of which he spoke. Was she so disloyal to her own family that she would ignore such a terrible slight to Winter Fawn? And, just as disturbing, why had she even been speaking about accompanying him when she was supposed to be in love with Hunter? *What kind of woman am I?*

While Bess was busy questioning her own integrity, Mr. Horton's face turned bright red; his mouth gaped. Then he began to sputter. "Why, Miss Megan! That was . . . that was a long time ago. You were just a child. You shouldn't speak about things you don't understand."

Megan opened her mouth to respond.

Bess cut her off before she could say anything else outrageous. "Megan, Mr. Horton has obviously had a long ride. I believe there's some lemonade left. Would you get him a glass, please?"

Megan bestowed on Bess an overly sweet smile. "Of course. I'll be right back."

As soon as Megan stepped into the house, their visitor said, "Forgive me for saying so, but someone should teach that young lady some manners."

"Perhaps," Bess allowed. "I believe she was just trying to help me, since she knows I have no memory of any of this."

"Of course," he said, all solicitous now. "I'm sure that's the case. You must believe me when I say that whatever happened concerning your brother's wife in the past was years ago. It has nothing to do with you and me, Bess."

"Mr. Horton—"

"Virgil. You've called me Virgil for a long time. I wish you would again."

"Virgil," Bess ceded with a nod. "I'm afraid my amnesia renders me at a disadvantage."

"Well, of course it does, my dear. But I assure you I would never take advantage."

"I'm sure you wouldn't." She wasn't sure of any such thing. "But until I regain my memory, you are a stranger to me."

"What are you saying?" he asked cautiously.

"You spoke of my accompanying you to an Independence Day celebration?"

"Yes. I see now that you don't remember. I asked you when we ran into each other in Pueblo recently. You and your aunt were returning from a trip to Atlanta. You seemed excited about the idea of going with me."

"Be that as it may, I'm afraid I can't possibly do so now. Surely you understand. As far as my memory is concerned, I only met you a few moments ago, when you rode up and said hello."

He lowered his gaze and picked a piece of lint from the leg of his tweed pants. "Perhaps if I called on you a few times between now and then, you could get to know me again, and feel more comfortable with the idea."

"I'm afraid not, Mr. Horton," she said gently. "But I thank you for your understanding."

And what, Virgil wondered in frustration, was a gentleman supposed to say to that? This was not the way things were supposed to happen. His father was going to disinherit him!

"Perhaps," he said to her, "I could call on you anyway, with no pressure about the Independence Day celebration?"

Bess clasped her hands in her lap. "I'm afraid that until I regain my memory, I won't be accepting callers."

He hung his head. "I understand." He gave her a small smile. "But when you regain your memory, I hope you'll remember how much you like me. Perhaps we'll plan something else at that time."

"Perhaps," was the best Bess could offer.

Without waiting for the promised lemonade, he said good-bye and rode out.

A moment later Megan returned to the porch with two glasses of lemonade. She handed one to Bess, then took a sip from the other. "That snake," she muttered with a glare at the retreating rider.

"Megan, shame."

"Don't *Megan shame* me," Megan fired back. "You really were considering going with him."

"But why?" Bess asked, bewildered. "You said I was in love with Hunter. Why would I want to see another man?"

Megan refused to meet her gaze when she said, "You wouldn't really have gone with him."

"I wouldn't?"

"No. I told you, you love Hunter."

"Then would you mind explaining why I would let this Mr. Horton think I would welcome his visits and go out with him?"

Megan took a big gulp of lemonade. "You were sweeping the porch?" she asked, spying the broom.

"Megan, you're stalling. What aren't you telling me?"

Megan heaved an exaggerated sigh. "You were trying to make Hunter jealous."

Bess winced. "I was? Why?"

"Because you were home from Atlanta several days and he still hadn't come to see you. You got it in your head that meant he didn't love you anymore. You went to his cabin to tell him you were going out with Mr. Horton, hoping Hunter would get mad and tell you not to. You were especially glad that Mr. Horton had asked you, because you knew Hunter didn't like him because of that business over Winter Fawn years ago. You thought—you said that if he didn't get mad, that would mean he really didn't love you anymore. That's why you were at Hunter's when the outlaws showed up."

"Gracious," Bess murmured. The dull throb started in her temple again. She pressed her fingertips there in hopes of easing it. "If what you say is true, I don't think I like the person I used to be." And that was putting it mildly. She was out-and-out appalled.

Bess did not mention her gentleman caller to Winter Fawn and asked Megan not to, either. If whatever it was that had happened all those years ago was bad enough to cause Carson to change banks, it must have been offensive indeed.

Winter Fawn not allowed in the bank? Why, there was no more beautiful, generous, wonderful person on earth than Winter Fawn. How could anyone who knew her do such a thing?

Bess would rather the subject not be brought up. She did not want Winter Fawn distressed by a painful memory.

Carson, Hunter, and two of the hands returned to the ranch less than an hour after Mr. Horton rode out. They came from the direction he went, which told Bess that it was likely they had seen him. Judging from the terse looks Hunter and Carson shared now and then during supper that night, their clenched jaws and forced smiles, Bess feared it was more than likely.

Bess felt her own smile grow more tense as the meal dragged on.

"Aunt Bess?" six-year-old April said. "Did you remember us yet?"

Beneath the table, Bess strangled the napkin wadded in her left hand. The poor little thing didn't understand Bess's lack of memory. Bess knew just how she felt. "I remember you from today, and yesterday, and the day before."

"Don't worry," April offered, repeating what she'd heard the adults saying for days. "You'll remember pretty soon. I know you will."

Bess's smile felt forced. "I'm sure you're right." But she wasn't. She wasn't sure about anything anymore. Her eyes began to burn and the room felt as if it were shrinking around her while all the air was being sucked out. She knew she had to leave the table or risk embarrassing herself and upsetting everyone else. "Excuse me," she murmured, scooting back her chair and making her escape out the front door.

Taking in big gulps of air, she hurried away from the house. To the south of the barn, lights burned in the cookhouse. Men's voices drifted out into the night. Bess went north, to the farthest corral. There she braced her hands on the top rail and stared up at the stars, letting her breathing even out.

The corral, when she finally looked, was empty. Like her,

she thought with a flash of self-pity. Then came another flash, this one of irritation. She wasn't empty, only her memory was. The rest of her was filled with too many emotions, too many questions.

Too soon she heard the front door of the house open, then close. The hollow sound of boot steps thudded across the porch and down the steps. She knew without turning to look that it was Hunter.

Not enough time. He hadn't given her enough time to steady herself.

She would have to make it be enough.

She heard him stop directly behind her. Then he said, "You'll get cold." He draped a shawl over her shoulders.

Bess took the ends and pulled it snug. "Thank you."

"You want to tell me why you walked out that way?"

She might not like what she was learning about the woman she used to be, but she vowed now to be different. She would start with honesty. "Because I prefer to have my bouts of self-pity in privacy."

"Wee April got to you, did she?"

There was sympathy in his voice. That was the last thing she expected from him. "I suppose."

"Anything else on your mind?"

No sympathy this time, she noted. There was a biting tone to his words now. "Anything else like what?"

"Like maybe that caller you had today?"

Shamed by what she had learned of herself earlier from Megan, Bess kept her back to Hunter and stared into the empty corral. "I didn't invite him. I didn't know who he was."

Hunter let out a gusty breath. "Do you now?"

"Megan told me. I . . . I'm sorry, Hunter. I can't imagine what I must have been thinking to have anything to do with him. I don't like what my actions say about the kind of person I am. Or was. If it helps any, I doubt he'll be back."

"I know he won't."

She didn't want to know what he meant by that. But there were other things she wanted—needed—to know. She turned and faced him. "Hunter, what were we to each other?"

"Bess . . ."

He was a large, dark shadow before her, yet a warm one. "Megan tells me I was in love with you."

"Dammit, Bess—"

"She says you were in love with me, too."

"Sounds like Megan's been saying a lot lately."

"Is she right? Did we love each other?"

"Bess—"

"I need to know, Hunter. I can't go on guessing and walking on eggshells. I need to know the truth. I need to know why, sometimes, you act as if you hope I don't get my memory back." A shiver of dread raced down her arms. "Are you hoping I won't remember so that I won't love you again?"

"No," he said fiercely, grabbing her arms. "No, Bess. That's not it at all. There are some things I hope you never remember, but loving me isn't one of them."

"So it's true? I did love you?"

Hunter felt a giant fist tighten around his heart. What should he tell her? How much? How little?

It worried him that she hadn't remembered anything yet, nothing other than a bit of knowledge here and there, like the hen. He'd heard all about that incident, and he'd let himself be hurt that she hadn't told him herself. What if she never remembered her past? Never remembered that she once loved him? Was it better to tell her about it, about how it was, or not tell her?

Suddenly she wrenched free of his hold. "Don't *do* that."

"Do what?"

"Stand there and try to decide what's best for me to know and not know. Don't deny me my own past, Hunter, even if you think I won't like what you tell me."

Hunter felt that fist tighten again around his heart. But she spoke the truth. It was her past, after all. Their past. Maybe if he told her everything, even things he'd never told her before, she might be more inclined to give him another chance if she did regain her memory. If she even wanted to give him another chance.

"Come," he said, reaching for her hand. "Walk with me."

She held back. "Are you going to tell me what I want to know?"

"Probably more than that, even. I'll tell you everything. Just walk with me."

Bess took his hand. It scared her a little to realize she would have walked with him regardless, even if he refused to tell her. Did that make her spineless? Desperate? *Or in love?*

And then he began. "The night we escaped our village—"

"Wait," she said with a slight laugh. "You've already lost me. Who is we, and why did we need to escape what village, and how did we come to be there in the first place?"

Hunter gave a rueful chuckle. "This is going to be harder than I thought. Okay. I'll back up. You know about our fathers, yours and mine. How they came to be friends?"

"What I've been told is that my father couldn't cope with my mother's death when I was a baby. When he heard about the gold rush here, he came West. That was in '58. I was four. Carson and Aunt Gussie raised me. Your mother had died, and your father had the same problem as mine—he couldn't cope. He left you and Winter Fawn with your grandparents. Our fathers met in the gold fields. Then my father decided providing beef to the miners was easier than mining, so he started this ranch."

"That's about it," Hunter agreed.

"Then the War Between the States broke out, and my father went back to fight for the South. He was killed near the end of the war at a place called Spotsylvania. But before he died, he convinced Carson to come West and help him build up this ranch. So Carson came, right after the war. I think he needed time alone. It was a year before he came back for Megan and me.''

''As the story goes,'' Hunter took up, ''the three of you ran into my father when you reached Pueblo.''

''Carson told me that. But he wouldn't say much else. All I know is that right after that is when we met you and Winter Fawn.''

They strolled past the cookhouse, and Hunter squeezed her hand gently. ''It was a little more complicated than that. To understand about us—you and me—you have to know all of it. The Cheyenne and Arapaho still lived here in those days. The Inuna-ina—that's what the Southern Arapaho call themselves—wintered in the foothills. Our village was near the Sierra Mojada—the Wet Mountains.''

''Not far from here?''

''That's right. There had been some trouble right before Carson brought you and Megan here. The Cheyenne had killed three whites just half a day south of Pueblo. The bluecoats went after them, but they never could tell one Indian from another. In retaliation for what the Cheyenne did, they killed three Arapaho. Hunters, out looking for a deer for a feast.''

''They weren't even warriors?'' Bess asked, getting caught up in the story.

Hunter shrugged. ''When there was fighting, they were warriors. That day they were hunters. But there were those who were always warriors, always looking for a fight. In retaliation for our men being killed for something the Cheyenne did, some of our Dogmen rode out and attacked you. They claimed they didn't see my father until it was too late.''

''Your father? What difference would that have made?''

''It should have made all the difference. He'd been considered a member of our tribe for more than twenty years, through his marriage to my mother. His friends—Carson and you girls—should have been safe. He was able to talk the warriors into turning you and Megan over to him, but they wouldn't release Carson. They wanted blood as payback for the three men we'd lost.''

Bess shivered at the thought of all that hatred, all the bloodshed.

"Are you cold?"

She shook her head. "No. Just thinking."

"Anyway," Hunter said, "they brought all of you back to the village, and there was a council to decide what to do. The Dogmen—the warriors who attacked you—wanted to kill Carson for revenge against the bluecoats. My father argued for setting him free. I don't remember why they didn't make up their minds that night, but the decision was put off until the next day. But during the night I overheard one of the warriors planning to kill Carson before dawn and be done with it. Because Carson was my father's friend, my sister and I helped all of you escape."

"That must have been a difficult decision for you to make," Bess murmured, wondering silently where all of this was leading. "To go against the wishes of your own people."

"Not really," Hunter confessed. "Our people hadn't decided what to do. They had vowed that nothing would be done until the next day. Carson should have been safe. To kill him in secret, against the agreement, was to dishonor all Inuna-ina. Besides, I would have ridden into hell for my father. No," he added thoughtfully, "the decision wasn't hard at all. The actual act of escaping, that was hard."

As they neared the trees along the river, Hunter slowed. "I was fifteen and suddenly responsible for getting all of us safely away in the middle of the night. It was as dark as the inside of a buffalo's belly. I was proud that my father trusted me to lead us, but I knew that if I wasn't careful, I could get us all caught, probably killed."

"It seems we met under extraordinary circumstances."

"That's putting it mildly. Do you remember the other day

when we rode down out of the mountains and you thought it seemed familiar to ride behind me?''

''Yes. I asked you if we'd ridden that way before. And you said, a time or two.''

''The first time was that night we met. Between the six of us, we had three horses, one saddle, and a loaded-down pack mule. We all rode double.''

''And I rode with you.''

''Aye,'' he said, leading her to a long, flat rock that hung out over the flowing water. ''I admit it was a young man's dream.''

''Escaping in the dark of night, on the run for your life?'' she asked, incredulous.

Hunter chuckled. ''No, not when you put it like that. But leading my father's friends to safety, being responsible for that, and having you wrapped around me like a second skin, depending on me to keep you safe. My ego puffed up like a toad about to croak. I was all full of myself, and your arms were around me, and my blood ran hot. You took my breath away, Blue Eyes. That's how we met.''

''And we fell in love?''

He tugged her down to sit with him on the rock. ''I guess so, but I don't think either one of us understood that just yet.''

Light from the quarter moon danced along the surface of the swiftly moving water. Delighted, with the dancing light and the story of how she and Hunter met, Bess smiled. ''No wonder I fell for you. You were a hero.''

Hunter chuckled. ''If you don't count the fact that I almost led us right through the middle of a Cheyenne war party camped at the edge of the foothills.''

''I take it we made it, though. So you were a hero.''

He shook his head. ''I was trying to impress my father. And you.''

''I'm sure you impressed us all.''

"You fascinated me," he confessed. "I'd never met any white people before, other than my father."

"How did we talk? I don't speak Arapaho, do I?"

"No. Winter Fawn and I were brought up speaking both languages. But I was usually so tongue-tied around you once we settled in here, it didn't make much difference that I spoke your language."

"You seem to have gotten over it since then."

"Aye. I got over it when Winter Fawn got bit by a rattler and we all thought she was going to die. It was only a few weeks after we came here. I found you here, by the river, crying. You were afraid for Winter Fawn, but you said you were also afraid that if she died, I would leave, and you didn't want me to leave."

A wave of deep emotion washed through Bess. Despair. Fear. Longing. Was that what she had felt that day?

"That's when I knew."

"Knew what?"

"That beside you was where I belonged. That I would never leave you."

Bess let out a little, breathy "Oh" and leaned against his shoulder. "Oh, Hunter, how could I not have loved you? How can I not remember it? I don't understand."

Hunter slid his arm around her and relished the feel of her against him. He had wondered, during these past few days, if he would ever have the chance to hold her again. If she would ever want him to.

But now, he had to tell her the rest. The truth.

CHAPTER FOURTEEN

"It's possible," Hunter said quietly, "that you had changed your mind about me by the time you were kidnapped."

"Don't say that," she cried. "That can't be true."

"We were so young, Bess, back when we first knew how we felt about each other. Too damn young," he said grimly. "You started going to school, met other kids your own age. I was too old. I wasn't about to go to school for the first time at the age of fifteen and let a bunch of white kids laugh at me because I couldn't read. I let your brother and my father convince me to step back and let you grow up."

Bess straightened away from him and glared. "They said that? And you listened?"

"I tried. But it didn't stop the way we felt. I slept in the bunkhouse with the men. I used to sneak out at night and come down here to the river. I'd whistle, making the call of the mountain bluebird. It's a morning bird, so if you heard it at night, you'd know it was me. You would climb out your bedroom window and run down here and meet me."

"I snuck out of my room? How shameless of me."

He heard the smile in her voice. "Not quite shameless," he told her. "At least not in those early years. Mostly we just sat and talked."

"What about?"

"Everything." He shrugged. "Nothing. Just . . . I guess we just wanted to be together."

"You said those were the early years. What happened in the later years?"

"We grew up," he said simply. "And so did our feelings, and our bodies and our needs."

Heat blossomed in Bess's cheeks and in the pit of her stomach. She had a flash, just a flash, of two young bodies entwined on soft summer grass, their blood running hot, their kisses deep, their hands greedy.

Her heart thundered in reaction. Was it a memory? Or only her imagination? *Or wishful thinking.*

"You're awfully quiet all of a sudden. Have I shocked you?"

"I . . . I don't know. Did we . . . I mean, did we . . . you know."

In the moonlight, Hunter reached out and stroked his fingers down her cheek. "No, Blue Eyes. We kissed, we touched, but I would not dishonor you that way. I knew we couldn't get married yet, and to take you, then not marry you . . . I couldna do it," he said, the burr slipping into his voice.

Another shiver slid down Bess's arms, but this one was hot. "Had we talked about getting married?"

"Aye. Many times. Talked about it, planned for it."

"Then what happened, Hunter? Why did we not marry?"

"Because I am a fool."

"I doubt that. I doubt there's a foolish bone in your body."

"Ah, lass, that's because ye canna remember."

"Tell me."

He was silent for a moment. He pulled up his knees, spread them and braced his elbows on them, letting his hands hang limp and loose. "One night, under one of these trees—that one," he said, pointing to an old cottonwood that split into a Y about three feet from the ground, "things almost went too far."

That hot, tingling sensation in the pit of Bess's stomach spread lower.

"The hardest thing I ever did in my life, up until then, was pull away from you that night. You were eighteen and I was twenty, and we were so hot for each other, we damn near set the grass on fire."

Bess swallowed hard. She wanted to say something stupid, like she wished she had been there. "How it must hurt you to know I can't remember."

"Aye," he confessed. "That it does, but I know 'tis none of yer doing, so don't fash yerself, lass. It canna be helped. And I'm not telling you this so you'll feel guilty for not feeling the things you used to."

"Why are you telling me this?" she asked with a calm she didn't feel.

"Because I *don't* want you to feel guilty. I don't want you thinking you have to try to make yourself feel the way you think you used to, the way you think you should."

She heaved a sigh and looked up at the stars blinking through the overhead branches. "It's not working. I do feel guilty."

"You won't when you understand that I've spent the better part of the past two years hurting you."

"On purpose?"

"No," he admitted. "The hurting you wasn't on purpose, but the distance I deliberately put between us was."

From down the river a night bird called. A gust of wind stirred the leaves overhead. Bess pulled the shawl closer around her. "You wanted distance between us?"

"I couldn't trust myself around you after that night under the trees. I couldn't be alone with you again. I was afraid I didn't have enough control to stop myself the next time, and every time I saw you, I wanted you more. So I figured we'd both be better off if I stayed away from you for a while."

"You . . . you didn't want to marry me, then?" she asked hesitantly.

"It wasn't a matter of not wanting to." He picked up a small stone and rolled it over and over in his hand. "At least, that's what I thought at the time. I was drawing pay from the Double D, working for your brother, living in the bunkhouse. How was I supposed to support a wife? Where were we supposed to live? No." He shook his head. "We were both too young, and you were used to having nice things, living in a nice house. I couldn't give you any of that."

"Is that what I wanted from you? Nice things and a nice house? That seems so foolish of me."

"I never asked you if that's what you wanted. It's what I wanted for you. We never talked about it until that day you came to see me after you got home from Atlanta."

"The day I was kidnapped?"

"The day I let those bastards just walk in and take you," he said fiercely, throwing the stone in his hand into the river with a hard jerk of his arm.

"We aren't talking about that," she warned him. "I'd rather hear what happened before that. Megan said I went to see you because you hadn't come to see me, and I'd been home for several days."

"That's right, and to try and make me jealous by dangling that goddamn Virgil Horton under my nose. That was low, Bess, that was really low."

"I agree. Did it work?"

"Did what work?"

"Were you jealous?"

"I was sick with it. I didn't know—still don't—if you really meant to go with him or not."

"Why would I do such a thing?" Bess wondered, truly dismayed. "Why would I have anything to do with someone like him? Just what did happen with the bank? Megan was pretty vague about it.''

"She was probably too young to remember. Then, too, she wasn't there. For that matter, neither was I.''

"But you know what happened?''

"Aye. Carson had his money in Horton's old man's bank. This was back, oh, five years ago, I guess. One day when he went in, Winter Fawn was with him. He said they all looked down their noses at her. When he came home, he was fit to be tied. Next time he went, Winter Fawn went to the bank without him, while he was over at the lumberyard. They had a sign up at the door saying no Indians allowed. Wouldn't let her in. Benjamin Horton himself escorted her right out the door. When Carson found out, he damn near exploded. He walked in and pulled all his money out then and there and took it down the street to the other bank. Hasn't been back since.''

A sick feeling stirred in the pit of Bess's stomach. "I don't like what it says about me, that I would even speak to someone I knew was connected to such an incident. And to throw him in your face the way I did.'' She shook her head. "I can't believe I would do something so horrid. Why, Hunter?'' she cried. "Why would I throw him in your face the way I did? Did I know who he was?''

Hunter stroked her cheek with the backs of his fingers. "You knew him. I don't know for sure why you decided to go with him, though. I think maybe you were giving me one last chance to declare myself and my intentions once and for all, or tell you flat out that I didn't want you anymore.''

The night seemed to press down on Bess, making her feel small and insignificant. She knew from things he'd said from the very beginning that if that had been her ploy, it hadn't worked to get him to declare himself. Still, she couldn't stop herself from asking. "What happened?''

What happened. A simple enough question, Hunter thought.

He just wished he had an answer that made sense. Wished he had any kind of an answer.

"Hunter?"

"We . . . talked."

"Talked?" she asked, surprised. "Sounds to me like you should have yelled at me, and if I thought I was right, I should have yelled right back."

Hunter swallowed. "Yell? You would never do anything so unreasonable, so unladylike as to yell."

Bess's eyes widened. "You have to be joking. Of course I would yell. Any reasonable person would yell over something so important as her whole future. That's what this came down to, didn't it? If you didn't care whether or not I went with this Horton character, that would have been the end for us, wouldn't it?"

"But I did care," Hunter said. "You knew I cared."

"But you didn't tell me not to go with him?"

"Hell, Bess, I don't remember what I told you. I just felt everything slipping away. You, the things we used to talk about and plan for. You . . . you wanted to get married, you said. I wanted to wait."

Bess let out a short breath. "I don't understand any of this. I was forward enough to tell you I wanted to get married, but too well-behaved to yell at you? I wanted to marry you, but I would hurt you that way, throwing that man in your face? It makes no sense. Are you sure you're telling me everything?"

"I can't tell you what was in your mind, your heart. We haven't been close enough for the past couple of years for me to know that. And that's my fault. That night here under the trees, when things got out of hand . . . nothing was ever the same after that between us. I must have scared you worse than I thought. Or hurt you."

"But according to you, I still wanted to marry you. I still cared enough to try to make you jealous."

"It might be," he said slowly, "that what my father was worried about happened anyway. At least to you."

"And what would that be?"

"That we were too used to each other. He was afraid that we would get it in our heads when we were young that we would get married one day, and we'd just plod along in that direction because it was expected of us, because we expected it of ourselves, instead of because we . . . well, instead of because we really wanted to get married."

"That wasn't what you were about to say."

"Dammit, Bess, we should never have started this conversation. What good does it do to talk about it now? It's only adding more confusion and pressure on you, when that's the last thing you need."

"I agree. But I asked you for the truth, and I'm glad you told me. But what were you about to say, Hunter?"

"What difference does it make?"

"Maybe none. But you're going to a lot of trouble not to tell me, so it must be important. You say we loved each other for years, but that wasn't a good enough reason to get married."

"That's not what I said."

"That's what it boils down to. What else should we have felt, if not love?"

A gleam of moonlight slid along the bunched muscle of his jaw. He threw another stone into the river and said nothing.

"Dammit, Hunter—"

"All right," he said, his voice tight with leashed emotion. "Fire."

Just the word, despite the way he flung it at her in a bitter tone, had the power to heat her blood.

"We should have burned for each other, the way my father burned for my mother, the way he and Gussie burn for each other, regardless of their ages. The way Carson and Winter Fawn still burn for each other. You can see it in their eyes when they look at each other when they think no one is watching. The way we used to burn for each other until that night out here under the trees, when I killed it in you.''

It took Bess a long time to be able to speak. His words shook her. Surely he was wrong about killing the fire in her, the fire that burned for him. Otherwise, why would she be feeling it now? ''I don't understand,'' she managed. ''What do you mean, you killed it?''

''I pushed too far, asked too much of you, took advantage. You weren't ready for what I wanted from you that night.''

''I pushed you away?''

Hunter closed his eyes and tilted his face up to the night. ''No,'' he said, his voice tinged with sadness. ''I think you would have let me have you, right here on the grass.''

''I wanted you.'' She knew it was true. It wasn't a memory so much as a certainty within her. She had wanted him.

''Aye. You did. Almost as much as I wanted you. But after that night, you changed. You pulled inside yourself. Became so controlled, so . . . I don't know what to call it. You never raised your voice to me again, no matter what I did. If I got close enough to touch you, you moved away. When you laughed or smiled, it didn't reach your eyes.''

''Wait,'' she said, holding a hand out to stop him from continuing. ''You told me that it was you who put distance between us. Now you say you tried to touch me but *I* pulled away.''

''I didn't say I was any good at staying away from you. I did put distance between us. But I couldn't stay completely away. I didn't know how to do that and still keep breathing. And when you wouldn't respond to me anymore, I knew I'd done the right thing by backing off.''

''Did you ever think,'' she said quietly, ''that maybe it was your backing off that caused me to act the way you describe?''

''No.'' He shook his head. ''One of these days you'll remember for yourself. Before that night, if I'd done something you didn't like you would have ripped into me and told me exactly what you thought. But after that, you were so controlled, so damn polite all the time. And agreeable, almost always agreeable. And so sweet. Always sweet, even if you disagreed with something I said.''

He was quiet for several minutes before he spoke again. ''I thought—hoped—that if I gave you enough room, and saved up enough money so I could build you a real house instead of that cabin, you'd come around. Then all of a sudden, there you were that day last week, telling me you wanted to get married right away. You didn't want to wait for a house.''

''And I dangled Virgil Horton under your nose for proper motivation, to get my way.''

''I suppose that was it.''

''How you must hate me,'' she said sadly.

''No, Bess, you're wrong. I could never hate you.''

''That's all right.'' She pushed herself to her feet and turned back toward the house. ''Right now I think I hate myself enough for both of us.''

''No, Bess.''

She didn't see him reach out for her. She made her way through the trees out into the open and kept walking, heading for the house.

Hunter sat for a long while, watching her progress, cursing himself. Damn his hide. He should have kept his mouth shut. He didn't know what to hope for now—that she would regain her memory and understand everything that had gone wrong between them, or that she wouldn't. That their slate might be wiped clean, that they might have the chance to start over.

Finally he lowered his outstretched hand. He couldn't for his life think of a single reason why she should come to care for him again.

Bess slept poorly that night. First, she lay awake for hours, troubled by all Hunter had told her, trying to understand and come to grips with the girl-woman he had described. It was a fruitless effort. Her actions and her relationship with Hunter continued to baffle her.

Oh, not the loving him part. She could fully understand why she had loved Hunter MacDougall. He was kind and generous, strong and decent. Not to mention the way the mere sight of him backed her breath up in her throat.

But none of that explained her behavior as he had described it. Surely there was something he hadn't told her. Or perhaps something that he himself didn't know about her feelings.

That made the most sense to her. But until she regained her memory, she had nothing else to go on. And it was driving her crazy. She tossed and turned so much that her bedcovers tangled around her legs.

She must have eventually worn herself out and fallen asleep, for she awakened well before dawn covered in icy sweat, with fear clawing at her throat, yet no memory of the nightmare that had so terrified her.

Hunter did not come in for breakfast. Bess was hesitant to ask about him, but Winter Fawn felt no such restraint and asked Carson where her brother was.

"He's chopping wood." Carson then looked at Bess with an odd quirk of his lips. "He's been doing a lot of that lately, chopping wood."

"But we have plenty," Winter Fawn protested, starting to rise.

"Leave him be," Carson had told her. "He's a grown man, honey. Let him do what he needs to do."

"But he doesn't need to chop wood," Winter Fawn insisted. "Sometimes," she added with a lift of her brow, "grown men behave like little boys."

Carson gave her a devilish grin. "That's not what you thought last—"

"Carson!" Winter Fawn's dusky cheeks showed red just before she slapped her hands over them.

And the only thing Bess was able to think was, *they burn for each other.*

Shortly after breakfast the rumble of hoof beats announced the arrival of half-a-dozen riders at the ranch, led by County Sheriff Jim West.

As Carson, Hunter, and several of the hands gathered to meet them, Bess, Winter Fawn, and Megan stepped out onto the porch.

"What's the occasion, Jim?" Carson asked the sheriff. "Not that we don't appreciate a visit from you, but this"—Carson waved toward the men who rode in with the sheriff—"looks like a posse. What's up?"

Jim West was a big man, with light brown hair streaked with gray and a nose that had been broken more than once and looked like it. His brown eyes tilted down, and so did the ends of his mustache, giving him a perpetually sad look that was misleading. He had a thick neck, a barrel for a chest, and thick, meaty arms. He had a reputation for being tough and honest, a little mean when he was crossed, but the first to laugh at a joke.

"There's a rumor surfaced in Walsenburg yesterday that Miss Bess—" West paused and tipped his hat to Bess and the other ladies on the porch. "Howdy, ma'am, ladies." He turned back to Carson. "A rumor that Miss Bess went and got herself kidnapped by the Rawlins gang. Come to find out if it was true."

Bess touched Winter Fawn's arm to gain her attention. "I'll go make sure the coffee's hot."

"You won't mind talking about it?" Winter Fawn asked her.

Bess shrugged. "Why should I mind? I don't remember any of it."

Winter Fawn nodded. "All right, then." When Bess went inside, Winter Fawn left the porch and walked to her husband's side. "We've got coffee. Why don't you and Hunter bring the sheriff inside and be comfortable."

A few minutes later, Sheriff Jim West, Carson, Hunter, Bess, and Winter Fawn were seated around the table as Megan poured coffee for everyone. The rest of the sheriff's men were watering their horses, waiting for Megan to make it outside with coffee for them.

"So," West said. "Is it true?"

"Fine damn time to be asking," Hunter muttered. "A week or more after the fact."

"Well, now, you've got a point there." West blew on his coffee, took a sip. "I've told the powers that be a dozen times if I've told them once that situations like this are going to crop up, but the dang fools just can't see their way to fitting a crystal ball into the county budget. 'Course, if some of our county citizens would bother themselves to let their sheriff know when there's a problem, the sheriff would probably stir himself to give chase in a more timely manner."

Hunter rolled his eyes. "All right. But we'd have all been a lot happier if you'd caught the bastards before they made it to my place."

"So would I, son, believe me." He took another sip, then set his cup down carefully. "We took out after them when they hit the bank, but they had about a ten-minute head start on us, and they headed straight for the thick brush. We lost their tracks at the river. Followed it a considerable ways, but by then it was raining hard. We figured the rain must have wiped out their tracks, 'cause we never did pick 'em up again. You say they came to your place?"

"That's right. Bess was there. It started raining, so we went indoors. About five minutes later, Rawlins and his gang burst in on us."

Bess had remained silent, having nothing to contribute to the conversation. Her head was starting to hurt, as it did whenever she tried to remember. She forced herself to breathe slowly and just listen.

"You're sure it was the Rawlins gang?" the sheriff wanted to know.

"Positive," Hunter said.

"All four of them?"

"Aye," Hunter said tersely, "but one of them had to be carried."

A flash of pain struck through Bess's temple.

"That'd be the one Herschel Pilgrim shot before they killed him," the sheriff said.

"They killed Mr. Pilgrim?" Winter Fawn asked. "Ach, that poor man. His poor family."

"Yes, ma'am." West turned back to Hunter. "So they caught you by surprise, burst in on you and Miss Bess. Then what?"

"They made Bess bandage up the wounded man, then they tied me up, knocked me out, and took her."

"But—"

All eyes turned to Megan, who stood with one hand holding the coffee pot, the other clamped over her mouth, her eyes wide.

"Megan?" Bess asked.

With her face as red as a late summer apple, Megan lowered her hand and started edging toward the front door. "I'll just— uh, take this coffee to the men outside."

Now what, Bess wondered, was that all about? What had Megan been about to say? What did she know that Hunter wasn't telling?

"Miss Bess," the sheriff said. "Do you know where they took you?"

The shaft of pain in her head turned vicious. She pressed her fingers to her temple and bit back a moan. "The mountains."

"Which mountains? North or south?"

She sought Hunter's gaze. "I—"

"They took her north," Hunter said, answering for her.

"I'm assuming you went after her, got her away from them.
I'd like to hear about that."

Hunter took a drink of coffee to give himself a minute. He
couldn't tell the sheriff they'd shot him without explaining how
he'd been able to get up and ride after them. It didn't matter,
as that had nothing to do with the sheriff's business. But he
would stick as close to the truth as he could, anyway.

"It was too dark to trail them when I came to, so I rode
over here to get help, but Carson wasn't here."

"Innes and I had gone to Pueblo to look at a bull I was
thinking about buying," Carson explained.

"So I rode back home and waited for it to get light enough
for me to pick up their trail," Hunter continued. "Trailed them
a day and a half up Greenhorn Mountain to a cabin."

"And I suppose you just politely asked them to hand over
Miss Bess."

Hunter ran his tongue along the inside of his cheek. "Something like that."

The sheriff turned to Bess. She tensed and found herself
holding her breath. "Were you treated roughly?" he asked
gently.

Bess glanced down at the cup before her, then back up into
kind brown eyes. "I believe I was, Sheriff, but I have no
memory of it."

The sheriff sat back in his chair and frowned. "You have
no memory of how they treated you?"

"I have no memory at all, of anything that happened to me
before Hunter rescued me." She gave him a lopsided smile.
"I'm only hoping they're not all pulling my leg when they tell
me my name is Bess Dulaney."

Sheriff West stared blankly around the table. "Well. Well,
I swan." He looked to Hunter. "How . . . what . . ."

When Hunter spoke, he kept his gaze on Bess. "She took a
hard blow to the head during her escape. Knocked her out. I
had to carry her out of there. She didn't come to until the next

morning. When she woke up, she didn't know who she was, or anything about herself or what had happened.''

"Well," the sheriff said again. "I swan." Frowning, he took another drink of coffee and drained the cup. Then his gaze focused on Hunter again and sharpened. "Did you kill any of them?"

"I'm sorry to say I didn't. But I don't see how that wounded man could have still been alive. He was gut-shot. I didn't see him up there. I caught two of them—the younger ones—by surprise and left them gagged and tied to a tree. I was circling around the clearing to come up on the rear of the cabin when Bess made her break. Right before she ran out the front door, I heard a noise.''

"A noise?"

"Kind of a gong-like noise." Hunter's lips twitched. "Unless I miss my guess, I think Bess must have whacked Rawlins on the head with an iron skillet, 'cause that's sure what it sounded like to me.''

The sheriff slapped his hand down on the table. "Good for you, Miss Bess."

Bess grinned. "I'll say. Do you really think I whacked him?"

Hunter smiled. "You did something that bought you enough time to get out the door and halfway across the clearing before he tried to stop you. He wasn't looking any too steady on his feet when he staggered to the door and took a couple of potshots at us.''

The sheriff heaved a sigh. "You coulda saved us all some grief if you'd gone ahead and killed the no-good scoundrel.''

"Don't think I didn't want to," Hunter said grimly. "But Bess fell and hit her head on a rock, so I had to carry her. My first priority was to get her to safety. I ever see the bastard again, I'll tell you right now, he's a dead man.''

The sheriff studied his empty coffee cup and nodded his head several times. "I hear ya, son. But if it comes to that, do this old man a favor and lie to me. Tell me it was self-defense.

Can you take me and the boys up the mountain and show us that cabin?''

"I can find it easy enough," Hunter said. "But you know they're long gone from there by now."

"I'm sure of it. But I need to see it, anyway. Maybe they left some clue as to where they might be headed. I'd be remiss in my duty if I didn't check it out. I'd be much obliged if you'd ride with us and point the way."

"All right," Hunter said. "If you think it'll do any good."

Bess lifted her cup with both hands, took a sip, then set it down carefully. "Sheriff, if you don't mind, I'll be going with you."

"Now, Miss Bess—"

"Bess, you can't do that," Carson broke in.

Bess's back stiffened. "I beg your pardon?"

"Be reasonable," Carson cried.

"Reasonable? You're telling me what I can and cannot do as though I were twelve instead of twenty, and *I'm* supposed to be reasonable?"

"It's a hard ride up mountain trails, and for what?" he demanded.

"For a chance to get my memory back," she stated firmly.

"What?" Carson shook his head. "Bess, losing your memory isn't like losing a handkerchief. You can't just go back to the last place you know you had it and expect to find it lying around waiting to be found."

"Carson." Bess reached across the table and placed her hand on his. "I know it's a chance, and not even a very good one. But maybe by going back to where it happened, something there will jar my memory. I can't live the rest of my life with everyone else knowing more about me than I do. I want my life back. If riding up a mountain trail will give me that, it's a small price to pay. And if nothing comes of it, I'll have spent a few days in the saddle. I appreciate your concern, but I'm going." She released his hand and stood up. "If someone can have my saddle put on a reliable mount, I'll be ready to leave in fifteen minutes.''

She didn't dare look at Hunter as she left the table and made her way quickly upstairs.

Sheriff West and Virgil Horton were not the only people to hear of Bess's kidnapping and subsequent rescue. The man known to the Rawlins gang as J.T. also heard the tale, and he was furious.

Damn those fools. He'd *told* them to get rid of the girl. To kill her.

Dulaney. Shit. If he'd known she was a Dulaney, he'd have killed her himself on the spot rather than count on Rawlins to do what he was told.

But how was he to recognize her, with that bandanna wrapped around her face and her hair all scraggly? Besides, she'd been barely more than a child the last time he'd seen her, back when her brother first came out and took over his father's ranch. Damn shame the Yankee Army hadn't taken care of Carson when they'd got his father during the war. It would have saved J.T. a great deal of headaches over the years since. Damn uppity Rebs, anyway.

At least the girl had been blindfolded. There was no way she could identify him to anyone.

And rescued by a MacDougall. Goddamn. If there were any two families in that godforsaken county he didn't need to tangle with, it was the Dulaneys and the MacDougalls. They were too well respected, too influential with their neighbors.

Well, this would finish things between him and Rawlins. J.T. could not afford to continue doing business with someone so careless. He had his future planned out, and nowhere in his plans had he left room for a prison sentence or a noose.

His only regret was the loss of income from the holdups.

He was going to have to come up with another source of funds if he was to achieve his goal.

But that shouldn't prove too difficult. After all, he was an important man in Colorado Territory, and he planned to be an important man—the first elected governor—when Colorado became a state. He would find the money. Somewhere.

CHAPTER FIFTEEN

The mountain trail forced the posse to ride single file. Hunter took point, with Sheriff West behind him. Bess followed the sheriff, and the rest of the men—all from the county seat of Walsenburg—trailed her.

When they'd first left the ranch, the land was flat and they were able to ride abreast of each other, which gave Bess a chance to get to know the other men a little. It helped take her mind off what lay ahead; in addition she was going to be spending four or five days with these men. She wanted to know with whom she was riding.

Directly behind her once they were forced to ride single file came Martin Pilgrim. He managed a hotel in Walsenburg, Pilgrim's Inn, and it was his brother, Herschel, who'd been killed by Ned Rawlins during the holdup at the bank the week before. It seemed that the late Mr. Pilgrim had hired on as a special guard for the shipment of money the bank had just received.

Bess was certain that under ordinary circumstances, Mr.

Pilgrim—the one riding with the posse—was a nice enough man. But right now he was crazy with grief and out for blood. The skin along the back of Bess's neck prickled, knowing he rode directly behind her, with his right hand resting every minute on the butt of his revolver as if he expected Rawlins to suddenly appear before them. Martin Pilgrim was ready to shoot.

Behind him came Antonio Lopez. In his late fifties, his face was creased in permanent smile lines; he looked as if he was ready to burst out laughing any minute, and he did so frequently. His everyday job was as a cook in the restaurant at Pilgrim's Inn, but he had a talent for tracking, which the sheriff often made use of. He spoke excellent English with only a slight Spanish accent. Except when he wanted to make a point or get a laugh, then he laid the accent on thick and heavy.

Next rode Godfrey Reinhardt, a blacksmith with massive shoulders, and hands that looked as if they could bend cold steel. He had a wife named Geraldine and four daughters, named Giselle, Gerta, Gretchen, and Genevieve. His horse's name was Griswold. The packhorse, which he led but which did not belong to him, was Bert, but Mr. Reinhardt swore it was a good horse, even if improperly named.

The seventh rider was Don Jackson, a deputy marshal for the city of Walsenburg. He had a quiet nature and hard eyes that missed nothing. He took it as a personal affront that the Rawlins gang had dared to rob a bank in *his* town. He wanted the outlaws caught, tried, and hanged.

Bringing up the rear was one of Sheriff West's county deputies, Peter Gorman. He wasn't any happier about the robbery than any of the others. As they rode away from the ranch, he had stated that his fondest wish would be to find Ned Rawlins napping in this cabin up in the mountains, but he knew it wasn't likely. His gut, and his five years as a county deputy, told him Rawlins was headed for Mexico.

As she rode behind the sheriff, Bess thought about the men

behind her and their various reasons for joining the posse.
Concentrating on them kept her from thinking about what
might, or might not, happen once they reached their destination.
If the sight of Hunter, or her own family, her own home, had
not jogged her memory, what hope was there that the sight of
a cabin she'd seen only once would help her remember?

But hope was a cat with nine lives, and hers had not run
out.

Hunter had seriously mixed feelings about Bess making this
trip up the mountain with the posse.

He understood her need to try anything that might help regain
her memory. There were things in her past he hoped she never
remembered, such as what she went through at the hands of
her kidnappers. But he only had to look into her eyes to realize
how lost and confused she felt at not knowing her own past,
her own nature.

This trip, for her, was a gamble, because there was certainly
no guarantee that seeing that cabin again would help her
remember.

But Man-Above, he hated to see her pin all her hopes on
this. They'd been on the trail less than one full day so far and
already she looked exhausted. How anyone could perch on the
side of a horse in that stupid excuse for a saddle while taking
a steep switchback up the side of a mountain was beyond him.

To her credit, Bess was an excellent rider, especially considering the handicap of a sidesaddle. For two cents, he'd take
the damn thing and throw it off the next cliff, except then she'd
have to ride astride, and he remembered, vividly, the chafed,
bruised condition of her inner thighs when he'd changed her
out of her wet clothes when she'd been unconscious. Never
did he want her to have to go through that again.

At any rate, it didn't matter whether he agreed or not. She
was there, and she was handling it. He'd lost his chance to

protest when he had clamped his jaw shut back at the house when she'd announced that she was coming along on the trip. If she asked for his opinion, he would give it. Until then, he was doing his best to let her make her own decisions.

And damn, it was hard.

He called a halt just short of the spot where Rawlins and the gang had camped for the night—the place where he'd found Bess's hat and the bloody hatpin. Lopez, the tracker, wanted to look around the site. While he did that, the rest of them dismounted to stretch their legs and give the horses a rest.

Lopez was good. If there were any signs left after so many days, the Mexican would find them. With his years of experience, he might even find something Hunter had missed. But it wouldn't help them find Rawlins. Hunter doubted that anything up here on this mountain would help them do that, unless the gang had left tracks deep enough to find after a week.

Hunter didn't much care what, if anything, Lopez would turn up. His attention was on Bess.

He shouldn't have told her about their past. He could practically see her thoughts on her face. She was trying to figure it all out, reconcile what he'd told her with what she now felt, and dammit, it just wasn't going to come together for her. He knew that. She couldn't make herself feel the things she'd felt before.

He hurt for her. But he hurt for himself, too. She'd forgotten him. She'd forgotten that she used to love him. No matter how many times he told himself that wasn't her fault, it still twisted like a knife in his gut.

She came toward him now, determination on her face and in her stride. "We camped there?" she asked, pointing to the clearing up ahead, where Lopez was going over every inch of ground.

Hunter nodded.

Bess turned away and strode toward West. "Sheriff, when Señor Lopez is finished, I would like to take a look around before we ride on. If you're in a hurry, I can catch up with you when I've finished.''

Hunter clenched his jaw shut to keep from swearing. He'd be damned if they'd ride off and leave her, and she knew it. West practically fell all over himself assuring Bess that she could take her time looking around as soon as Lopez was finished.

"We wouldn't think of leaving a lady out here alone on the trail," West protested. "Of course," he added slyly, "we do need to get our business concluded and get back down the mountain as soon as possible. These men here, they've all got work to get back to, and some of them have families waiting, worrying about them. But we'll be glad to wait on you, Miss Bess."

So, Hunter thought, biting back a grin, West wasn't quite the pushover Hunter had thought. It was plain on Bess's face that the sheriff had gotten to her with that remark about families waiting and worrying. She wouldn't dally long and be the cause of the men being kept away from home longer than necessary because of her.

And she didn't dally. When Lopez returned, reporting to the sheriff that there was plenty of sign, but none of it helpful, Bess wondered about the sidelong glances the tracker kept throwing her way. What signs had he seen that might pertain to her?

But Bess wasn't interested in signs. She wanted her memory back. She walked to the edge of the clearing and stopped, looking around, hoping something would look familiar.

Trees, shrubs, a small, trickling stream cutting across the trail at the edge of the clearing. She walked the perimeter. She crisscrossed the clearing. She stood in the center and turned slowly around. Nothing unexpected. Nothing out of the ordinary. Nothing familiar. Nothing but that damned, dull throbbing that struck her temple whenever she struggled to remember.

Suddenly she felt a presence at her back. Without looking, she knew it was Hunter.

He placed a hand on her shoulder. "Are you all right?"

Those were the first words he'd spoken to her since she'd left him at the river last night. They eased some of the tightness in her stomach. His touch soothed her even more. She had loved this man. Why, God, why couldn't she remember loving him? Why did it feel as though she still did?

"I'm fine," she finally answered, turning toward him. "I'm ready to go now. There's nothing here for me."

That night when they camped, Bess worried that she might have another nightmare and humiliate herself by waking everyone, but she decided she wouldn't let herself care what the others thought. They were nice men. They would probably feel sorry for her. She would hate that, but it couldn't be helped. She was too exhausted after being in the saddle all day to even think of staying awake. And there was tomorrow to consider. Hunter claimed they would be at the cabin by noon. That meant all morning on the trail again, and they might not stay long, which would mean all afternoon in the saddle again.

No, she could not stay awake. Although if she didn't fall asleep soon, she thought after more than an hour, it might become a moot point.

It was disconcerting, however, to lie in her blankets and relax, knowing she was surrounded by men. Strangers.

But Hunter was there, not more than three feet from her side in his own bedroll. She wasn't afraid, as she must have been with her kidnappers.

At the thought, twin flashes of pain and terror shot through her.

Hunter heard her emit a soft cry and was instantly up and kneeling at her side. Her face was ashen, her eyes staring blindly through him. "Bess?" He wanted to touch her, take her hand, pull her into his arms. But he didn't dare. Not if she was finally remembering something. "What is it?"

He watched as she wrenched her mind away from whatever had frightened her. "Hunter."

"I'm here. I'm right here. What happened? You looked like you'd seen a ghost. Did you remember something?"

"I . . ." She shook her head. "Feelings. I remember feeling afraid. And . . . empty." She fumbled around until she could get a hand free of her blankets. She gripped Hunter's hand in hers and squeezed hard as she closed her eyes and swallowed. "As if I had no reason to live."

Not knowing what to say, Hunter raised her hand and pressed his lips against her knuckles. When he saw tears seep out from beneath her lashes, he gripped her hand tighter and nearly moaned.

"I'm all right," she whispered. "I'm all right now. But I wish . . ."

"What do you wish, Blue Eyes?"

She swallowed again and opened her eyes to look at him. Her long, black lashes were damp and clumped together. Her blue eyes were dark with emotion. "I wish we were alone, and that you were holding me."

"I do, too," he said with feeling. But they weren't alone. The sheriff was stretched out on Bess's other side, and he was raised up on an elbow watching them.

"Everything all right?" West asked.

"Aye," Hunter told him. "Just a bad dream."

With a low grunt, West lay back down and rolled over, presenting his back to them.

When Hunter looked back down at Bess, she was biting her lower lip. "What?" he asked her.

She worked her other hand free from beneath the blanket and wiped her cheeks. "It wasn't a dream," she whispered.

Hunter sucked in a sharp breath. "A memory? You remembered something?"

"No. Like I said, the only thing I remember is the feelings. I was lying here trying to go to sleep, and thinking that it was okay that I was surrounded by strange men, because this time it was the posse, not the outlaws, and . . . and suddenly, it was just there—the fear, the emptiness. Why would I feel fear and emptiness at the same time?"

"It was a bad time for you, Blue Eyes. But even if you do remember it, if it all comes back to you, you have to also remember that it's over. It's done with. You survived it, and you're here with me, and I swear, Blue Eyes, I swear I'll keep you safe."

The minute the words were out, Hunter wanted to call them back. How could he make such a promise, when he hadn't been able to keep her safe in his own home? But she'd needed to hear him say it. And, he thought, he'd needed to say it. He needed to believe he could do it, that he could keep her safe, because, by damn, he would die trying.

"Here." He placed her hand atop her blanket and let go of her. "Hold on." He dragged his bedroll closer, crawled beneath his blankets, then reached for her hand again.

They slept that way, their hands joined, fingers entwined, resting on the scant few inches that separated their blankets.

There were no nightmares to plague Bess that night.

The sun was still making its climb toward high noon when Hunter led the posse up the final leg of the switchback that led to the shoulder of Greenhorn Mountain.

Earlier in the morning the sheriff had been delighted with the discovery of the bags of gold coins Hunter had hidden. Rawlins had not found them. The two Wells Fargo bags, along with the third one, which Hunter had given to the sheriff back at the ranch, were now safely secured on the packhorse.

"The bank put up a reward for recovery of the money," West told Hunter. "I'll see that you get it."

The thought of taking money from a bank owned by Horton turned Hunter's stomach. "Give it to Mrs. Pilgrim," he told the sheriff. "I'm sure she could use it now that she's got kids to raise on her own."

"Why, that's right generous of you," West said.

"Damn generous." Martin Pilgrim shook Hunter's hand. "My brother's widow will be grateful, MacDougall. I thank you."

Hunter had shrugged away the thanks and led them on up the mountain.

Now, a dozen yards ahead, he could see the end of the trail where it spilled out into the clearing. It was about there, a dozen yards short of the clearing, when the smell hit him.

The skin on the back of his neck crawled. There was no mistaking the sickly sweet odor of rotting flesh. Reining in his horse, he raised his hand to signal a halt to the others.

"What's up?" West called from behind him.

Hunter twisted in the saddle. "You smell that?"

West sniffed the breeze like a bloodhound. His lips firmed, his jaw tightened. "Son of a bitch. Ten bucks says that's not an animal."

"Ten bucks says you're right." Hunter nudged his horse on until he broke out into the clearing. There he reined aside and let the others, except for Bess, go ahead. He called Bess aside. "I want you to wait here," he told her.

Bess smelled the odor and heard the men muttering curses to themselves. The last thing she wanted to do was stumble across a dead body, so she agreed to wait.

With her promise, Hunter left her at the edge of the clearing and followed the posse toward the source of the smell—the cabin.

The door to the cabin was closed, and the shutters were barred across the single window, but nothing could keep the smell confined within the walls. Claw marks marred the door, small ones at the bottom and along the dirt in front of it, and large marks higher up. But the door had obviously held against the predators that had been drawn by the smell of rotting flesh.

With bandannas tied across their faces to help filter out the smell, the men lingered outside for several minutes, looking around. Even the sheriff was reluctant to enter.

Hunter pointed out the remains of the brush corral, and the general direction where he'd left the two men tied up. He described his actions and movements on the day he was there, but again left out mention of Bess being shot. He wouldn't be able to explain why she had no wound to show for it.

Finally it had to be done. West tugged on the latch string and the door opened with a loud creek. Martin Pilgrim jumped at the sound. A cloud of flies rose from a dark form near the back wall, buzzing and swarming straight at the men.

They all jumped.

There was nervous laughter from a couple of the men, and the sound of hard breaths being drawn through bandanna-covered mouths—anything to avoid drawing air through the nose.

It was dark inside. Someone opened the shutters to let in the light.

"Whoo-ee," Jackson, the town deputy said. "I always figured those outlaw bastards were rotten to the core. Looks like I was right."

There was more nervous laughter at his grim pun. The body stretched out along the back wall had been dead a long time. The skin was black and rotting.

"We try to move that," Lopez said pragmatically, "it's gonna shake like jelly."

"I don't see any need to move it," Pilgrim muttered.

"We got to bury the poor bastard," Reinhardt said. "Don't we?"

"I reckon," the sheriff allowed. "Look there. Is that a bandage wrapped around his middle?"

Lopez squatted down to look, and the others stepped aside

to give him more light. "*Sí*. Must be the one your *hermano* shot, Martin."

"That'd be Cecil Smith, according to the description."

Hunter nodded. "They called him Cecil."

"Ah," Lopez said. "It appears someone was in a hurry for this one to die."

"How's that?" West asked.

"Look there. That's a bullet hole in the middle of his forehead."

To a man, they all leaned forward to look at what used to be a man's face but was now nothing more than black ooze with indeterminate features.

"Hmph." Reinhardt straightened and backed away. "How can you tell?"

"I can tell," Lopez assured them all.

"I'll go get the shovel and start digging a grave. It would be best, I think, if Miss Bess did not see this."

"I agree," Hunter said grimly to Reinhardt. "Let me know when you get ready to carry him out and I'll make sure she can't see."

Humor danced in the sheriff's eyes. "You're not going to help us carry ol' Cecil out?"

"I don't remember anybody deputizing me," Hunter said. "I'm just the guide, remember?"

They buried the unlamented outlaw Cecil Smith behind the cabin, while Hunter made sure Bess did not get an inadvertent glimpse of the badly decomposed body.

With the body gone, the majority of the flies vacated the cabin, but by no means all of them. When Bess finally ventured inside against Hunter's wishes—and holding a kerchief over her nose and mouth—she had to continually wave her arm in front of her face to keep the flies away.

Hunter wished she had stayed outside, but he understood her

need to seek out anything that might trigger her memory. So he stuck to her side at her every step.

"Yep," said the sheriff, who followed them inside. "Look there. Now, I ask you, what's a skillet doing on the ground over by the window, when the fireplace is clean over here? If that's not where Miss Bess dropped it after clobbering Rawlins, I'll be a ring-tailed cat. Does anything look familiar, Miss Bess?"

Bess gave the sheriff a wan smile. He and the other men had been so solicitous of her the entire time she'd been with them, it was sweet. She looked around the one-room cabin that was all but bare. "No," she finally answered. "I would say I've never been here before, but I know that's not true."

"Well, you just take your time and look around all you want." He stepped outside and left her alone with Hunter. Lopez had already gone over the inside of the cabin, determining there was nothing there that would help them find the rest of the gang.

Nothing, indeed. There had been blankets and a dead body, but those were gone. All that was left were a few cooking utensils, the iron skillet, and a man's felt hat.

Bess stared hard at each item, each wall, the floor. Her temple throbbed. She'd been here. She knew that, but only because Hunter said it was so.

Why? she cried silently for the millionth time. Why couldn't she remember? Just one little thing. Anything, to give her something to hold on to, to feed her dying hope that one day her full memory would return. *Anything.*

But there was nothing. Nothing but this stabbing pain in her temple. In defeat, she turned toward the door, anxious to feel the sun on her face. She took one step, and the room began to whirl. Blindly she reached out to steady herself.

Hunter caught her hand and slipped an arm around her shoulders. "Bess?"

Something . . . something was stirring in her head. "I—"

The pain in her head blinded her, but she didn't need to see her surroundings now. She squeezed her eyes shut, the better to see the picture that was forming in that dark, empty part of her mind.

A hand. Large. Pale. Clean. A scar down the outer edge.

A man's boots. Black and glossy. Not a speck of dust. Expensive looking.

Then . . . nothing.

Bess cried out, reaching out with one hand as if she could pull something more from the depths of her lost past. But there was nothing there. Only emptiness.

"Ah, damn!" she cried. "Damn them, damn them to hell for doing this to me!"

"Talk to me. Tell me, Bess."

Hunter's voice, tense, concerned.

Her heart was racing. She was breathing too fast. She opened her eyes, dreading, fearing what she might see. What she might not see.

There was only Hunter, standing with her, holding her, in this empty cabin. But—

"I remembered something," she said, suddenly elated. "It isn't much, but if I can remember little things, surely the big things will come, don't you think?"

"What did you remember?" he asked, his eyes a mixture of concern and dread.

"I remember seeing a man's hand. It struck me as odd that it was so smooth and neat, as if he'd never done hard work. There's a scar down the outside of it. A narrow, white scar. And boots. They were . . . I'm sure they were his boots. Shiny black, polished. No dust. I . . . I remember wondering how he'd managed to ride all the way up here without getting dust on his expensive boots."

"Here?" Hunter asked. "You remember being here?"

"I . . ." She shook her head and pressed her fingertips to her temple. "It's all so jumbled. I remember the hand and the boots, and what I thought of them. I don't remember being here. I mean, I don't *remember* the cabin. But I just . . . I know it was here, because I wondered how he'd gotten all the way up the mountain with such clean, shiny boots. It didn't . . . yes! I remember thinking that it didn't seem logical that he would bring his boot polish just to . . . to . . . to what? Damn.''

She concentrated hard, pressing her fingers to her temple again because it seemed to help. ''Just to meet a bunch of outlaws. That's it! That's what I thought. He wouldn't carry his boot polish in his saddlebags just to meet with a bunch of outlaws. Hunter! I *remember* it.''

She threw her arms around his neck and laughed. ''I know it's not much, but it's something, isn't it?''

Aye, Hunter thought, it was something. If he was right, it was something none of them had considered. ''Come on.'' He led her outside, his arm still around her. ''You need to tell this to the sheriff.''

The men were gathered near the empty brush corral watching Lopez look around. At Hunter's urging, Bess repeated the few sparse memories she'd recalled.

The sheriff took off his hat, scratched his head, then put the hat back on. ''Well, now. Don't know if it helps us any, but it's interesting. Anybody here remember if one of those fellas has a scar on his hand?''

The men looked at each other and shook their heads.

''I'll tell you this,'' Hunter said. ''None of the men who took Bess was wearing boots that could have been polished up the way she remembers. They all wore brown boots, beat up and scarred. And how many outlaws have you ever heard of who carry a pair of fancy boots along, and wear them around their own hideout? I think what we've got, sheriff, is a fifth man.''

The sheriff repeated the ritual of taking off his hat, scratching his head, then donning his hat again. ''Well now. That puts a new wrinkle in the blanket, if you're right.''

"He is right," Bess said, more than certain of that tiny bit of memory. "He came here to meet the gang that brought me here. I remember that much, Sheriff."

Lopez joined them. "Ay, Chihuahua. A fifth man, you say?"

"He met them here," Hunter said. "Which means he didn't ride up the trail with them. He was gone before I got here."

"You're sure?" the sheriff asked him.

"If not, he was awfully quiet and had his horse hidden. There were six horses in the brush corral—one for each man, a packhorse, and one of them was Bess's mare. This fifth man either came up ahead of them, or came by a different trail. If he'd left by the trail they came up, I would have run into him. There has to be another trail. Which would explain why we didn't cut any sign on our way up of them coming down. A back trail."

Lopez narrowed his eyes and hummed. "Or no real trail. They could have cut through the forest. You," he said to Hunter. "How did you come up?"

"I left my horse a couple of miles down the trail and came up on foot."

Lopez looked down at Hunter's feet. "Wearing those boots?"

Hunter grinned. "Moccasins."

"Me, I think I won't find any tracks of yours, half-breed. We need to look for another trail. They may have left by it. Wait," he said as the men started moving out to search. He eyed each of them, then shook his head in mock dismay. "You city gringos stay here. Me, I don't trust your tracking skills. I will search north and east. You," he said to Hunter, "take south and west. The man who finds something whistles. If no one comes running, fire off two quick rounds."

Hunter left Bess in the care of the sheriff and started walking the south and west edges of the clearing. If he didn't find anything there, he would move in among the trees, moving farther out each trip until he found something.

He hadn't made it halfway along the south side when Lopez whistled and men shouted.

Hunter joined them at the stream near the east edge of the clearing. On just about the spot where Bess fell when she got shot there lay a human skull.

The sheriff took his hat off and scratched his head again. "Well, hell. Begging your pardon, Miss Bess."

"No need," she said. "I was thinking worse myself. Who do you suppose it is? Was?"

Hunter gave Bess a close look, but she seemed to be handling this discovery all right. At least a skull picked clean by predators was a damn sight easier on the eye—and the stomach—than what they'd found in the cabin.

"At least this time," Hunter said, "the bullet holes in the skull are plain to see, front and back."

Hunter and Lopez squatted side by side and studied the skull.

"Tooth marks are still pretty fresh," Hunter observed.

"*Sí.* I would say not much more than a week."

"You mean he died about the same time as the one we just buried?" Jackson, the town deputy, asked.

Sheriff West knelt across from Hunter and Lopez. "It appears that could be the case."

"Yeah, well," said Gorman, the county deputy. "Where's the rest of him?"

They fanned out to search. Hunter stopped before Bess. "Are you all right?"

She'd been staring at the skull, but looked up at him. "Yes. I want to help. I need to help."

Hunter started to object. Searching through the brush for bones and body parts was no chore for a woman. Shouldn't, he acknowledged, be a chore a man had to do, for that matter. But he understood her need to feel useful, to take an active role in finding out all they could about her kidnappers.

"All right." He took her by the hand. "You can help me search." He wanted to look at those spots where he'd left two of the gang members tied up. He had a feeling those boys never saw daylight again.

CHAPTER SIXTEEN

It turned out that Hunter was right.

They found enough bones scattered in a fairly small area to account for two bodies. The predatory wildlife had picked every bone clean in the week since Hunter had last seen the two men alive. The second skull, like the first, bore a bullet hole front and back. Pieces of the rope Hunter had used lay near the trees where he'd left them bound and gagged.

"Billy Rawlins and Woody Smith," Hunter said. He turned to West and looked him square in the eye. "Sheriff, I swear to you that when I carried Bess out of here, those two men were alive. Unconscious and tied up, but alive, with no bullet holes in their heads."

West nodded and waved away his words. "Don't fret about it, son. I believe you. 'Course, if you want to change your story, there's a reward out for these two."

Hunter shook his head. "I'm not saying I didn't want to kill them, but at first I left them alive in case I needed to trade something or someone to get Bess free. Then, once I had her, there wasn't time to come back and kill them. I was too busy ducking Ned Rawlins's bullets and trying to get Bess to safety.''

"Could a couple of those bullets . . . ? Naw." Reinhardt answered his own question. "He couldn't have hit them accidently in the middle of their foreheads, just like that other one.''

"No," the sheriff allowed. "No, not by accident. What we've got us here, boys, is another new wrinkle. I've heard of outlaws turning on each other, but by Hannah, it looks to me like Ned Rawlins killed not just his partners, but his own kid brother.''

Lopez crossed himself. *"Madre de Dios."*

"Coulda been the other one," Don Jackson offered.

"Cecil Smith's kid brother?" Peter Gorman asked. "Naw."

"He's mean enough," Jackson pointed out.

"Yeah, but he's not smart enough," Sheriff West asserted.

"What about Billy Rawlins?" Martin Pilgrim asked. "I hear he was mean enough to kill his own mother.''

"I suspect that's true enough," the sheriff said.

"That," Hunter said, pointing to one of the skulls, "is Billy Rawlins.''

The sheriff eyed him a minute, then looked down at the skull in question. "By damn—begging your pardon, Miss Bess— you're right. Look at that broken front tooth. Yep, that's Billy Rawlins, all right. And until I have reason to think otherwise, I'm working under the assumption that Ned Rawlins killed all of them and kept the money for himself.''

"What about the fifth man?" Bess ventured.

The sheriff shrugged. "He's the wild card in the bunch. We don't know who he is or why he didn't ride with them.''

"An inside man?" Hunter suggested.

The sheriff frowned. "Could be. But inside where? They've hit banks and stages all over the southern half of the territory. He'd have to have a bodacious amount of information at his disposal to be an inside man on more than a job or two. I'm

going to have to think on this. Yes, sir, wrinkles on top of
wrinkles, that's what we've got.''

The sheriff had to put his foot down when Martin Pilgrim
insisted they leave the bones scattered where they lay.

"They got off too damn easy as it is. They should have been
hanged,'' Pilgrim argued. ''Slowly, so they'd have time to
think about what they've done. Time to be afraid, like my
brother was afraid when they shot him.''

"Martin," the sheriff said. ''I know just how you feel, son,
and if you were on your own, I'd say maybe you've got the
right of it. But the Huerfano County Sheriff's posse doesn't
ride around leaving dead bodies—or parts thereof—lying out
on the ground. Godfrey's right. We're going to bury them. You
don't have to help.''

Martin Pilgrim did not help.

Bess watched it all, the argument, the digging of the grave,
the rather haphazard way the bones were tossed into the single
hole in the ground, with a detachment that both bothered Hunter,
and relieved him.

He was relieved that she wasn't upset by the sight of the
remains, or the argument over whether or not to bury them.
But the Bess he knew ... well, to be honest, he didn't know
how the old Bess would have reacted. On the one hand, she
was so softhearted that she would have been appalled at the
idea of bears and mountain lions ripping apart a man's body—
even if the man was already dead. On the other, these were
two of the men who had kidnapped and abused her. The Bess
before him now seemed stronger than before. Maybe he
expected her to be glad the men were dead.

And maybe, he thought, resigned, he should quit trying to
predict how she would react to things.

As for Bess, she was mildly surprised by her own reaction.

Or rather, her lack of one. Surely she should feel something, she thought. Sorrow? Gladness? Something.

Instead, she felt nothing. She'd been so elated over the small bits of memory she'd regained. But as the sun peaked and started its downward slide and the rest of her memory remained locked away from her, she'd felt her energy and her interest in what was going on around her wane.

There was nothing else for her in this place where she'd been held against her will.

And raped.

The reminder whispered viciously through her mind, robbing her of peace. She was grateful that the few small memories she had regained were not of what her captors had done to her. Please, God, may she never remember that.

If she did eventually remember it, would she forever be afraid to be around men? Would she cringe away from being touched?

She looked around the clearing at the men she had ridden here with. Men who had treated her with the utmost courtesy. Family men, officers of the law, businessmen. Hunter.

Would she have been able to make this trip if she remembered being savaged by thieving, murdering outlaws?

She could feel Hunter's gaze on her and turned slowly toward him. She could not imagine ever fearing his touch. She could not imagine spending a day without knowing he was near. Did she love him? She thought so. But was this her old love she was feeling, or something new?

He walked toward her and touched her cheek. "Are you all right?"

"Take me home, Hunter."

"I will, Blue Eyes. We'll be finished here before long, then we'll head back down."

Bess closed her eyes for a moment and shook her head. "No, not home. I need to see your cabin," she told him. "I need to go back to where it started. Maybe then I'll remember. I need to remember, Hunter. I need to remember so I can put it behind me.''

"All right, Bess. I'll take you.''

Ned Rawlins was grateful—sort of—to his little brother Billy, and to Cecil and Woody, for helping him rob that bank so he could have all this money to ease his way when he got to Mexico. He figured he was in tall cotton now, and it would be taller still south of the border.

But first he needed a change of horses.

He had plenty of money, of course, to buy new horses, and he'd shaved off his beard, he reminded himself, rubbing a gloved hand along his clean cheek, which meant no one would recognize him. He had half a mind to ride right in to the livery at Walsenburg, bold as brass, and shell out the cash.

But he wouldn't do it. No, sir, he wouldn't.

It wasn't the money, it was the principle of the thing. Ned Rawlins had not paid cash money for a horse in nearly ten years. Where was the challenge in that? No, it would be much more fun to steal one. Or two, he figured, deciding he'd trail a packhorse to Mexico. Needed the extra horse to carry all his money, if nothing else, he thought, laughing out loud.

He knew it was just a trick his ears were playing on him when the laughter that echoed back sounded not like his own voice, but like the half-breed's. The dead half-breed who came after the girl.

Ned shook away the uneasiness that crawled along his skin every time he thought of those two—the woman he'd meant to kill and the man he'd killed but who hadn't died.

Maybe, he thought grimly, he'd just take himself a little ride back up that goddamn canyon to that cabin and finish the job right this time.

* * *

Hunter and Lopez had circled the clearing and met along the north side when they found the back trail that led east down off the shoulder of the mountain. It was a narrow, little-used game trail. Little used, except for some time in the recent past when a number of shod horses had traveled it.

The posse mounted up and took that trail. Hunter and Bess left the clearing by the same trail they'd taken to get there. It was the quickest way back down to the Huerfano Valley.

Bess wasn't sure how she managed to stay in the saddle until Hunter finally called a halt for the day. She was utterly drained.

He led them off the trail and into the trees to make camp. When he lifted her down from the saddle, Bess sagged against him. "Have I always been such a weakling?"

"A weakling?" Hunter couldn't seem to stop himself from taking advantage of the situation and wrapping his arms around her. He rubbed his hand up and down her back, cherishing the feel of her pressed against him. "You're no weakling, Blue Eyes. You're just not used to so much riding, that's all."

"All I want to do is collapse."

Hunter chuckled in sympathy. "Before you do that, you need to walk around some so you won't be too stiff to ride in the morning."

With a sigh, she straightened away from him and untied the bow that held her hat in place. "I may as well make myself useful and gather some firewood while I'm at it."

With great reluctance, Hunter let his arms fall away from her. Together they made quick work of setting up camp. Bess seemed to revive herself for a while, but once they had eaten, she folded her riding jacket, skirt, and petticoat neatly and, using them for a pillow, crawled between her blankets and fell asleep wearing her drawers and chemise. The night was mild, so she should be warm enough. But just in case, Hunter pulled one of his blankets from his bedroll and draped it over her.

For a long time, he sat on his remaining blanket two feet away from her and watched her sleep. He smiled briefly when he realized she hadn't worn a corset. He remembered her thanking him that first day for not putting it back on her when he'd changed her clothes.

He'd been surprised today when she'd remembered those few bits and pieces up at the cabin. He hadn't really thought . . .

Maybe, he admitted to himself, he'd hoped . . .

Ah, damn, how selfish could a man get? Had he really hoped she wouldn't remember anything?

Closing his eyes briefly, he called himself every foul name he could think of. This was her life he was talking about. He had tried more than once to imagine what it must be like to have no memories. No memories at all. To not remember his mother's smile, his father's big, booming laugh. To not remember Bess.

No, he could not wish such emptiness on her. He would take her to his cabin as he'd promised, and pray that it would help her regain more of her memory. If she remembered everything, and wanted nothing more to do with him when she recalled the way he'd treated her these past couple of years, it would be no more than he deserved.

At least, he thought fatalistically, he would have his memories of her, which was more than she had right now.

Deep in the night, Bess began to dream. It was an ugly dream, of hard hands, putrid breath, an evil leer. A gaping evil leer with a broken front tooth.

The hands hit her, grabbed at her, threw her to the ground. The breath gagged her. The leer paralyzed her with terror.

Then he was on her, this grinning, evil man. Billy. His name was Billy, and he called her name in Hunter's voice. She tried to scream, but it wouldn't come. She shoved and twisted and tried to dislodge him, but his weight easily held her down.

His hands were everywhere, pinching her, bruising her, tearing at her clothes. She tried again to scream, but the sound was locked in her throat. She prayed for a gun, a knife, any kind of weapon with which to defend herself, but there was no weapon. Only a hatpin. A puny, laughable hatpin.

She tried to scream again. It came out as a hoarse croak as she tore herself awake. But the nightmare continued. A dark shape loomed over her. Hands reached for her. Hunter's voice called her name.

"Bess. Come on, Blue Eyes, wake up. You're having a bad dream."

Ah, God, how cruel to hear Billy Rawlins speak in Hunter's voice!

"Come on, Blue Eyes, wake up."

Blue Eyes. Billy Rawlins wouldn't—

With a gasp, Bess sprang upright. "Hunter!" She threw herself into his arms. "Oh, God, Hunter." Violent tremors, part remembered fear, part relief, shook her. She buried her face against Hunter's neck and held him tight. "It's you, it's you."

"It's me, Blue Eyes. I've got you. You're safe."

Oh, but his arms were warm and secure. Yes. She was safe. This was Hunter.

"It was only a dream," he murmured. "Just a dream."

"No," she said with a gasp, pushing back enough to see the shadow that she knew was his face, but not far enough to break his hold. "Not a dream." Lord, her heart was still racing, her breath still coming in short pants. "It was Billy. Billy Rawlins."

Hunter bit back a curse. "You dreamed about Billy Rawlins?" He knew he shouldn't have let her go to that damn cabin. She'd seen the skull and heard them talk about Billy, and it had given her nightmares.

"Yes," she said. Then, "No. It wasn't a dream, it was a memory. It was real. It happened."

Hunter smoothed a thick strand of hair from her face and

pushed it over her shoulder. His hand shook slightly. He forced himself to ask, "What happened, Blue Eyes? What makes you think it was real and not just a nightmare?"

"Because I remember it," she said earnestly. "Not the dream. I mean, yes, I remember the dream, but I remember what happened on the trail, too. He . . . he hit me, knocked me down." She touched a hand to the spot on her cheek where the bruise had been.

It was all Hunter could do to keep from swearing out loud. He wished in that instant that Billy Rawlins was still alive so he could tear him apart with his bare hands and leave his bones scattered just the way they'd found them today.

"We struggled, but he was too heavy for me to push away."

Rape? Was that what she remembered? Damn, Hunter didn't want to hear this. But she needed to tell it, so he clenched his jaw and let her talk while he kept his arms around her.

"His hands . . . God, they were everywhere," she cried as a shudder ripped through her.

"Bess—"

"I couldn't fight him off. I remember thinking, if only I had a gun, or a knife. But all I had was a hatpin."

When she fell silent, Hunter knew that she needed to get the rest of it out before it poisoned her. "Is that when he forced himself on you?"

Bess sniffed. "I don't know. That's all I remember. Except I remember pulling out my hatpin and thinking how puny it was. But it was all I had."

Hunter smiled to himself grimly. "Where were you? Do you remember where you were when this happened?"

She shook her head and sniffed again. "No. On the ground. In the dirt."

"Not at the cabin?"

"I don't . . . no. No. It was out in the open, and there was a . . . a fire nearby."

Hunter brushed her cheek again, just to feel the satiny texture of her skin. It was damp from tears. "I don't know if you're really remembering, or if you just dreamed about the things you saw and heard today."

"No, it's real," she insisted. "The dream was distorted, like dreams are. But the memory—it's real, Hunter, I know it is."

"Okay," he said to soothe her. "Okay. Then if it's real, it happened on the trail, where they camped that first night."

"The spot you showed us? I stood right there and didn't remember a thing. And now, this. I know it's real. I can remember pulling the hatpin out of my hat. I didn't do that in my dream."

"And nobody ever told you that you'd been wearing a hat when they took you," he realized aloud. She hadn't worn a hat or been around anyone who had since he found her and brought her home, until this trip. But the hat she wore yesterday and today had ties. No hatpin. She would have no reason to dream of one.

He'd never given her ruined hat back to her. The torn and bloody dress had been a bad enough, vivid enough reminder of her ordeal. He'd kept the hat stuffed in his other saddlebag and took it home with him when he'd ridden there the day after he got her home. No one had ever mentioned it, so neither had he. So, he thought, this must be a true memory.

"Have you remembered anything else?" he asked.

"No." She sighed and leaned against him. "I wish I could pick which things to remember and which to forget. I would choose to remember something more pleasant than trying to defend my honor with something so pathetic as a hatpin."

Hunter debated with himself for a moment, but remembered his vow to always tell her the truth and let her make her own decisions, let her cope with the things she needed to cope with. He knew, then, that he needed to tell her.

"Blue Eyes, I don't know how much it helped, but I think you put that hatpin to good use."

"What makes you say that?"

"Because I found it."

She leaned back to see his face, what she could see of it in the dark. "You found my hatpin?"

"And your hat. At the campsite on the trail."

"The place where we stopped yesterday?"

"That's right. Your hat was torn and smashed and dirty. I found it in the scrub growth at the edge of the clearing. I found your hatpin on the ground. I . . . I saw the spot . . . the spot where what you remember happened. That's where I found the pin. I'd say you put it to good use. It had blood on it. It wasn't your blood, because you didn't have any holes." He found himself smiling, despite the grim subject. "You must have jabbed him a good one."

"I hope so," she said vehemently.

Hunter thought of the signs he'd read on the ground that day, of what he'd felt, the coldness that had settled in his heart when he realized she'd been reduced to defending herself with a meager hatpin.

"I was so proud of you when I found that pin with the blood on it. You didn't have much, but you kept your head and used what you had."

"For all the good it did me."

The desolation in her voice was almost more than he could stand. He pulled her onto his lap and held her close, pressing his lips against her hair.

Bess reveled in his embrace. This, *this* was what she wanted, what she needed. His arms around her, his warmth seeping into her. It felt so wonderful to be held by him.

"I wish," he whispered to her, "that I could take it away, Blue Eyes. The fear, the pain. You haven't remembered the worst of it yet, but I know you think about it. I know it hurts you. I would take away the hurt if I knew how."

"Kiss me, Hunter," she whispered, tilting her face up to his. "Kiss me."

He hesitated, and for a moment she feared he would deny

her. Then his head lowered, and with so much tenderness that it made her throat ache and her eyes sting, he brushed his lips across hers.

Bess gasped at the exquisite touch, so light that she couldn't think of it as a kiss, but couldn't think beyond it at all. And then he was back, his lips settling on hers lightly at first, so lightly. "Oh, Hunter," she breathed, threading her fingers along his scalp. "You take my breath away."

Her words took his. If he'd thought about it, he might have feared that with this latest memory of hers, she might find the feel of a man's lips on hers disgusting. He was glad he hadn't taken the time to think. He stroked his hand down her bare arm and felt her soft skin rise in gooseflesh. "You're cold," he murmured.

"No," she whispered against his lips. "I'm not cold at all."

He kissed her again, harder this time, and felt his pulse leap. She met him fully and parted her lips for his tongue. He tasted her and couldn't stifle the low moan that rose from his chest. Man-Above, she was so sweet.

Sweet and generous, and she set his blood on fire. It had been so long since they had kissed. So damn long. That fast he wanted her, burned for her.

He told himself to ease away, that she had only asked for a kiss, not everything else he wanted to give her. But he ignored his own warning and deepened the kiss, teasing her tongue with his and feeling his heart stop when she returned the favor.

By the time he came up for air, his breath was coming hard and fast, and his heart was pounding. He kissed her jaw, her cheek, her closed eyelids.

"You make me feel all hot and jittery inside," she confessed, turning her face up to give him better access. "Why did you stop?"

"Because," he said, working his way down to her neck, "I was about to get carried away."

"I don't care," she whispered fiercely. "I want you to get carried away."

Hunter groaned and buried his lips against her neck. "Bess, I—"

"Tonight I remembered a man's weight pressing me into the ground," she told him. "And it's the wrong man. Take that memory away, Hunter. Let me remember your weight on me, your hands on me. You wanted me once, Hunter. Can't you want me again?"

"I didn't want you once," he said fiercely. "I want you always. I want you so much right this minute that I don't trust myself to be gentle with you, and you need to be loved gently."

With her fingers threaded through his hair again, she raised his head and brushed her lips across his. "If you kiss me again the way you did a minute ago, I won't want you to be gentle."

Her words shot through him like lightning, leaving white heat in their path. He wished he could see her face. Her eyes. Her eyes would tell him the truth. Did she really want him, or did she only want to wipe out the memory of Billy Rawlins?

"Don't," she begged him. "Don't think about the other, because I'm not."

"Ah, Bess." He took her hand in his and pressed his lips against her palm. He wasn't sure how to interpret her quiver of response, until his name left her lips on a sigh.

She does want me, he thought with wonder. For the first time in more than two years—since that night beneath the trees when he'd nearly taken her—she wanted him.

She had wanted him that night, at least in the beginning. And he knew he would drive himself crazy trying to figure out what had killed the fire in her. But it was back now, that fire. If it was selfish of him to bask in it before she regained her memory, then so be it. He was a selfish son of a bitch. He didn't care. He only cared that she wanted him.

"Love me, Hunter. Please love me."

"Yes." He brushed his lips across hers once, twice. "I do.

I will.'' And three times. ''I am.'' And then he buried his lips against hers and took her gently down until they lay on their sides on the blanket. She might say she wanted to feel his weight on her, but there was every likelihood, in his mind, that if he moved too fast she might forget it was him and panic. And that would kill him.

So he took his time, with long, slow kisses. She responded openly and honestly, kissing him back, stealing his breath, making him ache to bury himself deep inside her.

He wouldn't be the first, but he would be the first she remembered. And, Man-Above willing, he would be the last man to ever love her, because he didn't plan on ever letting go of her again. He would hold on to her forever, if she would only let him. If, when her full memory returned, she still wanted him.

Don't think about that.

No, he couldn't think about it. Not just now, when she was so soft and pliant in his arms, so sweet and hot against his lips. The urge to rush filled him, then ebbed away. He'd waited so long for this moment—years. Now that it was here, he could take his time, savor every moment, every touch, every taste.

He raised himself up on one elbow, keeping his weight off her while he leaned over her. ''I want to touch you, but I don't want to do anything—''

She halted his words in his throat by the simple act of taking his free hand in hers and pressing it to her breast. ''Yes,'' she whispered. ''Touch me. Anywhere you want. Everywhere. Your hands . . . God, I love your hands, Hunter. They're so strong, yet gentle. When you touch me, I feel safe, I feel cared for.''

Hunter cupped her breast and gently squeezed. ''You are safe, always safe with me. And I will care for you as long as you'll let me, Blue Eyes.''

When he kissed her this time, Bess felt her entire body tingle, head to toe, inside and out.

This, she thought with wonder, was what it felt like to be wanted, cherished.

His thumb rubbed across her nipple, shooting fire to her core. And she stopped thinking. She might have cried out in sheer pleasure, but she wasn't sure, didn't care. She only cared that he not stop, that he never stop.

Then he was touching her everywhere, it seemed, everywhere at once as he kissed his way along her jaw, down to her neck. Lower.

Was that moan his, or hers?

What did it matter? His gentle, clever fingers traced down to her belly and back, and cool night air touched her skin from waist to neck. Then his mouth was there, trailing hot, moist kisses down the middle of her chest to her navel, where his tongue dipped in and had the amazing effect of making her back arch clear off the ground.

She had barely caught her breath when he kissed his way up again, to the spot between her breasts, then up one slope. His hot breath teased across her nipple. She could all but feel him kissing her there, yet he stopped just short. Instinct told her she wanted what he was about to give her, wanted it desperately.

And then he gave it. His lips, his tongue, his teeth. They sipped and tugged and scraped and shot fire to that secret place between her thighs. She cried out his name and used both hands to press his head to her harder, to make sure he never, ever left.

Her response had Hunter's blood roaring in his ears. She was so willing, so eager, her nipple so hard against his tongue, the skin around it so silky soft, he had trouble remembering that he wanted to go slowly and savor each moment.

But he wanted to savor her, because no one else ever had. He wanted this to be as different from what had happened to her as day from night, so that when she remembered, she would remember him. Only him.

Touching and kissing, he made his way across her body, and

down, along arms and legs, peeling clothing out of his way as he went. Tasting, touching, wishing he could see her, but seeing her in his mind's eye, creamy pale skin soft over sleek, feminine curves.

Something tugged on his shirt, and it took him a moment, involved as he was, kissing his way up the outside of one thigh, to realize it was Bess who was tugging. With a high sound of frustration, she pulled his shirt free of his pants. With a warm, tantalizing sound of satisfaction, she ran her hands up beneath the shirt.

Hunter shivered at her touch. And he smiled. There was nothing shy or tentative about the way her hands explored his back. They felt greedy against his flesh. Possessive. He reveled in it.

He left her only long enough to whip off his shirt.

"Oh," she whispered, reaching for him. "Yes."

But Hunter didn't just lean down again. It was time to take that next step. Slowly, in case she objected, he slid one leg over hers and pulled her close. When she reached her arms around his ribs and moved her knee aside, he slipped into the cradle of her thighs and slowly let himself down.

When their bare bellies met, Bess sucked in her breath and held it, the sensation was so exquisite. He was so warm, so sleek. "More," she whispered, urging him down onto her. When his chest settled on hers, her breath trickled out, and she didn't care if she ever regained it. Glorious. That was the only word she could think of. His weight, his heat. She felt him all along her, from her feet to her shoulders. Never had anything felt so right, with his heart pressed against hers.

"Oh," she whispered again. "Oh . . . yes."

Hunter felt her welcome him with her body, her heart, and he was humbled. She was his. If her memory later returned and she changed her mind . . .

He wouldn't think of it. Couldn't. Right now she was his. It was enough. He would make it enough.

She trembled beneath him, and he knew it for eagerness. He trembled in response and crushed her mouth with his. Her hands were everywhere, fast and greedy. He wanted to shout with joy. No one had stolen her passion. It was there, inside her, and it was his.

She moved beneath him with a tiny cry of frustration. When she raised her knees beside his hips and arched against his hardness, fire shot through him. No woman had ever been so eagerly generous with him. No woman had ever responded so honestly, letting him know exactly what she wanted, even if she wasn't sure herself just what that was.

With a small whimper, she pushed at the waist of his pants. "Off," she whispered. "Take them off."

"Are you sure, Bess? You can still change your mind." *Please don't change your mind.*

She reached for the fastenings. "Off."

In seconds he had shucked his pants. Lying beside her with a knee across her near leg, he stroked a hand up one thigh, down the other. The skin there was as silky and sleek as a baby's. "You're so soft. I can't get enough of touching you."

Bess quivered, at his words, at his touch. Cool night air kissed her skin, but where he touched, she burned. When he nudged her thighs apart with his hand, her heart rose to her throat and fluttered there like a trapped butterfly.

And then his hand was there, at that hot, secret place between her legs. He was touching her there, making her burn, making her hips move of their own accord, and surely no man had ever touched her like this. Never could she have forgotten this singing in her blood, this soaring of her spirit.

She felt him probe at the entrance to her body. Felt her own moisture. Heard his low growl of satisfaction and eagerness. And suddenly she was filled with the power of her womanhood. Never could she have imagined the surge in her blood, the sheer headiness of it. She gasped for breath, and his name spilled from her heart.

When he positioned his hips between her thighs, she reached a new level of tension, part nerves, part anticipation. Without conscious thought, she spread her legs wider and raised her knees, the better to cradle him, the closer to hold him. The nearer to bring him to the desperate throbbing that only he could ease.

And then he was there, not with his hand but with that part of him that made his body so very different, so gloriously different from hers. Yes. Yes. She wanted this, needed it, needed to be joined to him.

The discomfort surprised her, then grew sharply worse. Instinctively she tried to back away from the pain.

Above her, shock held Hunter motionless and locked the breath in his throat. "Ah, damn, Bess."

"What's wrong?"

He forced a breath past his throat, then another. He knew, Man-Above, he knew he should pull away, but he couldn't move. "They didn't . . . Blue Eyes, they didn't rape you."

"They . . . but . . . Hunter?"

"It hurts, doesn't it?"

She swallowed audibly. "A . . . little. But I don't care."

"It hurts because you're still a virgin. If you want to stay that way, tell me now, Blue Eyes. Tell me now."

CHAPTER SEVENTEEN

The sky overhead was turning from black to gray. Bess could almost make out the features of Hunter's face. But she didn't need to see them. They were forever etched in her soul. This was right, being with him this way. Despite the pain, there was pleasure, too, a pleasure greater than any she had ever known.

In answer to his question, she gripped his hips in her hands and thrust her hips upward, impaling herself. The pain spiked, but she didn't care. He was inside her, a part of her. Forever.

Once again shock riveted Hunter in place. "Bess . . ." A giant fist squeezed around his heart.

She was in pain, he knew. He struggled to hold himself still when every nerve in his body screamed at him to move, to thrust. But he resisted, pulling control from some deep part inside himself that he hadn't known existed. A part that belonged only to Bess. Only to his Blue Eyes.

Gradually he felt her tension ease. "Better?" he whispered.

Her hips moved slightly, drawing a hiss of violent need from him.

"Yes," she whispered back. She moved her hips again. "Oh . . . yes."

Slowly, so slowly, he started to move.

This time it was Bess who hissed in need. The pain ebbed and pleasure returned, stunning her with its intensity. Her breath came in gasps as the pleasure mounted, the tension inside her twisting tighter and tighter until she feared she would simply explode into a million pieces right there in his arms.

And then she did. Lights flashed behind her eyes. Her body convulsed. She cried out Hunter's name.

Whatever control Hunter might still have had by then dissolved, drowned in her hot, tight depths. With a shout of his own, he followed her over the edge straight into oblivion.

It was the sobs shaking her that broke through Hunter's daze of aftermath. "Bess, Bess." He held her tight and kissed her wet cheeks, her swollen lips. "Bess, I'm sorry. Man-Above, I'm sorry." She'd been a virgin. He'd hurt her. He wanted to die of guilt for taking her.

"No!" She clutched him tightly in her arms. "Please," she managed between sobs. "Please don't be sorry. I . . . you . . . It was . . . so overwhelming, th-that's all. So . . . I didn't know. I didn't know anything could be so . . . wonderful."

Guilt stood no chance against her words. He wanted to shout with pure, male cockiness from the top of Greenhorn Mountain. Instead, he held her close and prayed, giving thanks that she had not been violated at the hands of her kidnappers.

He held her until her tears quieted. Held her while the sky lit with the first rosy hint of dawn. Then, reluctantly, he eased away. "We have to get going."

She placed her hand over the steady beat of his heart. "You're not sorry, are you?"

Hunter smiled. "I think I'm supposed to be asking you that question."

"But you know my answer."

"Aye. And no, Blue Eyes, I could never be sorry. I'm only sorry that your first time was not in a soft bed with smooth sheets, instead of on the cold, hard ground."

"If you want the truth," she said, her eyes glowing with remembered passion, "I don't think I would have noticed the difference."

"Careful," he said, only half teasing. "My ego will swell, and so will something else, and we'll be here in these blankets all day."

Bess laughed with delight, sliding her arms around his shoulders. "Would that be so terrible?"

"Only when some prospector, or worse yet, a bear, comes ambling along and stumbles across us."

"Oh, my." Smiling, she fluttered her lashes. "You are so romantic."

"And you," he said, planting a quick kiss on her lips, "are so greedy to want more."

Bess searched his face, traced a finger along his smiling lips. "Is that bad?"

Something dark and hot sparked in his gray eyes. "It's humbling. It's . . . it makes me admit that I'm just as greedy for you, if not more so. Bad? Oh, Blue Eyes, between you and me there is only good."

Bess felt as if her heart were filled with millions of tiny bubbles constantly bursting in sheer happiness and sending warm, tingling sensations clear to her fingers and toes, and to that secret place where Hunter had joined their bodies together as one. She wanted to fling her arms wide and sing out for all the world to hear.

Bess Dulaney loves Hunter MacDougall!

She managed to refrain from singing, but she could not contain a burst of delighted laughter.

Riding beside her as they left the foothills and reached level ground, Hunter smiled. "Something funny, Miss Dulaney?"

"Not funny—wonderful. I don't believe I've ever been so happy. Thanks to you." She laughed again, even while she blushed at her own confession. "It's just about the grandest day imaginable."

Aye, he thought to himself. It was a grand day. The sun was warm, the grass was green, and Bess Dulaney was his woman. And if she didn't quit looking at him as if she wanted to gobble him up, he was going to be damned uncomfortable in the saddle.

Suddenly he was in a hurry to reach the cabin. There he could carry her inside and close the door. The family didn't know when to expect them back at the ranch. One night at the cabin wouldn't cause any alarm. He wanted her all to himself for one more night before he took her home.

He nudged his horse into a gallop, and Bess urged her horse forward to keep pace. They crossed the Huerfano about an hour before noon and followed upstream the creek that ran the length of the canyon where Hunter's cabin sat.

At the mouth of the canyon, Bess reined in. Hunter stopped and turned back to her. "What's wrong?"

She shook her head and smiled. "Nothing. I just want to look at the place you chose to live."

Hunter braced his hands on the saddle horn and shifted his weight. The creak of the saddle was a familiar song in his ears. It was good land that they looked upon. Water all year, thick grass, trees along the creek and around the spring that bubbled up sweet and pure behind the cabin. Except for the open mouth, it was a natural enclosure, a good place to raise horses. A good place for a man to build something. A ranch. A family, he thought, looking at Bess and trying to judge her reaction.

Her smile gladdened him.

"Hunter, it's beautiful. Perfect. Look! Are those your horses?"

About a half mile up, half-a-dozen mustangs broke from a

stand of juniper and raced across the open ground, circling the cabin, the barn, the corrals, running for the sheer joy of feeling the wind in their faces.

"Aye," he said, his voice and his heart filled with satisfaction.

Bess forgot that her reason for coming here was to try to regain more of her memory. She was caught up with the knowledge that this was Hunter's land, Hunter's home. "I want to see it. I want to see all of it."

"Well, come on, then."

Bess kicked her horse into a gallop. Laughter trailed in her wake. "I'll race you to the barn!"

"Hey," he cried, urging his horse to catch up. "You cheated."

They were fifty yards from the barn when the first shot rang out. Hunter heard a slight buzz as the bullet whizzed past his head.

Shit!

Startled, Bess drew in on her reins.

"No!" Hunter bellowed. "Get to the barn! Around the side! Go! Go!" He'd closed the big double doors, so they couldn't just ride right in, but the shooter was up on the east rim of the canyon, and the small door was on the west side of the barn. He could get Bess to shelter there.

Without question, Bess followed his orders and raced toward the back side of the barn. With his heart in his throat and his eyes glued to her, Hunter followed, flinching as another shot rang out, then another. Off to his right, dust kicked up where a bullet struck the ground. As they slowed to round the corner of the barn, a bullet struck the building beside Hunter's head.

Son of a bitch. Who? Why? Rawlins?

With the bulk of the barn shielding them from the gunman, Hunter leaped from his horse and jerked Bess down from her saddle. "Are you all right?" he demanded.

Breathless, she ran her hands over his shoulders, down his arms. "Yes. You?"

"I'm not hit. Quick. Inside." He opened the back door of the barn and gave her a none-too-gentle shove, then gathered the reins of her horse and his and pulled the animals inside with them. Inside he dropped the bar across the door. "I want you in the tack room," he told her.

Her jaw stiffened. "Only if that's where you're going to be."

"I'll be in the hayloft. I might be able to get a shot off at him through the hay doors up there."

"Do you think it's him? Rawlins?"

"I don't know. I can't imagine anybody else mad enough to shoot me who wouldn't care about hitting you. Go." His shove was gentler this time, but firm enough to get her going.

She didn't like it, no sir, she didn't, hiding in the tack room while Hunter was up there taking a chance on getting shot. But Bess had learned at an early age that if a woman couldn't help in the fight, she needed to stay out of her man's way and let him get it over with.

She paused and stared at the tack room door she had just closed behind her. How in the hell, she wondered, did she know that? Where would she have learned such a thing?

From overhead at the front of the barn, she heard Hunter fire off a round from the rifle he'd carried in a scabbard on his saddle. The sound of the shot wiped the trivial question of where she'd learned to stand back and let a man fight straight out of her mind. Instead, she prayed, fast and furiously, for Hunter's safety.

Tucked away in the enclosed room at the back of the barn, she had no fear for her own safety. But for Hunter to return fire, he had to have opened the hay doors. Which meant he could be hit.

Another shot struck the front of the barn. Hunter fired again.

"Dear God, keep him safe."

Another shot. A curse from Hunter.

The sudden vision of Hunter being struck in the chest by a bullet paralyzed her. She could see it so plainly. Blood blossoming obscenely across his shirt. His eyes, wide and startled.

"No," she moaned. "No, no, no." She couldn't hide here in safety while he might be hurt. She wrenched open the tack room door and raced up the ladder to the hayloft, crying his name with every step. "Hunter! Hunter! Hunter!"

"Bess!" He rose from his crouched position beside the open hay door and rushed to her, grabbing her by the upper arms and holding her back. "What is it? Are you hit? What's wrong?"

"Oh, God." Frantic, she ran her hands over the front of his shirt. "You're all right? You're not shot?"

"I'm fine. Just mad. He's gone. I saw him ride off. I got off one last shot," he said, frowning over his shoulder at the hay doors. "But I missed the bastard."

"I thought you were hit." Bess closed her eyes and tried to catch her breath. "I saw it so clearly. I . . . oh, God." She collapsed against his chest. "I pictured you shot, and I couldn't . . . couldn't stay down there and hide. I had to know."

Hunter wrapped his arms around her and held her close. "I'm all right, Blue Eyes. I'm fine." But he wondered. "Tell me what you saw when you thought I was shot."

A deep shudder tore through her. "It was horrible. The bullet . . . it hit you in the chest. There was blood all over your shirt. And then you fell. Face down. In the mud." She pushed back and frowned up at him. "It was raining. Why would I imagine . . ." Her words trailed off; her eyes widened. "It wasn't my imagination," she cried. "He shot you, didn't he? When he took me, he shot you! Oh, Hunter!"

"Shh. It's all right, Bess. I'm all right."

"It's true, isn't it? It wasn't my imagination, it was a memory. I thought you were dead. That's why I felt such emptiness. I thought you were dead. But . . ." With hands that trembled, she fumbled with the buttons on his shirt, peeling back the fabric to see his flesh. There wasn't a mark on it. "I don't understand."

"Winter Fawn," was all he said.

Bess blinked up at him.

"After they took you, I came to and managed to get on my horse—sort of—and make it to the ranch. Winter Fawn did for me what she did for your scalp wound."

Bess closed her eyes and leaned against his chest again, her hands clutching at his shoulders. "Thank God for her. Remind me to thank her. I think I'll kiss her feet."

Hunter chuckled. "So, does this mean maybe you like me a little?"

Bess's smile turned poignant. "Oh, Hunter." She smoothed a hand along his jaw. "Yes, I like you. But more than that, I love you. I love you so much."

"Bess . . ."

"I know you're worried that once I remember our past, I'll change my mind. But I won't, Hunter. I don't think I could if I tried. Whatever happened before . . . I don't think I was very smart, or very wise, or even very adult. If that's true, I'm different now. I won't stop loving you just because I remember it. I won't stop loving you if I never remember."

Hunter pulled her close and closed his eyes. "I don't deserve you."

As much as Hunter wanted Bess to himself for one more night—this time indoors, with a bed—he refused to chance that the gunman might come back. When he told her he was taking her back to the ranch, she balked.

"Dammit, Bess, I promised to keep you safe."

They were inside the cabin—he'd allowed her that much, a look around to see if anything would jog her memory. Sunlight streamed in through the open door, highlighting, to Hunter's mind, the terrible meagerness of the place he called home.

"We're both safe inside these walls, aren't we?"

"Aye, if we don't mind getting pinned down in here. One man up on the rim could keep us trapped in here for as long as he could stay awake. Two men could keep us pinned down forever." He knew he was acting like a hen with one chick. If whoever had shot at them was of a mind to keep them pinned down, he had his chance, and chose to leave. But the thought of Bess in danger was crippling.

"You mean . . . we could be trapped here?" She smoothed a hand up his chest and inside his shirt, which was still unbuttoned. "Alone?" She leaned into him and teased his chin with her lips. "For days?"

"Well, hell." He pushed the door shut, dropped the bar down, and lowered his lips to hers. "If you're going to nag me to death." He kissed her. Slowly, softly at first, until remembered fear for her safety pricked his mind. Then he devoured her. The thought of a bullet striking her tender flesh made him weak.

He would never be able to concentrate solely on her, on loving her, until he satisfied himself that the shooter was well and truly gone. It took considerable effort to pull himself away from her, when all he wanted to do was carry her to his bed and lose himself in her.

"Will you stay inside with the door and windows barred while I have a look up on the rim to make sure he really left?"

"What are my other choices?"

"We wait in here until dark and then slip out and head for the ranch."

She looped her hands behind his neck and smiled. "Either way, I've got you."

"Aye, but if I satisfy myself that he's gone, you can have your wicked way with me all night long."

"Ach, then wot are ye doin' standin' here? Get yerself up on yon rim and be checkin'. And be fair quick about it, laddie."

His grin nearly split his cheeks. "Yes, ma'am," he said in a Southern drawl that would have done Aunt Gussie proud.

Hunter didn't purposely stay gone so long that when he returned, the anticipation had risen to a level that had them falling into each other's arms, but that was the effect of his careful search for the gunman who'd fired at them.

He'd found tracks, and plenty of them. One man, with the horse he was riding and either a horse carrying another man— a heavy man—or a pack-laden horse, loaded down with a cache of gold coins.

Hunter was betting on the coins. Double eagles, to be exact. According to the sheriff, there was still several thousand dollars unrecovered from the holdup. Hunter's gut told him that Ned Rawlins now had all that money, and it was Ned Rawlins who'd shot at him and Bess. There simply was no one else who would go to the trouble to shoot at them. As far as Hunter knew, he hadn't made any other enemies lately, and who but Rawlins would want to harm Bess?

No one.

But why, once he had them pinned down in the barn, had he given up and ridden away?

Ned Rawlins knew what his trouble was. He was bored. He'd made up his mind to swap his horses for fresh ones, he'd shaved off his beard, and he planned on heading to Mexico. He'd gone after the half-breed and the girl because it seemed like the thing to do. But hell, even his own mama wouldn't recognize him without his beard, so who cared if the breed and the girl lived to tell their tale?

He could have lain there on that goddamn canyon rim for a week of Sundays and not flushed them out of that barn. They obviously had a back way in and out. If the breed was half as smart at Ned thought he was, he'd slip that girl out of there come dark and get clean away.

At least he had put a scare into them, by God. He chuckled to himself, remembering the way they'd lit out for the back side of that barn when he'd opened fire.

He was a little disgusted with himself for missing his targets, but he consoled himself with the fact that even the best marksmen—which he knew he was not—didn't always hit a moving target at that range.

And where was the challenge of shooting fish in a barrel? Or people in a barn, even if they did have a chance to get away from him?

No, Ned was bored, all right. He needed a bigger challenge than that. But in addition to a challenge, what Ned really wanted was a good laugh. He wanted a laugh at the expense of the city of Walsenburg. That's where all this damn trouble came from. If that stupid guard hadn't decided to play hero and collect the reward on the infamous Rawlins gang, none of this would have happened.

Ned wanted to thumb his nose at the whole damn town in a way that would make them cringe at their own stupidity.

A slow grin came over his face. Yes, sir, he was starting to feel like his old self again, back when it was just him and Cecil, before J.T., before they'd brought Woody and Billy in with them.

Laughter, low and devious, trailed behind him as he rode toward his new target. He knew what he was going to do, by damn.

It would be a challenge, a risk, but a fool-proof one. It would damn sure be fun. And it would make the good folks of Walsenburg howl in humiliation.

Then he'd see about Mexico.

* * *

To be on the safe side, Hunter put his and Bess's horses in the barn rather than turn them out to graze. He wanted them nearby where he could get to them in a hurry if need be.

Not that he thought there would be a need. Rawlins—or whoever—was gone. Of that Hunter was certain.

As he put out grain and pumped water for the horses, he couldn't keep from glancing over his shoulder toward the cabin.

Bess had heard him return and stood leaning in the open doorway, watching him. He could feel her eyes on him, could feel the pull of her as if she were a flame and he the moth—helpless and not caring, as long as he could reach the flame. As long as he could reach his destiny.

He took his time, letting the need, the anticipation build, savoring it. Finally, when he'd done everything he needed to do at the barn, he turned toward the cabin. For a long moment, he stood there outside the barn, just looking at her, this woman who owned his heart.

She slowly straightened away from the jamb in such a way as to make his heart pound. She had taken off her jacket, and stood in her shirtwaist and riding skirt. He could see the rise and fall of her breasts as they pressed against the thin, white fabric of her blouse with each breath she took. With graceful movements, she reached up and pulled the pins from her hair, letting it tumble across her shoulders and down her back, her gaze never leaving his. From twenty yards away, he swore he could see the invitation in her eyes.

She had asked him to love her, and had given him her innocence. They were bound to each other now. She held him more surely in the palm of her hand than any man had ever been held by a woman. With strong, certain steps, he started toward her. By the time he reached her, his shirt was off and wadded in his hand. He didn't even remember removing it.

But Bess remembered. It was a sight she would never forget.

The sun streaming down, striking bronze highlights in his long, black hair. The way his hand tugged the tail of his shirt free of his pants while his eyes devoured her. Watching him whip the shirt off over his head and ball it up in one hand. The gleam of his dark golden arms. His chest, sleek, hairless, muscles flexing and bunching with each stride as he neared her.

By the time he reached her, she was breathless with the need to touch his sun-warmed flesh. But when he stepped up to her and she saw his eyes, she backed away, suffering a sudden attack of nerves. Had those gray eyes lit with such fierce intent last night, when it was too dark for her to see?

Oh, my. She took another step back and clasped her hands at her waist, suddenly unsure of herself and her ability to answer the challenge of a man whose virility threatened to overwhelm her.

He stopped just inside the door, flexing his fingers around the shirt still bunched in his fist. His gaze darted around the room and lit on the bed. "You've been busy."

She swallowed, uncertainty building in her stomach. "It was a mess." The blankets had been thrown aside and the top sheet had been in shreds. She'd found a replacement in the trunk at the foot of the bed. It had been something useful to do while waiting for him.

Now he turned away and closed and barred the door. The room was dark then, the only light being the thin cracks seeping in around the shutters.

He stepped around her. She skittered away, then scolded herself for a fool. He opened the shutters of the window in the back wall. Sunlight streamed in across the bed.

Before turning back to her, he took off his gun belt and placed it on the trunk at the foot of the bed. Then he turned and she saw the heat of passion simmer in his eyes.

She took another small step backward.

"You back away from me. Have you changed your mind?"

Changed her mind? Not want him? Not want to touch him

and taste him and feel his touch on her? Dear God. "No," she whispered, unclasping her hands and reaching for him. "Never."

When her small, pale hands touched his chest, Hunter tilted his head back and closed his eyes, the better to savor her touch. Beneath her fingers, his flesh quivered. His heart pounded. Then he was reaching for her, pulling her to him, devouring her mouth with his. Lifting her in his arms and carrying her to the bed.

There he stood her on her feet and eased away. "I want to see you. I want to see all of you."

Bess felt herself blush at the thought of standing before him naked. Then, when she thought of him doing the same, of being able to see him, all of him, in the daylight, to know him in a way that their joining last night had not permitted, a new heat surged through her.

She had chosen clothes for this trip that she could get in and out of without help. Now she was doubly glad, because she wanted to do this for him. She waited as he turned down the blanket on the bed to reveal the clean white sheets she'd just put on. When he turned back to her, she reached for the buttons on the front of her blouse, her hands, and her gaze, steady.

Hunter's mind shut down. Her nimble fingers made short work of the buttons, revealing the white camisole underneath. She pulled the tail of the blouse free, then removed it. She drove him crazy by carefully folding it and placing it on top of his gun. Then she unfastened the waist of her riding skirt and stepped out of it, again folding the garment and placing it atop her blouse. Her petticoat followed, and with each layer of clothing she removed, his breath came faster. When she reached for the buttons of her camisole, her cheeks pinkened, and he lost his battle.

He brushed her hands away. "Let me do this one." His

ingers weren't as steady as hers had been, but they got the job
done. Leaning down, he pressed a kiss to her collarbone, then
trailed his mouth down her center, where the camisole parted,
slipping the garment down her arms as he went. On his knees
before her, he leaned and placed the camisole atop her other
clothes. Not for his life would he toss something to the dirt
floor that she wore next to such precious skin.

When his lips met the waist of her drawers he leaned back
to look at her for the first time in the light of day. He skimmed
his hands up the creamy pale skin over her ribs to cup breasts
made to fit his hand. "You are so damn beautiful. You take
my breath, Bess."

His words made her dizzy with pride and pleasure. She
swayed and braced a hand on his shoulder to steady herself.
The feel of his warm skin beneath her hand distracted her from
any shyness that might have lingered. "Your skin is so smooth,
so warm."

He pressed his cheek against her abdomen and spread his
hands across her back. "I love it when you touch me."

She scarcely noticed when he untied the tapes of her drawers.
He eased them down to her knees, then sat her on the side of
the bed before taking them all the way off and adding them to
the growing pile on his trunk.

Then he stood and went to the bootjack in the corner and
took off his boots. But he never took his gaze off her face. She
felt warmed by his look. Her blood stirred, and in that secret
place between her legs, heat gathered and throbbed, readying
her for him. Waiting for him. Eager for him.

When he returned to her, he stripped off the rest of his clothes
and then stood there, letting her look her fill.

Oh, but he was glorious. A bronze, pagan warrior, and he
was hers. All of him, from his broad shoulders and muscular
arms, down his lean torso and the ridged muscles of his abdomen and his long, powerful legs. Even his feet were beautiful.

But it was that part of him that made men different from women that drew her gaze. Although she'd had a good idea what to expect, she'd never seen a naked man before. He was sleek and hard and . . . huge, she thought, remembering the feel of him inside her. When she touched him there, he jerked and sucked in his breath.

Her gaze flew to his face to find it contorted in pleasure, his eyes closed, neck arched.

Bess smiled. "You like my touch."

Hunter looked down at her hand curling gently around his erection and shuddered to keep from throwing her back on the bed and ramming himself into her. "I like your touch." He moved then, and took her down on the bed, stretching out to half cover her. "I would kill for it." He brought her hand back and placed it where she'd just had it, wrapping his own hand over hers and squeezing slightly. "I would die for it."

Then, because he couldn't stand any more without losing complete control, he took her hand away and held it above her head against the pillow.

"My turn now." He stroked a hand down the center of her chest and watched her skin quiver beneath his touch. Smiling, he trailed his fingers farther, farther, until he brushed the hair at the apex of her legs and felt her whole body vibrate in response.

"I want to watch your eyes when I touch you." And he did, holding those deep blue depths captive with his as he slipped his hand lower and cupped her.

Her eyes darkened and widened in response.

With one finger, he delved the secret folds at the core of her heat and watched as blue turned to flame.

He kissed her then, her mouth, her nose, her eyes. He'd never thought about how right it could be to love in the light of day, but this was perfect.

For Bess it was that and more. It was everything. He touched her everywhere, kissed her everywhere, numbing her mind with pleasure. She returned the favor, kissing every inch of his skin that she could reach.

Together they rolled over the bed, legs entwined, breaths mingling, hearts pounding to a primal rhythm. And then he moved between her legs and she opened for him, welcoming him home as he pushed his way inside and joined their bodies. They were no longer two people, but one. And it was glorious.

Everything inside her tightened, stretched, reaching for that pinnacle she now knew was there waiting for her, for him. For them. And when she reached it and everything inside her shattered with pleasure, she cried out Hunter's name and took him with her over the edge of the world.

They made love twice more before dark, and twice again before dawn. Each time that Hunter took her to that place where the world fell away, Bess fell more deeply in love with him.

Her world was perfect.

Until they were eating breakfast the next morning, Hunter wearing only his denims, Bess wearing only his shirt, and they heard hoofbeats pounding up the canyon.

Cursing, Hunter grabbed his rifle, slapped the shutters closed on the back window and cracked them open on the front one.

Then he swore again. "It's your brother."

They held him off long enough for the two of them to get dressed, but aside from any concerns for modesty, they might as well not have bothered. One look at the two of them, and Carson Dulaney knew precisely how they'd spent the night.

With narrowed eyes and clenched jaw, he glared at Hunter. "I trusted you."

Hunter stood straight and tall, just outside the cabin door, his own jaw clenched just as tightly as Carson's. "Trusted me to what?"

Carson's face turned red. "What'd you do, figure that since

the outlaws had already had her, you might as well, too? You son of a bitch.''

"Carson!" Bess had been standing just inside the cabin, because she had yet to put on her stockings and shoes and had hoped Carson wouldn't notice. Now it didn't matter. She flew to Hunter's side.

"Stay out of this, Bess," Carson ordered.

Bess nearly sputtered, so outraged was she. "The hell I will."

Carson's eyes widened. "Bess!"

"I was under the distinct impression that you were talking about me."

"It doesn't concern you, and you watch your language."

"It most definitely concerns me, and if I feel like swearing, I'll damn well swear, and you can go to blazes."

"Good God, man," Carson cried to Hunter. "What have you done to my sister?"

With her eyes narrowed, Bess folded her arms across her chest. "All of this brotherly concern is touching, Carson. Misplaced, but touching. What are you doing here, anyway?"

"I *thought* I was helping out a *friend*. I thought you were still with the posse, so I came to check on the horses."

"Thank you," Hunter said tersely.

"Don't mention it," Carson said, his voice dripping with sarcasm.

"Oh, this is ridiculous," Bess muttered. "Get down off that horse and come in for a cup of coffee."

"I'll get down, all right, but only long enough to saddle your horse, young lady. Then I'm taking you home."

Bess nearly sputtered again. "The hell you say."

"The hell I don't!" Carson bellowed.

"I go nowhere with someone who treats me like a child."

"No," Carson told her, "you're not a child anymore. You'll be a married woman before this day is out."

"Carson," she protested, appalled.

"No," Hunter stated firmly.

His objection struck like a knife straight to Bess's heart. They hadn't talked about it, of course. They'd been too well occupied with each other to talk much about anything. But she'd thought . . .

"No?" Carson said, his voice deadly quiet.

"No," Hunter repeated. He reached out and gripped Bess by the forearm. "Bess knows how I feel about her."

But she didn't, she thought frantically. She'd told him she loved him, but he'd never said the same to her. He'd said many things, sweet things that made her heart swell. But he'd never said he loved her.

"You'll not be forcing her to marry a man she doesn't remember."

"What is this?" Carson demanded tightly. "A convenient excuse? If she didn't need to remember you to sleep with you, she doesn't need to remember you to marry you. If you'd been so damn concerned with her memory, you wouldn't have taken advantage of her."

Guilt slammed into Hunter like a fist to the gut. His only excuse was that he'd wanted her so much, he'd lost his head. And what the hell kind of excuse was that? Who knew better than he himself that he'd taken advantage of her loss of memory? Her memory was starting to come back now, in bits and pieces. Surely that meant the rest of it would come in time. And then what? Would she still want him? Still love him? Or would she want nothing to do with him? If they were already married by then—Man-Above, he wanted nothing more than to make her his wife—she would be trapped. And she would hate him.

He forced himself to turn and face her. "We'll give your memory a few more weeks. If it hasn't come back to you by then, we'll talk about getting married. If you want."

It was all Bess could do to keep from crumbling to the ground before him and weeping. Never had she seen such emptiness in a man's eyes.

"No," she said quietly. "There's no need for you to marry me. I'll just . . . put on my shoes and go home with Carson."

CHAPTER EIGHTEEN

Bess rode home beside Carson, her back straight, her eyes burning. She gripped the reins so tightly that the leather cut into her palms. She'd forgotten to get her gloves out of her saddlebags. She didn't care enough to do so now.

"Bess . . ."

"Shut up, Carson."

"Bess, you're not yourself. He took advantage of your . . . your . . ."

"My what? Having amnesia does not mean I'm suddenly crippled or stupid. There was nothing for him to take advantage of."

"With your memory loss," Carson said urgently, "you've really only known him for barely more than a week."

"A day and a half longer than I've known you," she threw back. "But you expect me to trust you, to jump when you snap your fingers."

"I do not."

"Let me tell you about trust, Carson. When I woke up in

that cave last week, it's true that I didn't know who Hunter was. I didn't know who I was. I was terrified. I was angry. He was kind and gentle and more patient than I deserved. He didn't even raise his voice when I stole his horse and tried to ride off and leave him. For all of that day and into the next, Hunter MacDougall was the only person on the face of this earth whom I knew. He had plenty of time to take advantage of me, if that was his intent. But even when I threw myself at him that first night and begged him to take me—''

''Bess!''

''—he refused. Gently, and dare I say with some regret, but he refused.''

''Well, something obviously changed his mind since then.''

Bess slowly turned her head toward her brother and gave him her haughtiest look. ''I did.''

He muttered something under his breath that she was just as glad she couldn't make out. ''He wouldn't have touched you if you hadn't already been . . .''

''Raped? Is that the word you're trying not to say?''

''All right, raped. If not for that, he would have married you first, if he honored you at all.''

''Is that what you did with Winter Fawn? Married her first because you honored her?''

She made a direct hit with that comment. She knew by the way his face turned red.

It gave her little pleasure to add, ''Do you think I can't count? Do you think I don't know that April was not born six weeks early, the way you'd like everyone to think? Do you think that makes April or Winter Fawn, or even you, you hypocrite, any less in my eyes?'' Carson was staring at her in a way that made her frown. ''What?''

''No one told you that.''

''Of course not. I rem— Oh! I remembered!''

''Bess, that's great!''

She shrugged. ''It's been coming back to me, a little piece

here, a little piece there. But it's beside the point," she added. "I'm trying to remember that the only reason you're acting like such a jackass is because you love me."

"Of course I love you. And I'm not acting like a jackass. I'm only looking out for you."

"I know." Bess heaved a sigh and guided her horse around the large clump of sage the animal was about to walk through. Fine for the horse, but the small leaves would stick all over the hem of her riding habit. "I wasn't raped, by the way." She could put her brother's mind to rest on that subject, at least.

"I never accused him of raping you, only of taking advantage of the fact that someone else did."

"You misunderstand. I mean no man had touched me before Hunter. I was a virgin."

The muscle along Carson's jaw bunched. "This is not a proper conversation for a young lady."

Bess laughed. "You sound like Aunt Gussie, like you think I'm still twelve years old. I'm not a young lady, Carson, I'm a woman. And until the night before last, I was a virgin."

"Bess, I know you don't remember being with the outlaws, and that's probably a good thing." He paused a moment, looked up at the sky. "I guess if you want to believe they didn't violate you . . ."

"I believe it because it's true. At the risk of embarrassing both of us, I'll just say that my virginity became more than obvious two nights ago when . . . well, two nights ago."

Carson studied his sister's face. She believed it. She believed she wasn't raped, that it was Hunter who took her virginity. Maybe she needed to believe that. But she was so young and naive, he wondered if she really knew the truth.

He had a sudden memory of the day they'd climbed off the stage in Pueblo, Bess and Megan and he. He remembered the doubts and fears he'd had about being able to raise his two girls to womanhood on his own. He'd known nothing about raising girls.

Today he felt as if he'd let Bess down. That all this could somehow have been prevented if he'd only done things differently.

"You're right, you know," he told her as they crossed one of the many creeks that fed into the river.

She smiled at him with laughter in her eyes. "Of course I am. About what?"

"I do love you."

Her expression turned so tender that a lump rose in his throat. "I know, Carson. I know you do. Now all you have to do is learn to trust me to know what I want."

"And you want Hunter?"

"More than anything. I'm told I always have, although I don't remember that. I'm also told that you love him like a brother."

"I do, Bess. He's a good man. But it doesn't look to me like he's interested in marrying you. At least right now. He's a very prideful man."

"He's afraid that I'll remember I didn't love him anymore."

"What are you going to do?"

"I'm going to give him a little time." A very little, she thought, the fire of battle igniting inside her. "And then I'm going to change his mind."

Hunter stood in the dust of his yard and watched Bess ride away with her brother. Ride away with his heart.

Damn his hide, he'd done it again. He'd hurt her. In trying to do what he knew was best for her, he'd hurt her.

But she had to know, he thought desperately. She had to know he loved her, he wanted her for all time.

Did you tell her?

He'd told her in every way a man could tell a woman what was in his heart. Every way, he realized, except with words.

Carson and Bess were not yet to the end of his canyon when

he started for the barn, intending to saddle up and ride after
them.

Then he stopped. What would he say? That he was sorry?
That he really wanted to marry her, but . . .

But what? But she might one day remember that she'd given
up on him? That he had hurt and disappointed her and taken
her for granted too many times to forgive?

Bloody hell, he'd made a mess of things.

He turned and looked back at his cabin. The cabin he had
believed not good enough for her.

He'd wanted a love such as his father and mother had had.
Yet they had lived their entire married life together in a tepee.
He had lived the first fifteen summers of his life in a tepee.
And now a dirt floor was not good enough for him?

Bess hadn't seemed to mind. He could easily put in a plank
floor. He could buy a cookstove. It wouldn't be the same as a
real house, not like she was used to. And if he bought those
things, it would just be that much longer before he could afford
to build a real house for her.

He knew deep inside that Bess would not care. It was his
own pride that was standing in his way. That, and his fear of
what might happen when she regained the rest of her memory.

How long was he willing to wait on her memory?

How much time could he afford to wait? Nothing had been
said between them about the possibility of a child, but even
now, his son or daughter could be growing inside her. At the
thought, he felt an overwhelming sense of rightness settle into
his heart.

Yes. It was right. Him and Bess and babies. Right here in
this canyon. In this cabin, if need be, to start with. If she would
still have him. If he hadn't hurt her more than she could forgive.

Explaining Hunter's fear of her returning memory to Carson
made Bess realize that Hunter had not meant to hurt her with

his reaction to Carson's demand that they marry at once. But the less hurt she became for herself, the more she hurt for Hunter. It seemed incomprehensible that the strong, vital man she'd come to know could be afraid of anything. Yet his actions and his words told her that he feared her returning memory.

With that realization came anger. He didn't trust her. He didn't trust that whatever she had been like before, she was different now. Whatever he thought he'd done, however he thought she'd felt—all of that was in the past. He had to know that she would never stop loving him, no matter what.

But he didn't know it. How was she to convince him if she was here at the Double D, and he was out there in his canyon, alone, without her?

What if her memory never returned? Would he hold her at arm's length forever?

After being back at the ranch for two days, she still had no answers. Two long, lonely days. And nights. What was she to do? Wait to see what he would do?

Oh, Hunter, I miss you.

She missed his smile, the way he tossed his head to flip his long hair over his shoulder when it got in his face. She missed his warmth, the rare and precious sound of his laughter. She missed his touch, his taste, the masculine scent of his body that was like no other scent on earth.

And at night, alone in her bed, she missed the feel of his body next to hers, his weight settling between her thighs. She ached for the feel of him inside her, filling her clear up to her heart, making her complete and whole.

Her own thoughts made her restless. She tossed the tangled bedcovers aside and stood before her window, looking out at the moonlight dappling the vegetable garden, and beyond it, the dark line of trees along the river. The light wind made deep shadows dance beneath the trees. She could almost imagine she saw the tall, broad shape of familiar shoulders there beneath that crooked cottonwood.

The shadow moved away from the tree.

Bess raised her window and leaned out into the night, straining to see.

But no, it was her own wishful thinking, that was all. What would Hunter be doing in there in the middle of the night?

Then she heard it. The soft, warbling whistle of the mountain bluebird. And he was there, standing in the moonlight, staring at the house. At her window. At her.

Without thought, Bess reached out and grabbed the tree limb that arched beside her window. In seconds she was out and down and running between the rows of seedlings in Winter Fawn's garden, then beyond, not caring that she wore nothing more than her thin nightdress. She had to run, had to reach the tree line and the shadow that waited for her there.

So she ran, heedless of the rough ground, the rocks and sticks and sharp-bladed plants. She had only one thought, and that was to reach Hunter, lest he turn out to be truly only a shadow in the night, born of her desperate longing for him.

Snuggled in bed beside her husband, Winter Fawn heard the call of a bird that only sang in the morning, and smiled in the dark.

Then she heard a grunt, as if someone had just climbed down the tree that grew beside a certain upstairs window.

Beside her, Carson bolted upright. ''Someone's outside.''

''It's only the wind.'' Winter Fawn tugged gently on his arm, determined to keep him from getting up and looking out the window. She had been appalled when Carson had told her what had taken place at Hunter's cabin the other day. Not that he'd caught Bess and Hunter only half-dressed, and not that it had been more than obvious to him that the two were now lovers.

No, *that* Winter Fawn had been expecting for years. There

was nothing in Bess and Hunter's love for each other to appall her. It was her husband's reaction that had boiled her blood.

Oh, she knew, as Bess did, that it was only because he loved his sister and wanted the best for her. And Winter Fawn knew that Carson loved and respected Hunter, as a friend, as a brother-in-law, as a man. Carson had just been taken by surprise. He hadn't been prepared to let Bess grow up, especially not since she had lost her memory.

Winter Fawn sighed and smoothed her hand along her husband's shoulder. Men could be so silly about some things.

"Go back to sleep," she whispered.

He lay back down heavily, abruptly. "Now I'll just lie here awake all night, wondering what I thought I heard."

"Well . . ." She skimmed her hand down his chest, beneath the covers, and lower. "Since you're already awake . . ."

With a low laugh, he rolled and covered her with his weight. "You were saying?"

"Me? I would never be so bold as to suggest anything."

"Oh, come on." He kissed her chin, her neck. "Be bold."

There was no sound but the wind in the tree outside when she moved his hand to cover her breast. "Well, if you insist." And then she reached between their bodies and took him in her hand.

After that, Carson would not have heard an entire Arapaho war party thunder past the bed. He was too busy making love to his wife.

Bess ran until her heart threatened to burst, praying with every reach of her legs that she was not mistaken, that she hadn't imagined the whistle, that he wasn't just a shadow.

He was more than a shadow. He caught her up in his arms and squeezed the breath from her lungs.

"Hunter, Hunter, I've missed you." Frantic, she held his

face between her hands and peppered him with kisses. "I was afraid you'd never come."

"I couldn't stay away." He swung her up into his arms and carried her into the deep shadows beneath the trees, away from any prying eyes that might be watching.

He'd brought a blanket, and sat her on it. He kissed her, and tasted tears. "Ach, Blue Eyes," he whispered with his Scottish burr evident in his voice. "Dinna cry, lass. Ye tear me up inside with yer tears. I didna mean to hurt ye so."

Her delicate little sniff tugged at his heart. "I know you didn't. Do you love me, Hunter?"

"Never doubt it," he said, hugging her fiercely. "I know I never gave you the words, and I'm sorry for that. I do love you, more than my life, Bess."

"Then show me," she said, reaching for the buttons on his shirt.

"Bess, we need to talk." He tried to still her hands.

She wasn't having it. "We can talk later. Love me, Hunter, love me now."

Hunter couldn't have resisted her plea if he'd tried, but he didn't try. She didn't hate him. She wasn't turning him away, as she had every right to do after the way he'd acted. She wanted him and let him know in the way her hands sped greedily over him, the way her mouth took his fiercely.

There beneath the shadows by the river, on the very spot where he'd once turned away from her and put a distance between them that had nearly destroyed what they could have had with each other, they came together, two bodies, two hearts, into one.

Clothes melted away as if by magic. With hands and lips, skin to skin, they took and they gave everything they had, and when he emptied himself into her, he could not hold back the cry of her name.

It was a long time before the breeze dried the sweat from their bodies. Even longer before Hunter gathered the strength to move and relieve her of his weight. Longer still before either spoke.

"We weren't smart," Hunter finally said, "letting Carson find us like that."

"He's not angry anymore." Bess turned on her side to face him.

Hunter snorted. "I'll bet. He's probably calmed down from wanting to hang me to just wanting to geld me."

Bess's low laugh made his skin quiver. "Oh, don't worry." She cupped her hand between his legs and set him ablaze all over again. "I'll keep you safe."

"You're playing with fire, woman."

"Am I?" Gently, ever so gently, she squeezed him and took his breath away.

That fast, and he was hard again. "Aye." Whatever he'd been about to say to her flew right out of his head when she pushed him onto his back and straddled his hips. "Fire."

"Oh," she whispered with feeling as she leaned down to kiss him. "I do hope so." She sat up and reached down with both hands and positioned him. Then she took him home.

"You're a dangerous woman, Bess Dulaney." After she'd had her way with him, he had put her nightdress back on her and donned his pants. Now he held her in his lap and leaned back against the trunk of the tree that sheltered them from view of the house.

"Why, thank you." She nuzzled her nose against his neck. "That's one of the nicest things you've ever said to me."

Hunter chuckled. "Brat."

"Of course, if you're complaining, I could always turn myself back into that restrained, self-contained girl I was back when I had a memory."

"Restrained?"

Startled, Bess pushed herself from his chest and sat up. "I don't know why I said that. Is it true? Was I restrained?"

"Maybe. Some. Around me. And if you were, it was my fault for hurting you."

She placed her hand along his jaw. "Hunter, that's all in the past. Please don't let it ruin what we have now."

"What do we have now?" he asked her. "We're sneaking around in the middle of the night, your brother wants to kill me—"

"He does not."

"And I haven't even asked you to marry me yet."

Bess went perfectly still, her only movement the slight rise and fall of her breasts with each shallow breath she managed to draw. "Are you going to?"

"I can't build you a house yet. Not for maybe a year or so."

"What's wrong with your cabin?"

"Plenty," he said tersely. "That day you came to see me it started raining."

"The day I was kidnapped?"

"Aye. It was raining, so I sent you to the cabin while I stabled your horse in the barn. By the time I joined you, I was soaked. I stood there dripping water onto that dirt floor, and with every move you made, the hem of that pretty dress of yours got dragged through the mud. I couldn't ask you to live like that, Bess. I just couldn't. A floor that turned muddy, no stove to cook on, no furniture to store your clothes and things. My pride would not let you live like that, Bess."

She pinched the skin over his ribs.

"Ouch," he yelped. "What was that for?"

"This from a man who grew up in a tepee? Which brings to mind the fact that among the Arapaho, it is the bride's family who supplies the home and furnishings, is it not?"

"How do you know that?"

She shrugged. "I don't know. It just popped into my mind."

"You're not Arapaho."

"No, according to Aunt Gussie, I'm a Southern Belle. Southern Belles don't tan hides for clothing or build the home for their families. Instead, they come with a dowry. I come with a dowry, Hunter. The Double D stands for Dulaney and Dulaney, and I'm the second Dulaney of that pair, you know. I'm not penniless."

"I'm not touching your money. Don't even think it, Bess."

She sighed. "I didn't. Not really. If you're too proud to see me standing on a dirt floor and cooking over an open fire, you're certainly too proud to let me spend my money to do something about it. But we could compromise," she offered.

Warily, he asked, "How?"

"I don't know if it's a memory or not, but aren't there skins covering the floor of a tepee? We could put skins down in the cabin."

Hunter gave the top of her head a loud, smacking kiss. He wouldn't tell her yet that the reason it had taken him two days to come see her was because he'd ridden to Walsenburg for a load of lumber to put down a floor in the cabin. He wanted to surprise her, and he hadn't put it in yet. "Furs, huh? I don't care what anybody says, I like smart women."

"Now who's the brat?" She pinched him again.

"I don't know, though," he said thoughtfully. "You don't know how to work the skins. I'd have to do that myself. That's an awful lot of trouble just for a wife."

She pinched him hard enough to make him yowl this time.

"I can see," he said ruefully, rubbing his ribs, "that you're not going to be a complacent wife."

All urge to tease drained away from Bess. "Am I going to be a wife? Your wife?"

Hunter cupped her face in both hands and brushed his lips across hers. "I hope so, Blue Eyes. Man-Above, I hope so."

"Oh, Hunter." She melted into him. "You know all you have to do is ask."

He kissed her hard and deep. "I'm asking. But listen to me, Bess, and hear what I'm asking."

"I thought you were asking me to marry you."

"I am asking, if your memory returns by the end of summer, and you still want me, will you marry me?"

Startled, Bess pulled away. "The end of summer? That's *months* from now."

"When the first leaves turn. Will you marry me when the first leaves turn?"

"You still don't trust me, do you?" she said sadly.

He gripped her face again. "I trust you with my life. But I won't hold you to a promise you make while you don't remember."

"But what if my memory doesn't return by then? What happens then?" she cried. "Do we wait for winter? Next spring? Two years from now?"

"No," he said fiercely. "No, Bess. If you're willing to chance it, then so am I. I just want to give your memory a little more time first. Say yes, Blue Eyes."

Bess closed her eyes and willed the hurt to go away. He might say he trusted her, but he didn't. That's what it boiled down to. He still didn't trust her not to change her mind about loving him once her memory returned. And if it hurt her this much, how much more must it hurt him?

"Yes," she whispered to him. "I will marry you whenever you want, Hunter. How could I not, when I love you so much?"

Ned Rawlins chuckled to himself as he inspected his new haircut in the barber's mirror. Yes, sir, this was a hell of a lot more fun than taking potshots at some stupid half-breed and a girl. It wasn't as much of a challenge as he'd been after, but it was fun. That counted for something.

He'd circled wide around the city of Walsenburg when he'd ridden away from the breed's place. He'd gone more than twenty miles east of the city until he'd found a sleepy little farm with good-looking horseflesh.

He'd turned three of the horses loose long before he'd reached the half-breed's canyon, keeping only his and the girl's mare. He'd put the pack saddle on the mare, and the ol' girl took to it right enough.

At the little farm, he'd traded his horses in for fresh mounts, one of which, a stallion, was a fine, prime specimen of horseflesh. By the time he'd returned to Walsenburg, he thought maybe he'd just stick around long enough to enter this stud in the horse race on Independence Day.

Wouldn't that be a hoot? *Ned Rawlins wins county horse race—collects the fifty-dollar prize for first place.*

He laughed out loud at his own reflection as he remembered the idea striking him as he'd ridden beneath the banner strung across the main street at the edge of town.

"Something funny?" the barber asked him.

"Just laughing at myself." And the town marshal, he remembered, laughing again. When he'd hit town a couple of hours ago, he'd spotted the marshal on the street and rode right up to him. He'd introduced himself as John Robertson and asked where a man could get a bath and a haircut.

Polite man, that Marshal Anderson. Real helpful. Complimented Mr. John Robertson on what a fine horse he had, suggesting he run him in the county race next week. Pleased, it seemed, to make a newcomer feel welcome in his town—even to the point of inviting him to share a table at supper later on, over at the Pilgrim's Inn.

" 'Course," the marshal had said, "Lopez, the regular cook, he's not here, on account o' bein' off with the county posse that's chasin' after that Ned Rawlins scoundrel who robbed one of our banks a couple of weeks ago. One of my own deputies is with 'em, too, plus a county deputy, Godfrey Reinhardt from over at the livery, and, o' course, Martin Pilgrim. It was Martin's brother what got killed by that thievin' murderer, Rawlins.

Damn shame about that, yessir, but I don't mean to scare you off from our fair city. We're a right peaceable place, if you've a mind to settle here. And now's a good time to eat over at the Inn, 'cause when Lopez is gone, Mrs. Pilgrim fills in, and she's a much better cook, but I wouldn't be tellin' that to Lopez, if you know what I mean. He's got a way of burnin' your next steak that just plum ruins a man's meal, yessir.''

Once the marshal finally wound down—Ned didn't think he'd ever heard a man talk so long before without drawing breath—Ned had politely accepted the supper invite. It was just too much to resist.

So with his new packhorse and most of the take from the holdup hidden away in a little arroyo southeast of town, he'd had himself a bath and a haircut, and now he was headed over to take a room at the Pilgrim's Inn and change into the new duds he'd bought.

The outlaw Ned Rawlins was having supper with the marshal. What a hoot.

Maybe, just maybe, this was finally his chance at that respectability he and Cecil used to talk about. Supper with the marshal.

While the outlaw Ned Rawlins was having supper with Marshal Anderson, Willie Tomkins finished loading up his supplies in the back of his wagon. He'd be all night getting home, but the road was fairly straight and smooth, and there was a moon out tonight.

He was in a hurry to get home. He didn't trust his sons to take proper care of Vindicator, and that was one stud horse who deserved proper care.

As he drove past the hotel on his way out of town, wishing he had the money and the time to stay the night—and already counting his prize money when he and Vindicator won the race next week—he put his foot on the brake and drew the team to a halt.

Be damned! That horse looked just like . . . by Holy Hannah, it was! That was his Vindicator, wearing his own diamond box brand on his hip, the brand Willie had put there himself less than three weeks ago when the horse had arrived from Kentucky on the train. He hadn't had a brand until then. Had to make one up just for Vindicator.

If those sons of his had ridden that stud to town, he was going to skin them alive. He didn't care what their mama said about him being too hard on the boys.

Ned Rawlins, alias John Robertson, was enjoying himself a fine supper with Marshal Anderson when the hayseed farmer came into the dining room.

That's when the trouble started.

Standing there amid the finely dressed citizens of Walsenburg in his dusty overalls and crushing his hat in meaty fists, the farmer eyed every man in the room. Then, over the din of voices and the clank of dishes, he yelled, "Anybody see who rode in on that blood bay stallion out front with the diamond box brand?"

Well, shit, Ned thought.

"Why, that'd be my friend here," the marshal answered. "Mr. Robertson."

"That a fact?" Weaving his way through the tables, the farmer came and stood beside them. "Well now, ain't this convenient. Marshal, I'd like you to arrest this man."

Ned managed a credible job of looking shocked. For a split second, he weighed his options. He could make a run for it. The marshal was an old-timer, with enough gray in his hair to give Ned the hope that he'd be slow to respond. Through the dining room, across the lobby, out the door. Untie the reins, swing up in the saddle, and race that son of a bitching horse out of town.

Chances were fair to middling that he would make it. On

the down side, they knew what he looked like without his beard now. They might not know he was Ned Rawlins, but that just meant they'd have both descriptions, one on the poster for Ned Rawlins, and another, maybe not on a poster but certainly circulated, for John Robertson, horse thief.

Dammit, he'd have to leave the territory for sure, when he'd just made up his mind to stay. Might even have to leave the country, if they figured out he was really Ned Rawlins. The marshal had just told him that since the kidnapping of that girl, the reward for Ned Rawlins had been upped to two thousand dollars. "Folks around here don't much like having their womenfolk snatched right out of their homes," Anderson had told him.

Or he could sit still and bluff his way out. He was dressed respectable, wasn't he? He'd had a shave, a bath, and a haircut. He was dressed like a damn banker, wasn't he? While the man before him was rigged out in dirty overalls.

Ned was inclined to just sit tight. Until the farmer spoke again.

"That stud out there belongs to me. Bought him from a racing farm in Kentucky, I did. He come in on the train just three weeks ago. I gotta bill o' sale at home, and you can ask down to the depot, 'cause they'll sure as spit remember that horse and the papers that came with him. Papers that says he belongs to Willie Tomkins, and that'd be me."

Ned chuckled. "Surely, man, you're mistaken. I raised that stud from a colt personally. Marshal, you're not going to believe this fellow, are you?"

"Well, now, I don't know." Anderson used his left hand to scratch his jaw.

Anderson looked so relaxed that Ned sat easy in his chair and forked another piece of steak into his mouth.

The next thing Ned knew, he was looking down the barrel of Marshal Anderson's Smith & Wesson and wishing like hell he'd taken his chances and run.

"I suppose I got to believe him, Mr. Robertson," Anderson said in a kindly manner that set Ned's teeth on edge. "Seein' as how he's my wife's cousin's brother-in-law's nearest neighbor. Why, that makes him practically family."

Within less than five minutes, Ned found himself on the inside of a cell, a guest of the city of Walsenburg, Colorado Territory.

"It's not as nice as a room at the Pilgrim," Anderson allowed with a gleam of malice in his eyes, "but it'll do 'til Willie goes home and gets that bill o' sale to prove ownership. If he's lyin', o' course, you'll go free. But I wouldn't count on him lyin' was I you."

"Ah, come on, Marshal," Ned wheedled. "It's not like I left the guy afoot in the desert. Why, I even left him my own horses in trade. The only reason I did it was because I've got a ways to travel, and my horses needed a good long rest. I would have come back in a few weeks and traded him back."

"Whoo-ee." Anderson laughed and slapped his thigh. "That's a good one. Why, I oughta hire you to make up bedtime stories for the grandkids. You was gonna trade him back, my Aunt Fanny."

The next day Willie was back with his bill of sale. By then, of course, Marshal Anderson had questioned the employees at the train depot and verified Willie's story to his satisfaction. As far as the marshal was concerned, the bill of sale was a mere formality. What they had here was a gen-u-ine horse thief by the name of John Robertson.

But things got real interesting when Willie showed up. Not only did he have the bill of sale and a branding iron in the shape of a diamond with a box around it, but he also brought the two new horses he'd found in his corral.

One of them caused Anderson considerable consternation. There wasn't a body in Huerfano County that didn't know the

Double D brand on sight. That there was a Dulaney horse. What with the talk of Miss Bess Dulaney being kidnapped by the Rawlins gang, Anderson figured he might have more on his hands than a mere horse thief.

The man calling himself John Robertson didn't look much like the poster he had on Ned Rawlins, but a shave and a haircut had a way of changing a man's appearance.

Anderson believed he'd just hold on to this fellow until the circuit judge showed up next week. The Dulaneys would be in town about then for the Independence Day celebration. Maybe they could shed some light on this here little mystery.

CHAPTER NINETEEN

Because of the distance they had to travel, the Dulaneys left home on Friday, July 3, for Huerfano County's Independence Day celebration at Walsenburg the next day. Several of their hands, as well as Innes and Gussie MacDougall, rode with them, while Beau Rivers stayed home to oversee the ranch during the three days Carson planned to be gone. All in all, there were two buggies, a single box wagon with gear and children piled in the bed, and five riders.

Hunter, leading the horse he planned to ride in the race, met them on the road just past dawn.

Bess had chosen to ride horseback. As Hunter pulled up alongside her, she practically ate him alive with her eyes. She had not seen him in three days—since the night they made love beside the river. And oh, how she had missed him.

Hunter hadn't wanted to stay away from her so long, but because he had, the next time she stepped into his cabin, she would stand on a plank floor rather than dirt. He wouldn't tell her, though. He wanted it to be a surprise.

He'd also needed to work with the horse he planned to ride in the race. Pride and ego had reared their heads again. Bess would be watching, and he damn well intended to win.

The practical Scots side of him also admitted that winning would bring him some business when people found out he had other horses just as fast, horses he'd trained himself, and they were for sale.

Still, three days was a long time for a man to stay away from a woman like Bess Dulaney. "I've missed you," he said as he rode next to her.

"And who's fault is that?" she quipped.

"Ah, feeling saucy today, are we?"

"You couldn't find time to come see me, not even once, in three days?"

There was too much teasing in her voice for him to believe she was truly hurt by his absence. "Could have," he answered laconically, "but I was busy working on a surprise for you."

She smiled at him and batted her eyes. The look was pure Bess, from the old days, before he'd put that damnable distance between them, but with a hint of the woman she had become, rather than the young girl from before. "Oh," she said, laughing. "I like surprises. What is it?"

"If I told you, it wouldn't be a surprise."

"Did you bring it with you?"

"Nope." He shook his head. "It's too big."

"Hmm. Too big to carry with you. When do I get to see it?"

"I'll let you know."

"Tease."

Hunter turned serious. "I didn't ask you the other night. How are things with you and Carson?"

Bess glanced toward the lead buggy, which Carson drove, with Winter Fawn beside him. She couldn't see him for the canopy, but he had seen Hunter join them. Hunter had stopped to talk with him before he'd tied his extra horse, the one he planned to ride in the race, to the back of the wagon and joined Bess a moment later.

"He's trying to remember that I'm no longer a child. What did he say to you?"

"Not much." He shrugged. "Just that he expects us to get married."

"Did you tell him?"

"I told him to butt out and mind his own business, that you and I were going to handle our own lives the way we saw fit."

"You should have told him, Hunter. It would ease his mind."

"Maybe I don't want his mind eased," Hunter said tersely. "Not after the way he treated you at the cabin." After a moment, Hunter angled away from the road and hung back, letting the others pass them. "He's right about one thing, though."

Bess slowed her horse to stay beside Hunter. "What's that?"

When he didn't answer right away, Bess looked over to find him staring at her with a look of such intense love that her heart rolled over. "Hunter . . ."

"You could already be carrying my child."

Bess's hands trembled on the reins. With nerves. With longing. "Would you mind?"

Heedless of anyone watching, he nudged his horse next to hers and reached out and took her hand. Squeezing it tightly in his, he swallowed. "I would feel like the king of the world."

A deep shudder of love and yearning swept through her. She longed to be able to feel his arms around her.

"You'll tell me, won't you?" he asked. "The minute you know one way or the other? The minute you even suspect? Promise me."

"I promise."

It was a good thing that Carson had sent a man to Walsenburg last month to make hotel reservations for them. If he hadn't they would all have been sleeping out under the stars, along with a hundred or so other people who'd come to town for the big doings.

One of the things that had brought a number of people, aside from the horse race, picnic, and promised fireworks, was the talk of statehood. Territorial politician Jasper Trimble was scheduled to stop at the depot on his whistle-stop train tour on the Fourth to talk about Colorado becoming a state. It was high time, most folks said. Colorado was just as good as any state in the union, by God.

Carson pulled the lead buggy to a halt in front of Pilgrim's Inn and unloaded the women, children, and luggage. While Winter Fawn and Gussie got everyone checked in and organized at the hotel, Carson and the men would take the horses and vehicles out to the field behind the livery, where everyone was parking their wagons, and new corrals had been set up for the horses.

Because she was on horseback, Bess rode with the men. When they finished there, they walked as a group back toward the livery.

As they passed several corrals, Hunter was eyeing some of his competition in the upcoming race when a particular horse caught his eye. "I'll be damned."

Bess had been walking between her brother and Hunter when Hunter stopped. "What is it?" she asked.

She and Carson followed Hunter toward the corral where the horse stood.

"Oh," Bess said. "You're a pretty girl, aren't you?" She reached a hand through the fence, and the dainty little mare walked right up and nuzzled her fingers. Delighted, Bess laughed. "I think she likes me."

"She should," Carson said tightly. "You raised her from the day she was born."

"I did?" Bess asked, stunned. "But . . . what's she doing here?"

"That's what I'd like to know." Hunter stepped back from

the corral and shouted for the livery owner. "Comstock!" To Bess he said, "That's the horse Rawlins took when he took you. The same horse I saw up at his hideout in the mountains when I went after you."

The implications were staggering. Confusing. "But surely," Bess said, "a man with wanted posters out on him wouldn't just ride back into the town where he'd robbed the bank and leave his horse at the livery. That doesn't make any sense."

"I'm going for the sheriff," Carson said. "Bess, come with me."

"I'm staying with Hunter."

Carson started to argue, but the livery owner showed up just then.

"There you folks are," he said.

Hunter didn't waste time on niceties. "Who brought in this mare?"

"Funny you should ask." Comstock wiped his hands on a greasy rag tucked into the waistband of his pants. "Town marshal's holding the fellow. Seems he stole a couple of horses from a farm out east, left this mare and that roan gelding there in place of the ones he took, then rode right into town, bold as brass. Marshal says for you folks to come pay him a visit over to the city jail soon as you get a chance."

"Thanks," Hunter told him. "We'll just do that."

He and Carson each took one of Bess's arms and started through the livery toward the street.

"We'll leave Bess at the hotel," Carson said.

"You will not," she protested.

"Be reasonable, Bess," Hunter told her, picking up the pace. "If they've got Ned Rawlins in that jail, I don't want you anywhere near him."

Bess nearly had to run to keep up with them. "You be reasonable. If he's there, he's behind bars, so he can't hurt me. Seeing him might help me remember."

They slowed down in front of the hotel.

"No," Bess said, standing her ground. "I'll just follow you."

Over her head, Hunter and Carson looked at each other and silently acknowledged that they'd rather have her with them than trailing along behind on her own.

Bess sensed their accord and whispered a silent prayer that the two men she loved the most would not remain at odds because of her. Perhaps this one small instance of agreement would ease them back into their old friendship and mutual respect.

When they reached the city jail, they found not only the city marshal, but the county sheriff as well.

"Ah, good," Sheriff West said when they entered. "I take it you've been to the livery and seen Miss Bess's mare."

"Aye," Hunter said. "I hear you've got the man who had her."

"Marshal Anderson"—he pointed to the city marshal— "has him back there in a cell. Maybe you'll have more luck identifying him than we've had."

"You think it's him, don't you?" Bess asked. "Ned Rawlins."

"Well, that's entirely possible, Miss Bess, but all any of us have to go on is the poster, and what he looked like during the holdup, with a bandanna covering half his face."

"Let's see him," Carson said tersely. "I want to get a look at this bas—this man."

Hunter would have preferred that Bess not follow them back to the cell. It wasn't that he didn't want the sight of the man to bring back her memory, but he didn't want her to have to face Rawlins when and if that happened. He didn't want her anywhere near the son of a bitch.

Four cells lined the left side of the back room, leaving room only for a narrow walkway outside the cells along the right wall. The room was brick, the bars on the cells sturdy. Each cell sported a small, high window with equally sturdy bars.

In the back cell, someone snored. But it was the man in the first cell that interested them.

He was sitting on the iron cot with his back to the wall, his hands crossed over an upraised knee, with the other foot resting on the floor. At the sight of his visitors, he smiled. Until he spotted Hunter. Then his eyes widened and his shoulders stiffened.

"That's him," Hunter said harshly. "He's cleaned up some, shaved and cut his hair, but that's Ned Rawlins."

"You're sure?" the sheriff and the marshal both asked him.

"Positive."

"You're lying!" the man protested. "I never heard of this Ned Rawlins character 'til everybody started saying I looked like him."

"Then where'd you get that mare with the Double D brand?" Carson demanded.

"He got the mare out of my barn." Hunter took a step closer to the cell and spoke quietly. "You're going to hang, Rawlins."

"I tell you, my name's not Rawlins."

"Liar," Hunter said, his voice even quieter than before.

"Miss Bess?" Sheriff West looked to her. "Have you remembered anything else? Does this man look familiar?"

Bess stared hard at the man in the cell, trying to see if anything about him looked familiar. The harder she stared, the sharper the pain in her temple. She wanted to recognize him. Wanted it badly. Not just to back up Hunter, but so she could remember, once and for all, and put the episode behind her. She wanted her future. The future she dreamed of with Hunter.

But try as she might, she could not honestly say she'd ever seen the man before. "I'm sorry, Sheriff." Her gaze went to Hunter. "It's all still a blank to me."

The man in the cell looked thunderstruck at Bess's failure to identify him.

"What's the matter, Rawlins?" Hunter taunted. "You look surprised."

The man shook himself, then rose and strolled toward the bars. Grinning, he said, "Who, me? Why should I be surprised? The little lady says I'm not the man who kidnapped her. Isn't that right, honey?"

In the blink of an eye, Hunter reached through the bars and grabbed the man's shirtfront. With a yank, he jerked him forcefully into the bars. "Who," Hunter said, his voice deadly quiet, "said anything about kidnapping?"

"Come on, now, MacDougall." Marshal Anderson put a hand on Hunter's shoulder. "Don't go roughin' up my prisoner that way."

Hunter's grip tightened. "I'll turn him loose when he starts telling the truth."

"You're sure it's him?" Sheriff West asked.

"Positive," Hunter answered, still using enough force so that the bars of the cell cut deep into the man's cheeks.

"You're lying, you stinking Indian. Who's going to take the word of a half-breed over mine?"

Hunter twisted his fist and pulled him tighter into the bars. "You're just pissed because I didn't die when you thought I did."

The man's eyes lit with fire. "You should have died, God-damn you. I shot you myself. You're the spawn of the devil, that's what you are."

Hunter loosened his grip just enough to let the man breathe easy, then jerked him into the bars again. "Tell them when it is you think you shot me. *Tell them.*"

Realizing he'd said too much, Rawlins's eyes widened. "I made a mistake. I never shot anybody. You're mixing things up."

"You made a mistake, all right," Hunter told him coldly. "But if I were you, I'd start spilling my guts and pray they never let you out of this cell. The most they can do is hang you. If I had my way, you'd take a week to die, begging me to kill you every minute of that time. If I get my hands on you, there won't be anything so simple as a noose. Or a bullet between the eyes, like you gave your own brother. But you'll beg for it, and that's a promise.''

The marshal's grip on Hunter's shoulder tightened. "You can let him go, son. I've heard all I need to hear. You're right. Nobody told him about the kidnapping. Judge Hamlin'll be wantin' to hold us a trial. You'll need to testify."

It took Hunter another full minute to conquer the killing urge inside him. This was the man who took Bess. Who hit her and bruised her and terrified her. Who shot her, tried to kill her. It was all Hunter could do to keep from drawing his gun and shooting the bastard between the eyes, witnesses be damned.

"Hunter?"

Bess's voice reached him when the marshal's did not. Snarling, Hunter released Rawlins with a shove that sent the prisoner sprawling across the brick floor. "Trial or no trial, you bastard," he said in a quiet, deadly voice, "you're a dead man."

Hunter, Bess, and Carson were halfway back to the hotel before Hunter was calm enough to realize that Bess was unusually quiet. "Are you all right?" he asked her.

Her lips curved slightly. "Are you?"

"I asked first."

Bess would have brushed away his concern, but the look in his eyes said he wasn't going to let it go.

"I just don't understand why I didn't recognize him."

"Hey, Blue Eyes," Hunter said softly. "Why should you? You didn't recognize me, or any of your family. Besides, he didn't look like that the last time you saw him. He had a long, bushy beard, with hair down to his shoulders, and he was dressed differently. Don't worry about him anymore. He can't ever hurt you again."

"But if I can't remember him, maybe I'll never remember anything else," she said with dismay.

"I think you will. Look how much you've already remembered."

"But what if that's all there is? What if I don't remember the rest?"

"Then we'll live with it, Bess."

"Will we? Can you?"

"I swear it," Hunter told her solemnly, leaning close. "I swear it, Blue Eyes."

"I swear to God, Hunter," Carson said, surprising them. They had both forgotten his presence. "If you kiss her right here on the street, I'm gonna have to belt you."

Hunter grinned down at Bess, then up at Carson. "It'd be worth it."

Hunter did not kiss Bess while they stood on the street. He never got the chance to kiss her at all that day, as they never found a moment alone. The same was true the next morning, as all the festivities began.

More and more people poured into Walsenburg on the morning of July Fourth, eager for the race, the picnic and games, the speech-making, and the fireworks promised for that night.

Now that Willie Tomkins had his stallion back, he was the favorite to win the race.

"That," Bess told Winter Fawn and Gussie as they spread the blankets at their picnic spot in the middle of hundreds of other picnickers beneath the grove of cottonwoods near the creek at the edge of town, "is simply because no one here has ever seen Hunter ride. It's a shame he won't be riding bareback, wearing nothing more than moccasins and a loincloth." Then with a giggle she added, "It's just as well. It really wouldn't do to have all the ladies swooning in the streets."

"Why, Elizabeth Dulaney." Gussie's voice was filled with shock, but her eyes twinkled merrily. "A proper young lady would never think of a man in such a state, much less look."

Winter Fawn broke out laughing. "Ach, and yer so old, then, that you wouldna be lookin' a wee bit yerself?"

Gussie gave up her pretense and laughed. "There is something to be said for the beauty of the male animal in his natural state."

"But Bess," Winter Fawn said curiously, once the blankets were spread and the baskets set out. "Do you remember seeing Hunter ride like that?"

Bess blinked, surprised by the question. Did she? Had a new memory surfaced? Frowning, she sat down and closed her eyes and concentrated. The pain came first, as it always did, and then, suddenly, there it was. A picture in her mind—a picture that moved and breathed and raced across the canyon. Hunter, the morning sun—morning? Yes, it was morning—gleaming off the bronze skin of his bare back and legs, his long black hair streaming out behind him in the wind as he raced a mustang toward the creek, then took a flying leap across.

"Yes!" she cried. "I do remember!"

Winter Fawn and Gussie each squeezed one of her hands.

"That's wonderful, dear," Gussie said with feeling.

"Do you remember where it happened, or when?"

"I remember where." She closed her eyes, the better to concentrate. There was no more pain, now that the memory had come. "It was . . . he was riding across the canyon. I can see his cabin and barn in the background. It's morning." She opened her eyes and frowned. "But dammit—sorry, Aunt Gussie—I can't remember when I saw it."

"Can't remember when you saw what?"

"Hunter," Bess cried, jumping up. "What are you doing here?" It was nearing noon, but Hunter had said he wanted to stay with his horse until the race, which was scheduled for two o'clock, which would have it ending just about the time the train carried the politician to town for the speech-making.

"I got hungry." Hunter reached into the nearest basket and

pulled out a chicken leg. "Did I hear right? Did you remember something else?"

Her smile was huge. "Oh, nothing important."

"Ha!" Laughing, Winter Fawn poured her brother a cup of cider and passed it to him. "To my way of thinking, a half-naked man is not 'nothing important.' "

Hunter's eyes narrowed. "You remember seeing a half-naked man?"

Bess tapped a finger against her cheek and looked up at the cloudless blue sky. "Well, actually he was more than half naked. But not completely naked," she add. "I mean, his feet were covered."

Hunter took a menacing step closer. "What else was covered?"

Bess smiled. "Not much. And oh, he was magnificent."

"Bess." He drew her name out and held the cup of cider over her head. "It would be a shame to ruin that pretty yellow dress and get your hair all wet and sticky."

Laughing, Bess took a step back, and Hunter followed.

"You know, Winter Fawn," Gussie said thoughtfully. "I believe we've all misjudged these two. We've been thinking of them as adults lately, but just now they resemble a pair of naughty children set on tormenting each other."

"Except," Winter Fawn said gravely, "for the particular subject matter under discussion."

"This is true."

"Bess," Hunter growled again. "Tell me who this naked man is, or I'll dump this cider on your head."

Laughing harder, she brought her arms up to shield her head. "It was you. I swear, it was you."

"Bess!" he cried, his cheeks turning dark as he shot a quick glance at Winter Fawn and Gussie, who were so busy laughing that they could barely stand. He lowered his cup of cider and stepped back.

Bess plainly read the shock on his face. He thought she was

referring to something private, intimate, and that she had spoken of their lovemaking to others.

"Oh, don't worry," she told him, chuckling. "You were on horseback for this particular memory."

"I have never," he hissed between clenched teeth, "ridden a horse naked."

Emboldened by his lowering of the cup, Bess patted him on the arm. "No, you were wearing a loincloth and moccasins."

Understanding lit his eyes. Then his gaze sharpened. "When? When did you see me ride like that?"

She closed her eyes briefly and shook her head. "That I don't remember. All I know is that you were racing across the canyon on the same horse you're riding in the race today."

"Bess." He took her hand and squeezed it. "That's the day you were kidnapped."

Bess reeled, thrown off balance by the news.

"Do you remember anything else?"

"No," she said, frustrated.

"It's all right." He brought her hand to his lips and kissed her knuckles. "I told you you'd remember more. And you'll remember more still, you'll see." Then he paused and gave her a lazy, heavy-eyed look. "Magnificent, huh?"

"There you are." Carson arrived at the blanket. Atop his shoulders, three-year-old Innes Edmond squealed, delighted with the perch that made him taller than anyone. In their wake came Megan, with April and Bonnie in hand, and Innes strolling along behind.

Innes slapped Hunter on the back. "They're calling for all riders, son. Let's be gettin' to it. We'll be expectin' you to win, lad."

"You can count on it."

Bess went with Hunter and tied her hanky to his horse's bridle. "There. You now carry my favor. You'll be careful, won't you?"

Hunter smoothed away the frown line between her eyes with

his thumb. "And fast." He stroked his horse's neck and spoke softly to him in Arapaho.

"What did you tell him?" Bess asked.

"I told him our honor was at stake and that he should run like the wind."

Hunter's horse ran like the wind. That was what everyone said when he flew across the finish line, beating Willie Tomkins's favored stud by two full lengths.

Afterward there were cheers and toasts and laughter at the blankets where the Dulaneys and MacDougalls gathered to eat and celebrate.

Hunter was more than satisfied with the five offers he turned down from men wanting to buy his horse. "He's not for sale," he told each man, "but I've got others just as fast that are."

Carson shook his hand. "It looks like you'll be getting that ranch of yours off to a good start. I'm glad for you."

There was something else in Carson's eyes, something that might be approval. Hunter hoped with all his heart that it was, for he wanted this man's respect. "Thank you."

They were barely finished eating when the train whistle blew, announcing the arrival of the politician. The speechmaking was about to begin.

"Come on," Bess urged everyone.

"If you remembered Jasper Trimble the way I remember him," Carson said darkly, "you wouldn't be in such a hurry to hear him flap his jaw."

Surprised, Bess looked at her brother. "I know him?"

Carson shrugged. "You probably don't remember him. It was a long time ago."

"Isn't he that rather unpleasant Yankee who escorted me to your ranch when I came out from Atlanta?" Gussie asked.

"That's the one," Carson told her.

"Well, I don't remember him, so I don't care," Bess

announced. "I want to hear about statehood. We might not have as many people, but Colorado's every bit as good as any state in the union."

"She's got ye there, lad," Innes said with a hearty slap on Carson's back.

"If it's all the same—" Carson began.

"Oh, go on," Winter Fawn said, interrupting him. "You know you're interested. Just pretend he's someone else. I'll stay here. I believe your offspring are ready for a nap."

"I'll take Bess if she really wants to go," Hunter said.

"And I will accompany you," said Gussie. "I would like to hear someone explain how we can go about gaining statehood. Perhaps there is something we can all do to help the effort along. A man of your stature in the county, Carson, should definitely attend."

"If for no other reason," Innes murmured, "than to laugh out loud when he starts in tellin' about his old *war injury.*"

"War injury?" Bess asked as she and Hunter, Gussie, Innes and Carson wove their way through the crowd toward the train depot.

"War injury." So disgusted was Innes by the term that he turned his head aside and spat.

Gussie puckered. Spitting, in her book, was one of man's more distasteful habits.

"You know nobody believes that story about him taking a Cheyenne arrow and getting left with a permanent limp and early retirement," Carson told Innes.

"Hmph." Innes started to spit again, but glanced at Gussie and thought better of it. "Maybe not, but they let him get away with tellin' it. More likely," Innes continued, "the fool just fell off his horse. Or tripped over his own feet."

Bess *tsked.* "I don't see either of you stepping forward and leading the way toward statehood. Oh, look." She pointed toward the caboose sitting just past the depot. "The mayor's already introducing him."

They got as close as they could, but because of the press of people eager to hear about the possibility of statehood, Bess could not see over the heads of those in front of her. But she could hear, so she would settle for that.

"Ladies and gentlemen," said the mayor from the rear platform of the caboose. "Good citizens of the great territory of Colorado, I give you Colonel Jasper Trimble."

The crowd wend wild with applause and cheers.

"Thank you, thank you," the speaker said over the last of the applause. "Isn't this a glorious day to celebrate our country's independence?"

With the first words out of the man's mouth, a sharp pain stabbed through Bess's temple.

CHAPTER TWENTY

With a gasp, Bess pressed her fingers to her temple.

"Bess?" Hunter, already pressed against her side because of the closeness of the crowd, put his arm around her waist. "What's wrong?"

Bess shook her head and strained to listen over the distracting pain.

"I submit to you, citizens of this Colorado Territory, that it is time—nay, past time—that we should be allowed to elect our full complement of delegates to the United States Congress, and that these representatives have the right to vote."

"That voice," Bess whispered, the pain in her head increasing.

"Come on." Hunter gathered her closer and starting moving her through the crowd. "You're as pale as a sheet. I'm getting you out of here."

"No," she cried. "There." She pointed toward the caboose platform. "Take me there."

"Bess—"

"Please, Hunter."

"And I further submit that it is time and past time that the citizens of Colorado be allowed to elect their own governor—"

The crowd roared with approval.

Hunter gave in to Bess's urging and shouldered his way toward the front of the people lined up along the tracks.

"—rather than have one appointed for us by the President," Trimble went on. "As fine a man as he is, no president from back East understands the needs of Westerners."

Pain stabbed again, harder, sharper, through Bess's head.

The crowd roared again in approval of Colonel Trimble's words.

"Yea, fellow citizens, it is time for Colorado to become a state. And I say, let's get on with it!"

Above the shouts of "Statehood for Colorado! Trimble for Governor!" Bess kept hearing that final phrase of his over and over in her mind.

Let's get on with it. Let's get on with it. Let's get on with it.

Bess stared up at the man, unable to look away.

"Bess?" Hunter said near her ear. "What's going on?"

She shook her head.

"If you remember him," he said, "it's because you met him years ago."

"No. That's not . . ." That wasn't what she was remembering. But *remembering* was too precise a word for what was going on in her mind. It was chaos.

Names. Faces. Feelings. Smells. Everything flew at her at once in one gigantic rush until she cried out.

"Bess! That's it. I'm getting you out of here."

"No." It was there. All of it. From her earliest childhood memories on. "I remember." She had her life back! Just like that. "Hunter! I remember everything!"

But why now, she wondered, looking at the man on the

platform. Why should this stranger, his voice, call from her mind all those lost memories, when no face she *should* have recognized had done so? Not people she'd loved, not even the outlaw who had kidnapped her.

"Bess?" Hunter turned her to face him. "What do you mean, you remember everything?"

As she was about to explain, Colonel Trimble gestured broadly to make some new point, and she saw his hand. His right hand, with the scar running down the outer edge.

"It's him!" she cried to Hunter. "It's him. The fifth man at the hideout. That explains . . ."

"Bess." Hunter gave her a slight shake to make her look at him. "The man is a politician, not an outlaw."

"I don't care. It's him, I tell you." She had to shout in his ear to be heard over the thunderous applause as the colonel concluded his speech. "I recognize his voice, and I saw the scar on his hand."

Yet when she turned and saw the man in question descend the platform stairs and walk among the crowd, she noticed that he walked with a severe limp. The war injury, no doubt.

But the man at the hideout had not walked with a limp. She had heard him walk, seen his feet move through that narrow strip the misplaced blindfold had allowed, and his steps had been smooth and even.

By now Carson had worked his way through the throng to join Bess and Hunter. "What's wrong?" he asked.

"I don't know," Hunter told him. "Bess thinks she remembers. Something about Trimble."

Trimble stopped before them and extended his hand toward Carson. "Ah, Captain Dulaney. It's been a few years."

"Yes," Carson said, his handshake obviously reluctant. "It has. You remember my sister, don't you? Bess, this is Colonel Trimble. I believe he was a captain the last time you saw him." Bess looked into the man's eyes and read the surprise there. And the truth.

"Perhaps he was," Bess said with a sudden surge of rage. "But not the last time he saw me. Isn't that right, J.T.?"

For one eternal instant, shock registered on his face. Then he began to sputter. "Why, I'm sure I have no idea what you're talking about. You must have me confused with someone else."

"No, I don't, and you know it. I saw your hand that day up at the cabin. The scar on your hand."

The smile he gave her was so condescending, it made her want to retch. To Carson he said, "The young lady is obviously mistaken. Perhaps it's the heat."

"And *perhaps*," Hunter said, taking hold of Trimble's arm in an unbreakable grip, "we should just go pay ourselves a visit to the marshal's office. There's a friend of yours over there waiting to see you."

Seeing the look of murder in Hunter's eyes, Carson motioned for Innes, and together they got the marshal's attention and herded everyone to his office.

"What's going on?" Marshal Anderson wanted to know. "I need to be out there keepin' an eye out for trouble, and the colonel here needs to be out there shakin' hands, if he wants to be the first elected governor of the State of Colorado." Smiling, Anderson patted Trimble on the shoulder. "You've got my vote, Jasper, you surely do."

"Thank you, Marshal," Trimble said formally, shaking off Hunter's loosened grip as the door opened and Sheriff West entered. "Perhaps then you'll tell these good people that there's been some sort of mistake and that they should leave me alone."

"What's going on?" West demanded. "What kind of mistake?"

"No mistake," Hunter told him.

"No mistake indeed," Bess said hotly. "That man you've got in there"—she pointed to the open door of the room where the cells were—"and his cohorts kidnapped me. And it *was* him. I remember now. That man is Ned Rawlins."

"You remember?" West demanded.

"Yes, sir. I remember everything."

"Someone kidnapped you?" Trimble said, feigning outrage. "Why, no wonder you're so confused, you poor child. Who is this monster? I demand to know who would do such a thing. We can't have that kind of activity going on while we're trying to gain statehood."

Brushing past Hunter and the marshal, Trimble stepped through the door and up to the first cell. The sound he made sounded as though he might be about to choke. Then he cleared his throat. "Excellent work, marshal. You've managed to capture that despicable Ned Rawlins."

"Why, you low-down—" Rawlins began.

"I understand he had a gang. Did you manage to capture them as well?"

"No need," Sheriff West answered. "They're all dead. Either Rawlins there or his silent partner killed them all."

Trimble's eyes widened. "Silent partner?"

"Sheriff," Bess said. "Remember when I told you about that fifth man, the one with the scar on his hand?"

"I do."

"Take a look at his hand."

"What?" Trimble cried in outrage. "You would associate me with outlaw riffraff because I have a scar on my hand? I'll have you know that scar was honorably received in the line of duty in the United States Army."

"I don't care how you got it," Bess said heatedly. "All I know is I saw you at the hideout where the Rawlins gang took me. You were there waiting for them, waiting for your cut of the money, because you'd told them about the new shipment of gold coming in. Did you know they cheated you? Did you know they stopped before they reached the cabin and buried half the gold so they wouldn't have to give you your full cut?"

Trimble's face turned red. "Now see here, young lady. I can appreciate that you might have suffered a serious shock, being kidnapped as you *say* you were," he said, as though he didn't believe she'd been kidnapped. "But I had nothing to do with it. If there was someone waiting, as you say, why, it could have been anyone. *You* wouldn't have known who it was. You were blindfolded, after all."

The sheriff gave Trimble a sharp look.

The marshal gave a like look to Bess. "Miss Dulaney, is that true? Were you blindfolded?"

"I was," Bess said. "But I only just recalled that fact a few minutes ago. There are only two people alive today who know I was blindfolded. Ned Rawlins and the fifth man, the one who met him at the hideout. *This* man."

"Miss Bess," Marshal Anderson said cautiously. "These are serious accusations you're making against a highly respected public figure."

"Marshal Anderson, I know what I saw, and what I heard. I saw this man's hand, and I distinctly heard his voice. They called him the boss, and J.T. Except twice, when Ned Rawlins called him Colonel. He didn't like being called Colonel. He got mad, saying he'd told them never to call him that. And he told them to meet him here on July Fourth and he'd give them information on an Army payroll they were going to rob. Remember the words he used to close his speech just now? He said, 'Let's get on with it.' "

Trimble's face twisted in disgust. "I wouldn't expect a woman to understand about public speaking."

Bess clenched her fists at her sides. "You obviously don't expect a woman to have eyes and ears, either. Those are the exact same words—'Let's get on with it'—that you said to Ned Rawlins up at the hideout. Only you weren't speaking of statehood at the time. You were speaking of counting out the money from the bank robbery and giving you your share so you could leave. That was right after you instructed them to kill me."

"But Miss Bess." Marshal Anderson was clearly agitated at having his favorite politician accused of being connected to robbery and kidnapping. "What possible reason would the colonel have for involving himself with the Rawlins gang? He certainly doesn't need the money. Why, the man is rolling in it."

Carson scratched his chin and stared at Trimble with narrowed eyes. "Ever wonder where a retired Army colonel would get enough money to roll in?"

"This is preposterous," Trimble proclaimed. "One would assume that to get to this supposed hideout a man would have to travel some distance on horseback, would he not?"

"Jim?" Marshal Anderson asked the sheriff.

"That's right. All the way to near the top of Greenhorn Mountain."

"Well, there's your answer," Trimble said, smiling. "Ever since that run-in with the Cheyenne—"

Hunter snorted in disbelief.

"—I can barely mount a horse, much less ride up a mountain trail any distance at all. Why, I bet this man Miss Dulaney thinks she saw didn't even walk with a limp."

"How about it, Miss Bess?" the marshal asked her. "Did your man limp?"

Here then was the answer to that nagging sensation in the back of her mind. The man at the cabin had not limped. She'd seen and heard him walk, and he moved with a smooth, easy gait in those shiny black boots. Boots a lot like the ones Trimble now wore.

"Miss Bess?" the marshal prompted.

"No," she admitted, frowning. "No, he didn't limp. But he had this man's hand, and he spoke with this man's voice."

"Then I'm sorry, Miss Bess, but—"

"Hold on a minute, Marshal," Hunter said. He'd been watching Bess and knew that she believed Trimble was the man she saw. He'd been watching Trimble, too, and as far as Hunter was concerned, that comment about Bess being blindfolded had been as good as an admission. But maybe there was another way to prove Bess was right.

The thought of anything that might benefit Ned Rawlins turned Hunter's stomach, but Rawlins could always be dealt with later, if the need arose. For right now, he was safely behind bars and would stay that way until his trial.

"I've got a question for you," Hunter said to the marshal.

"What's that?" Anderson asked, shuffling his feet as though in a hurry to get this over with.

"If a man was accused of robbery and kidnapping, and maybe murder—"

"That would be our friend in the cell," Carson supplied.

"He'd fit the description, aye," Hunter agreed. "But if a man like that were to name his silent partner who supplied him with inside information on when and where large sums of money were being moved—are you listening in there, Rawlins?" Hunter called out.

"I'm listening, but I told you, my name is John Robertson."

"Aye, and you only borrowed that horse." To the marshal, but loud enough for Rawlins to hear, Hunter said, "Let's add horse stealing to the list."

"Yeah, well, what about him?" Anderson asked.

"If he were to name this silent partner of his, so that man couldn't go out and find himself a new gang to carry on with the robberies, would the judge take that cooperation into consideration at his trial when it came time to sentence him?"

Back in his cell, Ned Rawlins heard every word. He held his breath and waited.

"Well, now," Anderson said. "I suppose he might, as a matter of fact. Of course, I couldn't guarantee it, but it's a possibility."

"You hear that, Rawlins?" Hunter called out, turning toward the door to the cell room. "You're going to hang. You might hang anyway, even if you help us out here, but at least you won't hang alone."

Rawlins knew they had him cold. Even if he never admitted his true identity, they were going to convict him. And thanks to that fool at the bank who shot Cecil, Ned'd had to kill a man during the holdup. They'd call that murder, he was sure.

"Rawlins?" the half-breed called out.

"I'm thinking!" Goddammit, if he was going to swing, he sure as hell wasn't going alone. Never had liked that bastard, J.T., anyway.

"Think a little faster," the breed said. "We're getting old out here waiting on you."

"Preposterous, I say." There was that sneer in J.T.'s voice, Ned thought. The sneer that Ned hated almost worse than anything. "You certainly cannot take the word of a known outlaw over that of a respected Army officer."

"What's the matter, J.T.?" Ned called out. "You getting nervous that I might talk?"

Sheriff West went to the door of the cell room. "You have something to say, son?"

"Take off his boot," Ned told him.

"Pardon?" the sheriff asked.

"Take off his boot and look at the wedge inside. His limp is faked."

In the outer office, Colonel Jasper Trimble, U.S. Army, Retired, panicked. Everything he'd worked for for so many years was going to hell around him, and he didn't see any way to stop it. Sweat broke out along his collar. There would be no governorship for him, not when Colorado became a state, nor any other time or place. The only thing he knew to do was run.

He whirled toward the door, but ran smack into Carson Dulaney.

"Going somewhere, Colonel? Or is it J.T.?"

"Lies, I tell you! It's all lies!" Desperation lent him strength. He shoved Dulaney aside and leaped for the door. But his own manufactured limp tripped him up. Literally. He sprawled face down on the floor, his hand mere inches from the doorway to freedom.

But Jasper Trimble hadn't gotten where he was today by giving up easily. It took four men to hold him down while Hunter yanked off the man's boots.

Sure enough, there was a wooden wedge inside one of them that would definitely throw a man's stride off and give him a decided limp.

"Guess that answers that question," Hunter said, handing the doctored boot to Marshal Anderson. "There you have him, Marshal. The Rawlins gang's secret partner."

Carson and Innes pulled Trimble to his feet. Anderson dug around in his desk drawer and came up with a pair of handcuffs. "Colonel, it pains me to admit I was wrong about you. I'll take him now," he added to Carson and Innes.

When Anderson took him by the arm and turned him around to cuff his hands behind his back, Trimble, more desperate than ever, made his move.

He elbowed Anderson hard in the stomach, knocking the marshal's wind from him. At the same time, he grabbed the marshal's gun with one hand and Bess with the other. Before anyone could stop him, he was backing toward the door, holding Bess in front of him as a shield, with the gun pointed at her head.

Every man in the room froze.

"Now," Trimble said, his breath coming fast and hard. "The little miss with the big mouth and I are going to walk out of here. But before we go, you gentlemen are going to drop your guns and lock yourselves inside one of those cells back there."

"J.T.," Rawlins yelled. "You get me out of here."

"Rot in hell, Ned. Sheriff, get everyone back inside one of those cells."

"The hell you say," Sheriff West protested.

"Unless you want me to start shooting right now, with her." He nudged the gun hard against Bess's temple.

Bess winced. It was the same spot where Ned Rawlins's bullet had struck her. A surge of raw rage engulfed her. She was getting damned tired of being injured by these men. She'd been kidnapped, terrorized, beaten, shot, and left with no memory of those she loved. Now this man wanted to take her away from them again. He would kill her, she knew. If he got her out that door, he would kill her.

Bess's eyes locked on Hunter's across the room. His face was hard, his gray eyes hot with fury and fear. Fear for her.

"Shoot him," she said. "Shoot him!"

Trimble jabbed her head again with the gun. "They're not going to shoot me, because they know I'll kill you if they do."

"You'll kill me anyway." Her gaze stayed locked on Hunter. "They know that, too."

Trimble dragged her backward toward the door.

Bess took her chance. With all her might, she stomped down on his stockinged instep.

Trimble howled and stumbled backward.

Bess lunged from his grip and dodged sideways.

Hunter drew and fired. His bullet struck Trimble in the high center of his chest.

An almost comical look of surprise crossed Trimble's face as he crashed backward against the door. A moment later he fell to the floor, dead.

With a cry, Bess flew into Hunter's arms.

The rest of the day was total chaos. The shots drew a crowd demanding to know what had happened to the popular politician. The marshal had to call in his deputies to help control the crowd and keep everyone out of his office.

They could not, however, keep out Winter Fawn and Aunt Gussie. Their men and Bess were in that office, and no mere man with a mere gun—tin star or not—was going to keep them out. When they learned what had happened, Winter Fawn was upset, but grateful that everyone important to her was safe.

Aunt Gussie was not so easily pacified. She spent fifteen minutes lecturing the sheriff, the marshal, her own husband, and Carson on their inability to keep their ladies safe. "If y'all are not going to give us the vote," she told them in a haughty Southern accent, "the very least you owe us, gentlemen, is to keep us safe. Come along, Bess, dear. I'm sure you'd like to go to the hotel and rest after this ordeal."

"Maybe later, Aunt Gussie," Bess said, pressing closer to Hunter. "Hunter and I have some things to talk about. You go on without me."

"Very well, dear. You," she added to Hunter, giving him a kiss on the cheek, "are the hero of the day. I thank you for sending that unpleasant man to his just reward and saving our Bess. I believe it's time I started working on wedding arrangements for the two of you."

With his mouth hanging open, Hunter watched helplessly as Gussie followed a grinning Winter Fawn out of the marshal's office while everyone else laughed. He opened his mouth to say something—he didn't know what, but surely something intelligent would have come out. But he never got the chance.

"Give it up, lad," his father told him with a slap on the back. "That woman will have her way, no matter what."

Hunter shot his father a look. "You're her husband. Can't you do anything with her?"

"Me?" Innes splayed his hand across his chest in feigned shock. "What can I do? I'm the one she generally has her way with."

"And gentlemen," Gussie said from the doorway, pretending she hadn't heard her husband's remark. "Far be it from me, a mere woman, to tell you how to conduct your business—"

Innes made a choking sound and coughed into his hand.

"—but you might wish to consider disposing of the beast before he starts to smell." Without looking in that direction, she waved a dainty, gloved hand toward the body of Colonel Trimble, which the men had dragged out of the doorway while waiting for the undertaker to arrive. "The day is overly warm. He won't keep long. And he is ever so unsightly."

The round of laughter and guffaws that filled the room the instant she closed the door behind her went a long way toward easing the tension among the men left standing in the jail.

It seemed like hours, but was probably no more than ten minutes after Gussie and Winter Fawn left the marshal's office, before Hunter was able to get Bess out of there. He admitted, but only to himself, that he was suddenly reluctant to be alone with her, now that she had her memory back.

Would she remember that she had given up on him? That she had meant to come to this very celebration with another man? Would the love they'd found together during these last couple of weeks be able to withstand the strain of the past two years of distance and pain?

But then, he decided looking around at the hundreds of people clogging the streets, it didn't look as though being alone with Bess would be possible any time soon.

On the other hand, the troubled look on her face was tying his gut in knots. "Bess?"

She looked up at him anxiously. "Where can we go to be alone, so we can talk?"

"The next county?" he said, only half joking as he glanced around at all the people.

"Don't do that," she begged him.

"Do what?"

"You're thinking that since I've got my memory back, maybe you don't want to hear what I have to say."

He smiled ruefully. "You know me that well?"

"And I love you that much," she said, not caring who might overhear.

He snuck her up the back stairs at the hotel and into his room. He was probably the only person in town with a hotel room to himself. It was a risk, taking her there. If anyone saw them, Bess's reputation would be in shreds. But it was the only place he could think of, short of a two-mile hike into the countryside, where they could have privacy.

Inside his room, he closed the door and leaned back against it, taking her by the shoulders and drawing her close. "How much do you remember, Bess?"

She met his gaze for a moment, then looked away. "Everything."

When she didn't go on, Hunter flexed his fingers against her shoulders. "Come on, Blue Eyes, talk to me. You're killing me here."

She bowed her head as if in prayer. "I don't know where to start. I don't know how to apologize and make up for the past two years."

"Bess, no." He squeezed her shoulders. "What could you possibly need to make up for? The fault was mine for pulling away from you the way I did."

"But you had your reasons for that." She looked up at him, and he couldn't read all the emotions in her eyes. "I won't say I like them, but to you they were important. You've explained that to me. It's what I did after that. I . . . I took something you said that night when we almost made love and I blew it all out of proportion."

"It doesn't matter, Bess. As long as you love me now, none of that matters."

"But it does. I hurt you, Hunter. That day I was kidnapped, I hadn't come to make you jealous. I think you knew that."

There it was, then, Hunter thought. He rested the back of his head against the door and looked at the ceiling rather than see what was in her eyes. "You came to tell me we were finished."

Bess couldn't stand to see the pain on his face. She pulled

away from him and turned her back. She had to say this, had to get through it so they could put it behind them. "I didn't know what else to do. We were growing farther and farther apart. I was dying inside. We'd been so close once. Remember how it used to be, when we would talk and laugh and tell each other everything?"

"I remember," he said quietly.

"Then came that night, and I thought you turned away from me because of what we almost did."

"I don't follow you."

"You said . . . you said something about a proper young lady shouldn't let a man take so many liberties."

"I said that?"

"You did. I remember it because it's something Aunt Gussie always said. A proper young lady always does this. A proper young lady never does that. When you said it, I thought that meant that you didn't want me to respond to you the way I had that night."

"Bess, you know I didn't mean that you'd done anything wrong." He straightened away from the door and turned her into his arms. "Man-Above, you know how much I love the way you respond to me."

"I know that now." She laid her head on his shoulder and sighed. "But I was young and stupid and thought the world revolved around me."

Hunter kissed the top of her head and tightened his arms around her. "My world does."

Bess felt her heart melt. "Oh, Hunter, how could you still love me after all that time of my being so stiff and formal and restrained around you?"

"I've always loved you. You know that. I thought you were acting that way because I was hurting you. I stayed away from you most of the time. I tried never to be alone with you. I was afraid if I ever got you alone again, I'd just devour you, I wanted you so bad."

Bess sniffed and rubbed her cheek against his chest. "You were pretty good at hiding that. But then, I guess I was, too. I wanted so many things from you. I didn't want to wait to get married. I thought once we were married, everything would work out. You would want me again, and I wouldn't have to pretend I didn't want you. I could let myself feel again. I could laugh or yell or cuss, and you would still love me if we were married. But you wouldn't even talk about getting married."

"That was my pride, I'm ashamed to say. I didn't want to marry you and not be able to buy you the things you were used to, provide you a big house like you were used to. I was working like crazy saving my money to buy that land. When I finally got it a few months ago, I thought maybe things were going to work. You'd be twenty-one this fall, so Carson wouldn't object. I should have told you what I was doing, but I was just too stubborn, I guess. Then you went to Atlanta with Gussie without telling me, and I thought I'd waited too long. That I'd lost you for good."

"And when I came home, you didn't come see me."

Hunter smoothed his hands up and down her back. "We're a pair, aren't we? I guess I was trying to pay you back for not telling me you were leaving. But I couldn't stand it anymore. I was going to come see you that afternoon. You just beat me to it."

"And I threw Virgil Horton in your face."

"Yes," he said quietly, remembering the pain of that.

"Oh, God, Hunter, I can't believe I did that. Of all the people in the world. And the worst part is, I chose him on purpose, because I knew it would hurt you. I don't know how you can forgive me for that."

"It's over, Bess. Over and done with."

"I said I didn't come to make you jealous, but I think in my heart I was hoping you still loved me enough that you'd ask me to marry you rather than see me go with him."

Hunter chuckled, but there wasn't much humor in it. "I

might have done just that, if Rawlins and his gang hadn't shown up. You were wearing me down, you know.''

Bess raised her head and looked at him with a tentative smile. ''I was?''

''I was about ready to threaten you with bodily harm if you went anywhere near Virgil Horton or any other man.''

Bess smiled widely. ''How sweet.''

A burst of laughter escaped him. ''I was doing all right until you touched me.''

Her smile softened. ''What happened when I touched you?''

''I nearly picked you up and carried you to the bed. If Ned Rawlins had been five minutes later . . .''

A thoughtful frown creased her brow.

''Does the thought of my taking you to bed make you frown like that?''

Her cheeks pinkened. ''You know better than that. But I'm not sure how I would have handled it at the time. I think I'm a lot more mature now than I was three weeks ago, Hunter. I know my feelings for you are deeper, stronger.''

Hunter held his breath. ''Do you still love me then, Blue Eyes, even after all I've put you through these past two years?''

Bess cupped his face in her hands. ''The girl I was then still loves you with all her heart, Hunter MacDougall, and so does the woman I am now.''

Hunter felt his lungs expand with a new breath. ''I love you, too, Elizabeth Dulaney.'' And he kissed her, gently at first, then harder, deeper, as relief swamped him and his heart soared.

EPILOG

Bess and Hunter didn't wait until the first leaves turned to be married. They barely waited until sundown, and only then because Hunter wanted to honor both sides of his heritage, and Bess agreed with him.

In the way of the white man, Hunter went in search of Carson. Bess followed, because she wasn't about to miss this for the world. They found Carson, along with the rest of the family, back at their spot on the picnic grounds, sprawled on the blankets and drinking cider.

"There you two are," Carson said. "I was getting ready to come looking for you."

"No need," Hunter said. "I have something to ask you."

Something in Hunter's tone or stance must have alerted Carson, for he set his cup aside and rose to his feet.

"I'd like your permission to marry your sister."

Innes jumped to his feet and shouted, "Hallelujah!"

Carson shot him a quelling look, then turned back to Hunter. "Don't you mean *court* my sister?" he asked sternly.

"No, sir, I don't," Hunter said respectfully, if tersely. "I've been courting her since the night we rode out of our village and came to your ranch. We mean to be married, Carson. We'd like your blessing."

"Well, now." Carson folded his arms and pursed his lips.

When he said nothing else, just continued to eye Hunter balefully, Winter Fawn said, "Carson."

He glanced at his wife and winked. "I'm just trying to decide how long I can make him sweat."

"Carson," Bess cried. "He's asking for your blessing."

Carson couldn't hold back his grin any longer. He stuck out his hand and said, "You know you have it. I'd be honored to have you marry my sister."

It was with great relief and a glad heart that Hunter accepted the handshake. And the blessing.

"How many times," Carson wondered aloud after the cheers and laughter and congratulations had died down, "can I welcome you to the family? I welcomed you when I married your sister and you became my brother-in-law, then again when my aunt married your father. Let's see. That made you my stepcousin, I think. This time you're my brother-in-law again, from the other direction."

"Ties upon ties," Bess said, wrapping an arm around Hunter's waist. She was so happy, she thought she might burst. "I've got you now. You'll never get away."

The look Hunter gave her was hot enough to set the grass on fire. "Who's got who?"

"Now, now," Innes said, taking Bess by the arm and pulling her away from Hunter. "There'll be none o' that 'til after the wedding."

Hunter nodded. "I'll be going to find the preacher now."

"Now?" Gussie cried, aghast. "You mean to be married *today?* You can't possibly—"

"Yes," Carson said, cutting her off. "They can, and they should."

Gussie's eyes grew wide and round, and her mouth made a perfect O.

Bess wondered if her own face was as red as Aunt Gussie's. She would have liked, at that moment, to bury her face against Hunter's shoulder until her cheeks cooled. But when she turned, he was gone. So, too, she discovered, was Winter Fawn.

"Now where'd those two bairns o' mine get off to?" Innes demanded. "A fine time for a mon to disappear."

"They'll be back," Bess assured him.

And they were, in just under ten minutes. With them was Reverend Brown from the Methodist church, and the horse Hunter had ridden to victory in the race earlier in the day.

It was obvious to Bess that Innes now understood what was going on. His expression softened and his eyes turned misty.

Hunter stood back from the group as Winter Fawn led the horse and stopped before Carson.

"In the way of the Inuna-ina, I come as my brother's only living female relative to give you this horse as a token of my brother's high regard for your sister. Three other horses, trained to work cattle, go with this one. My brother seeks your permission to have your sister to wife."

"But he already did that," Megan said.

"Hush, child." Gussie took Innes's hand in hers and squeezed. "He does this to honor his mother and her people."

"The gift of these horses," Winter Fawn explained, "should rightly be given on the day of the wedding, after consent for the union has been granted. Forgive us for doing everything at once. But with your consent, this *is* the day of the wedding."

"Oh," Megan said with a sigh. "How romantic. Say yes, Daddy, say yes!"

Carson smiled. "I have my orders. My answer is yes."

Another round of cheers and laughter and congratulations occupied them for several minutes, then Reverend Brown led them all straight from the picnic to the church. Dozens of nearby acquaintances and total strangers followed and witnessed the joining of Elizabeth Blue Eyes Dulaney and Hunter MacDou-gall.

Just after sunset, in honor of the wedding—or so Hunter and Bess would tell their children in the years ahead—the city of Walsenburg shot off dozens of spectacular fireworks high in the night sky.

ABOUT THE AUTHOR

Janis Reams Hudson's romance novels have earned numerous awards, including the coveted National Readers' Choice Award, two Colorado Romance Writers Awards of Excellence, and two *Romantic Times* Reviewer's Choice Awards. She is also a three-time RITA finalist and has more than two million copies of her books in print. She lives in Choctaw, OK, where she is currently working on her next Zebra romance. Visit her Web site at http://www.JanisReamsHudson.com.

Put a Little Romance in Your Life With
Fern Michaels

_Dear Emily	0-8217-5676-1	$6.99US/$8.50CAN
_Sara's Song	0-8217-5856-X	$6.99US/$8.50CAN
_Wish List	0-8217-5228-6	$6.99US/$7.99CAN
_Vegas Rich	0-8217-5594-3	$6.99US/$8.50CAN
_Vegas Heat	0-8217-5758-X	$6.99US/$8.50CAN
_Vegas Sunrise	1-55817-5983-3	$6.99US/$8.50CAN
_Whitefire	0-8217-5638-9	$6.99US/$8.50CAN

Put a Little Romance in Your Life With
Janelle Taylor